BAD BILLIONAIRES 3

BILLIONAIRE'S CLUB #7-9

ELISE FABER

BAD BILLIONAIRES 3
BY ELISE FABER
Newsletter sign-up

BILLIONAIRE'S CLUB

Bad Night Stand

Bad Breakup

Bad Husband

Bad Hookup

Bad Divorce

Bad Fiancé

Bad Boyfriend

Bad Blind Date

Bad Wedding

Bad Engagement

Bad Bridesmaid

BILLIONAIRE'S CLUB CAST OF CHARACTERS

Heroes and Heroines:

Abigail Roberts (*Bad Night Stand*) — founding member of the Sextant, hates wine, loves crocheting

Jordan O'Keith (*Bad Night Stand*) — Heather's brother, former owner of RoboTech

Cecilia (CeCe) Thiele (*Bad Breakup*) — former nanny to Hunter, talented artist

Colin McGregor (*Bad Breakup*) — Scottish duke, owner of McGregor Enterprises

Heather O'Keith (*Bad Husband*) — CEO of RoboTech, Jordan's sister

Clay Steele (*Bad Husband*) — Heather's business rival, CEO of Steele Technologies

Kay (*Bad Date*) — romance writer, hates to be stood up

Garret Williams (*Bad Date*) — former rugby player

Rachel Morris (*Bad Hookup*) — Heather's assistant, super-powers include being ultra-organized

Sebastian (Bas) Scott (Bad Hookup) — Devon Scott's brother, Clay's assistant

Rebecca (Bec) Darden (Bad Divorce) — kickass lawyer, New York roots

Luke Pearson (Bad Divorce) — Southern gentleman, CEO Pearson Energies

Seraphina Delgado (Bad Fiancé) — romantic to the core, looks like a bombshell, but even prettier on the inside

Tate Connor (Bad Fiancé) — tech genius, scared to be burned by love

Lorelai (Bad Text) — drunk texts don't make her happy

Logan Smith (Bad Text) — former military, sometimes drunk texts are for the best

Kelsey Scott (Bad Boyfriend) — Bas and Devon's sister, engineer at RoboTech, brilliant

Tanner Pearson (Bad Boyfriend) — Bas and Devon's childhood friend, photographer

Trix Donovan (Bad Blind Date) — Heather's sister, Jordan's half-sister, nurse who worked in war zones, poverty-stricken areas, and abroad for almost a decade

Jet Hansen (Bad Blind Date) — a doctor Trix worked with

Molly Miller (Bad Wedding) — owner of Molly's, a kickass bakery in San Francisco

Jackson Davis (Bad Wedding) — Molly's ex-fiancé

Kate McLeod (Bad Engagement) — Kelsey's college friend, advertiser extraordinaire, loves purple and Hermione Granger

Jaime Huntingon (Bad Engagement) — vet, does excellent man-bun

Additional Characters:

George O'Keith — Jordan's dad

Hunter O'Keith — Jordan's nephew

Bridget McGregor — Colin's mom

Lena McGregor — Colin's sister

Bobby Donovan — Heather's half and Trix's full brother

Frances and Sugar Delgado — Sera's parents

Devon Scott — Kels and Bas's brother

Becca Scott — Kels and Bas's sister in law

Heidi Greene — Kels' friend since college

Cora Hutchins — Kels' friend since childhood

BAD BOYFRIEND

BILLIONAIRE'S CLUB #7

PROLOGUE

Kelsey, Nine Years Prior

COLLEGE HAD BEEN an utter waste of time.

Though part of that was probably due to the fact that she was graduating with her Master's when her peers were snagging their high school diplomas.

She wasn't bragging. She was just really smart.

College courses at twelve. Bachelor's (with a double major in Mathematics and Computer Science) at sixteen. M.S. in Engineering by eighteen.

And . . . she'd never been kissed.

Never gone on a date.

Which was great news, according to her overprotective father, who wanted to pretend she would be his little girl forever. Not so great when she had the social life of a leaf. A fallen leaf, dried out and crunched underfoot in the middle of winter when all the other leaves had gone to the movies and prom and lost their virginity in the back of Tommy Peddlenton's car.

She digressed, but that was Kelsey. Her mind going in a

million different directions at once, even as she did something completely different with her hands.

Brilliant had been a description of her more than once, and again that wasn't bragging, that was merely how her teachers had always described her. It was why she'd been offered an outrageous sum of money to work for the government beginning in a few weeks, and also why she'd turned down a dozen other offers from the private sector. But her big ole juicy brain—she had her older brother Devon to thank for that lovely description —was also a big reason she was lonely.

She'd been untouchable, undateable. Yes, as complete and utter jailbait until her eighteenth birthday just the month before, she understood exactly why that was. She was glad for it, glad the men she'd gone to school with had treated her with respect and consideration and . . . fine, also like she was asexual.

So *that* part she wasn't exactly grateful for. The rest of it, for sure she was.

Sighing, she fixed her gown, adjusted the colored stole that signified her exit from graduate school, and strode out of her room. Most of her family was downstairs, all wearing proud smiles, even her brother Sebastian, who tended toward quiet and closed down and definitely not verbose with his praise pulled her into a hug and murmured, "Proud of you, Kels."

"Thanks," she murmured back.

"Devon is going to try to make it for the party, sweetheart," her mother said in her softly musical voice. "His plane was delayed, but he's going to get here as soon as he can."

"Okay," she said and meant it. Dev was a professional hockey player, and his team was knee-deep in the playoffs. The fact that he had left, that his coach had allowed it, meant more to her than him seeing her walk across a stage. "Warn him, he owes me extra hugs when he gets here."

Her mom's lips twitched. "I'll do that."

Dev gave the best hugs ever. Probably because he was a giant, and so being hugged by him felt like being enfolded against the chest of a very large teddy bear, but his hugs were also good because he didn't let go. Didn't treat hugging like cursory contact—a wrap and release. He held on like he meant it, and . . . it was impossible not to feel like the most precious object in the universe when she was in his arms.

More digression.

"You know," her dad said, holding out his arms. "I taught him to hug."

Her mom's eyes sparkled. "I'd like to think *I* had something to do with his hugging ability."

"Nope," her dad said. "He got his slapshot from you. His hugs are all mine."

Kels laughed.

Sebastian grinned.

Her mom made an affronted noise and reached for her, but no sooner had her mom's arms closed tight than Kelsey found herself tugged out of the embrace and against her dad's chest. She giggled, then she was tugged away again, but this time into Sebastian's arms. He rivaled Dev in the hugging department, and she was enjoying the contact, the attention, when she was tugged away once more.

She let herself slide free, went willingly, assumed it was her dad claiming her again.

If she'd known who was reaching for her, she never would have allowed the contact. But she'd had her eyes closed, was soaking up her brother laughing and joking and being so fun and loose, a rarity compared with Sebastian's normal demeanor, and so she wasn't paying attention to who'd snagged her.

Wasn't paying attention until she found herself smack nose-first into a chest that was hard and broad, but definitely *not* comforting. Spice and male assaulted her nostrils, and she went from laughing to quiet, every cell in her body standing at attention.

She knew that scent.

Oh shit, she *knew* that scent.

She'd stolen his sweatshirt because of it and wore it to bed every night, no matter how hot it was outside. The smell, the feel, the image of it covering all of Tanner's hard muscles never failed to have heat coiling through her limbs, soaking deep into her abdomen.

Quite simply, that scent made her want.

And the object of her want was currently holding her tightly against his chest, hands running up and down her spine.

He glanced down at her, one half of his mouth curved up. "What do you think, Kels?" Was it her imagination or was there a trace of heat in his expression?

"About what?" she whispered.

"Do I give good hugs?" He tugged her a little closer.

She rubbed her nose across the half-circle of skin exposed above the collar of his sweater, inhaled deeply, trying to absorb his scent into her pores. His breath caught and she leaned back, definitely not missing the heat in his eyes this time.

"Yes," she murmured. "You give good hugs."

His lips curved, his smile hitting her in the gut like a punch.

But it was a good punch.

Because that was the moment Kelsey Scott fell in love.

She'd been crushing hard on Sebastian's friend for years, though he'd never shown her the least bit of interest—other than acting like another brother who was there to tease and annoy and steal her Pringles.

That hug had changed her. Changed *them*.

She'd catapulted over the edge from mere infatuation to offering her heart on a platter when Tanner's arms wrapped around her.

Love. Heady, intoxicating first love.

But feelings aside, that was also the moment she promised herself she was going to get Tanner to hug her again, only the next time, neither of them would be wearing any clothes.

She grinned and stepped away, knowing this was just the beginning.

In some ways, she was right.

She got another hug that night—in fact, many more hugs in the weeks and months that followed—and some of them were of the naked variety.

Unfortunately, she was also very wrong. That moment wasn't a beginning.

It was an end.

And it wasn't first love, heady or intoxicating or otherwise.

It was first hate.

She hated Tanner Pearson with a passion.

ONE

SHE OPENED the door of Bobby's, the local bar she and her friends liked to frequent, and paused for a moment, enjoying the crispness surrounding her.

It was one of those perfect end of summer evenings, warm during the day, but with the promise of fall in the air. She snuggled into her hoodie and smiled, thinking about how happy her brother, Sebastian, and his fiancée, Rachel, had been that evening at dinner.

Of course, a lot of that had to do with the fact that Rachel was sporting a diamond large enough to blind Kelsey . . . and the rest of the Earth's populace.

But, seriously, she was happy for them both.

Sebastian and Rachel were perfect for each other, and they deserved all the happiness in the world.

She slipped out of the opening and let the door start to close behind her, but before she got too far, Sebastian caught it. He slid through, dropped an arm around her shoulders. "Let me walk you to your car."

"I'm fine," she said, shrugging him off. "Go enjoy your fiancée. It's not your guys' fault that my flight is ridiculously early in the morning."

He rolled his eyes. "You know you're not going to win this argument, so just accept my chivalry. It's my brotherly duty, after all."

"You sell it so effectively."

"Shut up."

"*You* shut up."

"No, *you* shut up."

"*No*—"

They broke off with grins, and Kels let Bas sling his arm around her neck, tugging her into a hug. "I love you, brat," he told her.

"Well, *I* don't love you."

"Rude."

"You know it." But she hugged him back before leading him to her car. "I am really so happy for you both, you know that, right?"

"Of course, I do," he said.

They spent the next few minutes discussing the wedding—the date and location were set, as was the food—and the whole crew of females, including Kelsey, were going honeymoon shopping—because apparently that was a thing—the following week.

"It sounds like you've got it pretty much sorted."

Bas smiled. "Rachel's a force of nature," he joked. "Seriously, though, she wanted to ask you this, but I preferred to do it myself."

Kels frowned. "Ask me what?"

"To be a bridesmaid. We were hoping you'd be in the bridal party." He lifted his hands, palms up. "No pressure, of course, but we'd love to have you in the wedding."

No pressure? This was her brother. But her brother was a

reformed anti-social and so she understood the gesture—him asking her himself—for what it was. He wanted her there and it meant something. See? That M.S. in Neuroscience she had done in her spare time over the last few years had paid off—or at least the psychology classes that had been required for it had. She put her mental detour to the side and let her lips curve up. "I'm happy to play whatever role you want, Bas."

"How about flower girl?" he teased.

She shot him a glare. "Seriously?"

"So bridesmaid it is then?"

Since they'd reached her car, she unlocked the passenger's side door, and tossed her purse on the seat. "Yes," she murmured. "I'd be honored." Then added, a little firmer, so he'd know she was serious. "As long as you're sure that's what you guys want."

"I know this is all last minute," he said. "But it *is* what we want. We're ready to start our future together and want our family to be part of it."

Aw. Rachel was so good for him, bringing Bas out of his shell, making it so her brother could say something like that when he never would have managed it before.

"Thank you." She pressed a kiss to his cheek. "And count me in. Thank Rachel for me?" She'd call her future sis-in-law later to sort out dress details, but based on what she knew about Rach, Kels figured the dress was already purchased.

"Done."

Kels rounded her car, paused with her hand on the driver's door handle. "Oh, besides Devon"—their brother—"who are the other groomsmen?"

"We're keeping it small." He shrugged. "Heather is going to be the maid of honor, you a bridesmaid, and Devon is going to be my best man."

She smiled. "And Clay is going to be the other groomsman."

Bas shook his head.

Kelsey had opened her mouth, ready to tease Bas about choosing to include Rachel's boss over his when her gut sank.

Small bridal party.

Two on each side.

One of which was *not* Clay.

Her quiet, often taciturn brother only had a few close friends growing up. None of whom she could see in the bridal party.

Except one.

Fuck.

But she was worrying for nothing. Bas hadn't talked to Tanner in years as far as she knew. They *hadn't* talked in years. They couldn't have—

"Who is it then?" she asked through stiff lips.

Because it couldn't be Tanner. Her brother didn't know about them. She'd made sure of it. They'd kept things on the down-low and then when the short *thing* between them had gone bad . . . she'd nursed her broken heart two thousand miles away.

"Tanner."

Her gut twisted.

Double fuck.

And a shit for good measure.

"That's fine, right?" Bas asked. "You guys always seemed to get along great." Concern rippled across his face. "Is there something wrong? Did—?"

"No," she said quickly, fingers clenching on the roof of her car as she attempted to clear her expression of old pain while still keeping her tone light. "That's great. I'm sorry. I'm just preoccupied with my new project."

He grinned. "Always work with you."

"That's me," she said weakly. "Always working."

Of course, work was safer than risking another broken heart. Not that she wasn't fully over Tanner, because she was.

Definitely.

Liar, her big, juicy brain declared, never one to let anyone—including herself—hide from the truth.

Whatever.

"Great," Bas said. "Since you'll be paired up with him. And I know it's been a while, but he's coming into town next week to catch up." He tapped the roof of her car, took a step back. "You want to grab dinner with us?"

"I'd love to," she lied before getting into the car, and with a wave that hopefully didn't show her dismay, Kelsey drove away.

Paired up with Tanner.

Been there, done that.

Got the souvenir broken heart.

Triple fuck.

TWO

Tanner

HE SHOULDERED HIS CARRY-ON, smiled at the flight attendant who'd been flirting with him since the plane had crossed the Rockies, and strode off the plane. It had just been one in the latest of many flights, his job as a photojournalist having taken him all over the world.

But it was also the last of many in a way.

Because his career was over.

He was almost thirty, at the top of his field, and . . . he didn't want to do it anymore.

Bypassing the baggage claim carousel, Tanner exited the airport. Bas was waiting at the curb, huge grin on his face as he lowered the passenger's side window and gestured for him to get in.

"You look great, bro," he told his friend, and it was the truth. Bas was happier than Tanner had ever seen him.

"Rachel does a man good," Bas quipped.

"I can see that." Tanner shoved his bag into the backseat and buckled in. "How is the fiancée?"

"Working like a crazy person." But Bas grinned and his tone made it clear that Rachel's working habits didn't upset him. "She's allocated me exactly an hour tonight."

Tanner raised a brow.

Another flash of teeth. "She's clearing the decks for our honeymoon."

"Where are you guys going?"

"Aruba." Bas sighed. "The surf. White sand. And, more importantly, no cell phones."

"That bad?"

"Not bad," Bas said, navigating the airport's exit. "But Rach and I both have a hard time turning it off sometimes."

"I know the feeling," Tanner agreed. "Always seems to be one more thing to do, another project to squeeze in."

A punch to his arm. "Which is why I appreciate you coming to the wedding. I know your work schedule is just as crazy as ours. Where are you heading next? Antarctica? Some uninhabited part of the Amazon? Or, to keep with A's, Australia?"

Funny story, Tanner wasn't actually going anywhere.

That's what happened when a man burned out at the top of his career. Or at least, that was the route *he'd* taken, fucking idiot that he was.

He just hadn't told anyone yet.

"Well, actually—"

Bas's cell rang. "Oh, sorry, man. That's Rachel. I should make sure she's—"

"Don't have to explain to me," he said. "Pick up."

Since Bas had already pressed the button to answer the call, his reassurance was moot. Rachel's—or what he assumed was Rachel's—voice filled the car's speakers.

"Hey, babe," she said. "I grabbed a table. Has Tanner's flight landed yet?"

"Yup. His ass is currently plunked into the passenger's seat."

"Tell him to not mess with my settings," she said, laughter lacing her tone. "I just got the recline perfect."

"Hi," Tanner said. "That recline sounds serious. I'll be on my best behavior."

"Hi, Tanner," she said. "I'm kidding about the seat, obviously. Live vicariously and recline all you want."

"Noted," he said. "It's nice to meet you."

"You, too." She had a nice voice—warm and kind. "I'll let you two catch up, though I hope you like tacos."

"Love them," he replied, smirking inwardly because at heart he was a twelve-year-old boy. And also because after spending the last six months in the most remote parts of Southeast Asia, it had been way too long since he'd had tacos of any variety, food, female, or otherwise. "Carnitas?"

"Of course. This place has the best . . ."

They spent a few more minutes exchanging pleasantries before Rachel broke off. "*Oh!* Kels just walked in. I'm going to grab her. See you guys soon!"

Click.

But he barely registered the sound of Rachel hanging up.

Because—

"Kelsey's here, too?" he asked, gut twisting. He hadn't heard from her in years, random call almost a year back aside. She'd phoned out of the blue, apologizing for being a bitch to him in the past, for ruining things between them, when clearly *he'd* been the asshole who'd blown it and then hadn't been able to recognize that in time to get her back.

He'd assumed the call had come because she was drunk, though she'd assured him otherwise. But why she was holding on to guilt about their fling going south when she hadn't played any part didn't make any sense.

He should have known better.

He should have *done* better.

The only thing he could make sense of was that they were both young and impulsive, and while neither of them were so young anymore, Kelsey didn't appear to have grown out of the impulsiveness.

Bas smiled. "Yeah. It's great," he said. "She moved out here not too long ago, so I actually get to see her now and then." Another nudge of his shoulder against Tanner's. "You don't mind walking her down the aisle, do you?"

And considering Tanner had once contemplated that very same action—before he'd panicked and ruined things—he couldn't do anything but force a matching smile and nod.

"Of course, I don't mind."

Whether Kelsey would, was a completely different story.

THREE

Kelsey

TACOS.

The only reason she could get through that night.

Well, tacos and nacho cheese dip and prickly pear margaritas.

Fitting that her favorite alcoholic drink involved the word prickly, given that she was feeling exactly that way. Spiked. Barbed. Desperate to keep Tanner at a distance. Of course, that wasn't exactly necessary because he was doing an admirable job of keeping his own distance, but the intention was there, and she was sticking to it.

She didn't hate Tan anymore. Or . . . at least the mature part of her didn't.

However, the eighteen-year-old who'd loved him desperately enough to give up her lucrative job and follow him around the world still did.

But she was older now, an actual grown-up who understood that he'd prevented her from making a huge mistake.

Seeing him still stung though.

Especially when he had grown up in the nine years since she'd seen him. He'd filled out, muscled up, and had all sorts of interesting scruff and lines and scars on his face. And he was tan, a lovely olive color that her pale ass skin could never achieve, mostly because of genetics but also because of her lifestyle and being married to her computer and lab.

"Here you go," the waitress said softly, deftly snagging Kelsey's empty glass and replacing it with a full one, and totally proving that the hundred Kels had slipped her early on had been totally worth it.

"Thanks," she murmured.

"Absolutely." Then the pretty blonde was gone, and Kelsey was slurping down her fourth—fifth?—drink. A prickling on her nape had her glancing up.

Tanner.

Chocolate eyes locked on her. Disappointed, judgy chocolate eyes.

Because she was drinking?

Or because she was just a general disappointment?

And wow, *now* that was the alcohol talking. She normally was a one to two drink girl because alcohol went to her head. But prickly pear margaritas were the best, and so sometimes she went up to three.

Never four or five because then she got like this.

Self-hating.

But if she managed to get to six, she was the freaking life of the party.

To hurry the process along, she chugged like she was in college again . . . or, well, she chugged pretending she'd been of legal—or near legal—age while she'd been in college.

A glass of water appeared in front of her.

"Drink."

Her eyes flicked up and, full disclosure, she lost herself in those judgy chocolate eyes for a good thirty seconds.

Tequila.

But then her favorite server in the history of all servers appeared next to her, and just like the genie from *Aladdin,* managed to swap out the empty for another full glass before Kelsey blinked.

Tanner, however, wasn't as impressed by her skills. He snagged her arm, ordering, "No more."

Yeah, no. He didn't get to do that. Ever.

"How many have I had?" she asked the waitress.

She opened her mouth, but he beat her to answer. "Six."

Kel glanced at the waitress, who nodded in agreement.

Damn.

She'd been hoping it had been five.

Six drinks was her limit, but not because Tanner had declared it. Six was her limit because seven meant she'd go from the life of the party to the puker of the party, and *that* was not a role she wanted to play.

"I'm done," she told the waitress, "but not because this asshole ordered it. I'm done because I don't want to upchuck at my brother's celebration."

The waitress nodded, lips twitching. "Seems like a good call."

Kels reached into her pocket and pulled out another hundred. "Thanks for being awesome. Water from here on out."

"You don't have—" The waitress tried to hand the money back, but Kelsey took her fingers and closed them around the bill.

"Next night off, enjoy a few drinks of your choice on me."

A beat of hesitation before she nodded and shoved the bill in her apron pocket. Then she made her away around the table, checking glasses and bringing more chips before announcing the entrees would be out any minute.

And all the while Tan stood by Kelsey's chair.

Since she'd chugged the previous, she made sure to savor this one. So freaking delicious—tart but sweet and cold enough that it slid down her throat with nary a burn.

Hence the reason she could suck them back like glasses of water, but also the reason they seemed to sneak up on her, if her spinning head was any indication. She grabbed a handful of chips, ignoring Tanner's glowering presence at her shoulder.

"Trying to kill yourself?" he muttered.

She glanced up at him sweetly. "Hi, Tanner. Lovely to see you. Hope your worldly travels have been fantastic." A beat. "Now, kindly *travel* your ass over to the other side of the table and leave me alone."

Fire in his eyes.

And not the good kind.

The lashing out, stinging type she'd felt that night nine years ago. The kind of verbal laceration that someone *never* forgot.

Or at least, she hadn't.

Her stomach clenched, preparing herself for the hit.

"Glad to see you haven't changed."

She'd had practice with this, dealing with asshole men of all sizes and shapes, so she knew she revealed nothing. Kelsey had grown up in a lot of ways over the years, but the biggest of which was getting really good at hiding her pain.

Tanner had taught her that.

How to pretend everything was perfect and amazing, even while her world was collapsing around her.

"Thank you," she said. "I hate to think I had gray hairs and wrinkles already."

Lame.

Not that she had any gray hairs, or visible ones anyway, because her stylist had her back and dyed those little fuckers immediately upon appearance.

He opened his mouth, but she managed to fake a little better. "I have, however, grown out of obsessing over the Jonas Brothers, even if I do love their new music. Prince Harry"—she put her hands over her heart—"he'll always be part of me here."

Bas nudged her shoulder, and she could have kissed him for his perfect timing. "Stop waxing poetic about your princely love and pass me the chips."

She scooped up a handful and plunked them on her plate before doing her sisterly duty and relinquishing the chips. "You know how much I love you, right?" she said, sufficiently drunk enough to move on from self-hate and diving right into the life-of-the-party stage. Which basically meant she teased and then enjoyed being teased back. Luckily, the parties involved—perhaps with the lone exception of Tanner—thought she was hilarious in this state. Apparently, it was the only time she let loose enough to not get her tender feelings hurt over said teasing.

Which may or may not be true.

Fine, it probably *was* true because she did like to dish it out, but often had a hard time taking it. Not fair, she knew, but Kels was well aware she wasn't perfect.

"Just saying, only the best sister in your family would be nice enough to offer you their chips."

"You're my only sister."

"Details, details."

Bas smirked. "Also, pretty sure they're the table's chips."

She shook her head. "Personal baskets."

"What?"

"There are ten baskets and ten of us," she said. "Hence, personal baskets." Oh, look. Her drink was right there. She might as well finish it. But when she went to lift it to her lips, Tanner was there, arms crossed and glaring down at her.

"There are not—"

Bas broke off, probably counting.

Meanwhile, she turned to Tanner and matched his glare, though his higher position meant she had to glare up, while he got to glare down, and everyone knew that glaring down was the better strategic position.

Tan opened his mouth, and Kelsey realized she really was drunker than she'd realized. Her normal mental tangents and taken her down a few very strange rabbit holes in the last minutes.

Personal baskets of chips.

Yikes. Time for some water.

She set the margarita down, feeling sad for wasting the deliciousness of the prickly pear, and picked up the glass of water.

"You know that cocktail doesn't have actual feelings, right?"

"Why are you still here?" she snapped.

Uh-oh.

Tanner's expression went deadly, but she'd drunk enough that her normally meager filters were gone. Finished. Done-zo.

"Excuse me?"

"You heard me," she said. "You didn't want me then, so you don't get to talk to me now."

The table had been loud and raucous up until the moment she said that, or rather *yelled* it. But all night, the restaurant had been beyond noisy, music blaring, people chatting and laughing, plates and silverware clanking. Yet, the moment those words crossed her lips, silence reigned. The music was between songs, conversations had lulled, and everyone heard that Tanner hadn't wanted her.

Everyone.

Including Bas.

Her brother's face clouded. *"What did you say?"*

She stifled a curse, the buzz of alcohol creeping away from the edges of her mind and letting soberness claw its way in. If she'd thought Tanner's glare had been deadly before, now it was positively nuclear.

Fuck.

Her laugh was forced and loud. "I'm kidding," she said, shoving Tanner's arm. It made her head spin, and that was *only* the alcohol talking, definitely not the fact that the contact had sent tingles up her arm. "Oh, look!" she announced at large. "Food's here! Thank goodness. Those margaritas are deadly."

More laughter, awkward on her part, gentle on the part of her soon-to-be sister-in-law's friends.

The Sextant, as they'd dubbed themselves—and they were fully aware that wasn't the proper term for a group of six, but apparently too much wine at book club had led to them googling while intoxicated and misnaming themselves. Still, it had stuck, and Kels had even gone to a few of their so-called book clubs. They were fun, beautiful women both inside and out.

But she also knew that she'd just prickled their drama-seeking antennae with that loud declaration.

Hell would be paid.

Though, not as much as what Tanner would be enduring from her brother, if Bas's expression was any indication.

However, the friendly server once again saved the day, moving around the table with practiced speed and depositing plates at regular intervals, including stepping between her and Tanner to set her food down. He shifted back to let the blonde beauty in—Kels really needed to find out her name because she owed a serious debt of womanhood—then he glared down at her for one more long moment before turning on heel and going down to his end of the table.

If only that end could be a little further away.

Say, Antarctica.

Yeah, he'd fit in with the penguins down there.

Kels smirked, imagining him waddling around and sitting on an egg for months at a time. He was patient, was well used to being still while waiting for that perfect shot. Further that, he'd *always* been patient. Not just behind the lens, but in bed, then at outwaiting her until she gave up on them as a them.

She'd picked up her taco while thinking those lovely thoughts, chowing down on the carne asada and whitefish varieties she craved on a regular basis because they were just that good, when the memory of how he'd out-patienced her reared its ugly head.

Suddenly the tacos weren't so tasty.

Cardboard had more on them. And maybe some shards of broken glass.

Or perhaps nuclear waste.

Whatever it was, the memory of Tanner breaking up with her, of his cruel words and her response to them—strike back, strike *hard*—brought the two emotions that always seemed to be roiling beneath the surface straight to the top of the pile.

Embarrassment and shame.

Cute.

Sighing, she set down the taco and pushed up from her chair.

"Be right back," she murmured to Bas when he looked up.

His brows drew down. "You okay?"

A forced smile, that really good one she'd perfected. "Yup." Her shrug was self-deprecating. "Too many liquids."

He relaxed and turned his attention back to Rachel, who was sitting on his other side, not taking long for his focus to be only her. As it should be. This was their night. But his concern for Kels, checking in, watching out for her—she was lucky enough that it was like that with all the male members of her family. Dev, Bas, and her dad were just really good people, always looking out for the people around them, loving the ones who had a piece of their heart without reservation. Even when Bas had gone through his distant stage, he'd still been kind and considerate and protective.

And she'd never resented the care.

Mostly because being in the spotlight of it didn't feel like she was stuck in a jail cell, but also because she and her mom gave that same care back. Having been in one relationship that had been on the wrong side of that line, when protection had felt smothering, was a life experience that made sure she knew and appreciated the difference fully now.

Lucky for her, she'd gotten smart and dumped the guy.

Even though the bathroom wasn't actually her stop, Kelsey didn't risk drawing attention by going for her jacket as she walked from the table. Instead, she left it and slipped down the hall that lead to the back doors of the restaurant.

There was a tiny patio there, and while it was often packed on summer days and evenings, this fall night was too cold. The chairs were stacked along one wall, the umbrellas collapsed, and the tables were topped with condensation. But it was quiet, and for her rapidly sobering brain—*thanks to you for that, memories* —it gave her a moment to breathe.

Clear enough to see the stars and cold enough that her breath fogged in front of her, Kelsey leaned back against the wall and closed her eyes.

Breathe. Just breathe.

It was going to be fine. Everything would work out the way it was supposed to, and just because she was the single Scott who couldn't seem to find a person to love her for all her flaws, didn't mean she was going to die alone in her apartment with her seventy-two cats eating her face off.

Nope.

It'd probably be her seventy-two dogs, because she was much more of a dog person.

Speaking of that, maybe she'd get a dog. A cute little corgi with stumpy legs and a stretched-out body. Then again, dogs were a lot of work and she could hardly complete her own. Then again, *again*, Heather O'Keith had been bugging her to hire a few more lab assistants and punt off some of her grunt work.

Then again, again, *again*, she was purposely distracting herself from the real thing bothering her.

Tanner and the fact that she still had it bad for him.

His gorgeous face, the hint of a dimple on his left cheek, the bump on the top of his nose from a basketball injury in high school—and yes, she'd been at the game because she'd gone to *all* his games—the way his hair always looked a little disheveled, as though he'd just run his hands through it. How he smiled gently when people spoke to him, no matter if it was a stranger on the street asking for the time or Bas telling him a funny work story.

How he'd hugged.

How he'd kissed her.

How he'd taken her virginity—

"You aren't going to puke, are you?"

FOUR

Tanner

FUCK, she *was* going to throw up.

Her face was pale, no hint of the lovely peaches and cream coloration he'd spent way too many nights dreaming about after they'd—*he'd*—broken things off. Her lids peeled back, and her brown eyes were slightly hazy.

Brown wasn't the right description of those eyes, the one word could not nearly begin to encompass the breadth of color and depth. More whiskey than mocha, but with hints of espresso running through, and the right one had a perfect gray ring around its pupil. Hell, he figured he knew Kelsey's eyes better than his own. He'd sketched them, photographed them, stared into them while naked and felt way too many emotions for a boy who'd had nothing and suddenly felt everything.

Her eyes closed again. "I'm fine," she said, and the tone was *almost* perfect. If he hadn't known her so well in a past life, it might have fooled him. Especially when she added, "Just trying to puzzle out a work problem." A beat, lips curving but lids staying shut. "As one does."

He leaned against the wall next to her, seeing her stiffen, but Tanner had to give it to her, she didn't move away, didn't do anything but stay where she was and keep breathing.

"What's the problem?" he asked after a few minutes.

"What?"

"The work problem you're puzzling."

Her lips tipped up into a faint smile. "Oh, I puzzled that already. We were missing a critical line of code." She shrugged, as if her solving a work problem was as easy as breathing. And knowing her and how brilliantly smart she was, it probably was just that easy.

"So, now, what's your excuse for being out here?"

Silence, pretty eyes on his. "Because I can never seem to tear myself away from you." Her mouth curved into a rueful smile. "Though *you* don't seem to have that problem."

He jerked, opened his mouth to say something, but nothing came. The words stoppered up in his throat, and he could only stare at her like an imbecile.

"Though," she said. "I think you actually did me a favor. Made me grow up. Helped me learn when to suck it up and cut my losses." She pushed off the wall. "Everyone has a first heartbreak, the one that teaches you how things can go bad. I think I was lucky that I had you doing the breaking. Someone else, and I might have ended up doing something really stupid." Her fingers found his forearm and squeezed. "Thanks for looking out for me."

And then she was gone, the spots she'd touched burning, but the hole in his heart an absolute crater.

———

By the time he made it back inside, Tanner was a little more centered. Kelsey was, too. Or at the very least, she was beautiful and laughing and putting on a great show for all parties involved.

"Then," she said, the story not breaking its pace as he took his seat, "Bas came out of the bathroom, teeny tiny washcloth over his manly bits, the only white part left on his body."

Rachel and her posse cackled.

"And he was *all* green?" the pretty brunette he thought was named Abby asked.

"Yes!" Kels laughed. "Devon and I replaced his body wash and shampoo with animal-safe dye. He looked like a stalk of broccoli, skinny but with his mop of hair flopping all over the place."

Bas grinned good-naturedly. "I don't know what I was thinking, bleaching my hair that summer."

"Me neither." Kels smiled back at her brother. "But those blond locks really made the green dye pop."

"Brat." But he tossed his arm over her shoulders and reached up a fist to noogie her hair. "Only took me about thirty showers to get it so I could leave the house and not look like an alien."

Kels squirmed away. "Green is not your color."

Bas shook his head. "You and Devon put me through the wringer, you know that, right?"

Rachel rolled her eyes. "No playing the martyr, love. I seem to remember a certain brother who took all of his sister's stuffed animals and held them for ransom. Not to mention replacing the tip of your lovely sister's eyeliner with that of a permanent marker."

"That was in response to the broccoli incident!"

Tanner snorted.

First, because he'd bleached his hair that summer, too, and second, because he'd seen the outcome of both pranks.

The Scotts were vicious.

Case in point, when Bas pointed across the table and declared, "And Tanner, I thought he was my friend, but it turned out he was in on all of them."

"What?" Kelsey's eyes flicked to his.

"He gave Devon the dye *and* he thought of the eyeliner prank."

Ice from her end of the table. "And what about Mr. Snuggles? He never recovered from his incarceration."

Meaning, he and Bas had accidentally shoved Mr. Snuggles in an access panel for some plumbing, not realizing that the pipes got really hot and that the synthetic fur of Kelsey's favorite unicorn toy would melt.

She'd cried when they'd returned the misshapen toy, and he'd never felt more like an ass.

Except perhaps when he'd broken things off with her.

"I was in on that, too."

Definite frost, but she continued putting on her show, and so her lips curved. "You monster."

"No brothers and sisters to torment meant I had to find my own way."

Some of that ice melted, her knowing what it had been like growing up in his house. Not an uncommon story, his upbringing. Parents who worked too much, who spent all their time either uninvolved in his life, or feeling guilty for not being there and suffocating him.

At first, he'd eaten up the attention, been so starved for it.

But then work would inevitably become more important, and he'd been shuttled to after-school care or, once he'd become friends with Bas, the Scotts had let him hang out at their house every afternoon.

Sebastian's mom was the best, framing it like he was doing them a favor so Bas wouldn't be alone while she shuttled Dev to hockey practice and Kelsey to her extra academic courses. He hadn't cared why they'd let him stay. Besides Bas being his best friend, meaning extra hang out time was great, he'd also just loved being part of the hustle and bustle of a big family. Cars coming and going, voices talking over each other at the dinner table, laughter and teasing echoing through the halls.

His house was quiet.

Bigger and undoubtedly fancier than the Scotts', but so much colder.

No soul.

The only good thing his parents had ever done for him, besides the whole feeding and clothing and giving him a safe place to live—because those couldn't be discounted, even if he had been neglected in almost every other way—was buy him a camera. But after spending fourteen years shooting profession-ally, nine of those moving from place to place, never settling down, never having a home base for more than a couple of weeks, now he wondered how much he'd missed out on while using his job, his cameras as a shield.

Intimacy for sure.

At first, there had been lots of women, but that had gotten old quick.

At first, he'd loved flitting from place to place without being tied down.

But eventually he'd begun to miss home, to miss the noisy Scotts, to miss Kelsey and her brain that never stopped.

That had been a year before.

That had been because Kelsey had called.

He'd been looking through the lens of his camera, searching for the perfect shot, the perfect composition that would fill the hole inside him, and her phone call had made him see.

It would never be filled.

Not with photography, anyway.

He wanted to come home. He wanted to see his friends, his family—that would be the Scotts, not his biological parents.

And . . . he needed to see her.

To find out if it was the same.

The gnawing need, the draw that seemed to never waver, even though he'd done his best to stretch it to snapping by moving all around the world. Because he'd known at twenty-one, and he knew now.

Kelsey was it for him.

And just like then, that knowledge was absolutely terrifying.

Laughter drew him out of his head, the conversation having carried on while he'd been deep in thought. He reached for his beer and slugged back a fair portion of it.

"Got it bad," came a voice from his right. It was New York through and through and belonged to a gray-eyed beauty whose blond hair and gorgeous looks no doubt made most men underestimate her.

Tan didn't, however.

He saw the sharpness in her gaze, the shrewdness in her expression. That, paired with the fact that she was one of the most famous lawyers in the country at the moment—having won a big case against a corporation who was taking advantage of their hourly employees, a case that was currently all over television—meant that he knew Bec Darden to be a very smart human.

"Heard about your case," he said. "That was huge."

A flash of white teeth. "Thanks," she said. "But your pathetic attempts at distraction don't work with me."

"Becky baby," her husband, Luke, said. "This isn't the courtroom. Let the man enjoy his beer."

The fierce lawyer wrinkled her nose. "But he's got it bad."

"Anyone within a three-mile radius can see that, but still, the man should get to enjoy his beer."

Tanner sighed.

"But—"

"And I think I've had enough of tonight," Tanner muttered and stood, crossing to his friend and Rachel. "Sorry to say, but jet lag is hitting hard."

Bas started to stand. "I can drop you at your hotel."

Tanner shook his head. "Stay. I'll just grab my bag from your car and call a Lyft."

Sebastian's eyes flicked toward Kelsey, who was laughing with Abby. "Actually, maybe you can drive Kels home? She mentioned her car is here, and she doesn't want to drink and drive. If you take her, she wouldn't have to come and grab it in the morning. Her apartment is just a couple of blocks from your hotel."

Sensible.

But hellish.

And yet, what could he say aside from, "Sure. Sounds like a plan."

"If you even still have a valid license."

Tan rolled his eyes. "I do."

"And you've driven something more than a horse and wagon over the last year."

"Does a Range Rover count?"

It was Sebastian's turn to roll his eyes. "Always so fancy."

"All I got."

A snort before Bas turned to his sis and said, "Tanner will drive you home so you don't have to come back for your car tomorrow."

"I'm just going to get a—"

"You just told me you were leaving. Tanner is jet-lagged and needs to get to his hotel." Bas smiled. "Two birds, one stone."

Tan watched as Kelsey considered her options.

It didn't take her as long as him to realize they didn't have any. Either she went with this and pretended it was no big deal for a family friend to drive her home, or she admitted she didn't want to be trapped in a car with Tanner and why that was.

She chose option one.

Plastering on her fake smile, she pushed back her chair and stood. On went the jacket, waves and goodbyes were extended all around, a hug to Abby, to her brother, to Rachel, then she scooped up her purse and turned for the front of the restaurant.

Tanner followed her, but not before he saw the knowing expression on Bec and Luke's faces.

Yup.

He had it bad.

And he had the feeling that pretty soon everyone was going to know that.

FIVE

Kelsey

HELL.

A full seven circles.

Or maybe eight.

Ten?

Maybe *that* was a little far, after all. She may be trapped in a car with Tan, but it wasn't like he was driving them over a cliff. In fact, he seemed to be maneuvering very carefully through the streets of the city.

They hadn't talked except for her to give him the address.

Which was perhaps that eighth circle.

Sexual tension—on her part. Memories. Heartbreak.

Maybe ten wasn't so out there after all.

But traffic wasn't terrible, and they were nearing her place. Soon she could change into the cozy pajamas that Rachel had gotten her hooked on, down some water and preventative ibuprofen so she didn't die tomorrow when she had to get up for work, and then turn on *Outlander*.

She was way behind and needed to get caught up before she got together with her friends on Friday.

Spoilers were the worst.

Right behind the silence in this car.

They slid to a stop at a red light, her staring out the window, him with his eyes on the road.

"Did I ever apologize to you?" he said.

Shit. Why hadn't she turned on the radio? At least if she had, she could have pretended not to hear him. Instead, all she had was silence and a rapidly rising pulse.

Turn green. Turn green. Turn—

Fingers on her cheek.

"Kels."

She kept her eyes pointed out the window, the prickly pear goodness was totally gone now, but she answered him. "No."

A curse. "I'm an asshole."

No denying that.

He chuckled darkly. "I'm guessing you agree."

"Light's green."

The car moved. "Definitely agree."

Kels sighed and leaned back against the seat. "Fuck, Tan, what do you expect? We spent the summer fooling around and hiding things from my parents and my brothers while you promised me we were building something more, something permanent." She shook her head, hair catching on the fabric of her seat. "I know we were young and both made mistakes and that I reacted to you leaving like a spoiled brat. But I've apologized for that, and it also doesn't change the fact that"—another sigh, her voice dropping—"you said we were more—"

He'd said she was *everything*.

"—and then you just threw it away." Threw *her* away.

"You're right."

She froze, having expected him to latch onto the young and made mistakes part rather than agreeing with her.

"Yes, I was young and too fucking stupid to recognize exactly how good I had it. And"—he glanced in the mirror, changed lanes—"I was also a scared asshole who panicked because I had it so good. My head was messed up, Kels. My teenage and college fantasies were about you, and yet I spent every day pretending to just be your brother."

Yeah, that *had* been a little strange.

She'd never thought of Tanner as her brother, but they had pretended their relationship was like that when her family was there. Partly because it was fun to sneak around, but mostly because they were too young and cowardly to declare themselves a couple.

Her brothers wouldn't have liked it, and she didn't think her parents would have either, considering exactly how much time Tan and she had spent alone.

"We made a mess," she said softly.

He snorted. "Yeah. A big one."

"I liked the time we spent together."

And just when she thought the prickly pear was out of her, she had to go and admit that. Kels bit her tongue until it stung, reading Tanner's silence for exactly what it was. He'd liked it, too, but there was no going back.

"Like I said," she added as he pulled into her underground garage, "it sucks that it went down that way, but it also was probably for the best."

More silence. This time she didn't break it with her blathering.

"My spot's on the left. Six down."

He parked, and she stifled a sigh. "Thanks for driving me back. If you're going to walk, I'll let you into the lobby so you can cut through to your hotel." Her gaze drifted up and over to his.

He nodded.

Great.

She popped the door and hopped out, reaching back in and between the seats in order to grab her coat and work bag. The first went over her arm, the second . . . got snagged from her hand.

"I've got it," Tanner said, gripping the rather large tote like it was a clutch. She shivered. It might have been nine years, but she distinctly remembered the feel of his touch, the sensation of those big, calloused fingers trailing down her skin, slipping between her thighs—

La. La. La.

Kels needed to focus and not on how good Tanner had been in bed, or how off the charts their chemistry had been.

She'd had good sex over the years. Not great. But it had been pretty damned good. Plus, she had *Outlander* to look forward to and a set of really good vibrators that would make her Jamie experience even better.

Tan reached across her and closed the door. Then he clicked the locks, handed her the keys, tossed his own bag over his shoulder, and picked up his duffle.

Her signal to move so they could get this over with.

And since she had her Jamie and her Platinum—yes, her vibrator was named after the precious metal and no joke, it was worth as much as a bar of the stuff—to look forward to, she sucked in a breath and led the way over to the elevators. Security in her building was good. She had to swipe her card to access the room with the elevators and then swipe it again to get the elevator to move.

She hit the buttons for the lobby and her floor, and a few seconds later, the doors opened to reveal the marble-floored space. Kels put her hand out to prevent it from closing back up then pointed. "Just go out the doors and to the left. Your hotel is two blocks down." Tanner glanced in that direction and nodded, but didn't get off.

She raised a brow.

"I'll walk you up first."

"I don't need—"

His expression went mulish, and she knew it was either spend the next five minutes fighting with him and knowing that any argument she might put up would be ignored anyway, or she could just accept that he was going to walk her up and then get on with her evening.

Rolling her eyes, she let go and stepped back, allowing the elevator doors to close and the metal death box to rise the six floors to her apartment.

"You didn't use to give in so easily."

She leaned back against the wall and stifled a sigh, since they would counteract her next words. "Meet new and improved me."

Half of Tanner's mouth tipped up, but his gaze drifted down to her toes, and if she wasn't totally mistaken, Kels would say there was heat in those chocolate depths. But then again, she was probably just delusional due to the prickly pear's yummi-ness. "Improved how?"

She glanced down then thought—thanks prickly pear—what the fuck? Her hands came up and she cupped her breasts, jabbing herself in the left one with her keys. *Ow.* "These are new since I've seen you."

Tanner choked. "You got implants?"

A frown dragged her brows down. "No," she said. "Pig."

The doors dinged open, and he held them for her. "Just saying, I'm not the one cupping them and drawing attention to the hottest set of tits I've seen in ages."

She couldn't fault him for that.

Dropping her hands, she moved off the elevator. "My point was," she said, "that I've grown up since I last saw you."

He moved so he was walking next to her. "Grown up or filled out?"

This made her snort, and she punched him before admitting, "Both."

"Yeah," he said softly, "I noticed. What else has changed in nine years?"

"Hmm," she said, slowing her pace. Her head wasn't fuzzy, and she had gotten over her embarrassment with Tan. All that was left of her night was a pleasant warm sensation in her stomach from the cocktails. Or maybe that was just Tanner. "I've got my own place," she told him. Her apartment was around the corner, the last one in the hall. Although it was smaller than the other units on the floor, the placement in the building meant that she had lovely views of the bay.

"That is very grown-up," he said. "I don't have an apartment." At her look, he added, "Got rid of mine after a while. Was paying for a place that I was never in and so when I come home, I usually just bunk on someone's couch."

"Bas never mentioned you staying with him."

"Probably because I've been home to the states maybe six times since I left, and four of those were for jobs." There was a hint of something in his tone that she couldn't place in his expression, but then his face cleared, and he nodded at the door they'd stopped in front of. "This you?"

She nodded. "Yup."

Her keys were slipped from her fingers and before she knew it, the door was open, and he was nudging her inside. Immediately, because it was the first thing she always did when walking into her apartment, Kels stepped out of her heels and pushed them to the side. In proximity to the shoe rack her neat freak of a friend, Heidi, had bought her, but not on it.

His eyes slipped to her feet, and she glanced down to see her bright pink nails.

There those lips went again, curving upward just the slightest bit, even as his gaze seemed to be cataloging everything about her. Damn. Why did he have to be even sexier than before? Broader shoulders, slender hips, fine lines on the outside of his eyes that spoke to him having spent at least part of the last nine years laughing. His skin was tan and when he lounged back against the doorway crossing his arms, she noticed a tattoo on the inside of his forearm.

"What else has changed, Kels?"

She turned and walked further into her apartment, hanging up her coat, pulling out her laptop and plugging it into the charger she had on her kitchen counter. Then she stepped to her sink, reached into the cabinet, and pulled out a glass.

She held it up in his direction. "I have matching glassware? Want some lemonade?"

His half-smile went full, and he stepped into the apartment, closing the door behind him. "So, some things haven't changed, have they? Do you still make your lemonade with approximately two pounds of sugar?" He prowled toward her, and Kels's heart skipped a beat.

"Maybe just a pound now." She shrugged and grabbed another cup, setting it on the counter before turning toward the fridge to retrieve her pitcher of lemonade. "I haven't seemed to be able to grow out of my sweet tooth."

"Hmm."

Two glasses poured, she returned the pitcher and handed him one. "Thanks for the ride." A beat. "In my car. With my gas. But thanks anyway, I suppose."

"Just remember me when you don't have to get up early in the morning to go and get it." He took a sip and winced.

"Still too sweet?"

"There are some things that can never be too sweet," he murmured, reaching past her to place the cup on the counter, and she knew he wasn't talking about food or drink so much as people. Or maybe her?

But he'd left.

"How's work?" she murmured, pushing that thought away.

The change that overtook him was instant and all-encompassing.

Relaxed shoulders stiffened, softened jaw clenched, lips pressed flat, and his eyes . . . those went cold, frostier than a chocolate shake. "Fine."

Since that *fine* both spoke to things not being at all fine and also him putting up several rolls of caution tape, Kelsey set down her own glass and brushed by him, heading toward the door.

"For what it's worth," she said. "I'm glad you drove me home and we got to talk. Will make that trip down the aisle a lot easier."

He'd been lost in thought for a moment but jolted as her words reached him.

Then his head came up, and he closed the distance between them. "Thanks for the drink."

A nod.

"Apartment's nice."

Another nod, and he reached for the door.

"Tanner?"

"Yes, baby?" He was distracted by whatever was in his brain and probably didn't mean that baby at all, but the endearment was enough for her filter-less, impulsive tongue.

"About the car—" He frowned, so she hurried to add,

"About remembering you doing me a favor by driving me home—"

"Baby, I was just kidding about that."

Another baby. *Really* distracted. Still, she kept going.

"I didn't need the reminder to think of you," she admitted. "I've thought of you every single day since you left me."

It was as though he'd suddenly been prodded with electricity. Every muscle in his body went taut, and he rotated to face her. "What did you say?"

Oh shit.

She shook her head. "Forget it—"

He kissed her.

One second, she was ready to run away or beg the floor to swallow her up so she could forget what she'd admitted, and the next moment his mouth was on hers, his tongue down her throat, and sparks exploding along her spine.

Her knees wobbled, her panties got soaked, and her arms slid around his neck.

Hell, she was never going to catch up on *Outlander* now.

SIX

Tanner

FUCK, had it always been this good between them?

Tan had thought it was pretty freaking great kissing Kels nine years before, but now his mouth on hers was fucking incendiary. He slid his tongue across the seam of her mouth, and she opened immediately, letting him in at the same time she wrapped her arms around his neck and tugged him closer.

She tasted of tequila and flowers, sweet with tang, but she also tasted of Kelsey.

His Kelsey.

His from the first time he'd laid eyes on her, eight years old with tears in those pretty brown eyes because she'd fallen and scraped her knee. He hadn't known what she was to him then, just that he hadn't liked seeing her hurt and crying, so he'd hugged her and helped her inside to her mom.

But she'd been his since that moment.

That hadn't changed when he was in middle school and she was taking college courses, books sprawled on her kitchen island and pencil marks on her face. He hadn't been able to help her with her homework—in fact, she usually helped *him* when his own math problems stumped him—but he'd been self-sufficient for a long time. He knew how to make good snacks, and since she'd often forget to eat when completing whatever complicated work her professors had assigned her, Tan had made it his responsibility to feed her.

Even when they'd gotten older, when he and Bas had spent more time out of the Scott house than in it, he'd still checked in on her.

She'd been pretty then, but still so young, and he'd been in high school then college and after what most boys that age were. Kels had been both jailbait and his best friend's sister, so she was beyond off-limits. She was absolutely, impenetrably untouchable.

He'd tucked away the *pretty*, focused on the *sister* . . . until the day she'd graduated with her Master's, and he'd made the mistake of hugging her.

So right in his arms. So much fiery desire from such innocent contact.

Like now—

But also unlike now.

Because his mouth was on hers, and she was kissing him with far more confidence than she'd ever done before.

Her fingers drifted to his head and wove into the strands of his hair, tugging firmly, making prickles of pain dance on his scalp. Rather than really hurting, it enhanced, taking his cock from mostly hard to granite and sending his control scattering.

His hands swept down and cupped her ass, scooping her up. She didn't hesitate to wrap her legs around his waist and, fuck, that felt incredible. Lungs screaming for oxygen, he broke from her mouth, sucking in air while nipping at her throat, running his tongue along the shell of her ear. She moaned when he sucked on the lobe, fingers clenching on his scalp again, and he felt a bolt of satisfaction in remembering her spots, in discovering they hadn't changed.

But he also knew this was too much too soon, so he didn't drift lower when he desperately wanted to. Instead, he went back to her mouth, nibbling at the corner before taking it in a slow, easy kiss that helped him garner some of the tendrils of his control. Finally, he eased back, returning to reality to find that he'd pinned her against the wall, his groin nestled against the sweet softness of her pussy, and that reality meant that his control almost went scattering again.

Luckily—or perhaps *un*luckily, depending on how one looked at it—Tan glanced to the right and saw the eight-by-ten of her family hanging on the wall less than a foot from her head.

The whole gang was there, her parents, Grant and Megan, Devon and his wife, Becca, Sebastian and Rachel, and Kelsey. Brown locks shining, huge smile on her beautiful face, and bright brown eyes proudly focused on the camera.

Everyone else was laughing, no doubt because she'd said something smart ass.

They were happy.

And he wasn't there.

Carefully, Tanner set Kelsey back on her feet, trying to ignore the piercing pain that reminded him of exactly how much he'd missed when he'd run. It took her a moment to come to, her lids opening slowly to reveal eyes hazed with desire. His cock twitched again, but he ignored it and stepped back after making sure she was steady.

That made the haze clear slightly and a pang of regret shot through him, but seriously, what the fuck had he been thinking? He was fucked up. He didn't have a job, had put his camera equipment in storage—or all but his favorite DSLR—and he didn't even have a place to stay. Spending the last years as a nomad meant that he didn't have any ties, didn't know how to be part of a family, let alone a close one like the Scotts, and he knew that the moment he got involved with Kelsey, he'd be all in.

Which meant that inevitably he'd fuck things up with her.

And then he'd lose what he had with *all* the Scotts.

"Fuck," he muttered, turning away and shoving a hand through his hair. He needed them in his life, needed *Kelsey* in his life, and that meant he had to get a handle on this desire and go back to being a surrogate brother. If he didn't, he'd lose them all.

"Good to know that my kissing still makes you react in the same way."

At that smart comment, he almost turned around and slammed his mouth back down on hers. It took locking every muscle in his body tight to keep from doing it, but he managed. Then he sucked in a breath, took two steps, and reached for the doorknob.

He heard a noise—a rustle, a whoosh of something falling to the floor.

He shouldn't have looked. He knew that in his bones.

But he also knew he couldn't have *not* looked to save his life.

Tanner had made the same mistake all those years ago—underestimating Kels—and why he did the same thing in that moment was beyond fucking stupid. Regardless of his mental capacity, he glanced back.

Oh fuck.

She was standing opposite him . . . wearing nothing but her bra and panties.

He looked. He had to *fucking* look.

Turquoise lace that did nothing to disguise the dusky pink of her nipples, the brown hair between her thighs. Her breasts and hips were larger. She'd been slender before, almost a reed of a girl, but now she was all woman. Still tall and thin, but with curves that his palms ached to caress.

"Tan," she murmured.

He was frozen.

Then she unhooked her bra and dropped it to the floor.

Fuck.

Her breasts, holy shit, he'd thought the lace hadn't concealed much, but he'd been wrong. Seeing them naked, bouncing softly as she moved toward him, was going to be burned into his brain for all eternity.

She closed the distance between them, getting close enough that her breasts brushed his chest. Hard nipples through the cotton of his T-shirt, floral scent of her hair, soft breath catching in the back of his throat. His hands were in fists at his sides, desperate to touch her and yet terrified of what might happen if he did.

A kiss to his throat, floral scent getting closer, inundating his senses when she rose on tiptoe and whispered in his ear, "Come to bed."

Then she dropped back down and turned, fingers slipping into the waistband of her underwear, hips doing a little shimmy that did absolutely fantastic things to her ass, and that turquoise lace hit the floor.

Hot brown eyes over her shoulder, shining brown locks dancing on her back.

He took a step forward and he watched her smile grow.

Then she disappeared through a doorway that no doubt led to her bedroom.

Tanner took another step.

But his gaze caught on the family portrait again, and he froze. He had to leave, and he had to leave in that moment. Otherwise he was going to cave, walk into that bedroom, then make love to Kelsey in every single way he'd imagined over the last nine years.

Which meant they'd probably never leave.

But it also meant that he would have ruined things.

He spun, scrambled for the doorknob, opted for the stairs, and hustled his way out onto the street. It wasn't running. Rather, it was him protecting the most precious thing in the universe.

Or at least, that's what he told himself to convince him to keep walking.

SEVEN

Kelsey

SHE SIPPED her one beer slowly, because after her experience with six prickly pear margaritas, she'd decided to take it easy on alcohol.

As in, she was never drinking tequila again.

Beer made her a little loopy after one or two glasses, but tequila made her stupid.

Or maybe that was just because she'd had six.

Either way, it was Friday. It was girl's night and she was just going to hang with her buds and pretend that Wednesday night hadn't happened.

"Oh, you started without us," Kate said, flicking her long red ponytail over one shoulder. "What's wrong?"

Cora took one look at Kelsey's face and knew. Cora had been her closest friend since elementary school and even though they'd only been in the same grade for one year before Kels had started skipping grades, they'd remained close. She was also the only person in the universe who knew about Tanner.

Heidi, meanwhile, was studying Kelsey closely. "No book,

even on book club night. Beer in hand, even though she only normally tolerates it because we like beer. Hollow look in her eyes—"

Kels smacked her. "Stop. My eyes are *not* hollow."

Cora plunked down into the booth next to her. "They kind of are." Her book smacked on the table. "Let's forget talking about this. It sucked, and I only read the summary online anyway."

"Cora!" Kate said. "How could you?"

Heidi narrowed her eyes. "We have one rule for book club. You read the book or—" She made a slicing motion across her throat.

That, at least, made Kels smile. "Since when?"

"Since we stopped reading all the books we were *supposed*"—she made air quotes here—"to be reading and just started going for the ones we wanted to read."

"Well then, what happened with this month?" Cora asked, pouring herself a beer. "Admit it, none of us wanted to read it."

She looked at Kels, who nodded and shrugged. "It's true."

Heidi winced.

Kate gasped. "I thought you guys were into—"

"The existential crisis of the white man?" Cora said. "Not so much. Especially when the first half is about how difficult their lives are."

"It's difficult having all that power," Heidi muttered.

"It was at the top of the bestseller's list and—"

Cora gasped. "You didn't read it either! You bitch!"

Kate bit her lip, cheeks turning pink. "No," she admitted. "Honestly, I suggested it as a joke and couldn't believe you guys agreed to it."

Heidi smacked her. "I spent fifteen bucks on the ebook! *Fifteen!* What the hell!"

Kelsey snorted.

Her friends looked at her, Cora beyond affronted, Kate blushing though her expression was quietly mischievous, and Heidi's eyes sparking with frustration.

"I love you guys," she said and felt a tear streak down her cheek.

The book by a well-known asshole, albeit a damned good prank on quiet Kate's part, was forgotten and her friends all began talking at once.

"Tears, Kels? Holy shit, did you get fired?" Heidi.

"Is your family okay?" Kate.

"Tanner." Cora.

She sucked in a shuddering breath and released it, dashing the tear away and thankful that one of the very few social things she'd learned during her time in college was how to put on makeup that stayed. The older girls had thrown her a solid. Big time. Big—

"Kelsey!"

She blinked and stepped back on the conversational road. "Sorry," she murmured. "Family is fine. Great actually. Devon and Becca had their baby, and I'm going shopping with Rachel soon for stuff to wear on her honeymoon. Work is busy but good."

"Which leaves Tanner," Cora said.

"Who's Tanner?" Kate asked.

Kelsey didn't know where to begin, but as usual, Cora had her covered. She shoved the book aside and filled Heidi and Kate's glasses. "Tanner is Bas's friend, and Kels has been in love with him for her entire existence."

"Not entire," she muttered.

"Okay, since she was eight years old and Tanner helped her get a Band-Aid or something."

"It was a Band-Aid *and* ice," Kelsey corrected. "And my mom."

"Aw," Kate murmured.

"How come we've never heard about Tanner?" Heidi asked.

"There was no point," Kels said. "We were together one summer, for a couple of months. He dumped me and left the country and hasn't been back for nine years."

"But we've been friends for nine years," Heidi protested.

"Part of the reason I went back for my post-doc was because of him. I needed something to fill my time."

Cora rolled her eyes. "Only you would consider getting a PhD as something to fill your time outside of a normal forty-hour workweek."

"Well," Kate said, reaching across the booth and squeezing Kels's hand. "Whatever reason you went back to school, I'm glad you ended up in my path." She smiled. "I got a good friend out of it."

Cora rolled her eyes again. "Stop being sappy," she snapped. "You're making us look bad."

"You're the worst," Kate snapped.

Heidi sighed. "Can we focus on why Tanner and Kelsey only lasted a few months?"

Kels shrugged. "Things were good, or so I thought. Insepa-rable for almost the whole summer, but then adulthood was call-ing, and my job had started, and I wanted us to tell my family. At first, sneaking around was fun, but eventually I wanted us to just be a real couple, you know?"

"Seems reasonable," Kate said.

"I thought so, too, and I thought he was on board. I suggested it, he agreed, but then the next day he called and broke up with me." Kels took a sip of her beer. "Then he left the country and didn't come back."

"For how long?" Heidi asked.

"He came back two days ago because he's in Bas's wedding.

Apparently, he's been keeping touch with my brother but not me."

"Well, he was Bas's friend first," Cora said. "It makes sense that they'd stay friends."

"That's it!" Kate exclaimed.

"What?"

"He must be hung up on the fact that Bas is your brother."

"That's stupid," Kelsey said.

Cora considered for a moment. "Stupid on his part, yes, but it is feasible. Men get stupid when it comes to sisters."

Considering that Cora had six brothers, Kelsey figured she understood the concept well. And she supposed it could be true, though she'd never considered the fact that the reason Tan had left was because of his relationship with her brothers. Given Bas's tendency towards aloofness when he'd been younger, she'd always just figured Tanner's interest had been there, but he'd waited until she was old enough. He and Devon had been close, too, but Dev was older and not home much. He'd been as engaged as he could be, of course. Just as a professional athlete, he hadn't had a ton of time for her or the rest of the family.

But Tanner had. He *always* had.

He'd been at her house sometimes more frequently than her own brothers.

She'd always figured that was because of her. But what if it hadn't been? What if he only wanted her because of her family?

She groaned and plunked her head on the table.

"What?" Cora asked.

"He's an only child. His parents are shit. Mine basically took him in when he was in middle school."

"Oh," Kate and Heidi said, though this wasn't news to Cora.

"He didn't have something to lose if things went wrong with you, Kels," she said. "He had it *all* to lose."

Kelsey glared up at Cora. "Why didn't you ever say anything?"

Cora put her hands up in surrender. "We were eighteen. I didn't exactly have a wealth of experience with boys back then."

True. Considering she was the youngest of six very protective brothers and her dad had passed shortly after she'd been born, that was *exceptionally* true. Cora had barely been allowed to go to prom, and that was only because Kelsey had gone as her date. Her brothers continued to meddle in her life to this day.

"Sorry," she said, bumping Cora's shoulder with her own.

"Not offended. But now that we all know what happened in the past, it's time to talk about the present."

She wrinkled her nose. "Technically what happened with Tanner was two days ago, so that is the past, too, and I'd just as soon pretend it never happened."

Heidi pfted. "In what world do you think we'd let you get away with that?"

Kels turned sad eyes to Kate, but even her sweet friend didn't soften. "Dish," she said. "Now."

"Ugh. Guys!" Kels's cheeks got hot just thinking about what had happened. "It's so embarrassing."

"More than me puking on my boss's shoes?" Kate asked.

"Yes."

"How about me having two too many beers and then puking on the hot, tattooed bartender?" Heidi asked.

"Yes," Kels snapped. "And you're lucky he let you back in here. Bobby's is the shit, and it would suck infinitely to have to find a new place to hang out."

"I bought him an entire new outfit," she admitted, "and promised to only have one beer a night for the rest of my time in Bobby's." They all glanced toward the bar, where sexy as sin, Kace, reigned supreme. He lifted a brow, lips curving the slightest bit, but then he returned his attention to his work.

Though, Kels watched a little longer, maybe he was pretending to work because—

"He's got a thing for the redhead working in the corner," Cora murmured. "Wouldn't have thought she was his type."

"Lucky girl," Kate said.

Heidi just sighed, and it was all jealous.

Kelsey knew the feeling, though she thought sun-kissed photojournalists were more her speed. She picked up her cell. "Oops," she said. "I forgot I have a conference call in the morning. I should—"

"Don't get distracted, girls," Cora declared. "She's trying to give us the slip."

Kate shook her head. "Tomorrow is Saturday, babe. Even you don't work on Saturdays."

"I—"

Heidi pointed a finger at her. "You. Share your embarrassing tale of woe now or so help me, God, I'll make next month's book an autobiography."

Kels shuddered.

"I'll do it," Heidi pressed.

She would and since it was her month to pick, they all had to shut up and take it. *Ugh.* What a metaphor in a time like this. When all *she'd* wanted to do was shut up and take it from Tan. But that wasn't happening.

"Fine," she said and began detailing the entire sordid tale. By the time she got to the point of taking off her bra and stepping out of her panties, her friends were gaping at her. "Then I walked into the bedroom, expecting him to come right after me."

Cora's voice was quiet. "He didn't?"

"No." Kels's eyes prickled again. "I waited and then I heard the door shut. When I peeked back in the hallway, he was gone."

"Oh shit," Kate said.

"Yeah." She pressed her hands to her cheeks. "The thought of seeing him again, after him just leaving . . . I don't know how to cope with that."

"Not to be an asshole," Cora said. "But, for Bas's sake, you're going to have to figure out a way."

Kels groaned. "I know." She plunked her head back down onto the table. "So, what's the play? I pretend nothing happened?"

"Hell no." Cora.

"Yes." Kate.

"Yes *and* no." Heidi.

Kelsey looked up at her friend. "Explain yourself."

"From what I've heard, it sounds as though Tanner really likes you—"

She snorted, disbelieving.

"He wouldn't have kissed you if he didn't like you," Heidi pointed out. "And he kissed you first, so that's big. It means he's into you, even if he doesn't want to be."

"Great. Ringing endorsement." She leaned back in the booth and crossed her arms. Into her even though he doesn't want to be. Perfect. Such a confidence booster.

"Shut up and listen," Kate said, and that snapped her out of her pity party, because Kate wasn't tough and rarely lost her cool. If she was telling Kelsey to focus, she should do just that.

"It's the typical tortured hero," Heidi said, speaking of one of their favorite romance tropes. "Tough past. Scared of bringing that into the future, so he either lashes out to push the heroine away *or* he does everything in his power to keep his distance." She picked up her glass and took a large swallow, looking awfully proud of herself.

As she should be.

Kels sat up straight.

"He did both," she said, stunned. "Pushed me away and ran."

"And this time he ran again," Cora said. "So the pushing away might be coming next."

Fuck. "That's true."

"What you need to decide," Kate said, "is if he's worth trying to force your way through the barricades and fire he's going to put in your path."

"And," Heidi said. "This isn't a book. It's real-life. Happy endings aren't guaranteed. Which means you may put yourself out there and not get the guy in the end."

Kels traced her finger along the outside of her glass. "You all are sure building my confidence tonight."

"If you wanted confidence building, you wouldn't be friends with us," Cora said. "We love you, but we always give it to each other straight. No bullshit."

Kelsey sighed. "So basically, I need to decide if pursuing things with Tanner is worth my potentially getting my heart stomped on again."

"Or run over by a train." Kate

"Or put through a blender and making a heartbreak smooth-ie." Heidi.

"Or having your ass hanging out there where none of us can do a damned thing to protect it from getting spanked." Cora.

"Cruel, but true," she said to Kate. "Gross." To Heidi. "And thanks for putting it in that particularly poetic way." Cora. She sighed, finished off her beer then picked up her glass of water. "Now, can we please talk about something else aside from my embarrassing as shit naked exploits?"

"How about we talk about that time you got locked out of your apartment with three gallons of ice cream and tried to eat them all so they wouldn't melt while you waited for the super?" Cora put in helpfully.

Kels shook her head, but she was smiling. "You guys really are the worst."

"And if by worst, you mean the *best*, then yes."

Thankfully, Kate took pity on her and changed the subject to *Outlander*—which Kels was now caught up on, thanks to the all-nighter she'd pulled after Tanner's escape act on Wednesday —and they spent the next few hours discussing all the merits of Jamie and Claire and how the show compared to the books thus far.

Getting lost in the fictional world of her favorite highlander meant that by the time they were walking out of Bobby's, Kelsey felt much more like herself again.

Or at least she wasn't going to expire of embarrassment.

She said goodbye to her friends then drove back into the City and to her apartment, but the quiet of the road brought everything back into the forefront of her mind again.

Tanner was her weak spot. He always had been.

And she'd demonstrated that fact quite clearly—cough, *painfully*—after he'd been back in town for only a few hours.

Her hands tightened on the steering wheel. Fucking pathetic.

Her. Him. The whole situation.

This wasn't a fairy tale. She couldn't fix him. And frankly .. . she didn't want to have that kind of responsibility. She'd been destroyed by his issues once, and that was more than enough. Or maybe it was less that he had issues and more that he didn't want her. Or want her enough to deal with the flack that was sure to come from her brothers.

That thought was almost as painful as the embarrassment she'd felt from his leaving her naked and wanting.

It also reinforced the fact that she needed to get her head on straight, to keep her heart safe.

And to make a commitment to never get naked in front of Tanner Pearson again.

Decision made.

Her ass would be staying safely in her pants from here on out.

EIGHT

Tanner

HE WOKE WITH A START, hard and aching and sweating, his cock about two seconds from exploding all over his stomach.

A wet dream.

About Kelsey.

It wouldn't be the first time he'd had one.

Or even the first one this month.

But it was the first time he'd had one and hadn't woken up without at least having finished. Embarrassingly, he was disappointed by that fact, disappointed that he couldn't share an orgasm with Kelsey, even in his dreams.

"Shit," he muttered, and because it was four in the morning, because he was jet-lagged and throbbing, he gripped the length of his erection and started stroking. Pink-tipped nipples, turquoise lace, lips that had parted the moment his had touched hers, a tongue that wasn't shy as it had stroked against his. Long legs around his hips, hands in his hair, a husky moan in the back of her throat—

He came for a long time, cock pulsing, spine bowing, sweat dripping down his temples into his hair.

"Fuck."

Tanner reached over to the nightstand and grabbed the box of tissues he'd started keeping there. Like a fucking teenager. Christ, next thing he knew, and he'd be keeping some lotion there as well. To prevent chafing.

Cute.

Sighing, he pushed out of bed.

The jet lag was getting better, even if he was up at 4:16 in the morning. He was used to early mornings, used to getting up before the sun rose and getting into position to capture the best light.

But there wasn't a reason to get up anymore.

He'd stopped taking new contracts a year ago, had told his agent to no longer send him queries because he was taking an indefinite break.

Something Tom wasn't the least bit happy about since he got a percentage of every contract. But Tan didn't give a shit at this point. He'd worked his way up from taking photos at family and friends' events to traveling on a shoestring budget, picking something that struck him as compelling to capture then hoping like hell he might find someone who might want to buy his photographs. Eventually, he'd landed Tom and become in high demand for nature magazines. But after a portrait he'd snapped of a friend of a friend—who'd turned out to be a famous celebrity he didn't know because he spent most of his life away from the Internet—he'd been asked to take photos for various industry events and high fashion magazines.

He'd done it all.

Because he'd been hungry to prove himself.

But also because he'd been motivated to forget.

Then Kelsey had called him.

It had all begun unraveling then. He'd started dreaming of her at eighteen, of their time together—and not just sex dreams because he wasn't a total pervert. He'd remembered curling up on the couch, sharing a bowl of popcorn and laughing like loons at some comedy he probably wouldn't find funny nowadays. He remembered the way her smile used to change, just minutely, when she met his eyes, as though she held him in a special place in her heart.

And he remembered what he'd said to her to push her away.

The way her breathing had hitched when he'd wounded her.

For years he'd tried to forget it all, to bury it in work.

And a thirty-second phone call had made him realize how absolutely useless all the years of hiding had been. He'd never been able to get her out of his heart or brain. He had the feeling he never would.

Suddenly the fast-paced cities he was photographing in Asia had seemed dull, the beautiful beaches and ocean uninspired, the people faceless. Tan had gotten the necessary shots, had done his job because he was a fucking professional, but he'd hated every single moment of it.

Then he'd come home.

Or back to the states, at least.

Back to Kelsey.

But nothing had changed.

She felt like home, was captivating and brilliant and gorgeous. Still tempted him like no other woman ever had, and she still had the ability to burrow deep into his soul. Yet, *nothing* had changed. He was broken inside, so what could he possibly offer her?

He ran when things got tough.

His parents hadn't even wanted him.

All he could give Kelsey was an uncertain future and one half of a man.

The urge to hit the road and find whatever means necessary to disappear was intense, and the only thing that was stopping him from bolting was Sebastian. He might be a dick and screw-up, but the last thing he was going to do was fuck up his friend's wedding.

Tanner also knew that even if he ran again, even if he took all the jobs Tom wanted him to, that he'd never be able to shake off the feel of Kelsey in his arms.

Before he'd relegated the memories to the back of his mind, tucked safely away.

Now they were out and just like Pandora's Box, there was no going back to the way things were.

Sighing, he buried the tissues in the garbage can, took a quick shower and dressed, then grabbed his backpack and went down to the lobby. It was habit to check his bag for his camera, along with additional batteries and a handful of extra memory cards—a photographer never wanted to run out of disk space or for their camera to die mid-shoot.

Outside the sky was dark and the morning commute was just beginning, lines of lights trailing through the street, white coming toward him, turning red as they passed, but he could see just the barest glimmer of sunlight in the East.

As he walked, he'd pause at whatever struck his fancy and take a shot. With the changing lights and traffic building, it was a lesson in balancing technique with his artistic presence. But really, he was just playing around, pointing his camera in any direction, even purposefully ruining some pictures with too much light or not enough focus.

Sometimes good things happened when he broke the rules.

His camera had been pointed at the dark silhouette of a gothic building against the lightening sky when he'd had that thought, but the moment it crossed his brain, his lens drooped, and he ended up getting a shot of a pigeon's head peeking around the eaves.

See what he meant about good things?

But he couldn't appreciate the irony of that statement when he was shocked senseless by what he'd just thought.

When he broke the rules in his work, good things happened.

So why was he so terrified of breaking the rules where Kelsey was concerned?

He lifted his camera and hit the button, capturing the shot he'd imagined before, but it was even better than he'd thought it would be because he shot a little later, because there was more light available, and—

He was terrified of breaking the rules because Kelsey was so much more important than a picture. Quite simply, the stakes were higher.

But, with that piece of information straight in his head, he continued moving, kept doing his best to fill those memory cards, and by the time the sun was high in the sky, he'd found some of the happy that being behind the lens used to give him. The world focused to just a small circle, one that he could control and move as he saw fit. Tan was king of that lensed world, even if his subjects occasionally got a little squirrely and uncooperative.

Eventually, his arms got tired, his eyes tired, and his empty memory card supply dangerously low, so he decided to head back to the hotel.

Since he'd been wandering for hours without paying much attention to directions or landmarks, he pulled out his cell and spent a few minutes with the map to plot his course home. Then he started walking, larger intersections transforming into smaller twisting streets and nicer apartments.

A flash of green caught his attention just as he turned the street corner, and for a moment his breath caught in his lungs.

So fucking beautiful.

Fog hugging the ground, the sun having burned away the pockets overhead, but this little enclave of green was shadowed by the buildings surrounding it, and so the fog lived on, curling mist that garnished silver and black stones.

A cemetery perhaps wasn't the most obvious choice for beauty, but this one was.

Or perhaps it was the man kneeling over a flat headstone, brushing away the leaves and dirt before placing a bouquet of yellow daffodils on its surface.

Tan lifted his camera to capture the moment—sun drifting through the fog, highlighting the yellow flowers, silhouetting the man against the gray mist, the green grass bright, the black and white of the other headstones making the entire image otherworldly.

The *click* of the shutter startled him.

He dropped his camera, realized he was intruding on a private moment.

Shit.

As painful as it was, he'd delete the image when he got back to the hotel.

"Don't."

The raspy voice startled Tan, and he glanced up to see that the old man had made his way over to him, beige jacket darkened in speckles where the moisture had clung to the air.

"I'm sorry," Tan said. "I'll delete the photograph. Usually I ask before I shoot, I was just so taken by the moment . . ." He cleared his throat. "It was beautiful."

Pale brown eyes studied him for a long moment then the man pushed open the gate to the small cemetery. "Come."

Tan bit his tongue, swallowed his questions, and followed the man through the path to the grave he'd been kneeling at.

Rosario Hernadez, Loving Wife and Mother.

"My Rosie was beautiful," the man said softly.

"Were daffodils her favorite?" Tan asked.

A nod. "She'd get the biggest smile on her face when I'd bring them to her." His voice went sad. "I'd give anything to see that again."

The dates on the headstone told Tanner that the loss had been recent, and he found himself clasping the man's shoulder. "Did you have a lot of years together?"

Tears glittered, but the man nodded. "We did. Almost fifty, and yet it seems to have gone by in a flash."

"What were some things you loved about her?"

He smiled. "My Rosie was very competitive. Never met a board game she didn't have to win." Mischief crept into his expression. "Or an argument. She always made sure I had the type of drinks I loved, only cooked the meals I hated when I really made her mad."

Tan laughed.

"And she gave me a beautiful family. A beautiful life."

The tears were still in the man's eyes, but there was also something else—peace. Relief in knowing that even if the time spent with the woman he loved was ephemeral, he still held tight to those memories, those emotions.

"I wanted forever," the man said. "Even knowing that wasn't possible. And now that I find myself without forever, I still know I wouldn't change a single day."

Nothing was permanent.

Tanner lifted the camera without thinking, capturing the love on the man's face, how even though his heart was shattered because the incredible thing he'd had was now gone, he still understood he'd had something precious, and that precious thing was to be protected.

The man blinked, glanced at the camera.

"Sorry," Tanner said. "I—" He shook his head. "I'll delete them."

A warm hand stayed his when he began fumbling with his camera. "Don't." Then the old man reached into his pocket and pulled out a card. "Will you send them to me?"

Tan held his breath for a long moment, then carefully pocketed the card. "Yes."

"Good man," he said and turned back to the headstone.

"Would you—" Pale brown eyes found his again, warmer this time, and that gave Tan the strength to finish the question. "Would you do it again?"

The man opened his mouth to reply, but Tanner pressed on because that wasn't quite the question he'd wanted to ask. "I mean, if you knew you were going to screw things up, that there was no way that you could keep Rosie forever because you weren't good enough for her, couldn't give her everything she wanted . . . would you still go for it?"

The man was quiet for a long time.

Then he said, "Yes."

And that was it.

Tanner swallowed hard and nodded.

"You're going to screw up," he said when Tan started to turn away. "There are going to be times when everything you have to give her isn't enough. Life isn't fair or easy. It takes courage. Courage to leap and grab hold. Courage to hope that you'll be able to figure out what *is* enough." He pointed at Rosie's headstone. "Together."

The man bent and swept off one last leaf then squeezed Tan's arm as he left.

Tanner didn't know how long he stood there, staring off in to space, processing the words the man had said, feeling them shift all the pieces in his mind and heart around until they all started to make sense.

Maybe he *could* be enough.

His cell buzzed, jolting him out of reverie. He left the cemetery, turning back in the direction of the hotel, and he pulled it out of his pocket to see that Bas had sent him a text inviting him to dinner at his parents' place that night. With all three of their kids in the Bay Area, the Scotts had sold their house in the Midwest and moved to a town east of San Francisco.

It was smaller than the home they'd raised their kids in and supposedly quite a heap, according to Devon. But Grant had recently retired and wanted a project to keep him busy.

Or maybe it was more accurate to say that Megan, who'd quit her job as a classroom aid when they'd moved and whom Grant was driving absolutely crazy, had wanted to give him a project.

At least, this was all according to Bas.

But the Scotts were a close-knit family, and Tanner figured it was accurate gossip.

Poor Megan had probably imagined California as all sunny beaches, fruity cocktails, and avocado toast, but as most people who made it to the northern part of the Golden State eventually discovered, the north and south were vastly different. The southern part had the warm beaches, while the northern part had the frigid, only-swimmable-if-someone-was-crazy ocean. Cocktails were more likely to be wine, though avocado toast *was* prevalent.

He made a mental note to buy Megan and Grant a trip to Hawaii for Christmas that year then typed out a quick response to Bas saying he'd be there.

To which Bas replied:

Great. Want to get a ride with Kelsey? She's driving over.

The universe hated him.

Kels okay with that?

Which was really fucking unlikely given the way he'd left her on Wednesday night.

Of course, she'll be. I'll send her a text.

Oh, for fuck's sake.

I've got her number. I'll make sure it's not an inconvenience.

A few seconds passed.

Why do you have her number?

He cursed, pushed his way into the lobby and considered telling his best friend that he'd spent a summer boning his sister and then the nine years since imagining doing it in all the ways his twenty-one-year-old self had been too uninspired to think of at the time. Probably unwise. Snorting, he sent something safer.

Dude, I have every Scott's number. It's an occupational hazard of being practically adopted into the family.

Then.

Heading into an elevator. Will see you tonight.

As the floors sped by, he considered his options. One, he could ignore Bas's suggestion and take BART—the local public transit—to the east bay. This might be the safest option—well, not safe in terms of potential for bodily harm, but safe because he wouldn't be in close proximity to Kels. However, there were some sketchy stations if Bas was to be believed, and then there would be an explanation required for why he didn't actually ask for a ride. Second, he could ask Kelsey for the ride and risk her running him over in the parking lot of her building. Third—

Third . . . he could give up the fight, accept that it was impossible to keep Kelsey at a distance, and just go for what the universe had been telling him.

Third was the scariest.

NINE

Kelsey

HER PHONE BUZZED when she was mid-bite, and the contents of the text message made her oatmeal slop off her spoon and onto the table.

"Are you fucking kidding me?" she hissed, dropping the utensil into the bowl and trying to resist the urge to launch her cell across the room. She'd committed to forgetting Tanner, to closing up her heart and moving on from Tanner.

And now he was texting her, asking her to voluntarily spend the equivalent of two hours trapped in a car with him.

She plunked the phone on the counter then picked up her bowl.

"Stupid *fucking* men." She set the half-full bowl in the sink. Set, not tossed because she'd gotten her dinnerware at a really kitschy store that was no longer in business. The pieces were hand-thrown, each one a little different and all glazed in iridescent blue. Kels had loved the way they were edged, loved how the slight wave reminded her of a flower.

She'd bought a full set of twelve bowls, dinner plates, and

salad plates, and since she hosted meals at her house exactly *never,* that hadn't been an efficient use of her funds *or* cabinet space.

Still, she'd loved them, so she'd bought them then had dealt with the fallout of sacrificing an entire kitchen cabinet to store them.

Sometimes in life a woman had to make sacrifices.

Snorting, she filled the bowl with water before turning to rest her hips against the lip of the counter.

One day and her resolve to keep her distance from Tanner was kaput. Because, frankly, there was more than one type of distance. Emotional as well as physical, and riding in a car with him was about as far from keeping her physically away from Tan as possible. Then there was her reaction to his request.

Joy.

Excitement to be in his presence.

And then fury because she was such a fucking idiot. If he'd wanted something more than friendship from her, he would have taken it on Wednesday night. Even if he'd thought they were rushing things or that they should slow down and take a breath, he would have made it clear that he was leaving because of that and not disappeared out the door like a freaking ninja.

Seriously, if it hadn't been for her trail of underthings, she could have almost pretended she'd been hallucinating.

But the trail had been there, and her embarrassment was undying, and—

No, she couldn't be trapped in a car with him for two-plus hours!

So she texted him back.

Sorry. Can't.

Lame, but it saved her, and that was what she needed.

Setting her phone on the table, she started for the shower. She'd slept in that morning, watched a few new episodes of *Killing Eve,* then had subjected herself to an hour of Pilates.

Now it was lunchtime and she'd lost her appetite for her oatmeal, which conveniently was the only semi-palatable food she had left in her house. Maybe she'd treat herself to Molly's. They made the most incredible pear and walnut salad, and they probably had their new soups of the day out.

Yes. That was the perfect plan.

Drown her sorrows in raspberry vinaigrette and candied walnuts—

Buzz buzz.

How about a ride home then?

Ugh. She snagged her cell and headed for the bathroom, starting up the shower and debating what to say.

In the end, she settled on,

Sorry. No.

She wasn't sorry, but it definitely was a no, and so she left it at that and put the phone down again. By then the shower was warm, so she stripped off her sweaty clothes. The hot water hitting her skin was everything she needed in her life, sluicing down her hair, warming her from the outside in.

It soothed the muscles she'd tortured during her workout, and it also effectively blocked any noise of her cell's potential vibration.

Eventually, she'd pruned herself up enough and turned off the water.

No sooner had she toweled off, then her eyes found her cell.

Sure enough, a text was on the screen.

Understood. But you're going to have to think up a reason to tell Bas why you're not available to drive me when he knows you are coming to dinner and already offered you up as a ride option.

"Shit," she muttered.

He was right, of course, Bas had called her earlier that day, asked her what she was doing, and like an imbecile, she'd dished about her plans to do nothing but veg out before going to the family dinner.

Maybe she could think of some excuse at work?

Wait. Damn, that wouldn't work. Not so long as she and Bas were working on the joint RoboTech/Steele Technologies project. If she lied and said there was an issue with the product that she had to go into work to deal with, but didn't tell him immediately, he'd be beyond pissed.

Yes, they were siblings, but they were also partners on this product, and RoboTech didn't screw over their partners—or leave them out of the loop on potential problems, fake or otherwise.

Not to mention that lying about the project would quite possibly get her fired, and she really liked her job.

So work was out.

Maybe she could fake the sudden onset of the flu?

Bas wouldn't buy it.

An existential crisis that required her to stay in and gorge on Oreos she'd ordered in on InstaCart?

Ick.

There was a reason that she tended to lack a filter. She didn't like lying, and while yes, she had to admit that lying wasn't a skill she'd managed to hone over the years, she also didn't like lying because it made her feel bad inside.

Usually, she just gave her answer with as little of the negative details as possible.

Hence, *Sorry. No.*

So she either—

And dammit, she flung her cell onto the bed and stormed to the closet, thinking that her life over the last few days had been filled with way too many *eithers* and ultimatums.

She either drove him or lied.

She either offered her heart up to potentially be shredded by Tanner or she let him go.

She either put aside how much he'd hurt her nine years ago or she ruined her brother's wedding.

She either sucked it up and pretended everything was fine . . . or—

What else could she do?

Kelsey had had plenty of experience with pretending things were fine.

This would be just another day. Her fingers moved across her cell's screen.

Be in the lobby by four.

THANK God for Molly's and their perfectly caramelized walnuts.

Those nuts in her mouth were the only thing getting her through this day—yes, insert snort there—but the point was that Molly's fabulous salad was distracting her from what was coming in T-minus one hour.

Sighing, she closed her paperback and started gathering her things.

She needed to change before Tanner showed up, to put

herself together in a way that would allow her mom to miss that she was falling apart inside.

Though, with the wedding rapidly approaching and Devon's baby newly born into the world and altogether adorable, Kels's mom was missing plenty these days.

Still, she didn't need to slip up and get on the radar.

These were dark, dark days.

Potential motherly intervention before, during (or truthfully, *after*) Bas's long-awaited wedding—complete with the giant cake and seat covers and white poofy dress—wasn't something Kelsey wanted to deal with.

And more importantly, she wasn't going to mess up a single detail of her brother's big day.

Bas had waited a long time to be happy, and Rachel had been put through the wringer. Rachel's ex-husband was—or had been—a creep of the worst kind. He'd abused her repeatedly then had come after her in California when she'd tried to divorce him. Plus, her mom had left, her father was cruel and mostly absentee, and her grandparents, who'd basically raised her, had treated her like garbage. Things had worked out in the end, but Rachel had suffered in the process, spending a good deal of her life trying to escape her past.

Hmm. Kind of like Tanner and his escape act.

Not that his childhood was anything when compared to Rachel's, but he'd been obviously neglected and not a priority to his parents in the least. That had to leave scars.

Kels wondered if that was a Scott family trait, finding partners that were wounded and needed rescuing.

It wasn't like their lives growing up had been bump free or all sunshine and rainbows, but they'd had two parents who'd loved them, a steady home, food on the table. That was a lot more than most.

But also maybe that made her and her brothers choose lovers who hadn't had it as good.

Share the wealth of good.

She snorted.

Might as well don a crown and hold a fairy princess wand. She didn't wield that sort of power, couldn't change someone or make their past better. She was just a girl, living her life, and trying not to fuck up too much.

Still, it did bear some pondering, that Scott tendency to rescue.

Dev had rescued his wife, Becca. Or at least, he'd helped her out when she'd been in a tough spot and quite literally had protected her from some creep who'd been trying to hurt her.

Bas had rescued Rachel, though she'd resent the term and say the rescuing was mutual. Which it was. But according to Heather, Rachel's boss, Rach had been shut down and scared and hurting, with Sebastian as the only one to penetrate those layers of heavy, steel armor around her heart.

And Tanner.

When she was eighteen, she'd thought she might be enough to fill that hole inside him.

But in dramatic, teenage-broken-heart fashion, she'd been proven wrong.

Painfully wrong.

Ugh.

Enough.

She shoved her book into her purse, left a tip on the table, and bustled out of the restaurant. Twenty minutes later, she'd swapped her comfy leggings for jeans, her sneakers for flats, her scarf for a jumble of necklaces.

No primping.

As in, she wasn't going to allow herself to put any more effort into her appearance than she normally would for a visit to her parents' by resisting the urge to glam it up and shove in Tanner's nose exactly what he'd been missing out on Wednesday.

But she'd already shown him everything, and look how that had turned out.

So instead, Kels did the bare minimum, made sure she had a playlist on her phone—no way was she making the mistake of not filling the silence in her car this time. Then she grabbed her purse, jacket, and keys and headed for the door.

The knock greeted her just as she arrived.

"Fuck," she muttered, having no idea that Tanner was saying the exact same thing on the other side of the door.

TEN

Tanner

"FUCK," Tanner muttered after he'd knocked, trying to resist the urge to shove his hand through his hair.

He was equal parts convinced this was the stupidest thing he'd ever done and also maybe the smartest.

Kelsey was—

The door opened, and his breath caught.

Absolutely beautiful.

He could almost imagine that this was a real date, that he hadn't fucked her over twice and that they were making a real go of this.

If she hadn't looked like she wanted to kill him.

Blue eyes sparked with annoyance, and Tan was probably kidding himself, but he could have sworn there was a trace of heat in her expression. If it *had* been present and not a figment of his imagination, then it was gone in a millisecond, a tight mask of annoyance locked in place over her face.

Still beautiful, even when furious.

She didn't say anything, just stepped out, closed and locked the door, then headed for the elevator.

"Hi," he said.

Nothing.

"Good talk," he couldn't resist saying.

Kels spun around so fast that her ponytail smacked her in the face. "What did you say?"

He caught the ends and rubbed them between his fingers, and fuck, that simple touch was enough for him to *remember*.

Hairs tangling over his face as she slept sprawled across his chest, tendrils escaping her ponytail as she'd sat across the table from him working on some multiple-page proof, long strands damp from the shower and smelling like roses.

Roses she still smelled like.

Kelsey jumped back, wrenching her hair from his fingers, the ends catching in a way that had to be painful. Her wince of discomfort made him feel like even more of a shitbag.

"Don't touch," she snapped, wrenching back around in a way that made *him* wince, or at the very least, worry for her spine.

Yet, even furious, she was still the most beautiful thing he'd ever seen.

And for a man like him, one who'd seen more breathtaking landmarks in just a few years than people saw in their entire lifetimes, that wasn't easy to do.

It wasn't bullshit either.

Her brown eyes rivaled the desert sand of the Sahara, her hair as lush and thick as the foliage in the jungles of the Amazon. Kels's skin was softer than the merino wool he'd touched in New Zealand, her scent more delicate than the roses he'd photographed in the Queen's garden in England. She was . . . well, putting aside his pathetic rambling, Kelsey had always been with him.

As he'd gone through his memory cards, deleting most of what he'd shot, only saving the couple that might be good enough for publication—even though he was technically retired, old habits died hard. But then as he had studied the photographs from the cemetery, witnessing the love and devotion on the man's face all over again, feeling those same emotions pulse in his heart when he thought of Kelsey, Tan had come to the realization that no matter how far he'd traveled, she had always been in his heart.

So, he'd decided to go with option three.

He was going to keep her.

The thought of fucking things up with her still terrified him. He didn't know how to do something good, but he also didn't know how to be in this world and not have Kelsey. And he'd take on any of the Scotts who had a problem with that, whether it was Devon or Sebastian or Grant or Megan. He'd prove to them that he could make her happy.

He just had to figure out how to convince Kels to let him.

Figures, he'd already dug himself a giant hole in that department.

Back stiff as a board, she jabbed at the elevator button. Repeatedly.

Tan held on to his hope. The no touching thing, the irritation in his presence, the purposeful ignoring . . . all of those were good things. Well, not *good* exactly, because he'd prefer to go back to Wednesday and make a different choice, but those emotions also meant Kelsey was still feeling something for him.

Annoyance was just a hairsbreadth away from makeup sex.

Yeah, sure it was. But makeup sex or not, she felt something, and so that meant he wasn't going to give up.

Of course, annoyance was also very close to dead-to-her, and so Tanner needed to make sure he didn't fuck things up further.

Internally sighing, he followed Kels to the elevator, purposefully standing very close, but also not touching. Yes, he was an asshole. Yes, he planned on pushing that very boundary. No, he wouldn't cross the line she'd drawn without her asking him to. Still, that didn't mean he couldn't soak up as much of her as possible, starting with the scent that had been imprinted on his senses.

"Did you just *sniff* me?" She turned slightly, ponytail whipping around again, though this time it slapped *him* in the cheek.

Play it cool.

"Hmm?" he asked.

"Did you—"

The elevator doors opened with a ding, and Tan hurried in front of Kels, partly to ensure the metal panels didn't close on her, but mostly to avoid having to answer her question.

He pressed the button for the garage. "You coming?"

Her nose wrinkled, but she stepped onto the elevator, positioning herself with her back to the corner.

The one furthest from him.

Yeah. She felt something. He just had to convince her doing something about that *something* was worth it.

They rode down to the garage in silence, but she surprised him by handing over the keys as they approached her car. "I can't stand driving," she told him. "And you might as well make yourself useful."

"Putting me to work?"

"I should put you *somewhere*," she muttered, plunking herself down in the passenger's side and reaching for the seat belt.

He beat her to it, grabbing the buckle and stretching it over her lap. Her breath hitched and because he'd purposefully put himself as close as possible without actually touching, he felt those warm puffs of air on his neck.

Hot. Damp.

Fuck.

Now he *felt* it somewhere else.

He closed his eyes, struggling to call up some control. Him taking option three (his keeping Kelsey . . . permanently) didn't mean he could just waltz back into her life and fuck it up more than he'd already done. He needed to move slow, to move with caution. To show her he knew he'd fucked up, but that he wasn't going to do it again.

To prove that he wasn't going to hurt her again.

Kissing her senseless and then tossing her in the backseat to ravage her like a teenager on prom night wouldn't prove anything.

So he sucked in a breath, braced himself against the dizziness that came from having so much of her intoxicating scent in his nose, and buckled her seat belt.

The *click* was gunshot loud in the quiet garage.

Tanner blinked, started to shake his head to clear it.

Fingers in his hair, along his jaw.

He shuddered. The hand on his face shook.

His eyes swung to the side, saw her brown ones were clouded with desire. Lush, pink lips parted. "Tan—"

A car alarm went off, making them both jump.

Then the fingers slipped away, tucked back into the safety of Kelsey's lap. He shifted, straightening out of her sedan, and trying to remember that he was *not* going to ravish her in the backseat.

Swallowing, he retreated a step and closed the car door.

He'd been looking forward to the drive initially, thinking it would be a good start to him proving himself.

Now he was thinking that two-plus hours trapped in a metal box with Kelsey was going to be hell on his self-control *and* his plan to win her back.

Hell he probably deserved.

Hell he was going to soak up as precious anyway.
Because it was Kelsey. It was him.
It was them.
And he wasn't going to waste a *them* moment.
Not ever again.

ELEVEN

Kelsey

SEBASTIAN KNEW.

She didn't know how she knew that, but the prickling between her shoulder blades that had been her constant companion since they'd walked into her parents' place told her that the jig was up.

At least with one brother.

Which meant that it was soon going to be up with the other.

Sighing, she picked up another dish and began to rinse it in the sink. Her mom had cooked, normally a treat in and of itself, but because Tanner was there, she'd also baked. And *that* was a gift from God herself.

She set the plate on the drying rack then moved to the next, scooping up a piece of pie crust from the apple crumble her mom had baked before she began rinsing.

Probably not the most sanitary, but that crust was like gold.

It couldn't go waste.

There was a reason she'd offered to do the dishes, and it

wasn't just because it was an effective way to get out from under Bas's intent stare. It also was because the leftovers became hers.

Cue evil laughter.

That crust? Hers. The spoonful of homemade ice cream Devon didn't finish? Hers. Also, eating to soothe her feelings. No way that could go wrong. Especially when it involved her mom's—

"You always did have a sweet tooth."

Kels shivered. Tan had snuck up on her just as she'd shoved the spoon in her mouth, so it took her a moment to fumble out an answer.

"Y-you shouldn't be here."

A stuttering response, and yet an absolutely perfect one for the situation.

After Wednesday, after the scene nine years before, he shouldn't be in her space.

He'd had his chance, he'd blown it, and she was done.

But then he leaned back against the doorframe, smiled his rueful smile, and her stomach did a little flip. "Dev and Bas are arguing about who the Gold should pick up in the draft, and your dad has chimed in with lots of thoughts."

Kels bit the inside of her cheek and turned back to the dishes. "I'm guessing you didn't watch much hockey while you were traveling."

A chuckle. "Not so much."

"I followed Dev's career," he continued, "Which reminds me, I haven't teased him about being the Sexiest Man of the Month or whatever his title was."

"Year," she corrected, rinsing another plate before eyeing the next. The one that was committing a crime against people who loved baked goods. Three-quarters of the slice of lemon cream her mom had also baked was just sitting innocently in the corner. Probably Becca's, since she was on a quest to lose the quote-unquote baby weight.

Meanwhile, Kelsey thought her sister-in-law had never looked more beautiful.

Also, she was going to eat that slice of pie, even if it made her sick.

"You should go do that," she said. "Dev hasn't gotten his share of sibling smack talk of late."

"Is that what I am?" Tanner's voice was closer. "A sibling?"

Typically, her impulsivity was her downfall. This case was no different. "It's all you're ever going to be," she blurted. "It's all you'll ever *let* yourself be."

Silence.

Stupid. Why had she taken the conversation there?

It had all been going, well, not exactly *fine* but now—

A fork appeared in front of her face.

"Eat the pie." Tanner reached across her and picked up the plate.

"What?"

He handed it to her. "You want it." A soft murmur. "You should have everything you want, even if people are scared they won't be able to give you all you deserve."

"People?"

"Me."

"Scared?"

Tanner speared a bite of pie and lifted it to her mouth. She hesitated, then her lips parted and the tangy-sweet hit her tongue.

"Scared," he confirmed. "Then. Now. But I've been think-ing"—she snorted, and he grinned but continuing talking—"scared isn't always bad, not when scared can be a means to make a person give a shit." He touched her cheek. "And I give a shit about you, Kels. Always have."

Probably not the most romantic sentiment ever spoken, but his tone made up for it. And his eyes, too, sincerity pouring from the chocolate depths.

She swallowed, set the plate down. "I—"

"You guys done?" Bas asked, sticking his head in through the doorway. "We're starting a new Monopoly game since Tanner's home."

Kelsey groaned. "God, no. That's a horrible idea."

"You're only saying that because you thought you were going to win the last one."

"I *was* going to win it." She'd been kicking the entire family's butts.

Bas just shrugged and said, "We have to start fresh so Tanner can join."

"Oh," Tan said, eager to remove himself from the Monopoly war. And no joke, it *was* a war because her family took their board games seriously. "I—"

Bas didn't dispute further. "Hurry up with the dishes. Game's on in five."

She plunked her hands on her hips. "Bas—"

But he was gone, the stink. She frowned and picked the plate back up, shoving a huge, and not ladylike in the least, bite of pie into her mouth. "I had Park Place *and* Boardwalk," she grumbled. "Plus, a hotel."

Tan whistled. "Totally gonna win."

Kels glanced at him and couldn't hold back her smile. "Yes," she said. "I was."

He picked up a plate, started drying it. Amongst the many projects on her dad's to-do list in this fixer-upper was replacing the dishwasher that had died. But for right now, her mom had grunt work, and that meant Kels should get down to business. With a sad look at the pie, but a high five to her self-control, she dumped the rest of the slice in the trash then went back to rinsing. Tan stayed, and she washed and he dried in contented silence for a few minutes, time during which she felt her shoulders relax, the tension that had been making them ache ever since she'd learned the news of Tanner's return dissipating.

Maybe they could do this. Find a happy medium. Be friends —*just* friends—again.

"Tanner—"

"I fucked up, baby."

Baby.

She dropped the glass she'd been washing, and it hit the bottom of the sink, shattering. But she'd barely registered the sound of it break, the shards glittering in the bright lights of the kitchen. Because . . . *baby*.

His hand dropped onto her nape, and she startled.

"Careful," he murmured, sliding his fingers down her arm, slipping them around her wrist. He picked up one hand, lifting it away from the shards that she'd been absentmindedly reaching for, reeling from the contact, from his tone.

And she couldn't move.

Because the way he'd called her *baby*.

"Hey." Tan tugged, turning her so she faced him, so they were toe-to-toe, chests only a hairsbreadth apart.

"You—"

"I've spent too long running," he murmured.

"Tan—"

"I want you, Kelsey."

Her breath caught. "I—"

He kissed her.

Then Bas came into the kitchen. "Hey, the game's—"

All hell broke loose.

TWELVE

Tanner

OKAY, so he'd broken his promise not to touch her until she asked, but that was because she'd been about to cut herself.

He'd needed to do it.

Yeah, keep telling yourself that.

Frankly, it was easy to do that, the delusions of grandeur, when Kelsey's mouth was on his, her breasts pillowed against his chest, roses in his nose.

"Hey, the game's—"

Kelsey jumped, tearing her mouth from his and all but leaping back. Her hands flailed, and concerned one of them was going to land in the sink, Tanner nudged her out of the way. Which also meant that she ended up cuddled to his side, but as far as he was concerned, that was a good byproduct.

Even if Kelsey's face said she felt differently.

"I knew it!"

Bas was grinning as Devon popped his head in the doorway behind him. "Knew what?"

Tanner's gut sank, but he sucked it up. Choosing option three meant he knew this was eventually going to happen—that he'd have to lay it out there for all the Scotts, including Kels' brothers, and that they might want to kick his ass for even considering touching her.

She was worth it.

He'd figured that out earlier, too.

Tanner wasn't twenty-one years old, thinking he was a man when really, he was still a boy who didn't know his ass from a hand grenade.

He'd prove he was worth the risk. To Kelsey. And he'd tell her brothers to go fuck themselves if they had a problem with it.

In a nice way, of course.

But the point was Kelsey was his, and while the exposé al la Scotts had happened a lot sooner than he'd planned—mainly because *his* plan had included some wooing and maybe getting her to not hate him before he shared his feelings with the whole clan—this was also always going to happen.

So he had to roll with it.

"Kelsey has a thing for Tanner."

She gasped.

"Well, duh," Devon said.

"What?" Her ponytail flicked as she glanced from brother to brother. "You knew that?"

Bas rolled his eyes. "Hard to miss, Kels, when you were drooling after him every chance you got."

"I was—"

"Were, too," Tanner murmured.

Mouth agape, she stared up at him. "You knew?" she whispered, horror laced through the question.

His nod in response made her cheeks flush, and she tried to pull away. Since he liked her right where she was, he slipped an arm around her waist to keep her in place. "I knew because I had it bad, too," he said softly.

"How long?" she asked, relaxing against him.

Tanner's mouth tipped up. "Probably want to have that conversation without prying ears."

Kels jumped again, and he liked that she'd forgotten about her brothers in the room, liked that she'd leaned against him.

He just liked *her*.

Head swiveling, she glared at her brothers. "You two are horrible brothers."

"No," Bas said. "Horrible brothers would be horrified that my best friend is interested in seeing our sister."

"What?" Tanner asked.

Bas snorted. "Dude," he said. "You were as obvious as Kelsey, always asking about her, what she was doing for work, if she was seeing anyone serious."

Fuck.

He had.

His gut twisted. "Was that why you asked me to come back for the wedding?"

Sebastian sighed and rolled his eyes. "Seriously, man? I've stayed in touch with one person from high school, and that was you. Even when you were on the opposite side of the globe, we made an effort to talk," he said. "You're more than a friend. You're a brother."

"A brother who wants to see your sister."

Bas wrinkled his nose. "Well, when you put it like that, I can't condone it." A beat. "But if I think about my best friend, a man I've known my whole life, a *good* man watching out for my sister, then I can't think of anyone better."

Fuck.

Out there. Just like that.

And also the moment that Kelsey had had enough.

She shoved out of Tanner's arms, plunked her hands on her hips, and glared at each of them in turn. "First, I don't need anyone watching out for me. Second, I don't even know what the hell Tanner and I have—"

"So figure it out," Devon said, interrupting her before she went full rant.

"I—"

Dev slipped by Bas and crossed over to Tanner, toes almost touching, leaning down so his nose was mere inches away. "I'm going to say this *one* time—"

"Dev—"

They both ignored her.

"You hurt Kelsey," Dev said. "And I hurt you."

"I wouldn't expect anything less," Tanner said.

Devon straightened, a smile tugging at the corner of his lips. "But good luck trying to pin that one down. She's wily."

If they knew he'd had the chance to do it—twice—and had fucked up—twice—Tanner had the feeling that Dev wouldn't be quite so cavalier. Still, he kept that information to himself and nodded. "Thanks for the advice."

"You'll need all the help you can get."

Kels sighed loudly. "I'm right here."

"Also," Dev said, grin slipping free. "She hates when you talk about her like she's not in the room."

"I'm starting to remember that."

She huffed and turned back to the sink, picking up the shards of glass and tossing them into the trash.

"Careful," he, Bas, and Dev all said at once.

To which she shot them a glare that should have turned their dicks to popsicles.

Okay, not the best analogy, because now he was thinking about Kels sucking his cock and doing it in front of her brothers, and the last thing he wanted to be doing was popping a boner in the vicinity of her family.

Bas lifted his palms in surrender and slipped from the room. "I'll tell mom and dad that we'll be rescheduling Monopoly," he said over his shoulder.

Having dealt with his fair share of scary peeps in the NHL and not cowed by her glare in the least, Dev put one large hand on Kels's stomach and nudged her back from the sink. "Seems you have a long drive ahead of you. Probably should hit the road."

The last he said to Tanner, while looking over Kelsey's head.

Tan nodded. "I'll go say my goodbyes. Kels, you coming?"

Frosty brown eyes jumped to his face, and he was surprised when she nodded without argument. She rose on tiptoe and kissed her brother's cheek. "Bye." Then she walked out of the kitchen.

"Tan?"

He turned his gaze back to Dev, saw his friend had stuck his hand out.

"Be careful with her," Dev said when Tanner's palm met his. "She's a lot more than the tough, smart chick that shows on the surface."

"I know." And Tan kept his eyes on Devon's so Kels's brother would understand he knew exactly how precious she was. "She's it, Dev."

Dev's fingers tightened on Tanner's before letting go. "I know. Glad you finally got around to accepting it."

"You both knew?"

Dev released him. "Yeah." He started plucking up the remaining glass.

"Then, why?"

Why hadn't he said something sooner? Why hadn't they

told him to come back? Given their blessing? Hell, just done *something?*

"You weren't ready."

Quiet words. Truthful words.

Tanner acknowledged them with a nod. Then he left the kitchen and went to find his woman.

They had lost time to make up for.

THIRTEEN

Kelsey

SILENT CAR RIDES were the best.

Yes, that was sarcasm.

No, it wasn't the good version.

Sighing, she pulled her phone from her purse and plugged in the cord, cueing up her playlist. Anything to ease the pressing silence, anything to erase the knowing looks on her brothers' faces, the dawning glee on her parents' when Tanner had come up behind her and dropped a kiss to the top of her head.

She would have given anything for that at eighteen.

Nine years later, she just felt conflicted.

Tanner didn't say a word as she filled her car with the cheerful pop gloriousness, just as he hadn't said a word as he'd helped her into the car, or buckled her seat belt again.

Chivalry she shouldn't have accepted.

And yet she had.

Part of her knew it was because of what he'd said in the kitchen.

But could she trust it?

Should she?

How much of an idiot did it make her to sign up for a triple dose of potential heartbreak?

Tanner hit pause on the stereo.

"Hey!"

His lips curved, and Kels's heart skipped a beat. He had such a great smile. She remembered when they were teenagers and getting that smile pointed in her direction had been the best feeling in the world.

Even just seeing the edge of it now felt damned good.

Which was part of the problem.

Groaning, she pressed her fingers to her temples. This was the problem with her. She'd keep going in circles until she'd exhausted every potential avenue and outcome. The positive with that was she thought things through. The negative was that it took her away from living her own life.

It was safer in her own head.

But also probably why she hadn't had a boyfriend since Tan.

Crap or get off the pot, she imagined Cora telling her. And her friend would be right. She couldn't keep living like this, frozen in time. Not just with Tanner, but with every man she'd had in her life—

Fingers on her cheek startled her.

Kels realized Tanner had pulled the car over onto the shoulder. "Baby, what's wrong?"

Her life was a mess and her eyes were stinging, *that* was what was wrong.

She shook her head.

He made a noise of frustration and then the car shook as he shoved back his seat. "What—?" But she didn't get the chance to finish the sentence because the next thing she knew, her seat belt was undone, and she was in Tan's lap.

And tears.

Because she was a giant, swirling stress hurricane, her thoughts spinning in circles while the outcome seemed destined to bring devastation.

"Sweetheart," he murmured, hand cupping the back of her head, fingers stroking through her hair. "What's wrong?"

She sniffed, pushed against his hold so she could glare down at him. Her eyes were probably a puffy mess because she wasn't the type of girl who cried pretty. But dammit, how could he possibly ask her that question?

"What's *wrong?*" she growled, shoving harder against his chest. "Seriously? Fucking *seriously?*"

His eyes flashed, hands clenching on her waist. "Yes, seriously," he said quietly.

"Fine. You want to know?" she asked. "Here goes, little man. You'd better hang on to your hat. *You're* what's wrong with me," she snapped. "You. You and your walking away from me nine years ago. You leaving me on Wednesday. You pushing the ride today and then all but telling my family we were together." Kels threw her hands in the air. "You skipped over about a dozen steps, including apologizing to me for all of the crap you pulled."

"I apologized," he said.

Frustration made her back teeth ache. Well, that was probably because she was grinding them so tightly.

See? Her giant brain was useful for *something*.

And look at her go with the sarcasm, the good version this time.

Tanner shifted, drawing her focus back to the present. Namely, the fact that they were on the shoulder of a highway, rolling brown hills on either side of them, and cars whizzing by. Oh, and there also the fact that she was still in Tan's lap.

But when she went to pull away, he held her in place again.

"I apologized," he said again. "When you called, I said I was sorry."

"Did you?" she asked, voice soft. "Or did you take the 'we were young and stupid line' I was throwing you and agree that we each took an equal share of the blame for that?" She jabbed him in the chest. "Also, this just in, you *haven't* apologized for leaving me naked and wanting on Wednesday, have you? Hmm?"

Calloused fingers wrapped around her wrist, brushing gently back and forth, back and forth.

But Tan's eyes were unfocused, as though he were reliving the conversation they'd had more than a year ago. Then his gaze snapped to hers, and regret crossed his expression. "You're right," he said. "Fuck. I'm so sorry, sweetheart. For then. For now. For being such a fucking idiot."

"Words a woman lives to hear," she joked because the words calmed that hurt inside her.

He shook his head, chocolate eyes sad. "I know I said it before, but I fucked up."

Kelsey sighed. "It's not all your fault, Tan. I—"

"No," he snapped. "You don't get to own my fuckups, Kels. *I'm* the one who ended things. *I'm* the one that stayed away. *I'm* the one who finally figured out that I can't keep my distance from you any longer, and that I want you in my life—"

"For how long?"

He froze. "What?"

"For how long?" she asked. "How long until you leave again?"

"I'm not."

She sighed again. "Tanner, your work takes you all over the world. It's just—"

"I quit."

Her jaw dropped open. *"What?"*

His face took on a mulish expression. "I'm burned out," he said. "I finished my contracts, and I'm taking a hiatus."

Hiatus. Right. And he'd fill it with her until he panicked and ran off again and left her behind, brokenhearted . . . or maybe just broken. She shifted, and this time, Tanner let her slip back into her seat.

But he turned to face her, eyes earnest. "I've seen more of the world than I ever could have dreamed of," he said. "What I want now is to be home."

"You didn't grow up here."

"But here is with you," he said. "And so that means my home is here."

Her heart was pounding, her eyes stinging again. God, how many times had she dreamed about hearing those words? The only trouble now was Tanner had hurt her enough that she didn't believe them.

She also didn't know how to tell him that.

But Tanner knew. *Of course* he did.

"I know it'll take time for you to trust me."

And with that huge understatement, he tugged his seat forward and turned on the music. Then he checked for traffic and got them back onto the freeway.

Another long, uncomfortable drive.

Her favorite.

At least this time, Taylor Swift was filling the silence.

MONDAY MORNING MEANT she was due at work.

The only problem was that she was sick. Miserably, horribly sick with a fever and a hacking cough. So. Much. Fun.

She texted Bas to let him know she'd come down with a bug but to stay far, far away because his wedding was in less than a week, and the last thing she needed to do was be responsible for being patient zero that took out the groom and then the bride. But just typing the message: Sick. *Stay away. Contagious.* Had taken all of her energy, and so she collapsed back on the couch wearing a nice blouse and pajama pants.

The blouse because for a brief moment, she'd thought if she could just get out of bed and get dressed, she'd feel better. The pajama pants because that notion had clearly failed.

Then she spent the next hour wallowing in her misery, trying to summon the energy to get up and shower, if only to slip back into fresh pajamas. In the end, she decided to just try and sleep it off. A shower could come later.

Therefore, the knock on the door that came as she was just dozing off was wholly unwelcome.

So, she let her eyes slide shut and ignored it.

The knock came again.

"Oh, for fuck's sake," she muttered, shoving to her feet, wavering for a minute, then stomping to the door.

Like a moron, she didn't look through the peephole.

Instead, she flung it open and—

Tanner was there.

"You look like shit," he said.

Kels rolled her eyes, but the movement made her already wavering body falter more, and she stumbled.

"Shit, sweetheart." He rushed forward and grabbed her arm to steady her.

She batted him away, almost fell backward in the process.

"Right," he said, using his foot to close the door before sweeping her up into his arms. The lock clicked a moment later, and then they were moving toward her bedroom.

Totally different walk than she'd wanted the last time he was in her apartment.

"You're burning up," he muttered. "When did you take some medicine?"

He was slipping her beneath the covers of her bed and goodness that was lovely, so lovely, in fact, that she closed her eyes and burrowed deeper. Tan brushed her hair out of her face. "Babe. Medicine?"

"Don't have any," she said, and when he cursed, added, "Instacart. Should be here in twenty."

A sigh. "Okay," he said. "But if it's not here by then, I'm going out to get some."

Great. Now he just needed to shut up so she could sleep.

"Want a cool cloth for your head?" he asked softly.

Since that sounded like nirvana, she nodded, though she instantly regretted the movement when her head spun.

"Easy, sweetheart," he murmured, brushing his fingers on her forehead. They were cold, and it was glorious enough that she leaned up slightly to prolong the contact. But then he broke the contact, telling her, "Be right back."

Eyes still closed and much more comfortable now that she was in bed, Kels let her body relax and slip toward sleep again.

But she wasn't so far gone as to not hear the conversation in the other room.

"Hey, Bas," Tan said. "No, she's really sick. Fever, chills, cough. You'd better stay away and tell Rachel to do the same. The last thing either of you needs is to be sick for your own wedding."

A pause. The sound of a faucet turning on and off.

"No," he said. "I don't think it's serious. I'll get some medicine in her, and I'm sure she'll be better in no time."

Another blip of quiet then, "Yeah, I'll call you if anything changes. Tell your mom to call off the dogs, okay? We'll try to keep this contained and not bring the plague to your wedding."

"Okay, talk to you later," Tan's voice rose in volume, and

then the cloth was on her forehead and it was the best sensation of her life. "Rest, sweetheart. I'll be here."

Kels didn't make the mistake of nodding this time, but she did let sleep take her under.

THE NEXT TWELVE hours were a blur.

She remembered Tanner waking her up briefly to take some medicine and drink some water before she passed out again.

By the time she woke up, it was dark outside her windows and she was a sweaty, shivering mess, her blankets soaked, her clothes sticking to her body. Tanner was there, helping her unbutton her blouse and change into fresh pajamas he must have gone pawing through her drawers to find.

"Not the way I'd imagined you undressing me," she rasped.

"Me neither," he agreed before tucking a blanket around her and carrying her to the couch. He disappeared for a few minutes then reappeared with a cup of soup, coaxing her to drink.

After she'd managed a few sips, he gave her more medicine and carried her back to bed.

That's when she fell in love with Tanner Pearson again.

He'd changed the sheets.

She felt like shit, but he'd made her soup and changed her sheets and—

He tucked her in, placed a fresh cold cloth on her forehead, and started to straighten, but she caught his hand. "Tanner?"

"Yes, sweetheart?"

Maybe it was the soup and sheets, or maybe the cold had just filed down her defenses enough to allow him in. Or perhaps, Kelsey was just giving in to the inevitable. She squeezed his fingers lightly.

"Will you stay?"

A squeeze back. "Not going anywhere, babe."

"No," she whispered because her throat was on fire. "Will you stay? Will you hold me?"

His face clouded, and her stomach rolled over.

"Never mind," she said quickly, slamming her eyes shut. "I shouldn't risk you getting sick any more than you already are after being stuck here with me all day."

"Not stuck," he replied, and his voice sounded funny.

Kels opened her eyes. Turned out that was because he was bending over to take off his pants, his shirt already having hit the ground.

Too bad she wasn't in any position to enjoy the view.

"You still have a fever, sweetheart," he said. "Sure you want me in bed with you?"

In bed with Tanner, let her think about that.

She must have snorted, because his gaze found hers and he smiled. "Trying not to perv on you while you're sick here, Kels. Gonna give me a break?"

"When have I ever given you a break, Tan?"

He smiled, rounding the bed to slip under the covers on the opposite side. "You've already given me too much, baby." Carefully, he slid an arm under her middle and tugged her back against his chest. His breath ruffled her hair and he *was* warm, but it was still the most comfortable she'd been in her entire life.

Especially when he pulled her just a little closer and whispered, "Sleep now, baby. I've got you."

FOURTEEN

Tanner

CONSIDERING the close proximity he'd had to plague-ridden Kelsey, Tanner had expected to wake up the following morning feeling like shit.

Instead, he woke with a beautiful woman drooling on his arm.

God, even that was cute, he realized, using his free hand to retrieve the damp cloth from the night before and wiping his arm.

Kels would probably die of embarrassment if she realized she'd left a puddle on his arm, but Tan had spent more than enough time in some pretty rough places around the world to not get all worked up over a little saliva.

He brought his fingers to her forehead, relieved to find it was much cooler than the day before.

Then he slipped carefully from the bed and walked into the bathroom.

The strangling noise from the bed had him whipping back around in alarm.

But then he saw Kels's face, saw that she wasn't choking on her own spit and hadn't managed to strangle herself in the sheet in the last ten seconds. Instead, her color was high like it had been when she'd been burning up with fever, and her eyes were on his groin.

Tan glanced down.

Whoops.

His boxer briefs weren't hiding much, and he was sporting major wood.

"Kels?"

"Mmm-hmm?" It was garbled, and not because her voice was raspy. Then she ran her tongue over her bottom lip, and Tanner just about died. Or at least nearly passed out due to a loss of blood flow.

"Eyes up here, sweetheart."

Now it wasn't tongue but teeth on that bottom lip, and Tanner clenched his hands into fists at his sides, trying to stop himself from going over there and showing her exactly what he thought of her using her teeth and tongue.

Mainly that he wanted them off her lip and on his cock.

Instead, he sucked in a breath and asked, "Feeling better?"

She nodded, sat up. "Yeah, baby."

Baby.

Fuck him.

Literally, please, God, would she let him come over there and fuck her?

"Good," he said with a nod and took a step back. A tactical retreat because he was getting very close to forgetting why he couldn't just go over and show her that he never intended to pass up another opportunity like last Wednesday. But she was sick, or at least still recovering. She needed care, not fucking.

No matter what her eyes were saying.

"I'm going to shower," he announced. Mostly to convince himself that was what he was going to do.

"Okay," she said and lay back down.

Tan stood in place for a long moment, torn between returning to bed and trying to do the right thing. He did the right thing because Kelsey deserved that much. He'd discovered the shower was through one of the two doors in Kels' bedroom. The other one led to a walk-in closet that was bigger than he had expected for a one-bedroom apartment in the city.

Not that Kels had filled it. Her wardrobe seemed to consist mostly of T-shirts and jeans, with a small collection of work clothes. Though she did seem to have an inordinate amount of Converse—one in almost every color of the rainbow—and an affinity for lacy lingerie. The latter of which he'd discovered after searching for some fresh pajamas for her in the tall dresser that took up one wall of the closet. The top three drawers contained all manners of lace, and he'd be a liar if he hadn't said he'd explored. He had. The deep purple set had been his favorite.

Now, just to convince her to wear it for him.

Forcing his thoughts from lace and the temptation of Kelsey, he picked up the tube of toothpaste. He wasn't about to snoop while she was conscious, so he just had to content himself with squirting some on his finger. It wouldn't have been the first time he'd gone without a toothbrush, but at the very least, he had toothpaste and could do a minimal job at controlling his morning breath.

Morning breath. Morning wood. Ha.

Shaking his head at himself, he unscrewed the cap, and—

The door opened.

Kels walked in.

"Morning," she murmured, brushing by him and reaching into a cupboard to hand him a packaged toothbrush, as though she just opened the door and found him in her bathroom every day.

"Morning," he repeated dumbly.

She picked up her own toothbrush and made short work of brushing her teeth, then crossed over to the shower and cranked it on. Water was barely hitting the pan before she turned and pulled a stack of towels out from a cupboard. Enough to dry a small army.

Then she tugged off her pajama top.

Now it was his turn to make a garbled sound.

Especially when her pants followed the shirt.

"Umm." Not his finest moment.

Kels rotated back to face him, raising an eyebrow as she stepped into the shower stall. "You coming?"

No, but she would be.

His boxers hit the tile.

FIFTEEN

Kelsey

HER HEART POUNDED, her brain was as hazy as when she'd been sporting the fever, and . . . she couldn't believe she was doing this again.

Couldn't believe she'd stripped down in front of Tanner, again.

That she'd risked sending another invitation over her shoulder to him.

What the hell was wrong with her?

Too impulsive by far—

The shower door opened, and suddenly Tanner was there, pressing against her spine, hot and hard . . . and *hard*.

"Hi," he whispered, lips at her ear.

"Hi, baby."

Baby. Again. Just slipped out. And yet she loved the way his arms tightened around her when she said it. But most especially, she loved the way he spun her around, nudged her a little further into the water, and then dropped to his knees.

"Um, Tan?"

"Shh."

He lifted one of her legs and tossed it over his shoulder.

She gasped, but then his mouth was on her, his tongue finding her clit with short, firm flicks. Her gasp turned into a moan and *shit*, he'd learned a few tricks over the years.

The water sluicing down her back, the heat of his mouth, the tight squeeze of his hand on her hip, her thigh, all had her spiraling higher and faster than she'd even spun in her life.

"Tan!" she exclaimed when he hit *just the right* spot.

Thankfully he didn't stop, didn't stop or shift away at her exclamation. Instead, he seemed to redouble his efforts, tongue moving quicker, finger slipping inside and pumping slowly.

Oh . . . holy . . . fuck.

"Oh God," she moaned, hips bucking, her orgasm right . . . *there*.

Pleasure exploded from her center, spreading out along her limbs, and her eyes drifted down, half-expecting to see that her body had been set on fire. But it was intact, and the sight of Tanner's head between her legs, his chocolate eyes burning up at her was the most erotic thing she'd ever seen.

"Hi," he murmured, carefully slipping her leg from his shoulder and holding her steady at her hips.

She bit her bottom lip.

He was on his feet in an instant, his mouth on hers, his tongue in her mouth. He tasted of her, and somehow that was more intoxicating than she would have expected.

Or maybe that was just Tanner and the chemistry they shared.

Eventually, he pulled back and Kels rested her head on his chest as she caught her breath, dizzy from the orgasm and the kiss and from the bug she'd had. "I think that kiss probably just got you sick."

He kissed the top of her head. "Worth it," he murmured.

"Been thinking of doing that since I first saw those teeth digging into that pretty lip of yours."

Her breath caught, her hand slid down his chest.

He snagged it, brought it back up. "Not this time."

"Tan—"

"Shh." Wrapping one arm around her waist, he used his other to reach for what turned out to be her bottle of shampoo, squeezing some on the top of her head then massing it into her roots.

Not the most efficient way to wash her hair, but probably the only time in her life that she felt cherished while doing so.

He repeated the process with conditioner then soaped her up.

All the while, he kept her in the warm water, only nudging her aside to briefly rinse the shampoo from his hair, the soap from his body. Then she was back under the stream, barely having a chance to get cold.

On the other hand, it was probably the coldest shower that Tanner had ever had.

Not that he seemed to mind, and paired with the gentle way he handled her, the soft words and sweet smiles, and if she hadn't already fallen back in love with him, that would have done it.

Or maybe it was that she'd never fallen out of love, and now she just felt safe enough to admit it.

The water turned off, a towel was wrapped snuggly around her, but when she went to step out of the shower, Tan stayed her. "I've got you, sweetheart," he said, tucking a towel around his hips.

"I can walk," she said, though her eyes were drooping, and fatigue was sweeping back over her.

"I know." His palm cupped her cheek. "But this time, let me take care of you."

Could she?

Dare she?

In the end, with the past and the present all tangled up, with her emotions and love so raw, how could she not?

Tanner carried her to bed and held her close as she drifted off to sleep.

KELSEY WOKE late in the day.

She was no longer wrapped in Tanner's arms, and when she pulled herself from beneath the covers to peek into the front of the apartment, she saw she was alone.

Alarm blipped through her, but she pushed it down.

Tanner wasn't going away.

At least not until after the wedding.

Way to go pessimistic, Kate would have said.

And Kate would be right. Kelsey loved the man. She didn't know how or why, but she knew that even when she'd hated him, she'd loved him.

Sighing, she walked to her closet and snagged her fuzziest socks and the sweatshirt she'd stolen long ago from Tan. It was raggedy, with holes all along the seams, and she wore it more for comfort now than warmth.

Hell, who was she kidding? She'd worn it for comfort back then, too.

Regardless, she tugged it over her head, slid the socks on, then went to brush her teeth even though she felt tired enough to go back to sleep again.

A virus and an orgasm.

Who knew that was the way to keep Kelsey Scott down?

But she was hungry in addition to tired, so she made her

way to the kitchen to rustle up some dinner or whatever meal she was currently awake for.

Her eyes found the clock, and it told her the time was just after four in the afternoon. So dinner, that was what she was making herself. Then maybe she'd force herself to stay up an hour or two so she wouldn't wake up in the middle of the night.

And if all her plans went well, she'd be back at work tomorrow, playing catch up because her four-day workweek had now become a two-day workweek. So focused on her rustling of the cabinets, she didn't hear the front door to the apartment open, nor the footsteps as they crossed the floor.

But she did feel the hands on her waist.

She shrieked, spinning around and elbowing, colliding hard . . .

With Tanner's jaw.

"*Fuck*," he growled, hand coming up to cup the injured part.

"Shit," she exclaimed. "I didn't— You startled— *Shit!*" She patted his face uselessly for a few seconds before getting her head together and sprinting to her freezer for an ice pack. Swear to God, if she'd given Tan a giant bruise just in time for Bas and Rachel's wedding . . .

She hissed out a breath when she managed to get his palm away from his face.

A red welt was already rising on his jaw.

Shit.

Definitely a bruise then.

She wondered if she could pay the photographer to edit it out of the pictures. Or maybe pose him so the bruise was away from the lens.

Bas was going to kill her.

No, she corrected herself. *Rachel* was going to kill her. Bas would probably think it was hilarious that she'd bruised Tanner in the first place.

"So, you always abuse the people who take care of you?" he asked lightly.

She groaned. "I'm so, *so* sorry."

His warm hands went back to her waist, albeit slowly and from the front this time. "It was my fault, sweetheart. I shouldn't have snuck up on you like that."

"It's going to bruise."

A shrug. "Not like I haven't had one before."

"The wedding is Friday."

A brow rose. "I'm aware."

"You'll be bruised for the pictures."

His eyes danced as clarity dawned. "Well, lucky for the couple, they know a pretty good photographer who can easily make a bruise disappear."

Oh. There was that.

She bit her lip and heat replaced amusement in his expression. But he didn't kiss her as she'd half-expected. Instead, he just leaned close enough to rest his chin on the top of her head. "Were you looking for more medicine?"

"No. I feel fine. I was searching out dinner."

"How about I order a pizza instead?"

"I can cook," she started to protest.

"Show me that some other time, okay?" he murmured. "I'm guessing you're going to work tomorrow?" She nodded, and his arms went a little tighter. "So, at least take the rest of today off."

Kels hesitated before stepping out of his arms. Then she studied his face, looking deep into his eyes and hoping to figure out what the hell was going through his brain. "Why'd you come over yesterday?"

"Your brother texted me to ask if I was the reason you were sick and if you were playing hooky from work," he said.

"That's not your style, and when I called and texted, you didn't reply." A shrug. "So, I came over to make sure you were okay."

That tracked. Or was at least close enough to what she'd expected.

She supposed the bigger question was, "Why'd you stay?"

His chest expanded and contracted on a deep breath before he said, "Because I'd already left twice, and am not going to make the same mistake again."

"Oh."

"Yeah," he murmured. "Oh."

"You know, before the car ride on Saturday, I'd convinced myself that I was done with you." His jaw clenched. "Then ten seconds in your presence, and I knew it wasn't done, that I'd never been done."

Tan nodded. "I feel the same. I ran. I tried to shove it all down, but you were always there in the back of my mind." A beat. "And in my heart."

She sighed. "So, why did you leave then?"

"I had myself convinced that I could never be good enough for you," he said. "Fuck, it's still hard to believe that I'm going there with you now. And I was scared that losing you . . ." He trailed off, probably thinking that she'd be hurt if he admitted what she already knew.

"You were afraid to lose my parents, my brothers."

He looked away. "Yeah."

Okay, so she'd been thinking that, wondering on it, and the things her friends had said, and . . . all of it was so beyond dumb that she didn't hold back.

"How could you be so fucking stupid?" she snapped.

He jumped. "What?"

Maybe it was the bug she'd had—though probably it was more her impulsiveness—but she didn't have it in her to go easy on him in that moment. Not when he'd hurt them both so badly. Not when he'd stolen years from them.

"Never have I *ever* felt for another man what I felt for you at eighteen." Her finger went up even as she jerked out of his embrace. "*Never!* But you decided to be an idiot and take it upon yourself to deny us that—and don't tell me you didn't feel the same exact way, because you wouldn't have run for so long or so far if you didn't." She spun around then spun back, her finger waving as she ranted. "And you wouldn't be right back in my life the moment you did get back."

"You're right."

"And another thing," she growled. "Have I told you how fucking stupid it was for you to leave?"

She paced away then back, her irritation growing with every step. Kelsey didn't even fully grasp *why* she was upset, other than this vague notion that he denied them something they'd both wanted, and he'd done it for a long time.

"What if Bas hadn't invited you to the wedding? Huh?" She got in his face, shoved her hands against his chest, but when she went to pace away again, he kept them trapped there. "And another thing! How could you have been—"

"So stupid?"

His lips were twisting upward, as though he were valiantly fighting back a grin.

Ugh.

Even when she was furious, he was still beautiful.

"For a brilliant woman," he murmured. "Your arguments can use some work."

She opened her mouth to argue that statement—or more realistically, probably to call him stupid again—but then Tanner lowered his head and kissed her. Suddenly, there were other things on her mind aside from stupidity. Namely, how good it felt to be in his arms, his tongue rubbing against hers.

Eventually they had to do something stupid—aka breathe—and so Kels pulled away.

Tanner cupped her cheek, their lips only a hairsbreadth apart, hot, rapid breaths brushing each other's skin.

"Stupid," he murmured. "I know."

She chuckled.

"I love you."

She stiffened, reared back. *"What?"*

"Since forever," he said, hand sliding to her nape. "You know my parents," he said. "Know what they were like. They *never* told me they loved me." She sucked in a breath. She'd known they were selfish assholes, but she hadn't known they were that cruel. "Not once did I hear they were proud. And it took me a long time to understand that I'd taken that inside me, thought that it meant *I* wasn't worthy of love rather than realizing that they just weren't capable of giving it."

Her heart pounded in her chest. "How did you learn that?"

"You, babe." His fingers squeezed lightly. "Your mom. Your brothers. Your dad." Her eyes burned as he kept talking. "Do you know the first person who told me they loved me? Your mom. The first who said he was proud of me? Your dad. The first person to make me feel like I wasn't the most pathetic lost cause in the world and might actually be worth something? *You.*" The tears spilled over. "So yeah, I panicked when I realized I had all these big feelings and didn't know how to cope. I was so fucking stupid to not have talked about it with you or your parents or your brothers. Instead, I ran and kept contact to a minimum, thinking that at least if I had them and you in that limited way, even I couldn't fuck it up."

He gently wiped the tears from her cheeks.

"I was wrong. I missed—"

Kels rose on tiptoe so she could press her mouth to his. "You're here now," she said, dropping back down and taking his hand in hers. "Also, I've loved you since you helped me patch up my knee when I was eight years old."

She'd begun leading him over to the couch, but at her words, he froze. "What—?"

"Later," she murmured. "Right now, it's time for pizza."

He blinked. "Pizza?"

Kels nodded, knowing the admissions had rubbed them both raw and they needed time to process. "Pizza. Then a movie. Then you're going to hold me again while we sleep." She ticked off the orders on her fingers. "Think you can handle that, Pearson?"

"You okay?" he asked.

She nodded again.

"Then yes, I can handle it."

So they ordered a pizza—of which, Kelsey ate way more than she'd expected considering how sick she'd been just a day before.

Then they watched a movie—an older superhero one that Tanner had missed out on while in the wilderness somewhere.

Then she went to sleep with Tanner's arms around her.

It was the best rest she'd ever gotten.

SIXTEEN

Tanner

WHEN KELSEY'S alarm went off, he half-expected to have succumbed to the flu that had taken her out. But he woke with a clear head and no fever in sight, feeling more rested than . . . well, ever.

He especially liked the part where Kels rolled over and pressed a kiss to his mouth, leg slipping over his hips to get even closer. They kissed for a while, and he got a glimpse of blue lace under her pajama bottoms when he slipped his fingers between her thighs. She was so wet and hot and responsive that he almost came in his boxer briefs as he stroked her.

But then she toppled over the edge, and he got to kiss her as she found her way back down to earth.

Best morning ever.

Especially when he held her afterward and they talked about nothing for a bit, the movie, television shows she apparently needed to *educate* him on, his favorite place he'd visited. Eventually, she asked where he'd gone the previous day, and when he told her he went to get clothes from his hotel room, she shyly suggested that he get the rest of his things and stay at her place until he figured out what he was going to do apartment-wise.

Some might say too soon.

Tanner would tell them they'd waited nine years.

That was long enough.

Now, he was walking her to her office, his camera in his hand and the sun just rising over the hills in the distance.

"Text you later for lunch?" he asked.

Kels winced. "Can't. I'll have too much work, so I'll order in and eat through lunch."

"Dinner then."

"I might be really late."

He dropped a kiss to her nose. "Then we'll eat really late. Do what you need to do, sweetheart. I'll be waiting when you're done."

She nibbled at her bottom lip, and that meant he had to kiss the small hurt better, and so it was several long minutes before they came up for air and he watched her walk into the office building.

She waved from behind the glass windows, and Tan's heart squeezed.

Yeah, best morning ever.

HIS PLANS for a late dinner didn't materialize, mainly because he'd ordered takeout around nine, then jetlag had reared its ugly head, and he'd barely managed to stay up for its arrival.

He'd left it on the counter, along with plates and forks, then retreated to Kels' couch to watch a show and wait up for her.

Which had worked about zero percent.

She'd woken him up whenever she'd gotten home then left

him early that morning with a soft kiss. The wedding was that night, and she had a full day's work to get in before heading over to Rachel's.

Tanner understood, just as he understood Bas and Rachel's reasoning for a wedding on a Friday night. Their jobs were intense, projects were vast, and they wanted to make the most of their honeymoon by sandwiching it between two weekends. But thinking about not seeing Kelsey until she walked down the aisle that afternoon for the rehearsal stung. Plus, he wouldn't even be allowed to be alone with her after. The girls would all be swept away for hair and makeup while he did "guy stuff" with the male half of the Scott contingent.

Normally he liked "guy stuff." Or at least he had before it encroached on his time with his girl.

Then it sucked.

Still, he'd dealt with being apart from her for nine years, so he could deal with one more day.

In the meantime, he was going to call Tom, tell him he'd be sending him some photos to shop around for publication and that he'd take some jobs, but only so long as they were near the city.

He knew that some of the Hollywood types had big houses up in the hills around San Francisco, so if they wanted to hire him for some shoots, he was game.

His agent picked up his phone on the first ring. "Tanner," he said. "Let me guess, you've finally come to your senses?"

Tan chose not to touch that one. "I'm sending you some pictures. Shop them."

A beat then, "That's it?"

"No." Tanner sighed. "I'm at my friend Sebastian's wedding in San Francisco tonight and busy this weekend, but starting next week, if you have any inquiries for the Bay Area, I'll begin considering them."

"You're in California?" Tom asked. "How about coming to L.A.?"

"No."

"No?"

"I said the Bay Area." Tanner tried to moderate his tone. Tom was great at his job, but he was also good at steamrolling his clients into doing what he wanted them to do . . . and sometimes forgetting what *they* wanted.

But so long as Tan was explicitly clear with his agent, Tom seemed to get the message.

"No Los Angeles. Or Seattle. Or New York," he said. "Not right now, anyway. I'm not saying I'll take the jobs you offer because I need the break, but I will say that shooting in the city has reminded me of why I like photography again."

"Oh good. That's good."

"So, make some inquiries about the photos I send you, put together a job list, and I'll let you know if any of them interest me enough to pull me from my break."

"Consider it done," Tom said then hesitated. "Just to be clear. No L.A.?"

Tanner rolled his eyes and hung up the phone.

Then he grabbed his camera and headed out the door. There was an entire city to photograph, and he intended to find every nook and cranny.

SEVENTEEN

Kelsey

SHE POKED her head outside of the bride's room, made sure the coast was clear, then tiptoed down the hall. Her heels were still inside, along with the bride, Kelsey's mom, and Heather, the maid of honor.

The wedding was starting in less than an hour, but she'd gotten a text from Tanner, telling her it was urgent that she come and meet him.

Fuck. Her brother better not have gotten cold feet.

"Psst!"

Kels turned, saw the shadowy figure in the open doorway. "I swear to God, Tanner, you are asking for a matching bruise on the other side of your jaw."

He tugged her into the room and slammed the door shut.

Then had the inane thought that she was glad she hadn't put on her lipstick yet because Tanner's mouth came down on hers, and he somehow kissed her like it was the first time all over again.

Heart threatening to pound out of her chest by the time

they finally broke apart, she looked up at him curiously. "What was that for?"

"I missed you."

Now her heart skipped a beat, but she played it cool.

"Meh."

He grinned. "Meh? That's all I warrant?"

She floated closer, her breasts rubbing his chest. "I've had you around a few days now, I've over it."

Tan snorted and reached for her hair.

Kels jumped back. "Don't you dare!"

"What?"

"The wedding's in less than an hour," she exclaimed. "I barely have time to put on my lipstick, let alone fix my hair."

"An hour, you say?"

"Tanner," she warned.

His fingers brushed along the sweetheart neckline of the lilac bridesmaid dress she wore. Her previous supposition that Rachel had already purchased the dress had been right. It was also gorgeous and fit like a glove. "I like this."

"Because you can do that?"

A nod. "But also because I can do this."

This meaning slipping his hand beneath the skirt.

"Tanner," she said again. Okay, moaned. It was definitely a moan.

"I like *baby* better." His fingers slid beneath her panties. "Please, tell me these are the purple ones." He flicked up the skirt and groaned when he saw that she was indeed wearing a dark violet lace thong. "Thank you, God."

"How did . . . you know I had . . . purple underwear?" she asked, and it was punctuated with gasps as his fingers moved along her dripping pussy.

"Because I looked."

"Not now." She groaned when he circled her clit. "You knew before you looked."

"Because I looked in your underwear drawer."

She gasped.

He grinned.

"Perv."

"You like it."

If it got his fingers inside her like this, then, yes, she had to admit she liked it. Very much so. But she also had to admit that she'd come prepared for just this eventuality.

Reaching for the side zip on her dress, she slid it down, releasing her hold on the fabric so it puddled around her.

Tan had jumped back when her clothes had started falling off, probably thinking he'd broken something, so she took the chance to scoop it up and hang it on the doorknob, thus preventing the wedding photographer from having to do more work by editing out wrinkles alongside bruises.

"Baby?" he asked.

She reached into her bra and pulled out the condom she'd stashed there earlier.

Of course, she'd been planning on a coat closet or similar *post*-wedding, but this was even better. Bad bridesmaid etiquette, but she figured Rachel would understand.

She unhooked her bra.

Tanner didn't run.

She took a step closer.

He took one toward her.

She reached for the waistband of her panties.

"You're never going to let me undress you, are you?"

Kelsey burst out laughing and when Tanner's mouth hit hers, he was laughing, too. The amusement wasn't long-lasting, however, because his tongue drove in, rubbing alongside hers at the same time, his hand shoved down the dark purple lace. She was naked and he was fully clothed, and so she began unbuttoning his shirt as quickly as possible.

Not an easy task when she was holding the condom and he was still kissing her, his hands cupping her breasts.

She cried out when he rolled her nipples between his thumbs and forefingers, moaned when he broke off the kiss to suck one deeply into his mouth, forgot about his shirt altogether when his fingers slid back between her thighs.

Then it was all about his pants.

Wrestling the button open, yanking the zipper down, freeing the glorious hot length of him.

She tore open the condom with her teeth and rolled it over his cock.

"Baby," she panted, looking around frantically for any place he could take her without ruining the hairstylist's work. Table. Bad idea. Wall. No good. Well, good, but not for her hair. A counter would work or a chair or—

Tanner sank to the ground, shoving his pants down to his thighs as he went.

"I—"

He lifted up a hand. "Ride me, sweetheart."

She didn't need to be told twice. Kels dropped to her knees, straddled him, and took him inside.

"Fuck," he hissed and slowly slid deeper.

"Fuck," she agreed, bottoming out, barely able to take the hard length of him in this position. He twitched and she moaned, leaning forward to brace herself on his chest.

"That's it, baby," he said, gripping her hips and encouraging her to move.

She rocked back and forth, biting back a scream of pleasure when he tilted his pelvis so he was hitting her clit on the outside and her g-spot on the inside. So many new tricks to explore, positions to try—

But not now.

Not because there wasn't enough time—there wasn't.

Not because of her hair—there wasn't enough hairspray in the world to keep it completely unscathed.

Not because of the wedding—what wedding?

But not now because Tanner was deep inside her, his hands tracing her body, love shining in his eyes, and she knew there was no way she was going to last a long time.

"I love you, Kelsey," he said, hands reaching for her breasts again.

His words, his touch was enough.

She flew over the precipice, her orgasm crashing over her, even as Tanner thrust up into her faster and faster until he exploded with a long, low groan.

It was long minutes later that she finally came to.

"Tanner?" she asked, her face in the square of skin she managed to expose in her weak attempts to unbutton his shirt. At least she wasn't leaving makeup stains.

"Mmm?"

"How the hell am I supposed to walk down the aisle now?"

Tanner laughed and held her tight for another few minutes before they mutually decided they had to get their asses up and back to their respective bridal party rooms. Luckily there was a trash can and some tissues in this room, so they were able to clean up, then Tanner helped her back into her dress and zipped her up while she did up his buttons.

Thankfully, she'd regained feeling in her legs enough to stagger back down the hall.

"I love you," Tan murmured at the door.

"I love you, too," she murmured back.

"You okay?"

She wrapped her arms around his waist and loved that he wrapped his around her in return, but she most especially loved when he rested his chin on her head and inhaled, whispering, "Roses."

"I'm perfect, baby."

He pulled back, cupped her cheek. "Yes, you are."

"See you at the end of the aisle?"

"I'll be standing next to the groom." A flash of teeth. "Granted, he or Dev don't figure out what we were just doing." Her mouth twitched and he pressed a kiss to each corner. "Plus, I'll be there to walk you back down it when the carnage is over."

She snorted and rolled her eyes. "Really?"

"Got you to smile," he said. "Goal achieved."

Then with one more kiss, he was gone.

A moment later, she was back inside the bride's room, three women staring at her with smug expressions. Although, her mom's was laced with tears.

"Mom?" Kels hurried over. "Are you—?"

"I'm so happy that all of my babies are happy," she said and lost it completely. Kelsey and Rachel hugged her tightly, both sniffing and wiping their own eyes while Heather went for tissues.

"This is exactly why Abby is so obsessed with waterproof mascara," she muttered, shoving the box in their direction.

Eventually, they mopped up, touched up their makeup, and slipped on their heels. Just in time, too, because Kels's dad knocked at the door, told them it was game time, then escorted her mom to her seat.

"Ready?" Heather asked.

"Why'd I make this a big thing?" Rachel replied.

"Because you deserve a big thing," Kelsey said. "And Bas does, too."

"Right." Rachel nodded. "I can do this. I'm not going to puke on his shoes—"

"Oh my God," Heather said. "Do *not* tell me your pregnant."

Surprise flickered across her face. "How'd—?"

Rachel bit her lip, probably because Heather was thunderous. "You've been holding out on us! And we just had Wine Club last night, and—"

"I only found out this morning," Rachel said. "I didn't drink last night because my stomach was off. I thought it was nerves, but then I woke up feeling nauseous and took a test and . . . you can't say a word! Bas doesn't even know yet."

Heather appeared soothed. "I'm the first to know."

"Well, you *and* Kelsey."

Heather considered that. "I'll accept that."

Rachel met Kelsey's gaze and rolled her eyes. "Glad you feel that way. Now, can I trust you guys to keep this to yourselves for a few weeks until everything checks out?"

"No," Heather said. "But I promise to wait until after the wedding."

Rachel sighed. "*And* until I give you the all-clear that Bas knows."

Another considering pause. Then, "Fine."

Kelsey shook her head. "So, now that the negotiating is complete, maybe you can go marry my brother? He's probably getting a little nervous waiting at the end of the aisle by himself."

Rachel picked up her bouquet and marched to the door. "Let's do this."

EIGHTEEN

Tanner

RACHEL MADE A BEAUTIFUL BRIDE.

But Kelsey was a more stunning bridesmaid.

That was bias talking, but Tan didn't think Sebastian would fault him for thinking his sister was the most beautiful woman in the world.

He stared at her across the aisle until she caught him looking. Then he mouthed, "I love you," and got to watch the way her face softened whenever he said—or in this case, mouthed—those words. Either way, her expression was a beautiful thing and he vowed that he was going to keep that look on her face as much as humanly possible.

"You may kiss the bride," the officiate said, forcing Tanner to focus back on the ceremony.

Bas kissed his bride for a long, sweet moment before they broke apart and were announced as Mr. and Mrs. Scott.

That detail had surprised Tanner earlier during the rehearsal, Rachel being eager to change her last name, when he knew that Bas didn't give a damn. But then Bas had told him all she'd been through, and Tanner had realized that for Rachel, this was a clean start. A new life. A new family. A new name.

Yeah, he understood that.

Bas and Rachel held hands and walked down the aisle of the church, their small gathering of friends and family filling the pews. But the cheering was loud and the love in the room all-encompassing.

Tanner couldn't help himself.

He picked up the camera he'd held at his side and snapped a few shots of the receding bride and groom, of the space. He knew the photographer they hired was totally capable, but he also knew himself.

And for that reason, he also shot several dozen of Kelsey staring after her brother, huge smile on her lips, tears streaking down her cheeks.

And a few more when she glanced at him and he dropped his camera briefly to mouth, "I love you" again, capturing her face changing and knowing without a doubt that it would be his favorite photo he'd ever taken.

Then he crossed the aisle and offered her his elbow.

As they walked out of the church, he knew that someday soon, he was going to convince her to repeat the walk, only it would be in a wedding dress and with a ring on her finger.

THE CAKE HAD BEEN CUT, the bouquet and garter tossed, and Bas and Rachel were plastered against each other on the dance floor.

Kelsey *had* been plastered against him but was currently giving her feet a break.

Because apparently, the five-inch stilettos she was sporting weren't all that comfortable. Funny that.

But Tan kept finding these moments where he fell more in love with her.

Standing across the aisle from her.

The way she said, "Morning" when she woke in his arms.

How she'd handed him his camera then had told him to make Bas and Rachel's night by giving them "some fancy, over-priced photos from a fancy, famous photographer."

So he'd had a quick chat with the paid photographer to make sure he wouldn't be in her way or mess up her shot list, then had gotten to work.

The discarded bouquet with its ribbons drifting down over the table.

Fairy lights buried in greenery with just a glimpse of Bas and Rachel in the background, still dancing.

A discarded pair of white heels, the moon high in the sky.

Bare toes peaking beneath white lace.

Kelsey's shining brown hair, the updo having finally given way, tumbling down her back in a riot of curls.

He shifted the camera, wanting to get a shot of her profile, when he noticed she was talking to someone, her purse in one hand, her cell in the other. Her jaw was tight, shoulders stiff.

Who was—?

He dropped the lens and his heart sank.

She was talking to Tom. Or more accurately, it appeared that she was *arguing* with Tom.

"What the fuck?" he snapped, weaving his way through the tables to get to them. What the hell was his agent doing there, and why in the fuck was he talking to Kelsey? More importantly, what had he said that had upset her so much?

She put her palm up, cutting off Tom and standing.

Then she turned and hurried away.

"Kels!" he called, but either she couldn't hear him over the music, or more likely, whatever Tom had told her had royally fucked things up between them. He finally reached his agent, his wedding-crashing, now-fired agent, and grabbed the lapels of Tom's suit, shaking him roughly. "What did you tell her?" he growled. "What the fuck did you say to her?"

Tom winced and tried to push him away. "What the fuck, man?"

Tan held fast. "I asked. What the. Fuck. Did. You. Tell. Her?"

"Jesus, Tanner, get your shit together," Tom said. "I was already in the area when you'd called, so I put out some feelers. I got the normal offers." He paused. "Then I got a fucking *incredible* offer."

"Does this offer involve staying in the Bay Area?"

"Well, no," Tom said. "But I know you're going to take it because it's only three months, but it's in Antarctica and—"

"I'm not going to Antarctica."

"You love it there!"

"I'm *not* going."

"It pays—"

Tanner's hands, still locked in the lapels of Tom's suit, tightened further. "I don't think you're understanding this, Tom. I'm done with how I used to work. I want a life. A *real* life, and that means one with the woman I love. The woman who just ran off because you upset her. And *that* means you're fired."

"Tanner," Tom said. "I didn't— She was already—"

He didn't stop to hear any more of Tom's excuses. Fuck, really? Crashing a wedding, confronting his woman. What the fuck was wrong with him? Tan ran in the direction Kels had disappeared, out the side door that led to the parking lot.

She'd looked panicked.

Fuck.

He sprinted down the hall, pushed out into the cold, eyes scanning the lot for her car.

Still there.

His pulse calmed slightly.

She was still there.

But where?

He spun in a circle, trying to catch sight of her, but there was nothing.

Except . . .

He heard her cry out.

Shit, he'd made her cry. He'd hurt her again.

Tanner ran in the direction of the sound, turning the corner and going from panicked, worried, and slightly pissed-off to enraged.

Some idiot had his hands on her.

"Stop," Kelsey said, trying to shove him off and teetering on her heels.

The man gripped her hips, one hand snaking down to grab her ass. "I just want a little—"

Tanner stopped thinking. He reacted, ripping the man off her and punching him hard in the face. Pain erupted in his hand, but he didn't stop, just kept at him with his fists until he felt Kelsey's palm on his back.

"Tan. Stop."

Fuck.

He dropped the drunk, who was sporting a bloody nose and already forming a black eye and turned to her.

"I'm not going to Antarctica."

Her face changed, concern morphing into confusion. "Um, I know that, Tan."

"But Tom said he'd told you I was leaving."

She pulled out a tissue from her purse and wrapped it over his fingers. At the same time, a burly dude in an apron burst out of the restaurant. "I saw the whole thing, got it on video, too.

Cops are coming." His eyes went to Kelsey. "Sorry, I couldn't get out here in time to help. That guy is a fucking problem."

Kels sucked in a breath and Tanner saw her hands were shaking, even though she forced her words to sound light. "Luckily, I'm friends with Rebecca Darden. I think she'll be able to make him go away for a long time."

The fucker on the ground actually whimpered then started to push to his feet, as though he were going to run.

Thankfully, the chef stomped a foot on the man's chest and held him in place. "Got him," he said. "I'm Brent, by the way."

"Tanner," he replied.

"Kelsey," she said.

"I know, darlin'," Brent said, "I've seen you in here with your friends. But I think you'd better go sit down now."

She nodded, and Tanner slipped a hand around her waist, noticing that she'd gone from hands shaking to full-body trembling. "I'm taking her to the back. We'll be there if the cops need us to make a statement."

"Roger that," Brent said, and Tanner bustled Kelsey to the back room. The tables were decorated for the wedding, the remnants of a buffet along one wall, but thankfully most of the wedding party was out back on the covered patio, socializing and dancing.

He'd thought a bar was an odd place for a wedding, especially since everyone had been bustled out to the patio for dessert and dancing after finishing their meals, but now Tan was just glad to have a warm, empty room to bring Kels.

"I wasn't paying attention," she murmured as he sat her down on a chair and squatted in front of her. "I should have been paying attention—"

"That was *not* your fault," he said.

She blinked.

"No one has the right to touch you without you wanting them to. Got me?"

Hard words. Sharp words. But they seemed to snap her out of her trembling.

"Thank you," she said. "For being there. I couldn't get him off me a-and I was getting really scared."

Tanner wrapped his arms around her, holding her tightly against his chest, brushing his hand through her hair. "I'm not going anywhere, sweetheart."

"I know." He opened his mouth to tell her again that Tom was wrong, but then she shifted back, glancing down at his knuckles. "Still bleeding," she murmured, pulling back the soaked tissue.

"It's nothing."

"You came." She smiled up at him. "I knew you would come. That you weren't leaving."

"But you ran off, sweetheart."

Her face changed from hazy to focused and alarmed. "I need my phone."

"What?"

"Tanner," she said. "I need my phone. It's why I was out there. Why—" When he held it up from where he'd retrieved it and her purse from the ground, she snatched it from his hand and immediately began dialing.

"Hello? Mark? Yes, I'm okay." She sucked in a breath. "No, you have to reset the program, and . . ." She rattled on for several minutes in a language he didn't understand. "No. Not like that. It'll crash the whole system. You need to . . ." She kept talking, and Tanner finally began putting the pieces together. By the time she hung up after a, "Yes, exactly that. Now there shouldn't be any further problems, but call me if something comes up," he understood.

She set her phone on the table, still pale, but no longer shaking or out of it.

"You didn't leave because of Tom."

Kels shook her head, lips curving up. "I have my intern watching the new program we're testing this weekend." She shrugged. "He fucked up. Thankfully, it was salvageable."

"You didn't leave because he told you—"

Her finger pressed to his lips. "I didn't leave because of him or even because of you. If you'd checked your phone, you would have seen I texted you I was out front."

"But—"

"Also, I'm not a woman who changes her mind easily. So, when I told you I loved you, I meant it, and I'm not letting that go this time." Her finger lifted. "I should have fought harder last time, but then again"—her voice softened—"I think we both have a lot of should haves."

He touched her cheek. "Yes, we do."

"And I also understand why you left before. I mean, I think it was really fucking stupid, but you were also twenty-one," she teased. He snorted, but his lips were curving.

"Thanks for that," he muttered. "And for the record, I told Tom I would only take jobs in the Bay Area for now."

Her eyes went soft. "Baby."

"I want us to have a chance to get back to what we had, to build something strong."

"I don't care if you take the job in Antarctica. Or one in Australia. Or Timbuktu. I don't care because I know you'll come back, Tanner." Her forehead dropped to his. "And that is all I've ever needed."

"I love you."

More soft that Tanner soaked up and held tight.

"Also, I fired Tom."

"If it was because of what he said to me, that's stupid. If it's because he crashed my brother's wedding, then maybe he deserves it." Lips brushing across his. "But also, maybe I can help him learn some appropriate boundaries before you shitcan him."

"I don't think that's possible."

"I'm always up for a challenge." A beat. "But if he crashes *our* wedding, then he's definitely fired."

He laughed and kissed her gently, putting every bit of emotion and love into the contact, knowing that he was the luckiest man on the planet to somehow have found his way back into Kels's life.

"You do a lot of nude shoots, huh?" she asked as she pulled back.

"I'm going to kill Tom."

But he didn't get a chance because right then the police showed up.

EPILOGUE

Kelsey, Three Months Later

SHE WAS WAITING on the beach, toes in the sand, as Tanner picked his way through some tide pools several hundred feet away when suddenly he straightened and gestured for her to come and come quick.

Heart skipping a beat, she jumped to her feet and ran over.

Was there something wrong? Or was there something really cool?

She couldn't tell from his expression.

But then she got close enough to see and immediately relaxed. Not wrong, something in the cool column.

"Look," he murmured, dropping his lens and pointing slowly to the small pool of water.

"*Oh.*" Her breath caught as the cutest little hermit crab poked his head out of his shell. Long spindly legs, a pair of tiny eyes, and good lord, adorable little skittering as it made its way across the rocky bottom.

"He's so cute."

A tug of her ponytail. "How sexist to presume it's a boy crab."

Since he was right, she chose not to acknowledge him.

"Either way, it *is* cute. But I wasn't calling you over for that."

"Okaay." Her heart skipped another beat, and she fought the urge to bite her bottom lip. She'd been thinking a proposal was coming. Okay, well she'd snooped and found a ring, but it wasn't her fault he'd hid it in his T-shirt drawer. She liked to wear his shirts to sleep in. Still, with the waves crashing and the sun setting behind them, this would be the absolute *perfect* place for a proposal.

Tan pointed down again. "I think he or she is the answer to your delivery problem. Look how it maneuvers easily across the uneven surface."

Disappointment slid through her even as she watched the crab move and processed what he was saying. "Holy shit, Tan. You're right! If I could get engineering to model the legs after something more like this, we could study the movement and build in some of the better adaptations. This could really help—"

She glanced over, but he wasn't crouched next to her anymore. And when she spun to find him, her breath stuttered to a stop in her lungs, she found him down on one knee, camera in one hand, a ring in the other.

"Tanner?"

He lifted the camera, and she heard the click of the shutter. "Baby," he murmured, letting it hang from the strap around his neck, and reaching for her hand. "I love you more than life. I know that we're new and all, but will you—"

"Yes!"

Cue her impulsivity ruining whatever speech he had planned. But Kelsey didn't need it. She knew he loved her, knew they were meant to spend the rest of their lives together. She didn't need more words.

She just needed Tanner.

He grinned, nonplussed that she'd probably ruined a moment he'd been planning for a while, and slipped the ring on her finger. Then they were both on their feet and his mouth was on hers, the camera pressed between them.

Before she could adjust it, a wave slammed into them—well, mostly into Tanner's back—and later, when she saw the pictures, Kels was thrilled the precious piece of equipment had been safely stowed between them.

Her hair over one shoulder as she'd studied the crab.

Her surprised face when she'd seen him on one knee.

The love in her eyes when she'd said his name.

He'd captured them all.

Just as easily as he'd captured her eight-year-old heart with a Band-Aid and an ice pack.

Just as surely as he held her heart now.

And Kels knew she'd never want it any other way.

BAD BLIND DATE

BILLIONAIRE'S CLUB #8

ONE

Trix

SHE WATCHED HER FRIEND, Tanner, kiss his fiancée again then checked her watch, wondering two things.

First, why she'd come back to California in the first place.

And second, what the hell kind of drugs she'd been on when agreeing to this date in the first place.

The only good thing about it was that she had buffers: Tanner and his fiancée, Kelsey. Heather, her half-sister and the only decent member of her family, along with Heather's husband, Clay, who was pretty to look at and not *too* annoying.

For a man.

Probably not the best attitude to have going into a blind date, but she'd shown up, hadn't she?

Anyway, the dinner had also meant she'd been able to see Tanner. She'd met the photographer in sub-Saharan Africa almost five years before while she'd been working and he'd been documenting the health crisis for the Red Cross. They'd kept in touch, and he'd invited her to his wedding. It had been a surprise to both of them that they each knew Heather.

But that was the way the O'Keiths worked.

Infiltrating their way into everyone's lives.

Even if they didn't want it.

Regardless, she was back in California for the time being, ready to begin a new chapter in her life.

Apparently, that meant starting by dating.

At least, that was Heather's logic.

Or maybe Trix's own brand of stupid.

Still, whatever it was that had convinced her to come, she was there now and was going to make the best of it.

Or at least that *had been* her thought until she recognized who was approaching the table.

Him.

Trix slammed her eyes closed and counted to five.

It could *not* be him.

Could not—

She opened her eyes.

Clay was on his feet, shaking the man's hand, shaking *Jet's* hand, and making introductions all around. Heather looked thrilled, probably because Jet was gorgeous and funny and smart—

"And this is Heather's sister, Trix. She's a nurse."

Jet knew that.

Because he knew her. *Intimately*.

The doctor and the nurse. So cliché. So stupid on her part to think that things in her life might have turned out differently.

He'd been smiling as he turned to meet her, and it was almost comical to see his expression darken to fury. Or it *would* have, if that fury hadn't been directed at her. By then his hand was already in hers, mid-shake and *fuck* if his touch didn't still make sparks shoot down her arm.

She went to pull back, but he held fast then jerked her forward, as though he were giving her a hug in greeting.

No one at the table could see that he was hissing in her ear.

"What the fuck are you playing at, Trixie?"

She did some hissing of your own. "*Nothing*. I had no idea this date was you otherwise I sure as hell wouldn't have come," she snapped, ignoring the way his scent coiled her stomach, sending little tendrils of heat down between her thighs. "You're the last person I'd want to see at this table. And that includes my parents or maybe even Hitler, you freaking asshole."

"Trixie," he began.

"Fuck off, Jet," she said, then pulled back and plunked into her chair, not about to ruin everyone's night just because she couldn't stand the man she'd been set up with.

She'd endure.

It was what she did.

Jet sat down next to her, and she tried to force herself *not* to look.

She didn't succeed.

And what she saw on his face wasn't fury, not any longer. It was weariness.

Good. After what he'd done to her, she deserved a man treading around her with a bit of hesitation. She'd been hurt before—heartsick and sad, a few times even devastated—when her relationships had ended.

But Jet had broken her.

He was the *one* man she'd let in, with whom she'd shared her past and hopes, her pain and desires. So maybe he wouldn't understand how important what she'd shared was because she'd spent so long being closed down with everyone around her. Maybe he couldn't have realized how hard it had been for her to give what she'd given. But part of her felt like . . . he *should* have known. Especially since he'd shown about as much care with her exposed and vulnerable heart as a physician tossing a soiled bandage onto the floor.

For a nurse to pick up.

Because that was all she'd ever been to him.

A convenient place to stash his dick before he'd tossed her aside, dirty and used, and she had to cobble herself together enough to throw away those pathetic hopes she'd been hanging on to.

"Trixie," he murmured.

She smiled brightly and picked up the menu. "I've heard the prickly pear margaritas are delicious," she announced to the table at large.

As she knew it would, that turned the conversation to Kelsey, who had proclaimed her love of the cocktail far and wide as they'd all chatted a few minutes before. This jump-started the bantering with the table at large, and pretty soon, the waiter came over to take their orders.

All through dinner, she managed to keep the conversation light, to keep her physical and verbal distance from Jet while still pretending to get to know him enough to satisfy the others at the table.

Her fatal flaw began when she slipped away to use the bathroom.

Because when she came out, Jet was standing in the hall.

Sniffing, she started to move past him.

His hand on her arm stilled her.

"What, Jet?" she snapped. "What could you possibly have to say to me?"

A growl. "Nothing."

"Good."

"*Everything.*"

He kissed her, and the world went topsy-turvy.

TWO

Jet

IN FAIRNESS, the *smack* of Trixie's palm across his cheek was probably warranted.

They hadn't seen each other in nearly three years, not since he'd packed up and moved on to another assignment.

And part of the reason he'd packed up was because he'd known he'd never get what he needed from Trix.

Selfish? Yes.

The truth? Also, yes.

Cutting ties before he got even more connected, before it got even harder to leave? Painful, but necessary.

Trixie was beautiful. She was fun to be with, hilarious, and the most low-maintenance person he'd ever met. She didn't need anyone's help. She got her shit done and did it well.

Which had been part of the problem.

He hadn't felt needed, hadn't felt loved. He'd had scraps tossed his way or held back in reserve, and he *knew* he couldn't live with that.

He needed *more*.

And circling back to selfish. But look, he knew himself, knew how much he enjoyed being with Trix, but he also knew he couldn't have a future with a woman he felt shut out from, one who preferred to exist in two side-by-side lives rather than two intertwined ones. After his childhood, after spending so much time being shut out and trying—and failing—to earn his parents' love, Jet knew he couldn't go through that again.

It wasn't sustainable, and so he'd torn off the Band-Aid.

Quick and painless.

Of course, it had definitely been the first, just not the second.

But, back to the well-deserved smack. Trix shoved his chest hard, tearing her mouth from his, and skittering several steps away. "What the fuck is your problem?" she snapped, wiping the back of her hand across her lips. "I-I can't believe that you would think you had any right to touch me."

She was absolutely right. Not that he was going to tell her as much. "I just had to check on something."

Her teeth came together with a sharp *click*. "You're fucking unbelievable."

But he wasn't lying.

The rest of the table had cleared out while Trix had been using the restroom, ostensibly because they had work and life commitments, but Jet knew they'd been trying to give him and Trix some time alone, based on the knowing look that Clay had given him before his friend and Heather had taken off. Tanner was a cool guy, and his girl, Kelsey, had been a hoot. They'd both preceded Heather and Clay, Kelsey's cheeks flushed from the sheer volume of prickly pear margaritas she'd consumed over the course of the meal.

Based on the hot glances she'd been shooting Tanner as they'd prepared to leave, the other man was going to have a good night.

Unlike him.

"I was checking on you," he said. "Not whether we still had enough heat between us to spontaneously combust. Though"—he leaned back against the wall, crossing his ankles and arms—"in case you were wondering. We do."

Trix rolled her pretty gray eyes. "As I mentioned previously, you're fucking unbelievable."

Jet grinned. "Thanks."

"Not a compliment, fuck twit," she muttered, brushing by him and heading back to the table, not knowing the rest of the group had already left.

He trailed her, and because he was a total asshole already, he figured he might as well enjoy the view. And it was a *view*. Tight black dress, pointy heels she could stab him with, full sleeve of tattoos down both arms visible.

Jet had spent many an hour holding Trix close and studying those swirling colorful pictures, tracing them with his fingers.

Now she stopped, those arms falling to her sides as she took in the empty table.

Slowly, she turned, angry eyes coming up to meet his.

He held out her purse.

Two steps and she came close. Fire in her gaze, fury in her stride. One part of him thought she was going to smack him again, another thought she might kiss him when those gray eyes caught on his mouth before drifting up to meet his eyes.

The air in his lungs caught.

Fuck, yes. He'd had a taste and now he wanted more—that brief touch had been enough for him to crave her lips on his for a hell of a lot longer than a few seconds.

She leaned close . . . and snatched the purse from his hands.

Then spun around and high-tailed it for the front doors.

And he was again in the not-so-unfortunate position of having to follow her out.

Trix could *move* in those heels, *click-clacking* across the floor, pushing out the doors, ass bouncing as she strode to her car. Conveniently, the small gray hybrid was parked right next to his sedan.

She beeped the locks, yanked at the handle, and tossed her purse inside.

A sheet of dark brown hair flew over her shoulder as she spun to face him again. "Why the fuck are you following me?" she snapped then threw her arms wide. Jet noticed there was a new addition to the inside of her left arm—a curved line that was shaded with blue and purple. But before he could look closer, she let her hands fall to her sides. "This is your chance to go. So take it. We both know you're excellent at it."

He'd been amused up until that point.

But her words struck home, and as such, his temper spiked.

He crowded her against the car, close enough that he could smell the slightly tropical scent of her shampoo. Even in the middle of the jungle, with humidity making all the rest of them smell like ass, she'd still been all coconut and vanilla and pineapple.

Like a fucking piña colada and he'd been thirsty.

"I didn't *want* to leave," he growled, leaning in and inhaling that tropical scent into his lungs.

"More. Fucking. Lies."

"I *had* to go."

"Great." She shoved at his chest. "Sure. So, if you *had* to go, then why were you so pissed off to see me at the table?"

She had him there.

But he'd been pissed because he'd been blindsided at seeing her. He'd left three years before and then spent the entire time trying to pretend she hadn't existed at all, and now he was finally moving on with his life and had agreed to go on a fucking date after a long ass hiatus, *and* then of course, it had been Trix sitting at that table waiting for him.

Beautiful, fun, smart Trixie had been there.

Reminding him of everything he'd walked away from.

He ignored the fact that he'd initially felt a blip of pleasure at her presence then narrowed his eyes and focused on the knee-jerk pain of knowing that no matter what he did, what he gave, she wouldn't ever be able to meet him in the middle . . . and so he said something unforgivable, "I was pissed that you were flaunting your tits to the world in that dress."

Her cheeks flared pink. "How *dare* you," she gritted, shoving him back enough to sink down into the driver's seat. "How *fucking* dare you. As if you think you have some sort of say in my body, in my clothes."

She wasn't wrong.

He was just trying to be an asshole. To push her away like she'd pushed him, to keep her at a distance and remind himself of all the reasons she was wrong for him.

So he wouldn't forget all the bad and remember the good.

Trix in his bed, smiling up at him.

Trixie working alongside him, unfazed at whatever crisis thrown their way and always finding a way to get through it without losing her smile.

Trix who'd seen so much, and who'd always had his back.

Who'd never judged.

So, yes, insinuating that about her clothes, about her as a woman, was a low fucking blow.

But it was easier to despise Trix for that initial pulse of joy upon seeing her, easier to blame the fact that their relationship had been doomed from the start on her because she was so closed off and unavailable and—

"Oof."

Strong.

Caught in the past, he wasn't prepared for her shove. He stumbled back enough for her to slam the driver's door shut. He heard the locks click, the engine start up, then had to jump another pace back when she hit the gas and screeched out of the spot.

The glare she shot him as she pulled out made him glad he hadn't jumped in front of the car to stop her.

Because she wouldn't have stopped.

And he couldn't help but think that maybe he deserved it.

In many ways.

THREE

Trixie

SHE WAS RUNNING on about two hours of sleep and a half-cup of coffee because she'd gone on a fucking blind date the evening before instead of grocery shopping . . . and still needed to show up on time for her shift.

But that was nothing new.

She'd spent a decade working abroad, moving from country to country in under-supplied and sometimes dangerous conditions, often with a limited amount of caffeine.

Definitely not the way she preferred to work.

But she could push through.

She *always* pushed through.

Sighing, she tugged her scrub top over the long-sleeved shirt she'd slipped on, then pulled on and zipped up her hospital-branded fleece. Feet into sneakers, hair into a ponytail, home-made lunch in her purple insulated case, and she was ready to go.

Before she'd moved to San Francisco three months before, or rather before she'd moved to a town *south* of San Francisco—

because working for a nonprofit didn't exactly make a girl rich—she hadn't worked at an actual hospital for years. Now, she'd adjusted to her job. For the most part.

She still missed the kids.

The innocent smiles and the excitement when they came to help.

The ones here weren't terrible, but most of them also didn't know how good they had it.

She knew how good she had it.

Money hadn't been flush when she'd been a kid, even as an O'Keith—or well, she'd technically been a Donovan since her mom hadn't taken the O'Keith name. Regardless, her father might be a billionaire and the owner of a Fortune 500 company, and her sister, Heather, might be the newest named female billionaire in the world, but Trix wasn't in that circle. She had been part of his second family, part of *her mother's taint* (and thanks dear old Dad for those kind words when she'd gone to ask him for help paying for medical school).

Look, she got it. Her mom was a disaster. Flighty, burned through money faster than water flowing through fingers. She was selfish and . . . frankly, she could be mean.

So, Trix hadn't exactly won the parent lottery.

The dream of medical school had disappeared, and she'd worked her way through nursing school instead.

Pivoting, adapting, *that* she could do.

And it wasn't like everyone could have everything, could they?

"Nope," she muttered, agreeing with her inner monologue while grabbing her backpack and heading for the door. "They can't have everything."

But at the very least, she could do something to make the world a little better for someone else.

Her shift had been relatively uneventful.

Or, at least, uneventful for the ED—emergency department —because there weren't any gunshot wounds or people threatening to stab her. There weren't any potentially scary cases that might be ebola or another highly communicable disease.

A broken arm, a heart attack, and one stab wound.

Not exciting.

Okay, so maybe she had a high tolerance for excitement, but they had thirteen beds and a full staff of nurses and doctors twiddling their thumbs.

It was making her crazy.

At least in the field she'd always had something to do, something to occupy her time with.

There weren't empty hours to think.

About a certain unnamed doctor.

Okay, fine.

About Jet and how good he'd been in bed—

No. That wasn't fair, either, because, yes, they'd been great in bed together, their bodies seeming like they were made for one another, but the entirety of their friendship, even before the brief interlude when they'd transitioned into lovers . . . *that* had been good.

She'd been in love and Jet . . .

She hadn't been enough.

Not surprising.

Trixie didn't have a self-worth issue. She knew she had value. She was smart and capable and good at her job. But she also wasn't soft or emotive or the type of woman that would clasp her hands and flutter her eyelashes and let her man know he was her hero.

She didn't need a hero.

She *needed* a partner.

She'd thought Jet had understood that, had thought he wanted the same in return. *Sigh*. She'd thought *a lot* of things, but her being what Jet wanted as a future had been perhaps the most grievous of her errors.

Well, obviously Trix had been wrong, and now it was time to move on. No time to cry over spilled milk or keep up all her teenage girl level sighing. Stifling another of the said exhalations, she headed to the break room. So what, Jet was around. Her life was busy and full. It wasn't like she was going to open herself to him again.

Been there. Done that. Got the souvenir balloon, and it had popped.

Lucky her.

Trix opened the lock on her locker and pulled on her backpack then straightened the arms on her fleece before grabbing her lunchbox.

Time to wade through some traffic, order takeout, and get caught up on about ten years of quality—and she had to be honest, some *not* quality—television. She was going to forget all about Jet and their past, forget how good it had felt when he'd touched and kissed and held her, forget about—

The man walked into the break room.

Dressed in a lab coat, stethoscope draped around his neck, he was talking to the chief trauma specialist, Tricia Heldway, and didn't notice her.

Thank God for small miracles.

She whipped around, facing her locker, and doing her best impression of a sidle as they spoke. Neither stopping their conversation as she approached the door, and she started to slip out, only to be halted when something caught her backpack.

When a *hand* caught her backpack.

Jet's chocolate eyes met hers. "Hey, Trix."

Tricia's head tilted to the side. "Oh, do you know, Trix, Jet? She's one of our best nurses."

Trixie tried to tug herself out of Jet's grip, but he didn't release her. In fact, he exerted inexorable pressure on her backpack that she ended up very near his side. Close enough that she could smell the spice of him, close enough to sense the coiled strength of power, close enough that she had to smother a shiver when she remembered how well he'd used that power.

The humid heat on their skin that had made their bodies stick together, the way he'd held her tight, his fingers almost bruising, the thin cushion of the mattress as he'd pounded into her.

The sounds of the jungle, the smell of smoke and ash from campfires.

Feeling so incredibly exhausted and yet exhilarated because they'd made a difference, trailed by the moments of feeling so damned low when they hadn't.

Such an intense time in her life, both with her career and with her heart.

And now she had come full circle.

Back trying to find her own path to making a difference . . . right alongside Jet.

Who replied to Tricia's question with a, "Yup, I know her."

Ringing endorsement, that.

But Tricia smiled anyway. "Well, I'll let you two catch up. I'm going to wrap up my charting and get out of here." She waved and left.

Trix tried to follow her. "I should—"

The grip on her backpack stayed firm. "You're working here."

She sighed, chin dropping to her chest as she debated whether to push it. "Yup," she eventually said, echoing his earlier reply. "For a couple months now."

He dropped his arm. "Cool."

Slowly, she inched away. "Cool." Another step. "'Kay, bye."

One half of that mouth curved up. "Okay, bye."

Trixie escaped into the hall, narrowly missing being mowed over by a gurney. She sent an apologetic wave and chagrined look toward the patient and her coworker's way. "Sorry," she muttered, plastering herself against the wall as they moved by. Once they were gone and she started moving again, she half-expected Jet's hand to snag her backpack and tug her to a stop a second time. It didn't.

She wasn't disappointed. Nope. She wasn't.

Definitely not.

And yet the sound of her internal derisive snort still rang in her ears as she hurried to her car.

Fucking Jet Hansen.

FOUR

Jet

HE RESISTED the urge to chase after Trix.

On one hand, she wasn't in her car, so the threat of him being run over was minimal. On the other, there were no shortage of sharps—syringes and scalpels came to mind—within reach, and she was well-versed in using them.

But that wasn't why he stayed in the break room, why he walked over to the water dispenser and downed a paper cup full instead of following her, why he stowed his valuables in a locker then his lunch in the fridge.

Because he couldn't risk getting attached again.

It was bad enough that she was in the same state, in the same hospital.

But he'd been burned by the flame that was Trix Donovan once, and that was enough.

Sighing, he stretched his neck, wondering how in all of the hospitals in the world, how after his stretch of doctoring all around the globe he'd ended up here. With Trix.

Some might say fate or kismet.

Others might say hell.

If the way his cock had twitched just watching Trix, he was definitely going with hell.

And with that fateful thought, Jet straightened his shoulders, pushed his dick and its twitching in the vicinity of the gorgeous brunette down, and focused on the work. Just like he'd done for the last three years.

Just like he was going to continue to do.

SEVEN IN THE morning came slower than he expected. Then again, the department hadn't been particularly busy, and he wasn't used to working nights.

Or working in a hospital setting rather than in the field.

One of his other physicians on shift that night had assured him the calm wouldn't last, that there would be a full moon, or it would rain and then people would be flocking to the ED, that in the meantime, he should enjoy the peace.

Jet wished he could.

But the itch under his skin wouldn't abate.

It wasn't like he'd been constantly busy while in Lebanon, Haiti, or Syria, though there had been days on end where he hadn't taken a break, where he'd worked until he could barely see straight . . . and still, the itch had been there.

Missing something.

Missing some*one*.

"Fuck," he muttered, knowing that he needed to adjust back to civilian life, to being back in this setting. He'd burned out, needed to live some place with running water and electricity and a good mattress.

Maybe he'd go back.

Maybe he'd serve for shorter-term deployments or in more domestic emergencies.

But for now, the idea of just being home was paramount.

Perhaps then he'd be able to move on with his life. He wasn't a perennial bachelor by choice. He wanted to be settled, to have a family, with kids and maybe a dog and cat.

Not a picket fence.

But he'd take a wrought iron one.

Grinning at his idiotic and sleep-addled mind, Jet made his way to his car. He'd put an obscene deposit down for a condo near the hospital, one that would have been impossible to make without the money his parents left him.

Money he'd promised himself he'd never use.

Money he'd used anyway.

But then again, a lot of his principles had changed over the last six years. He'd been young, only a few years out of residency, ready to go out and save the world, all while shucking the rigors of his rich, privileged life—never mind that his rich, privileged life was what had enabled him to graduate from medical school without the crippling debt that some of his colleagues had. Now he was nearing forty—thirty-eight, if he was being exact—and he'd spent a long time chasing some utopian dream, only to find that it didn't exist.

No matter how far he ran, he was still himself.

And now, wasn't that a melancholy thought for so early in the morning?

Cool.

Sighing, he tossed his bag onto the passenger's seat and got into his hybrid. The car still smelled new, and it was. Another purchase from his trust fund, another ding against his conscience.

And yet, he'd needed a way to get to and from work.

So once again, convenience had given way to holding the line of his ethics.

Add self-disgust to the melancholy for a lovely mix of morning emotions.

"Fuck," he muttered, turning on his car and backing out of the spot. "I need to get some sleep."

Sleep away the memories. Sleep away the urge to go back. Sleep away everything but the work.

FIVE

Trix

SHE WAS face down in bed when her phone rang.

"Why?" she groaned, fingers fumbling on her nightstand as she tried to grab her cell. It buzzed out of her grip several times before she forced her head up, used her eyes to locate and her hand to grab it, then collapsed back onto her pillow and brought it to her ear.

Where it rang again.

"Fuck," Trix muttered, flopping over to her back, swiping her finger across the screen, and then bringing it up to her ear again. "'lo?" she grumbled.

"Trixie," Heather said brightly. "How's work going?"

That was both way too much cheer and way too much volume for this early in the morning.

She grunted in reply.

Which was a mistake. She should have sat up, blinked away the sleep, and reassured Heather everything was going fine. But instead, all Trix did was pique her sister's mother hen tendencies.

Her sister was recently married—well, she'd gotten married about two years ago. But now that she was happily hitched to Clay, and even Trix could say he was a good man, Heather was determined to see everyone around her happy.

If only she'd stayed abroad, then she would be safely out of Heather's crosshairs.

But Trixie had wanted to come home.

She'd missed northern California, missed its rolling hills and giant redwoods, missed the beaches and the mountains, missed San Francisco and its restaurants, Napa and its wineries, the little beach towns dotted across the coast.

After nearly a decade of escaping her family, she'd wanted to come home.

Not to her family, she thought with a shudder. But to California.

Heather's voice rose in volume, jarring Trix out of her thoughts. "Did something happen at work? Who do I need to kill?" She laughed. "Or sic Bec on, anyway."

Bec being Rebecca Darden, a famous employment law attorney and one of her sister's best friends. Friends as in plural, as in Heather was part of a group of cackling, intervening, happily paired women who thought nothing of sticking their noses into someone's business.

Into *her* business.

"I'm fine," Trix hurried to say, *now* sitting up and blinking the sleep from her eyes. "We had a couple of people call out sick last night, so I worked some overtime." She yawned. "I only just got home." Overtime both had the purpose of padding her bank account and helping to pass the hours.

So, she hadn't seen too many of those wonderful California features yet.

But she'd planned on it today, or at least driving to the coast and listening to the waves.

After some sleep.

"Want to grab breakfast?" Heather asked. "It's been a couple of weeks since our dinner. Did anything come of you and Jet? I want to know everything. Did he call? No, wait, you should just meet us at Molly's." *Us* being her group of friends, or perhaps, more aptly described, her group of intervening busybodies.

Not that Trix didn't like them. She'd actually hung out with the group a few times since moving back. The girls were funny and sweet but . . . they would also be the first to admit without apology that they'd earned an A+ at the whole intervening busybody thing.

And Trix didn't want the world to know every bit of her life, including the fact that she knew Jet, that he'd broken her heart three years before, and that they were now working together.

That would either get the matchmaking going, or have Heather truly siccing Bec on someone.

Someone being Jet.

And Trix was done. She'd moved on past the heartbroken, past the pissed and wanting to slash his proverbial tires or bog him down with some sort of legal magic Bec could whip up.

Trix had moved on.

The past was the past.

No use dwelling on it.

"I'm tired," Trix said then because she wasn't a total asshole, added, "I just got off after working twelve hours and have a shift tonight. Can I catch up with you guys another time?"

Even though she and Heather had never seemed to be able to find their stride as sisters, or rather, as *half*-sisters, Heather had always tried to bridge the gap between them, had always managed to find a way to check in with Trix over the years, whether by email or phone call or letter. In fairness, Trix hadn't always been open to the contact, but things had changed, she'd grown and matured. Her sister had weathered that process and so, at the very least, she deserved an explanation.

A pause.

Then Heather's voice was decidedly less chipper. "Sure, Trix. I understand."

Shit. "I would come if I wasn't—"

"Of course," Heather said. "I'll talk to you some other time."

"Heath—"

"Abby wanted me to tell you she said hi."

Trix sucked in a breath. "I say hi back—"

"Great, bye."

Click.

The call cut off.

Her guilt was a familiar feeling, but what Heather didn't understand was that Trix was trying, too. Yes, she'd moved home because she loved the towns and the beaches and the mountains and trees, but she could find those same features elsewhere. Part of the reason she'd moved home was also because her family was here. No, because *Heather* was here. Heather being the one person biologically related to her that had always tried to keep in touch.

Maybe she didn't know how to express that desire, but she was there, wasn't she?

That should count for something.

Trix dropped back to the pillows. "I *should* get points for trying," she grumbled. "Especially after working twelve hours straight."

Exhaustion weighed her limbs, made her lazy. She tucked the covers up to her chin and let her lids slide closed. But sleep wouldn't come. Aside from the well-familiar feeling of guilt she had in regards to Heather, the call had woken her brain enough that no matter how long she lay there with her eyes closed, cuddling into a pillow that was infinitely softer than any she'd used over the last decade, cool cotton sheets draped over her body, soft hum of the ceiling fan spinning . . . none of those creature comforts could lure her back under.

After an hour, she tossed back the covers and moved to the bathroom.

Since sleep wasn't an option, she was going to find comfort at the beach.

———

Waves were loud.

At least those of the Pacific Ocean variety.

But at least the noise of the water pounding against the shore had quieted the cacophony in her mind.

Part of her felt like she should have bypassed the beach and gone to meet her sister. Another piece thought that was too much too soon. Another . . . well she was trying not to think about her life.

Or Jet.

Or the fact she'd seen him almost every day she'd been at the hospital, short bursts of viewing as he'd come on and she'd left, a delicate floating note of his scent coating the air and sending a sharp pain through her heart.

Memories, such sweet, fucking memories.

Snorting, she pushed up from where she'd sat down on the sand, gathering up her flip-flops along with the paperback she hadn't ended up reading because she'd been too focused on the glimpses of the sky on the horizon, on the white caps dotting the blue waves, the curls of fog being blown to shore by a wind that tangled her ponytail and chilled the exposed skin on her face and neck.

It was summer in the city.

And summer often began with fog.

But that fog was burning off now, and it was going to be a beautiful day. Soon the beach was going to be crowded with couples and families, with kids off from school, instead of joggers and the occasional person walking their dog. They'd run in the waves, build sandcastles, dig giant holes.

Or maybe that was what she wished she'd been able to do when she was their age.

And *that* was a mental train she wasn't going down.

She would rather wax poetic about how good Jet had been in bed than think about the clusterfuck that had been her childhood.

Suffice it to say, it hadn't included trips to the beach.

It had barely included food in the pantry, never mind a ride to school. However, it *had* included plenty of red-bottomed shoes, plenty of purses and clothes, plenty of makeup.

All essentials according to her mom.

All things that did not grow a healthy child.

But that was the past. She was over it. She was fine now.

Or, if not *fine,* then at least she was at least functional.

And based on her upbringing, that was probably as much as she could ever hope for.

SIX

Jet

IT HAD BEEN two weeks since he'd first seen Trix at the hospital, and they'd crossed paths exactly seven times, mostly him coming in as she was leaving, but one time they'd brushed arms over the coffee cart in the cafeteria.

Brushed arms.

Next, he'd be talking about how the brief contact had made goose bumps rise on his arms.

For the record, it had.

Yes, he was losing his mind.

But tonight he'd come in and Trix was still working, black smudges of fatigue beneath her eyes, hair pulled back into a sloppy ponytail with small, curling tendrils escaping to dip across her forehead. He'd seen her eyes like that too many times to count over the years, knew she'd been picking up any and all overtime she could grab.

And that pissed him off.

They weren't in the field. She shouldn't be working herself to exhaustion instead of enjoying her life. Even though he'd called it quits on their relationship, it wasn't like he didn't care for her.

He'd wanted it to work between them. He tried and, in the end, he'd known it couldn't work, that they both needed more —*him* someone who was open, who could love him without reserve, *her* someone who could peel away the layers, make the effort to love the woman he knew she was underneath. He couldn't do that, not after spending so much of his life pathetically desperate and begging, urging and coaxing for just an iota of love from his parents.

Jet couldn't be like that again.

Not ever again.

But it also didn't mean that he wanted to see a woman he thought of fondly working herself to death.

She'd disappeared into a patient room by the time he walked to the computer and checked the charts then picked up his phone for the shift—so nurses and admins could reach him easily. Since the patient was one he'd need to see anyway, Jet headed into the room.

Trix was removing a blood pressure cuff from the man's arm as he walked in. She glanced up, freezing for one brief moment before her eyes darted away and she removed the thermometer from beneath the patient's tongue. One spin and she turned to the trash can where a flick of her fingers dropped the liner of the thermometer into the trash. Her next sharp movement gave him her back as she began to log the stats into the computer.

"This is Tom," she said. "His BP is 143 over 86. Temp is normal. Came in with chest pain. No prior cardiac episodes or history of heart issues."

Jet nodded his thanks and started to unwind his stethoscope. "Hi, Tom, I'm Dr. Hansen. Is it all right if I take a look at you and ask you a few questions?"

The chart told him Tom was sixty-four, but he looked good

for that age. Not overweight, good coloring, though he was a little pale. Still, chest pain was never something to discount.

Tom nodded. "Sure. Thanks, doc."

Jet began his rundown, listening to his lungs and heart, asking about his pain level—a seven—and what kind of pain Tom was feeling—squeezing. Neither of those made Jet think this was less concerning, so he ordered an EKG, blood tests, and asked Trix to start an IV and administer aspirin and saline, since Tom appeared a bit dehydrated.

"We'll get you taken care of, okay?" Jet told him, putting the stethoscope back around his neck and resting his hand on Tom's arm. "I'm going to go push those tests through so we can have some answers."

Tom nodded. "Thanks."

Jet left the room, heading back to the computers, getting the phlebotomist the orders, making sure the EKG happened as soon as possible.

By the time he finished with that, Trix had come out of the room, brushing a hand across her forehead. Even from ten feet away, he could see that it shook and that made fury crawl up his spine. He crossed to her, snagging her arm and pulling her down the hall. "What the fuck do you think you're doing?"

Stormy gray eyes blinked up at him. "What are you talking about, Dr. Hansen?"

"Jet," he gritted out. "And I'm talking about you."

"You gave up your right to talk about me three years ago." She jerked at his hold, snapping out, "Let go of me."

He dropped his hand but didn't back away. Partly because he was pissed she wasn't taking care of herself again, that she was clearly exhausted and working extra hours that she didn't need to take on. Partly, because she would keep pushing herself through this since some fucked up part of her thought that *this*— being a nurse, taking care of others—was her only worth.

She couldn't see, wouldn't *ever* see that she was so much more.

Jet sighed. "You're exhausted."

Her teeth clicked together. "I'm fine."

Fury faded, bleakness taking its place. "Still the same," he said. "Still can't see—" His phone rang, and he pulled it out of his pocket, glancing at the ID. "Do what you want, Trix. Work yourself ragged to the detriment of everything else in your life." He turned, started to walk away. "It's what you do best."

The phone rang again, but this time he answered it.

There wasn't any point in *not* answering it.

Trix didn't stop him from walking away this time, just as she didn't stop him from walking away then.

HE AND TRIX stayed far apart for the rest of the shift, aside from coordinating Tom's care. The EKG showed he was having a heart attack, and so he was quickly admitted and brought to the Cath Lab where he would have a catheter inserted and his arteries cleaned out.

His prognosis was good, however. He'd come to the ED quickly, had received rapid care. He was in good shape and healthy, and so likely would be heading home after a short time in the ICU.

Trix and Jet were in less than good shape.

They'd barely spoken a word to each other over the course of twelve hours, and now they found themselves both in the break room at the same time, all of four stalls apart as they gathered their stuff from their respective lockers.

With a heavy sigh, Trix slammed the locker door and turned to face him. "I don't need you to take care of me, you know that, right?"

Jet gritted his teeth, grabbing his cell from the locker and shoving it into his pocket.

"In fact," she said and crossed her arms over her chest. "It's probably best for our working arrangement if you *don't* interject yourself in my life."

"I'm not trying to interject myself—"

She sniffed. "Could have fooled me."

"I've worked with you enough to know when you're exhausted," he said, crossing his own arms. "And you're dragging ass, Trix."

"I'm fine," she said through clenched teeth.

Jet blew out a breath. "You're running on fumes. I know it. You know it. You just don't want to admit it because you're fucking stubborn."

Trix rolled her eyes, giving him her back as she shouldered her bag then strode to the fridge and grabbed her lunchbox. "Well, it's a good thing we're not fucking anymore because you don't have to give two shits about me or my *stubbornness.*"

Red was creeping into the edges of his vision. "I care about you, Trix," he growled. "You know I do."

"Pft." She headed for the door. "Why now, Jet? Huh? You're so desperate for someone to fuck that I'm suddenly on the menu again?"

He slammed his locker, intercepted her. "That's not fair."

"Well, you said 'fuck' to fair years ago," she snapped. "Why change now?"

Calm.

Calm.

He could manage a full ED with a short staff, could oversee a clinic without fresh water or electricity without breaking a sweat, but Trixie could make him madder than a toddler who'd had his lollipop stolen. She'd always been able to make him feel way too much.

"How was I not fair, Trix?" he said, coming closer, near enough to see the hint of blue in her eyes, to smell that tropical scent of her.

Her lids shut for a heartbeat, her shoulders lifting and falling on a long breath.

Jet felt a pulse of guilt. She'd worked two shifts. He knew she was exhausted, and now he was arguing with her. He should just let her go home and—

Those lids peeled back, and the pain in her gray eyes hit him in the gut.

"You left, Jet," she said. "I gave you more than any other person, and you *fucking left*."

The slice from her words was almost visceral, but the impact to his heart from witnessing the hurt in her expression as she spoke was definitely palpable. He didn't think, didn't bother with words.

He reached for her.

But she was already backing up, batting his hands away.

"Trix," he murmured.

"Don't," she said. "Just leave it, Jet. Just leave the past where it belongs."

She grabbed for the door handle, yanked it open, then ran out of the room.

This time it was *him* watching *her* go.

Unsurprisingly, this version of the scenario didn't feel good either.

And it felt even worse when she didn't come back to the hospital.

SEVEN

Trix

OH GOD, oh God, oh God.

Why had she said that? Why had—

"Fuck," she muttered, keeping her head down as she hurried to her car. Probably because she was as exhausted as Jet had accused her of being.

It *had* been a long week, all of the extra shifts she'd been racking up having taken their toll on her body, her mind, and clearly on her fucking out of control emotions. Why had she admitted that Jet had hurt her?

"I mean, not that it's not obvious." She sighed, unlocking her car and tossing her stuff inside.

She'd been devastated when Jet had gone.

But, come on, like she'd needed to confirm as much to the man?

Where was all of her the-past-is-the-past bullshit? Or maybe it was exactly that . . . *meaning* it was all bullshit. Her strength, her ability to be content in her life, to not wish for more or to want her life to have been different so she could be the type of woman a man like Jet might want permanently—

Stop.

She slammed her hand on the steering wheel.

"No. Fuck this," she muttered. "I am not this person. I am not this weak. I'm fucking *not.*"

But she wasn't sure who she was trying to convince.

Herself? Jet? The universe?

Some fucked up combination of all three?

All she truly knew was that she was too tired to ferret out the truth.

It was a special sort of hell to be on a girls' trip when she'd worked the number of hours she had in the last week.

Just the sheer volume of conversations alone was hell on her brain.

Trix had slept for twelve hours straight before frantically packing a bag and hustling her ass to Heather's place where a party bus—seriously, a *party bus*—had picked up her and the rest of the cackling busybodies.

Speaking of, they'd laughed hysterically when Trix had called them that upon first entering said bus and being peppered with questions about the blind date with Jet.

Sera had grinned when she'd pulled herself back together. "Yup."

Bec had fist-pumped and declared, "That's right! I'm finally recognized for something other than my law skills."

Heather had shaken her head though her lips were twitching.

Kelsey had nodded.

And then Rachel had shoved a protein bar into Trix's hand,

Abby had tossed her a blanket, and they'd left her alone to doze for the drive.

So the negative side to the term busybody wasn't exactly fair, not when their intervening came from caring. But since they seemed to get a kick out of her declaring it, Trix was going to keep it in her back pocket. She'd need some fodder to dish back the teasing this crew gave.

Trix had agreed to go on the trip in the first place because Heather had asked, but also because Heather's friends were cool and she liked them. She had come home because she wanted to start forming some meaningful relationships, and Heather's group of girlfriends had been super nice and welcoming.

Of course, they were still nosy as hell.

But now Trix understood that it came from a place of love and wanting their friends happy. Which made it perfectly acceptable in Trix's book—caring for other people was kind of her specialty.

She'd be happy to call them friends. She *wanted* to crawl out of her shell enough to be able to count them as friends.

But she felt absolutely raw inside, partly because she was still exhausted from working over twenty-four hours straight and partly because . . . Jet.

What else?

She'd been off-center from the moment she'd turned around in that restaurant last month and seen that six-feet-plus gorgeous male specimen walking toward her. He'd rocked her world, made her long for what she couldn't have, and he'd left.

Again.

Now he was back. Present in her daily life. At work, with her friends and family. She was trying to adjust to her new life, and Jet was already all over it.

"Yo! Wakie wakie!" Bec bellowed, making Trix jump. "We're heeere!"

In fairness, Trix had been dozing off over the last two hours, letting the conversation between Heather and her friends—Abby, Seraphina, Rachel, Bec, CeCe, and Kelsey wash over her.

It was comfortable in some ways, to be surrounded by gabbing women. She didn't know ninety percent of the inside jokes, but she did like the teasing behind it. Light-hearted poking fun, lots of laughter, embarrassing stories about Heather and her inability to hold tequila.

It had been nice to just sit back and listen.

She sat up and stretched her neck from side to side, finding the party bus—good lord—had, in fact, stopped. The other girls were lifting bags and hauling them onto their shoulders. All except Sera, who was arguing with Abby about carrying her bag.

"You're like a hundred months pregnant," Abby said, reaching for the bulging duffle.

Sera, a tall, statuesque blonde who easily could be a model, even in her one-hundred-months pregnant state, stepped to the side and blocked Abby.

Abby, Bec, and Sera had been friends well before Heather met Abby when she was interviewing Abby for a job at Robo-Tech. Abby was married to Heather's brother and had spent several hundred months pregnant herself while popping out kiddos left and right. Bec didn't have any kids yet, but based on the conversation on the bus, it wasn't because her husband or Bec didn't want them, rather that Bec was just trying to clear some of her caseload so she'd be able to have some work-life balance.

Either way, Trix knew enough to understand that Sera was thrilled to be pregnant and was blissfully happy with her spouse.

She was also about two seconds away from losing her shit because everyone was treating her as though she were glass.

Trix knew this came from a good place, had heard how Sera had been in a car accident early on in the pregnancy and had experienced some bleeding. But by all of Sera and her doctor's accounts, everything was progressing as it should and she was looking at a normal delivery in about six weeks.

Right in that moment, though, she was in the stabby zone, and so Trix did what she did best.

She intervened.

But smartly.

Slipping past the glaring friends, she bent, grabbed the bag, and walked off the bus.

It took both women some time before they realized what Trix had done, the conversation abruptly cutting off and then footsteps clattering across the floor before Abby and Sera appeared in a huff as they made their way down the stairs.

"Don't you dare," Sera growled when Abby made as though to extend her hand to help her descend the final one.

"Fine," Abby said, hands rising in surrender. "You don't have to be snarly about it."

Since Trix was feeling pretty snarly herself about the fuss Abby was putting on, she thought that Sera exercised an impressive amount of self-control when she came to a rest on the ground, extended her arms to the vineyard surrounding them, and declared, "I need wine!"

Bec snorted. "You got a few more weeks for that."

"You don't even like wine," Abby said.

Sera sniffed. "I don't mind it. You're the heathen who can't stand the stuff."

"I—"

"How about sparkling cider?" Rachel asked. The always-prepared exec at RoboTech pulled out a bottle from her bag.

Sera wrinkled her nose.

"And chocolate?" Rachel added, extracting a chocolate bar with a flourish.

More nose wrinkling, but Sera's eyes were dancing.

"How about we actually go inside the house and get settled?" CeCe said.

"Good plan." Kelsey moved to the lockbox of the AirBnB they'd rented and plugged in the code, extracting a set of keys.

Bec snagged them from her and opened the door, stepping back and declaring, "Preggos get to enter first!"

Sera huffed. "You guys are the worst."

"Accept the offer graciously," Abby called.

Sera whipped around and glared. "Sometimes I wonder why—"

"First in, means you get first choice of the bedrooms," Trix said.

Sera paused on the threshold, eyes meeting Trix's. "Good point." She addressed the group at large. "And I also think that being a hundred months pregnant means that I get to *assign* rooms." She strode into the house, tossing back over her shoulder, "And I declare that Abby is going to sleep in the bus."

"Hey—"

Their driver chose that moment to get back onto the bus. "Well, it's been a pleasure, ladies," he said and shut the door with a *snick*.

Abby looked from the bus, slowly backing down the driveway to the house, eyes wide.

They all burst into laughter.

Even one-hundred-months-pregnant Sera.

Then they carted their butts inside and got some wine. Well, except for Sera. She had sparkling cider.

And chocolate. Couldn't forget the chocolate.

It was two in the morning.

She couldn't sleep.

Probably because she'd basically slept the day away and then dozed on the bus.

But this wasn't a bad place to be stuck *not* sleeping.

Vineyards rolled over the surrounding hills, darkened shadows at this hour, their leaves barely distinguishable in the moonlight. She knew their branches would be heavy with grapes at this time of the year, though they were not ready yet for harvest.

Sighing, she brought her glass to her lips and took a sip of the Zinfandel, the sweetness of the rosé dancing across her tongue. Her father's winery produced a very similar variety, though thankfully none of Heather's friends were the type of people to support a total asshole.

Probably, because their own parents weren't much better.

There was something about money that changed people, turned them into . . . something selfish? Something self-absorbed. Something—

Well, that wasn't fair, was it?

She'd met plenty of selfish and self-absorbed people during her travels, knew those weren't necessarily traits that were isolated to the wealthy.

Maybe it was less that the rich were bigger assholes and more that the wealthy were able to facilitate their needs because they had the funds and power to do so.

She took another sip and set her glass down, reclining back on the chaise that was on the back porch of the house they were staying at.

It was a beautiful find, a one-story ranch with eight bedrooms and ten bathrooms—yes, she'd counted, yes, she'd also got the full real estate rundown from Sera on the way in. Apparently, Sera had tried to get her husband to buy the home when they'd first met and had fallen in love. Tate had waffled, someone else had bought it, and now she had to live here vicariously for one weekend.

But the house was set on a smaller vineyard, a hobby-type one that was more for show than production. Unlike her father's, which was somewhere over the hills, acres and acres of wine-grade grapes filling the vines, an army of workers tending the grapes, aiding with production, hosting tastings.

It was a lucrative business.

And yet, it was as important to her father as this hobby farm was to the owner of this house.

As in, it wasn't important at all.

Her father had made his money in tech and military contracts, but everything else he had his fingers in—wine, a cruise line, a professional hockey team based out of L.A., an airline—was just a hobby.

A billion-dollar set of hobbies.

Insanity.

And yet, no tuition for medical school. No donation to the medical organization she'd worked with when they'd been critically short of supplies after a hurricane in the Caribbean. Heather and Jordan had donated. Abby and Sera had donated. Bec had donated. Tanner, her friend, not yet having "made" it had donated even though he'd been struggling at the time. Trix also knew that even though she'd just met Kelsey, Rachel, and CeCe that they too would have opened their wallets.

But her dad. Nope. Her mom. Definitely not. She lived from alimony payment to alimony payment and, as a consequence, could rarely rustle up money for "extra" things.

Let it be noted that those extra things often included items like food. Or paying the electricity bill. Hell, until Trix had moved halfway around the globe, she'd received many a call from her mom wondering why the lights didn't work.

Ridiculous.

A grown woman with four children, who should have been set for life, who should have been able to take care of them easily, had just bailed on any and all responsibility.

It was no wonder that Bobby, Will, and Kevin had turned out the way they were.

Namely, assholes.

But they'd learned from the best.

And everyone coped in their own way.

She just . . . wished that things had been different. That her parents had gotten their shit together and actually acted like parents, that she could find a way to connect with her siblings, including pushing through the reserve with Heather, who didn't deserve her tentativeness. Trix should be able to connect with the one person in her life who'd been steady and there. She should be able to open herself up to the fact that Heather's wonderful group of friends was fine with including her and not making her feel like she was an obligation or something to be tolerated.

But . . . how to push through or be open?

It was absolutely terrifying.

She didn't stay and fight for things she wanted—didn't demand her dad pay for school or her mother get her shit together, didn't pressure Jet to stay or declare his unending love. That just wasn't the way she operated. Trix managed it herself and if for some godawful reason she *had* to ask and was turned down, she simply adjusted her expectations and surrounded herself with a safety net. That net kept toxic people out, kept her heart and mind and soul safe and . . .

Maybe it wasn't the healthiest, but she purposefully created distance between herself and all of the bad in the world.

From the disappointment, the heartache, the betrayals.

The being left behind, forgotten.

But after spending the evening with her sister's friends, after being wrapped up in conversation and included and laughed with, Trix had to wonder if the net that kept her safe was also hurting her.

Was the anxious feeling she'd been experiencing her mind revolting?

Telling her she'd been alone for too long?

That the net was harming her more than it protected?

Because if she was always behind that net, always hiding and safely ensconced from the world, then how could she ever be free?

So many questions. So unsettled.

Still, so alone.

Sighing, she picked up her glass, tilted her gaze to the stars, and kept drinking.

She wouldn't find the answers tonight.

But perhaps this was the first step to finding them eventually.

EIGHT

Jet

HE SPENT two days freaking out about Trixie not showing up for work before he broke down and by the third asked the charge nurse when she was scheduled again.

He'd made an excuse about wanting to follow up with Trix about their patient, Tom, and his prognosis, but Rosario didn't look like she believed him, and anyway, it wasn't like Trixie needed him to tell her about the patients when she could follow up about them herself.

Still, he'd probably looked like a moron, but he had found out that Trix's absence was planned.

Two additional days off, plus her normal three.

Like most of the other nurses in the area, she worked four tens on and then had three days off, while the docs in the department worked three twelve-hour shifts a week.

Regardless, Rosario had given him an assessing look and then told him that she'd be back on Wednesday. Wonderful. He was off until Thursday.

Which meant he'd been an ass and had to wait almost a week to apologize.

What was it that people said about doctors and egos? That they had them in the plenty and that they also weren't small. *Kind of like something else*, he thought and snorted at his lame high school joke as he gathered his stuff and took off for home.

He had a couple of days off before his next shift on Thursday, might as well make the most of them.

First, sleep.

Second, getting some furniture because his place was seriously lacking. He was thirty-eight and that meant he shouldn't be living off an air mattress with a wall-mount TV propped in one corner.

He needed a real mattress, a bed frame, maybe a couch, and a dining room table. Hell, he could even spring for some chairs.

Living the big life.

Ha.

His cell rang as he took his exit from the freeway. He glanced at the caller ID and saw that Clay was calling.

"Hey, man," he answered over Bluetooth.

"Hey." A beat before his friend's voice continued through the speakers. "I'm bored."

Jet was stunned into silence for a long moment. Probably because he'd never *ever* heard Clay say he was bored. Never. Clay Steele was a workaholic in the most classic sense of the world. They'd met when he, Heather, and Colin McGregor pooled resources and wanted to test using their artificial intelligence to get medical supplies and food to areas hit hard by natural disasters. Places where limited crews and shipments could get in, but where the need was intense.

Clay had unending energy, worked hours that compared with Jet's, and he always had about ten projects fired up and waiting on the back burner.

It was unfathomable that Clay could be bored.

Also unfathomable?

The pathetic tone of Clay's voice.

He sounded despondent, almost pouty.

"Heather take over all your work?" Jet asked.

Clay sighed. "No," he grumbled. "She extended her trip by a day, and now I'm home alone with no work because Sebastian won't let me take over his projects."

Jet laughed. "This is what happens when you hire people who are too good at what they do."

"That's what I'm saying," Clay muttered.

"How long has Heather been gone?"

"Since Friday, she and the girls went on a long weekend up to Sonoma," Clay said. "Now they're not coming back until tomorrow. Apparently, Trix found some sort of hot spring spa they want to try, so they extended their rental."

Jet's heart skipped a beat at the mention of Trix's name, and he deliberately ignored the pulse of alarm that trailed it. Probably because his dumb ass mouth was working. "Trix is with them?"

Clay grunted. "Eight women in that house. Drinking, watching marathons of *Magic Mike* and *Aquaman* and *Thor*, getting into trouble and—"

"Dude," Jet interrupted, navigating the stop-and-go that always crowded the last few blocks before his building. "You need to chill out. Order a pizza, grab a beer, and relax. Your girl will be home in twenty-four hours."

"I haven't seen her for four days."

Jet rolled his eyes. "Also, this just in, you're completely pussy-whipped."

"So what," Clay muttered.

"*So*, you should be okay being without Heather for a few days."

"I'm *okay*," Clay said. "I just don't like it."

"And you're apparently worried she's going to leave you for a stripper? Or a superhero?"

A long-suffering sigh. "No."

"Then relax. Enjoy being able to put your feet up on the table without getting yelled at. Have that beer, order that pizza."

"It's eight in the morning."

"Okay, wait a few hours *then* do both."

"Fine," Clay said, tone still grumbling. "Be reasonable, why don't you?"

"I will," Jet agreed. "Other than missing your wife, what have you been up to?"

They shot the shit as Jet pulled into the underground parking garage and made his way up to his condo, Clay telling him about some projects that were rolling out, including some cool innovations with AI that hospitals might be able to use shortly.

"You working today?" Clay asked as Jet walked into his condo.

"Just got off shift. Not working again until Thursday."

"Cool. Then you can order the pizza tonight. I'll bring the beer over to your place."

Jet dropped his stuff by the door. "Fair warning. My plan is to buy a couch today, but my furniture situation is a little sparse."

"Do you have a TV?"

"Yeah."

"Good enough for me." A beat then, "Should we bother with vegetables on the pizza?"

Jet kicked off his shoes, dropped onto the air mattress. "Nah."

Clay laughed. "Agree," he said. "Okay, I'm going to have my assistant send you some places that can have furniture delivered." There was a pause, as though Clay were glancing at the time. "I'm guessing you're going to crash now?"

Jet's eyes were already closed. "You'd be guessing right."

"Cool, I'll have Tristan email you the places."

"Not billionaire places," Jet said.

"Not billionaire," Clay agreed. "See you about eight tonight."

"'kay."

They hung up. Jet blearily managed to plug his cell into the charger and then tugged the covers up and over him.

He was asleep in seconds.

THE SUN WAS BLINDING when he woke, and Jet spent a few minutes mentally grumbling that he hadn't thought to shut the curtains. Realistically, it was probably a good thing since he probably would have slept until Clay came over and then they'd be sitting on the floor, a pizza box and beers between them, watching a TV that was propped against the wall in one corner of his condo.

That, at least, was enough to get him out of bed. Well, that and the sun shining directly in his eyes.

He crossed to the bathroom, showered quickly, and then got dressed.

As promised, an email from Tristan@steeletechnolo-gies.com was waiting in his inbox, containing a list of furniture stores, along with their styles, their inventory that was able to be shipped that day, and their location relative to his condo.

Tristan was scarily efficient.

Then again, after having recently met Sebastian—Clay's former assistant who had moved up in the company and trained Tristan—his friend didn't seem to accept them any other way.

Furniture shopping.

Yay.

Every grown man's dream.

Snorting, he tucked his cell in his pocket, grabbed a jacket, and got down to furnishing his condo.

Thankfully, the process wasn't too painful, and after a couple of hours Jet had a couch being delivered later that day, a bed frame and new mattress coming the next, and had filled his cart at Target to an obscene amount with new sheets and blankets, towels, pillows, and an area rug.

Even a man who'd spent more of the last few years in tents and sleeping on the ground, at worst, or an air mattress, at best, could be tamed by a walk through the home goods aisle at Target.

Now he was home, had mounted the TV to the wall, unpacked most of the bags, thrown the new sheets in the wash, and was moving his limited furniture to the side to make room for the kick-ass sectional he'd picked out. If Jet was becoming domesticated, he figured he might as well be comfortable at the same time, and so the pieces he'd chosen were solid and comfortable *and* had taken a giant chunk out of his paycheck.

Worth it, though.

If he was serious about wanting to settle down and have a family, he'd need furniture.

And it wasn't like he was going to be bringing a woman back to his place to get busy on an air mattress.

Come home with me, baby. I'll try not to fuck you hard enough to deflate the bed.

Yeah, that would be super smooth.

The buzzer rang, and his next hour was spent helping the guys bring the furniture in and then logging into all of his streaming accounts on the TV. Clay arrived with beer and the pizza in hand—having intercepted the guy in the hall, and they turned on a baseball game while making a respectable dent in the six-pack and extra-large pizza.

It was probably the most normal night he'd had in six years.

A friend, a game, some food, plenty of shit-talking.

"How'd it go with Trix?" Clay asked as they were carrying the empties into the kitchen.

"We going to have heart-to-hearts now?" Jet countered.

"Well, we already discussed in length how I'm severely pussy whipped," Clay said. "The least you can do is tell me my matchmaking efforts were successful."

Jet rolled his eyes. "Seriously?"

"Come on, man. She's perfect for you. She's smart, not interested in that giant wad of money your parents left you, and bonus, absolutely gorgeous."

Those were all true statements. Ones he knew, of course, being that he'd spent almost a year of his life learning everything he could about Trix—everything she'd allowed him to know, that was. The trouble was, Clay didn't know about that year. In fact, he doubted *anyone* did. Not only had their work often separated them, taking them on different assignments to different parts of the world, but during the times they were together, they'd needed to be discreet—not only because it was against policy to fraternize, but because some of the places they'd been were culturally different and they wouldn't have appreciated an unwed couple with a standing evening sex appointment to be administering their care.

It had been tricky.

It had been exciting.

He'd fallen deep and he'd fallen fast.

But Clay didn't know any of that.

And Jet wasn't willing to share it with the class.

"She's a nurse, Jet," Clay added when he didn't say anything. "She's traveled. She did the whole doctoring abroad thing like you, but for even longer. Heather hardly saw her for a full decade before she moved back home."

Jet knew all of that. Well, not the not seeing her sister part, though he supposed that wasn't too much of a surprise considering how all-encompassing that world had been. When they were on an assignment, it was hard to think of anything but what was right in front of them. Not only was it tough and exhausting, but oftentimes they weren't near any place where they *could* call home, even if they'd had the physical or mental energy to do so. But he knew the rest of it, that she'd lived abroad from almost the moment she'd graduated from nursing school, that she was brilliant and talented and could suture a wound better than he could.

He knew she could have been a doctor, would have probably been a better one than he was.

She was just that good.

But she'd barely been able to afford to put herself through nursing school.

Somehow despite being the daughter of George O'Keith, money had been tight. Jet didn't know the story as to why, whether O'Keith had refused to pay, or whether *she'd* refused, not wanting to be tied down. Yet, that probably as much as anything else, illustrated exactly why he and Trix couldn't work out.

A year together and he hadn't begun to understand her relationship with her family.

He shoved the pizza box into the trash and turned to face Clay. "She works at the hospital."

Clay's brows rose. "Which hospital?"

"*My* hospital," he said. "In the same department. It's too messy, even if she was interested in me. Which she's not."

"Did you even call her?"

Jet started sticking the empty beer bottles into the recycling can. "I saw her *at the hospital*."

Clay rubbed his chin, the bristle on his jaw making a loud scratching sound. "That is dicey. You guys work at the same time?"

He nodded. "Sometimes."

"Hmm." Clay shrugged. "Well, Heather's going to be disappointed. She wants everyone around her happy and paired off."

Jet straightened. "*I want to be happy and paired off, but as much as I like Trix, I'm not going to pursue something that puts both of our jobs at risk.*"

"Sometimes things work out better when you work together."

"That's easy to say when you're the boss," Jet said. "Meanwhile, I don't think *my* boss would be so happy about that scenario."

Clay grinned. "That's a fair point." He turned and grabbed his jacket off the back of the couch—which, note to the universe was really fucking comfortable. "You know what the solution to this is, right?"

Jet trailed him to the door. "What?"

"You become the boss, and then you get to do what you want."

Jet snorted. "So says the man with the giant HR Department."

Clay winced, hand on the knob. "It is obscenely large."

Jet paused, lips twitching. "Almost forty, and still so tempted to make a *that's what she said* joke."

Clay snorted. "Never too old for bad jokes."

"True." They shook hands. "Next time you need to forget you're missing your wife, I'm around."

"I'll take you up on that," Clay said. "Also, know that now

you're on Heather's and the rest of the Sextant's radar. So get ready for matchmaking efforts galore."

"What's a Sextant?"

Clay waved a hand. "It's a long story that involves an obscene amount of drunk Googling and a gaggle of women. The point is, Heather's got a good circle of friends, but they're all paired off. Now, they're looking for fresh meat."

Jet chuckled. "Well, consider me fresh meat then. If they have anyone as cool as Heather, I'd be all over that."

His eyes narrowed. "She's mine."

"That I'm well aware, my friend," Jet said. "My point was that you have good taste."

Clay grinned. "That I do."

"So, if there's another Heather around. One that's not yours," he added when Clay started scowling again. "Then, I'm in."

With a nod, Clay headed toward the elevator. "Just saying, there *is* another Heather around."

"Yeah?"

Clay pressed the button to call the car and glanced back over his shoulder. "Yeah. Her name is Trix."

NINE

Trix

SHE'D HAD fun with the girls, more fun than she would have expected, especially on their final day together, when they'd all blown off responsibility and had gone to the hot springs she'd nervously suggested the previous day in Calistoga.

They hadn't shot her down.

They'd actually extended their trip by a day and had all gone with her.

Trix grinned. So yeah, she had friends now.

Still, despite having grown up in the Bay Area, she had never done a lot of the touristy stuff. No cable car, no Alcatraz, no Hearst Castle or Missions.

When she'd bought her first car, she'd put as much gas in the tank as she could afford and then had driven wherever the tank would get her. To the beach, to Pier 39, to Tahoe once or twice when she'd really gotten good tips at work. But it had never taken her to Calistoga or Lassen or Death Valley. She'd never made it down to San Diego or even to Yosemite.

Trix had been all around the world and yet, had hardly explored her home state.

Well, that was going to change now.

First with Calistoga, and to be able to check it off her list felt good. Next week, she was going to do a tour of Alcatraz.

Feeling proud of herself both for surviving the weekend—because yes, the other women were great and fun and had included her in everything, but they were also a lot for a woman who wasn't used to that much socialization—but she was also proud for actually having a plan to live her life more fully.

For the first time ever she had goals and hopes and dreams, and she wasn't going to compromise them.

So, yes, Alcatraz and then Lassen and Death Valley and San Diego. Hell, maybe she'd live vicariously and take a drive down Highway 1.

Go her.

But for now, she had to go to work. The sightseeing and hopes and dreams would have to wait until her next few days off. She was on days from seven in the morning until five at night for the foreseeable future.

Which was a good thing, considering Jet worked nights.

If they had to work at the same place, at least they were on opposing shifts.

See? Look at her go with the bright side. She filled her coffee mug, shrugged into her backpack, and made her way down to her car. It would feel good to be on her feet for her shift, to walk off all that wine and cheese and lazing around she'd done all weekend.

Plus, Jet wouldn't be there.

She could work and focus on her job and not have to worry about betraying something to the man who'd broken her heart.

The one she'd declared that she cared about just a few days before.

"Ugh," she groaned, starting up her car, having almost forgotten that critically embarrassing moment.

Well, she had twenty-four more hours to get over it because Jet didn't work Wednesdays . . . and *go her* for having the wherewithal to have checked the schedule before she left.

The drive was its typical stop-and-go, but inching her way to the hospital at least let her get caught up on her podcasts.

That day's presentation was about a guy who let snakes bite him to build up his tolerance to venom, a la *The Princess Bride* and the Iocane powder Battle of the Wits, though no one had died.

Yet.

The nurse in her shook her head.

The woman who'd become obsessed with reality TV of late was fascinated.

But by the time she'd pulled into the parking lot, Trix had moved on to music and she was softly singing a song by Rhianna as she got out of her car and gathered her stuff.

"Always did have a pretty voice."

She jumped, narrowly avoiding banging her head on the frame of the car, and whipped around to glare at Jet.

"What the fuck?" she snapped. "You like sneaking up on women?"

A quick flash of white. "I never could resist doing it to you."

She rolled her eyes, tossed her backpack over one shoulder, then closed the door and locked her car. "I thought you weren't working today."

The moment the words were out of her mouth, she knew she'd made a mistake.

Trix had just all but told Jet she'd been aware enough of him to know his schedule. Paired with the whole *I-care-about-you* nonsense and—

Run.

As in, she needed to get the hell out of there.

"Well, good to see you," she said hurriedly and took off for the hospital.

He followed her.

Oh, good Lord.

She pointed toward the parking lot. "Shouldn't you go home and get some sleep?"

"Nope."

Her lips pressed into a flat line, irritation weaving through her, but she didn't snap back an answer like she wanted. Instead, she swallowed her retort and kept walking toward the hospital.

And Jet kept walking right alongside her.

Finally, ten feet from the door, she stopped and spun around to face him. "Seriously, Jet. What the fuck are you doing?"

He clipped on his badge, strode by her. "I'm going to work."

She followed him. "But you don't work this shift."

"That's twice you've mentioned my work hours." He leaned down, knowing eyes alighting on hers for a moment. "Keeping track of me?"

Trix sniffed. "Only as much as to know how to steer clear." She brushed by him. "Too bad that didn't work today."

At the doors, Jet reached past her and swiped his badge to open the panel. "I don't mind working with you. You're the best nurse in this place."

"I wouldn't say that too loudly," she muttered, striding through the door in front of him. "You have to work with all the rest of them, remember?"

"I remember."

"And why are you on days?"

"That was always the plan. I was just filling in for Dr. Joyce while she was on maternity leave."

Trix's gut twisted. "Oh."

They walked in silence the rest of the way to the break room, which was the point that she finally realized something. "Why don't you use the physician break room?"

A shrug. "It's a bit . . ." He trailed off.

"Stuffy?" she filled in.

"If stuffy means filled with arrogant assholes, then yes."

She snorted. Their department was pretty good, but Jet's point wasn't inaccurate. There were a lot of egos on the physician side of the ED. "So you decided to slum it with the rest of the staff?"

"I prefer to quote-unquote"—he did air quotes here and instead of being ridiculous or douchy, they made her smile —"slum it with the people doing the real work."

Trix smiled. "Laying it on thick, Hansen."

He lifted a brow, reaching in front of her to hold open the door to the break room. "That's Dr. Hansen to you," he said, tapping his chest self-importantly.

Pausing in the doorway, she stared at him for a long moment.

But then he made a goofy face and danced the slashes of his dark brown brows across his forehead. Between the eyebrow waggling, the banter, and the silly expression, she was reminded of exactly how it used to be between them. She broke out into laughter and he followed suit, still holding the door open. His body was close to hers, close enough his scent inundated her nose, made her thighs clench. Abruptly, her laughter cut off, the heat of him seeping through the thin layers of her scrubs, making her nipples bead against the soft fabric of her bra.

Jet went quiet, eyes flicking down to her chest, and she knew he saw her nipples standing out in sharp relief by the way every muscle in his body went taut, his hands clenching into fists at his sides.

"Trix," he murmured, voice raspy and scraping its way along her skin.

Not in a bad way.

Rather, it set every one of her nerves on high alert, raised goose bumps on her arms, the hairs on the back of her neck.

And his expression?

That was pure heat, threatening to incinerate her from the inside out.

"Baby," he murmured.

She leaned in, close enough that her nipples brushed his chest. He smelled *so* good and she knew he would feel good against her, those slightly roughened hands brushing up and down her arms, mouth dragging across her jaw until his lips found hers with a firm, but confident pressure, the wet heat of his tongue sliding against hers.

Jet bent slightly and she felt the hot, damp air of his breath against her ear. "Trix," he whispered and *fuck* how she wanted to turn her head, to allow his mouth to meet hers, to kiss and hold and *touch* him like she used to.

For him to wind his fingers into her hair, tilt her head, taste her deeply.

For the fingers to slide down and slip beneath the hem of her shirt, to drift across the skin of her stomach, to flutter up to her breasts—

A monitor alarmed and they jumped apart.

"Help!" someone yelled.

A millisecond later, a Code Blue—a patient's heart stopping —was called.

Trix hit her head against the door frame, hard enough to see stars, but that didn't stop her from lurching into the break room and throwing her stuff into her locker. Jet was right behind her, dropping his stuff before they both sprinted out of the room. A man was standing in the hallway, holding a woman who was covered in blood in his arms.

He wavered as Trix closed the distance between them, and she lunged the final few feet and stuck her shoulder beneath the man's, preventing them from crashing to the ground. A second later, Jet was there, grabbing the woman from the man's arms and barking out orders.

Half the department was in with the coding patient, and the rest sprinted out into the hall.

Two gurneys appeared and they hefted the patients onto them, calling out stats and injuries they saw as they rolled them into rooms. She and Jet ended up separated. He stayed with the woman while she got to work on the man with Dr. Harding. Her patient had a large laceration on his scalp, and what appeared to be a knife wound in his abdomen. He passed out in the middle of answering a question about what had happened but had at least told them his name was Ben and he was thirty-two. They kept working, addressing the injuries they could see, packing wounds, applying pressure, while she started an IV and began pushing fluids, stabilizing him enough to get him down to CT.

Trix knew the same was going on next door, and she also knew that somewhere in another room, her coworkers were also addressing the code that had been called, trying to restart the patient's heart while also doing their best to manage the pressing needs of their other patients.

It didn't matter that it was a shift change, that people might technically be off the clock. They banded together, worked efficiently and quickly to treat the patients in front of them.

Later, it would be time to breathe, to change their bloodied scrubs for clean, to splash some water on their faces, to suck in some air, shore up their spines, and go home or continue on with their shift.

In her room, they got the bleeding under control and moved Ben off to a CT.

She took the time to peel off her gloves and poke her head in next door. Jet's patient was awake now, but pale, answering questions as the team worked on her.

Trix moved to the next desk, made sure everything was under control.

Mostly everything was fine, but they were still trying to resuscitate the patient who'd coded, and it was nearing the time where they were going to have to call it.

Damn.

She stifled a sigh, tucked down the sadness. This was the way of life in the ED, in health care. Patients came, the staff did their utmost to help them, and even after they did everything they could . . . sometimes the patient didn't make it.

Trix spent a few minutes clocking in then walking down to the break room and making sure her and Jet's belongings had actually made it into their lockers with locks that were actually locked. Then realized her cell was still in her pocket, and so she disinfected it then stowed that away.

By the time she left the break room and made it back to the nurse's station, Susan was emerging from a patient room. Based on the expression on her face, Trix assumed it was where they'd had the code.

Susan tossed her gloves in the bin and came over.

"You okay?" Trix asked.

Susan nodded. "Yeah. Just sucks. He'd just been discharged yesterday."

"Oh? From where?"

"Here. He'd had a heart attack last week, a couple of stints were put in, but the prognosis was good."

Trix's breath caught.

"Was his name Tom?"

Susan's eyes met hers, and she nodded. "Yeah. Did you work on him last week?"

Trix nodded.

"Sucks."

Another nod. "Yeah, it does."

They stood together in silence for a few moments, knowing exactly what the other person was feeling—sadness because someone was gone, failure because there were always the "what if's," the "should have's," the "could have's," but also disappointment and fury and a teeth-clenching mix of *all* of those.

Because sometimes medicine didn't win.

Sometimes people died.

But as sad as that was, as heartbreaking, they still had a job to do.

Later, they could cry.

Trix sucked in a breath and released it slowly. "What else do we have?"

Susan was quiet for a beat longer then visibly shook herself and began rattling off the remainder of her patients and what needed to happen on Trix's shift. They discussed everything, got sorted, and then Trix made the rounds while Susan went home.

Those rounds, following up on Ben, administering meds, and checking on test results were *all* she focused on.

Otherwise, she'd think of Tom.

Of sweet, funny, kind Tom who'd joked and laughed and been quite wonderful and who was now . . . gone.

No.

Not thinking about that.

Work. She'd focus on the work, hold it in for the next twelve hours.

Then she could allow herself to break down.

IT WAS TEN PAST SEVEN, she'd just finished the shift change, and Trix was absolutely exhausted. Emotionally, physically, mentally, it was one of those days that she felt every minute of those twelve hours of work.

And she had three more days of the same in front of her.

One small miracle was that she had barely seen Jet for the entirety of her shift. He'd been focusing on the female patient, she'd been with Dr. Harding on Ben and then later dealing with the police when they'd come to investigate the car with its engine running in front of the ED, Ben's stab wound, and . . . oh yeah, the trunk filled to the brim with cocaine.

When she regained her sense of dark humor, that story was going to be a good one to tell.

She shrugged on her backpack, gathered the rest of her things, and headed out.

Jet was leaning against her car, arms and ankles crossed.

"Fuck," she muttered, but she was too tired to try and find a way to avoid this conversation. Instead, she kept walking, striding over to the passenger's side door and bleeping the locks. Her backpack went on the floor, alongside her dirty scrubs.

She briefly debated climbing over the console to get into the driver's seat, but that was too cowardly even for her. So this time, she stifled her f-bomb, backed out of the passenger's side, and rounded the hood.

Jet didn't move as she approached.

Fine. Whatever.

She yanked at the handle, trying to open the door, maybe his ass would get pinched in the opening.

A girl could hope.

But since he was heavy and she managed to get it open all of one inch—yes, she was strong no, she couldn't move a behemoth of a man who outweighed her by a hundred pounds all via a small strip of metal—she stopped and glared at him.

He looked down at her with patient eyes. "You heard about Tom?"

The name was a punch to her gut, and she sucked in a breath.

Jet moved, tugging her into his arms. "Yeah, you heard," he murmured into her hair, running his hand up and down her spine. "Are you okay?"

"I'm fine."

But she *wasn't* fine, and he knew it, and so luckily for her, she got to stay in the circle of his arms.

"It reminds you of Amare."

For as much as she tried to keep herself locked down, Jet always seemed to know exactly she was thinking.

"Yeah."

"That was a tough case."

"They're not the same."

Amare most likely would have lived if he'd had access to the U.S. healthcare system. Aside from his heart problems, he'd been otherwise healthy. And like Tom, he'd been funny and kind. He'd also been a great provider, and just a really special soul all around. Everyone in the clinic had loved him.

Everyone had grieved when they'd lost him.

"That doesn't make this any easier."

That much was true.

Jet dropped his arms and, no, she wasn't disappointed that he'd backed away. She couldn't afford to be sad at this point. It was a fact. He didn't stay, wouldn't *ever* stay long term. Still, regardless of the past shading their present interactions, Jet stepped back. Trix kept her eyes on her shoes, sucking in a few slow breaths, listening to his footsteps as he strode away.

That was fine.

He'd been nice about Tom. Friendly.

That was all she could ever hope for.

It would need to be enough.

A car door opened and closed and still she just breathed, eyes on her feet. Okay, good. Enough. She was going to go home and—

Warm fingers laced through hers.

Her gaze flew up, saw Jet had her backpack over his shoulder, the bag of dirties under his arm. "Come on."

"What—"

Before she could finish her question, Trix was in the passenger's seat of his car, her keys plucked from her fingers and her car's locks *bleeped*. Then faster than she would have thought possible, her seat belt was buckled, her stuff stowed in the backseat, and Jet was pulling out of the parking spot.

"Um . . ."

What had just happened?

"I'm sorry I was such an ass last week."

"Um . . ."

Double, *what just happened?* Because Jet was apologizing?

"I should have trusted you to know your own limits," he said. "I was out of line."

"Yes, you were."

He laughed. "Never one to let anyone off the hook."

Ouch. And just like always, Jet was able to cut her to the quick. Heart aching, she stared out the window, watching the red taillights moving past them for a long moment. The past, the present were tangled together, and she didn't realize for several minutes that they weren't heading in the direction of her place until he got off the freeway way to soon.

She needed to take it south for several more miles, not get off in the city.

"Jet—"

His eyes flashed to hers. "I wanted it to work between us. You know that, right?"

She forgot about the exit as irritation flowed over her. "And by wanting to make it work, you *left*? Didn't explain why you were leaving or where you were going or for how long?" Her palm smacked against her thigh. "We had what I thought was this incredible night together, made plans a-and you didn't return my calls, my emails. You just ghosted me and disappeared off the fucking face of the earth."

His jaw clenched. "I had to go to Haiti."

"Without a word?"

"It wasn't like there was an abundance of communication methods after the earthquake."

"You couldn't have left a note?"

"I . . . didn't have time."

She turned, meeting his eyes for long enough that the car behind them got antsy and honked. Jet hit the accelerator.

"You're full of shit," she said. "Whatever happened, you panicked and left."

"It wasn't panic."

"Then, *what* was it?"

"I knew we'd never work."

Trix huffed. "We seemed to work damned well for over a year."

Silence then, "That was before."

Her gut clenched. "Before what?"

He turned into a garage, hitting the clicker hanging on his sunshade, and pulling into a parking spot before he turned to face her. His eyes and tone were serious as he said, "Before I realized that you were never going to give me what I need."

Slice.

His words cut her deeply, gouging tracks through her heart,

her soul. She'd given this man everything that was in her power to give.

And it still wasn't enough.

She clenched her teeth against the burn in her throat, deliberately blinked to keep the tears in her eyes as she met his gaze. He was serious. He didn't get how much it had taken her to open up to him as much as she had. "I gave you more than I've given any other person."

"I think that's a pretty ex—"

"No," she said. "So maybe I didn't tell you about my parents and their pissing contest with money or how I had to fend for myself because my mother was too wrapped up in clothes and shoes and makeup to buy fucking food." Her breath was slow and controlled. "I tried very hard for *many* years to forget that. But I did tell you how there wasn't a lot of money growing up. I told you I'd dreamed of being a doctor, but had to give up on that and become a nurse instead." She reached into the backseat and snatched her backpack, but she couldn't reach the bag of dirty clothes. Fuck it, Jet could wash them if he really gave a shit. "I gave you . . . *so fucking much*," she snapped. "I gave you everything I could—"

He slammed his hand on the steering wheel. "But you didn't give me any of the why! You didn't tell me why you gave up on the dream, why your brothers left, why you had to fend for yourself. And you sure as shit didn't tell me what you felt about *any* of that."

"I—" She shook her head. "I'm not easy with feelings," she admitted. "I spent so much of my life shoving them down that *I'm* not even sure what I feel most of the time."

His eyes went sad. "And that right there."

She reached for the door handle. "What right there?"

"That," he repeated. "You don't know your own feelings

enough to discuss them like a rational human," he said. "You're not whole, Trix. Your past has cut you to shreds."

More slicing, more hurt tap-dancing on her heart.

"And what? I'm damaged?" she spat. "You didn't have the energy to heal me?"

Jet didn't deny that. Didn't say anything except, "I'm a healer of the body, baby. Not of the mind."

Ah. So that was it. The truth about why he'd left.

She was so incredibly fucked up that she wasn't worth the time and effort to learn what was beneath her armor.

She'd known that. Some part of her had understood. Hell, she was well familiar with her abilities to keep people at a distance. But . . . she hadn't kept Jet away, or hadn't meant to anyway, and that he didn't find value in how much effort it had taken her to give him all she had, to push herself out of her comfort zone as much as she had . . . well, that hurt almost as much as him declaring her damaged.

"Maybe my childhood fucked me up," she said.

"There's no maybe about it."

Anger hazed the edges of her vision. "Okay, so it *clearly* fucked me up," she gritted. "But you're just as fucked up, just as damaged. Maybe I wasn't open, maybe I had too much armor, but you're just as protected, Jet. You didn't even fight for us, didn't express what you needed from me, didn't bother to tell me that you had to have more in order for things to work out." She popped the door handle and started to push out, pausing to toss over her shoulder, "And the reason you didn't do *any* of those things was because you were scared. Scared shitless that what was between us might actually work out, scared *you'd* have to put yourself out there."

"That's—"

"Not fair?" she asked, stepping out and bending to glare at him through the opening. "What's *not* fair is you being in disbelief about the fact that *you're* damaged, too, that your childhood fucked you up just as much, that you're just as good at keeping people at a distance." She shook her head. "I didn't have a chance to learn the whys, the hows, and the emotions behind any of them. *You* didn't give me that opportunity." A beat. "The difference is that I was willing to give you the time and space to figure them out along with the *patience* and understanding for you to share them on your terms."

"Trix—"

"So, fuck you, Jet. Fuck you for calling me damaged. Fuck you for me not being able to live up to your impossible standards." She sucked in a breath and straightened. "And fuck you, for not loving me the way you should have."

With that, she slammed the door and walked away.

Fuck him.

Fuck Jet.

Fuck. It. All.

TEN

Jet

HE SLAMMED his hand on the steering wheel. "Fucking hell."

What the hell was wrong with that woman? Accusing him of being a coward. Was she actually serious? Jet threw open the door and got out, striding angrily over to the elevator and swiping his key fob.

"Impossible woman," he muttered. "Trying to make this seem like my fault—"

The elevator doors opened, and he froze, eyes unseeing as her earlier words washed over him.

You didn't fight for us.

The reason you didn't do any of those things was because you were scared.

Fuck you for not loving me the way you should have.

All of his words, including his so-called apology, crystalized into a perfect representation . . . of his asshole-ness.

Fuck. Trix was right. One hundred percent right.

He'd been *all* of the things she'd mentioned. Scared, cowardly, impatient. But the one that stung the most was the fact that he *hadn't* loved her enough, hadn't loved her the way he should have.

If he had . . .

Fuck it all, if he *had* he wouldn't have said those things today, wouldn't have left her the way he had, wouldn't have acted like such a—

"Shit," he muttered, spinning back in the direction of the parking lot.

He needed to go after her, to apologize and actually mean it this time.

But fuck, where had she gone? He'd all but kidnapped her, intending to take her back to his place and force some food in her over a movie, to try and distract her from what had happened, and now he'd run her off by being a total—

Twatwaffle.

"Shit," he muttered again, hurrying up the driveway and out onto the street. Trix was nowhere in sight, so he strode down the block, searching for an exhausted brunette in scrubs.

Nothing. Nothing. Noth—

There.

Thank fuck.

He rushed over. "Trix," he said. "I—"

She spun one-hundred-eighty degrees, not saying a word, not acknowledging him in any way. Instead, she lifted her phone to her face, and he saw that she'd ordered a Lyft.

More guilt. This time adding in the fact that she was paying for a ride home.

But at least he could solve this one.

He reached over her shoulder and snagged her cell, walking quickly back toward his building.

"What the fuck, Jet?" Trix exclaimed, chasing after him. Not answering, he rounded the corner and headed for the lobby of his building. "Give me my phone back," she snapped. "Now."

Jet opened the door, held it wide for her to precede him.

She stopped, glaring and reaching for her cell.

His only answer was to stow it safely in his pocket.

Trix studied him, seemed to be debating between making a scene by attempting to wrestle the phone from him or walking through the door he held open.

After a few seconds, she strode through the door.

"Jet," she growled when he walked past her and hit the button for the elevator.

He still didn't reply, mostly because he didn't know what to say. His thoughts were swirling with her words, with what he'd realized, and the realization that he couldn't begin to make up for everything he said to her.

He'd called her damaged, for fuck's sake.

That was the pot calling the kettle black.

He still revolted against using the money his parents had left him, had done his damnedest to do the exact opposite of what they wanted for him for years. Hell, even putting typical teenaged revolt aside, he hadn't discussed his parents with Trix at all, aside from the barest details about their deaths.

And yet he'd spent the last three years pretending he was both the victim and the person in the right.

Fuck, everyone always said that hindsight was twenty-twenty, but it still stung like hell to realize how truly screwed up he was.

Damaged.

Fuck.

The doors opened, and Trix glanced up at him when he held them open. He didn't move, didn't do anything except hold them. With another long-suffering sigh, she got on.

He pushed the button for his floor, half-expecting her to dart off.

But instead, she leaned back against the wall and crossed

her arms. Her eyes were as dark as rain clouds as she glared at him, fury pulling her brows down. One pissed-off—and well-deserved—woman threatening to dismember him with her stare, and she'd never been more beautiful.

Just like every other time he was in her presence, whether it had been that restaurant a few weeks ago, the hospital that day, Syria a few years before, every nerve in his body instinctively knew where she was.

It was like the heightened awareness of sensing when danger was near.

Except, it wasn't danger he was feeling.

Or at least, not the life-threatening type, proverbial dismembering glare aside.

Blinders. He'd gone a long time wearing them, not understanding the consequences, or perhaps, not being open to the fact that he'd played a role in them right alongside Trix. And that made him weak and cowardly and frankly, he was disgusted with himself.

But how to explain that?

How to prove to her that despite the bullshit he'd said not an hour before, he understood now that he'd been so incredibly wrong?

Yet, if someone came to him with that, flipping their opinions on a head after less than an hour, he'd tell them to fuck off and never come back. So, how to get her to understand that while he was still digesting the realization, he understood he was wrong, that he'd seriously fucked up, and though he'd stopped short of accepting responsibility for his part in the demise of their relationship before, he was ready to take ownership now.

All the right words.

All the right sentiments.

He wouldn't believe a fucking word of them.

Fuck.

But before he could go around in another circle in his mind, the elevator dinged, and the doors opened. Trix strode off, chin high, shoulders straight, backpack secured over both shoulders.

He should have taken that, too, so she didn't have to haul it so far.

Another should have, could have.

Ugh.

She stopped just inside the hall and looked—okay, *glared*—at him. But Jet was already committed to this fruitless (probably) venture, and so he slipped past Trix and headed down the hall to his condo's door.

Less than a minute later, he'd unlocked it and they were both inside, her backpack propped just beyond the threshold.

"Can I get you a glass of wine?"

One brown brow lifted.

Despite everything—the guilt, the disappointment, the frustration—that arched eyebrow had him biting back a smile, and he relaxed. Slightly. He'd lay it out there and not expect her to forgive him because . . . how could he?

"I'm trying to butter you up before I eat crow."

She turned on her heel and walked toward the windows. "You need to eat a fuck-ton more than crow. I'm talking fucking bald eagle level crow."

It was snark and her tone was acerbic, but it was what was underneath that surface level toughness that really sliced him to the quick. He'd hurt her, wounded her deeply.

"I'm sorry."

The second time that evening he'd said those words, but the first time he actually understood all he was apologizing for.

Trix turned, eyes searching his face for a long moment. Then she shrugged and rotated back to face the windows again. "Apology accepted." A beat. "Can I have my cell back now?"

Jet stifled a sigh and moved to the kitchen, pulling down two wine glasses—thanks Target—from a cabinet and a bottle of Zinfandel from the fridge. He remembered she'd mentioned liking it years before, and now he had to wonder how much of his blithely walking the aisles of the giant home goods store had been because he'd been trying to set up a house for himself and how much had been him knowing that with the two of them being in the same city, the same workplace, they would always have ended up in this exact place.

Though, if he was admitting every single one of his deepest, darkest secrets, he would have said that when he'd imagined Trix in his condo, he hadn't expected her to be quite so pissed at him.

He found the bottle opener, poured them each a glass, and then took a seat on one side of his island on one of his newly arrived barstools, his wine in front of him, Trix's glass on the opposite side.

Silence.

Still staring out the windows, Trix sighed. "Are you going to tell me why you've all but kidnapped me?"

"You followed me here," he pointed out, partly because it was true, but mostly because he hoped that it would piss her off and prompt her to face him.

The second worked.

Maybe too well.

"You know what?" she asked, throwing up her hands. "Keep my phone. I'll get a taxi." She moved to the door.

He jumped out of his chair and caught her arm. "Trix."

She wrenched out of his grip. "Fuck you, Jet."

"I deserve that," he said. "And more—"

"And another thing," she snapped, jabbing him in the chest with her finger, "you deserve a hell of a lot more than a *fuck you* after the shit you said tonight—"

"You're right."

"You were a fucking jerk, s-saying those things." At that slight falter, she tilted her head up toward the ceiling, eyes sliding closed. One breath in and out. Another. Then one more. Her face dropped back down, stare meeting his. "They were out of line, and I can never forgive you for them."

That made his stomach churn, but it wasn't anything less than he deserved. "I understand."

"So, then give me my phone and let me go."

He bent slightly, bringing his face very close to hers. "I can't."

Her tongue darted out, wetting her lips and drawing his focus there, to how much he was desperate to kiss her. Her pupils widened, shaky exhale escaping. He leaned in and—

No.

He couldn't.

He reached into his pocket and pulled out her cell. "I was beyond unfair and a total asshole. It was easier to blame you than admit I was scared to be in a relationship where I might care for someone more than they cared for me."

Jet clenched his hands into fists at his sides. "You were right. My parents were shit, and I never felt loved or like I was good enough to meet their exacting standards. But I didn't tell you that because . . . well, I don't know if it was because I didn't want to look weak or because I hadn't come to terms with it or if I was living in denial."

He gave in to the urge to touch Trix and gently cupped her cheek. "Neither of us was very good at sharing what was beneath our armor, but it was both of us, and for me to blame you wasn't right."

His chest was heaving, she was staring up at him with wide eyes, and their mouths were barely a few inches apart.

Jet bit back the urge to kiss her.

Instead, he picked up her palm and put her cell in her hand then bent, picked up her backpack, and gently set it on her shoulders.

"I know this isn't nearly enough to excuse how I left, what I said tonight, but I hope you'll believe me when I say I finally have clarity and that I really am sorry."

With that, he turned away, heading back into the kitchen. He grabbed his glass, mostly so he'd have something to do with his hands that didn't involve going back over to Trix, hauling her close, and slanting his mouth across hers.

First, that would get him slapped.

Second . . . that would get him slapped.

Smothering a sigh, he crossed to the windows and stared out at the city. The sun had gone down, only smudges of red and orange remaining as the navy and black of the evening crept forward over the sky. The buildings were mostly shadows, some lights on inside the nearby residential and office spaces, but many were darkened at this hour. Crimson taillights crawled through the skitter-scattered streets below, some sort of perverse version of Pac-Man.

And it was still odd.

To be in this busy of a city after so much time away.

He heard the thud of the door closing and let his shoulders drop, the glass of un-tasted wine descending to hang by his side.

Jet didn't know what he'd been hoping for.

Some miracle where he said he was sorry and Trix automatically forgave him and then launched herself into his arms and they made love beneath the moonlight?

He snorted.

Sure. Of course, it would happen that way.

Except, this was the real world and he'd fucked up, and things didn't always magically work out just because someone apologized. Plus, he didn't even know what he wanted and—

Lie.

A sigh.

Yes, that was a lie, and even though his conscience was a giant pain in the ass, it was still an untruth. For all their issues, Trix was the one woman he'd never been able to get out of his head.

He'd always thought about her—whether it was on a particularly tough case where it would have been wonderful to have her at his side, or what she'd smelled like after a shower—that tropical floral scent—or how she'd woken—slowly, incrementally, like a cat stretching after having been woken up from a nap.

He remembered how she'd kissed, how she held him tightly when he'd thrust home.

He remembered her joy at saving a baby in sub-Saharan Africa, her sadness in losing the baby's mother.

He remembered—

Everything.

Now they were together again, and he'd blown it . . . again.

"Fuck," he muttered.

"You know, generally, it's better to drink a Zinfandel cold rather than letting it sit out at room temperature."

He whipped around so fast that the wine in question splashed out of the glass, dripping down off his fingers and onto the carpet.

She hadn't gone.

The thud had been her backpack hitting the floor near the barstool, her sneakers silent as they'd traveled across the carpet.

He opened his mouth.

She shook her head. "I'm sorry, too."

"But, Trix—"

"Not tonight," she said. "I'll rake you over the coals again some other time." She lifted the glass to her lips and took a sip, eyes sliding closed, an approving hum escaping her mouth.

His cock twitched.

Not a surprise since it *was* Trix.

But then her pale lids peeled back, and her gray eyes met his. "Can we just be us again? For tonight, can we just pretend none of the bad stuff happened?"

Now his cock wasn't the affected organ. Instead, his heart rolled over in his chest, the vulnerable underbelly exposed and throbbing. How had he ever thought this woman wasn't worth the effort of peeling back the layers?

His eyes dropped to his feet, regret tearing through him again.

"Please, Jet?"

And because she asked, he tucked the emotions down, forced his gaze to meet hers again. "Yeah, sweetheart. We can just be us again."

An *us*.

He'd been an idiot in a multitude of ways, but perhaps the stupidest thing he'd done was not realizing quite how much he wanted them to be an *us* again.

Well, he burned that bridge quite thoroughly, and there was no going back.

But, part of him couldn't help but hope, maybe if they couldn't go back, they could still move forward.

ELEVEN

Trix

SHE SAT across the island from Jet and felt like a total idiot.

She could have left. She *should* have left.

But there had just been something so sad and arresting about the way he'd stood staring out the windows. All alone. She'd watched him stand there, and her fury had faded away. In its place was . . . not compassion, exactly, but understanding or maybe clarity.

They'd hurt each other.

They'd both said things that weren't kind.

They'd both made mistakes.

They were both very much alone.

Trix knew that feeling, looking out upon the world and not knowing one's place, standing on the outside and wondering how to make it different, how to slip inside. God, she knew it too fucking well, knew how it made her heart ache with longing, her mind cloud with sadness. A person wasn't designed to be alone forever. At some point that separation grew painful and they needed—

Connection.

Love.

Affection.

Friendship.

Plus, he'd opened a bottle of Zinfandel. She couldn't let that go to waste, especially when he'd even had it chilling in the fridge, allowing the sweet notes to sing but not overwhelm the palate.

Yes, she'd spent ten years abroad.

Yes, she still knew her wine.

Mostly because—

"Do you know why I like Zinfandel?" she asked when he sat across from her, setting the glass on the granite surface.

"No," he murmured, still appearing a little shell-shocked that she was still there. Hell, she was a little surprised herself, but she was also sad about Tom and though she also felt rubbed raw from Jet's words, he'd also apologized.

She wasn't one to hold a grudge for too long.

Take ownership, say sorry, don't do the behavior again, and everyone moves on.

Probably why she'd been hurt so often by her family.

Heather excluded, they could apologize till they were blue in the face, sometimes even pretend to change and take responsibility, but in the end, it always circled right back around—she was disappointed, they were themselves.

That was the way of life.

And maybe it made her a pushover, but she never could stop herself from giving a person another chance.

Probably also why her walls were so thick.

Don't allow anyone too close because they will inevitably fail you.

Such happy thoughts.

A warm palm settled over her hand. "Did you want to tell me why you liked Zinfandel so much?"

Not really now, but she'd brought the subject up, so she'd go with it.

"My father bought the winery when I was in high school." He nodded when she glanced up. "Even though I wasn't drinking age yet, I thought I could make myself useful by learning about the grape varieties being grown there, what types of wine were being made." She smiled ruefully. "I could name every variety and their preferred soil type, fertilizer, and growing season before I could legally take a drink. But when I was actually legal and could go on tastings, it turned out I could actually only stomach a couple of types."

"Zinfandel being one of them?"

She smiled ruefully. "I apparently have a sweet tooth, even in wine."

"I remember," he said. "I think you tried every type of chocolate bar from every place we visited."

"The airport shops didn't offer much else in most of them."

"True."

He brought his hand back and used it to raise his glass to his lips. "I seem to remember that you like champagne."

A laugh. "Only the expensive kind, remember?" She smiled. "How much was that bottle again?"

"Three hundred and fifty bucks." Jet grinned. "I almost fainted when we got the bill. Here I am, a simple man making a limited salary. We find ourselves in New York for a night, and I want to take my girlfriend out for a nice night."

She shrugged, lips twitching. "I made it worth it."

"You did," he agreed, smiling back at her. "I just nearly had to sell a kidney to be able to afford it."

Trix glanced around the condo, not having had to grow up with a billionaire father to know the place was expensive. San

Francisco real estate prices were outrageous, add in the doorman, the parking, the expensive kitchen, and the spacious living area, and this was in the multimillion-dollar range.

Plus, the HOA fees had to be off the charts.

"You seem to be doing okay," she said. "This kitchen alone is bigger than my apartment on the whole."

A shadow crossed his expression, and Trix prepared to be cut down, or at least told to mind her own business. Instead, the darkness left his face and he flattened his palms on the granite.

"My parents were like yours in a way. Lots of money, still critically unhappy."

Her heart skipped a beat.

"You know they passed," he said, and she nodded, remembering him telling her they'd both been killed in a car accident. "I bought the condo with the money they left me." He sighed. "After promising myself I'd never actually touch it."

She frowned. "But why? They wanted you to have—"

"They used it to control me." His fingers tapped on the granite. "Everything was a game, a test, a challenge. Even my allowance or paying for tuition. I always had to prove myself worthy to get it." He glanced up and his dark brown eyes met hers. "Did you know I never heard my father say *I love you*? Not once in my entire life."

It was her turn to cover his hand. "I'm sorry, Jet. I didn't—"

"Know?" he finished when she stopped herself. Trix nodded. "Well, no one knew. I didn't want to be that kid, the pathetic one looking for love, begging for it. I"—he shook his head—"I couldn't allow myself to be that person. For many reasons."

She wanted to ask about the reasons, but didn't have the courage that night.

She didn't want to be shot down, not when he'd shared something so big, not when *she'd* shared something big, too.

So instead, Trix said, "Parents suck."

He grinned, turned his hand over so their fingers interlaced. "I'm guessing your dad was about as impressed by your wine knowledge as mine was about my MCAT score?"

"Depends," she said. "What was your score?"

A squeeze of their fingers. "I'm guessing yours was higher."

She took a sip of wine, knew that hers was good. "526."

His eyes widened. "You missed two fucking points? That's it? Two off the whole thing?"

Trix shrugged, cheeks feeling a little warm.

"I took it three times to get a 512."

"I feel like this is the doctor's equivalent of whose penis is bigger." They both laughed and she took another sip of her wine, her head starting to feel pleasantly fuzzy. "Who cares? Scores aside, you went to medical school, I didn't."

Sad chocolate eyes on hers. "You should have gone."

Trix shrugged. "I couldn't have afforded it for a variety of reasons," she said. "Plus, I'm happy being a nurse." Her lips quirked. "Hell, with all the overtime I've been pulling, I think my salary is bigger than yours."

Jet laughed. "Probably." A beat. "Want to order something for dinner?"

Her heart twisted, and she carefully set her glass down on the counter. "I should probably go."

He nodded. "Yeah," he said. "Let me grab my keys, I'll drive you back to the hospital."

She shook her head, standing and heading for the door. "No, it's only a few minutes by Lyft. I'll be fine."

"I'm not making you pay for a ride when I all but kidnapped you."

"The kidnapping part is true," she agreed. "But I think it's good that we got the stuff out, don't you? Now we can move on." She meant it, too. What he'd said had hurt. Majorly. But maybe also, now that she'd told him a lot of what she'd felt and he'd *definitely* gotten out what was on his chest, they could go forward as friends.

She missed her friend Jet.

"I don't know if there could possibly be anything good about what I said." He'd stood, his hands fisted at his side.

Trix moved back around the island, standing next to his barstool and reaching for one of his fists. "No, there's not."

His eyes bored into hers, regret in their depths. She didn't understand what had changed so abruptly, but she'd learned after working in the medical field for the last decade that life was short and fragile and fleeting, that sometimes a person had to let go, to surrender to their instincts, and just live.

Nothing was served by letting the hurt from the past eat her alive.

So, she was going to let go, move on, and—

"I'm—"

"No more sorrys," she said. "Just don't be a dick, and we'll be fine."

"I'll make it up to you."

Jet's expression was earnest now, and he flipped his hand over so that their fingers were linked once again. God, even that simple touch felt good. Trix hadn't realized how much she'd missed touching another person, not to administer care or hurt them by cleaning a wound or starting an IV, but just for comfort or because it felt good or—

"I should go."

"I'll drive you."

She pulled back. "No, Jet."

Chocolate eyes on hers for a long time, and she prepared herself to stand firm against his argument. She was exhausted after the shift, after the argument, and the wine hadn't helped. Bed was calling, even more heavily than food.

He dropped his hand, nodded. "Will you text me when you get home?"

"I don't have your number."

His lips curved up. "We can remedy that." He held out a hand. "I can plug my number in."

Hesitancy slid through her, and she clutched her cell against her chest. "Are you going to try and keep my cell again?"

More curving, revealing a slice of white teeth. "Not this time," he said and leaned close enough to bump his shoulder against hers. "Come on, I won't even hold it. I'll just watch as you plug in the numbers to make sure you put it in right."

She narrowed her eyes.

His affected innocence.

A sigh. "Fine."

Victory slid across his face, but his tone was neutral as he recited his number.

"Can I walk you to the lobby?"

"Nope."

"Wait until the Lyft comes?"

Trix shook her head. "Nope."

"Can I at least pay for—" He reached for his wallet.

"Absolutely, not," she said and snatched up her backpack as she headed for the door. "Watch out the window if you're worried."

"This is the wrong side. The lobby—"

"We can't all have everything."

Jet rolled his eyes. "And even if it was, what am I going to do from twenty floors up?"

"Play Superman?"

His only response was to shake his head.

She reached for the door handle. "Bye, Jet."

"Bye, Trix."

He held the door open for her, and she strode out and down

the hall to the elevator. But he didn't go back inside until she got onto the car. At her hard look, he just grinned and waved. "Didn't promise not to watch you make it down the hall."

Trix sighed, hit the button for the lobby, and shook her head.

"Night," she called.

"Goodnight, sweetheart," he said just as the elevator doors shut.

That *sweetheart* stayed with her all the way through the ride back to the hospital, it followed her home and clung close as she powered through a bowl of cereal.

She heard it again just as her head hit the pillow.

And the husky endearment that soothed the raw edges of the hurt inside her was still nearby when she woke up the next morning.

TWELVE

Jet

HE BROUGHT Trix coffee to the hospital the next morning—an Americano with just a splash of cream. Meanwhile, his was diluted with four sugars and several healthy splashes of cream.

"It'll put hair on your chest," he teased, handing it over as she got out of the car.

This gave him two things—one, it distracted her from the fact that he'd been lying in wait near where she liked to park for the last fifteen minutes and two, with her hands busy bringing the coffee to her mouth, he snagged her backpack from the passenger's seat.

Her mouth opened on a sigh—caffeine-related, he thought, rather than the fact that he'd grabbed her heavy bag—and he took that as a victory.

"Just what I always needed," she said, lips quirking. "More hair on my chest."

He chuckled, shrugged on her backpack. "What do you have in here?"

"Is this where you fill in the blank with bricks?"

"I've got my dad jokes on point."

Smiling, she slammed her door, walked alongside him into the hospital. "Do you want to be one?"

He paused, eyes slanting down to her. "Want to be what?"

"A dad," she said, nudging him to the side and using her pass on the employee entrance.

"Thanks," he murmured. "And yes, I do want to be a father. I thought for a long time I didn't want to be, but . . . despite recent events, I think I'd be an okay one."

She touched his arm. "You've always been great with kids."

Not letting his behavior off the hook, but not sticking the knife in and twisting it. How had he been so blind to not realize how incredible she was?

Or maybe, like Trix had said, he'd known she was everything he wanted, but deep inside, he'd been too scared to truly accept that she was all of the things he'd wanted, and so he'd made up excuses to push her away, so he didn't put himself out there.

Too deep for this early in the morning.

And yet, he'd thought about little else except what he'd been thinking three years ago, the untruths he'd held on to since then.

"What about you?" he asked as they made their way down the hall.

"I didn't really think much about it for a long time," she murmured. "But I've always pictured myself married and with kids someday." Her eyes danced when she glanced up at him. "We're getting older now, though, so I guess someday is getting closer."

"True," he teased and tugged the end of her ponytail. "I think I even see a few gray hairs in here."

She smacked his hand away. "Rude."

He snorted and their entrance to the break room was significantly less eventful than the previous day. He slipped her bag from his shoulders and passed it over.

"Thanks," she said.

"No prob," he said.

They stowed their things then stared at each other for a moment—a long, awkward moment.

"Well," she eventually said, slipping off her sweatshirt and stashing it in her locker, "I'm going to go."

He didn't have anything smart or witty to say to that and so he settled on, "Yeah." Then watched her ponytail flutter behind her as her head bobbed and she spun away.

A second later she was out the door.

But he hadn't insulted her.

So Jet was counting that as a win.

It was Tuesday at lunchtime and when he pushed through the door into the break room, Trix was sitting at the table, reading a book, her lunch spread out in front of her.

She glanced up, those pretty gray eyes meeting his. "Hey."

He grabbed his lunch from the fridge, his cell from his locker, and hesitated. He and Trix had come to a tentative peace and he didn't want to overstep.

"I won't bite," she said. "Promise."

Jet grinned and sat down across from her, pulling out his very original PB&J and side salad he'd picked up from the cafeteria the day before but hadn't had a chance to eat.

So fine, his cooking skills weren't all that great.

But it was food and it would work.

He started in on the green stuff, silently scrolling through his phone, not wanting to interrupt Trix while she read, while also not really knowing what to say.

Trix closed the book and he saw that it wasn't so much a book as a guide.

For Alcatraz.

His brows shot up. "Have you never gone?"

She shook her head. "We didn't really do touristy stuff growing up."

There was a lot to unpack in that statement. A lot of undertones that went along with it, plenty of subtly Jet was just starting to understand had always been there in the first place.

"It's expensive," he said, knowing she'd mentioned that funds hadn't exactly been flush growing up.

"Yeah." She picked up her sandwich. "But it was more than that. My mom didn't want to do it"—a shrug—"which, in my house, meant it didn't happen."

He put down his fork. "That happened in my house, too," he murmured.

"Yeah." She nodded, took a bite, eyes glued to the pamphlet. "I'm going tomorrow actually. It's silly to go on my one day off this week, but I promised myself I'd start doing some of the stuff I missed out on and—"

"I've never been either," he blurted.

She paused, eyes flicking between the pamphlet and him. "Did you . . . um . . . did you want to come with—"

"Yes," he said instantly.

Her lips curved, expression warming. "Okay. I'm leaving about nine. Want me to pick you up from your place?"

"Works for me."

Teeth nibbling on her bottom lip, sandwich still clutched in her fingers. Knowing her break was almost over, Jet forced himself to shift focus. He didn't want her to miss her chance to eat, and so he began talking about the case he'd seen that morning. Discussing numbers and symptoms, asking her opinion, getting her perspective. It wasn't a technique to change the conversation away from personal so much as he wanted her to relax enough to go back to her meal and that her insights were always valuable.

And it worked.

Her shoulders lowered, her expression lost its hint of weariness.

They talked for much of the next fifteen minutes before she had to go back on. They discussed work and joked about funny things that had happened so far during the shift.

And Trix ate.

Small victories, but they were rebuilding their connections and so Jet would take it.

Fifteen minutes at a time.

———

His phone buzzed with a text saying Trix was out front and Jet hurried through the front doors of the lobby, pushing out onto the sidewalk and taking a few moments to spot her car.

He tugged open the passenger's side, sat down, and extended the cup of coffee.

Trix's eyes were excited, though tired, but when she saw the coffee, they brightened. "You're a god."

"I also have donuts," he said, holding up the white bag.

"I stand by my statement," she said, snagging one before checking traffic and pulling out onto the road.

It took a while to reach the Embarcadero, morning traffic slowing them down, but Jet didn't mind. Not when it gave him and Trix some time to ease past the awkwardness. They weren't quite back to their old pattern of banter and teasing, but they'd made progress.

They shot the shit about traffic and how it had been different in the places they'd traveled to until they parked and then about the places they *hadn't* gotten to and still wanted to visit on the ferry ride across, then caught up on what they knew was happening in some of their old colleagues' lives in line to get the audio tour. That was when they quieted down, listening to the story of the supposedly inescapable prison and the mystery of the three men who managed to get off The Rock.

"What do you think?" Trix asked, walking next to him as they headed down the gangway leading to the ferry that would take them to the city. "Did they survive?"

Jet shrugged. "It seems unlikely they survived the cold water and strong currents. What about you? Did they pull a Nick Cage and get off The Rock?"

She made a face as they went out onto the open deck, the ferry pulling away from the small island. "I'm not sure. I mean, kids make the swim all the time. It's not far. But in the dark, not knowing where they were going? I don't think they could have."

As she'd talked, she'd rotated around, watching them sail across the bay. Wind whipped up around them, tugging at the ends of the brown ponytail.

Jet's fingers itched to touch, to see if they felt as soft as he remembered.

But she hadn't given him permission to touch.

So he contented himself with leaning up against the rail next to her and continuing to try and puzzle out the rest of the mystery.

Just like he wanted to puzzle out the mystery of Trix.

Time. Patience. Care.

She deserved that much from him.

So he didn't touch, but he *did* tease and talk about the bad reality shows she was watching—promising to watch one about people who decided to get married without seeing each other— and then when they docked, he tempted her into the quin- tessential lunch of clam chowder in a sourdough bread bowl.

Jet argued with her about buying her a San Francisco emblazoned sweatshirt and then bought it anyway.

Though, he did relent and let her buy him some saltwater taffy.

He hated saltwater taffy.

But he didn't hate spending time with Trix.

THE NEXT WEEK PASSED UNEVENTFULLY. He continued to bring Trix coffee every morning when they were on shift together, kept their interactions light and easy, and while there weren't any more touristy days, there also weren't any fireworks between them.

Plus, their day to Alcatraz had eliminated a lot of the awkwardness. So, bonus.

They chatted while at work to pass the slow time between admissions, tag-teamed difficult patients, and generally recreated the connection they'd built when they'd first met abroad.

And it was just as good now as it was then.

If he'd needed confirmation that he'd been an idiot, then this week would have proved it to him. But he'd already known that, and so it did nothing more than confirm he was doing the right thing.

His phone rang as he headed out to his car, having stayed later than Trix that evening. He'd been waiting on some test results to come back, wanting to make sure he'd made the right call before admitting the patient he'd been working on—and considering the CT had shown the man had a brain bleed, Jet was glad he'd stayed.

"Hello?" he said, bringing his cell up to his ear.

"I hope you were serious about wanting that family," Clay

said. "Because Heather apparently has found the perfect woman for you."

Was that woman Trix?

If not, he could guarantee she wasn't.

"She—" There was a grunt and then muffled voices. "Hey —" Clay's voice cut off a second time, a scuffle loud enough to make him wince came over the airwaves, and then a cheerful female voice came on.

"Jet? It's Heather."

He grinned as he unlocked his car and sat down in the driver's seat. "Hey, Heather."

Keys in the ignition, doors locked, call on Bluetooth.

"Listen," Heather said. "I have the perfect woman for you. Her name is Molly, and she owns a local restaurant. The food is off the charts. She's sweet, she's funny, she's—"

"Heather."

Her words cut off.

"I appreciate the thought but—"

"I know that you and Trix didn't hit it off like we'd hoped. She mentioned that things were fine, but there wasn't a spark."

That made Jet's teeth clench together. "I didn't—"

"It doesn't matter. I get it. No doctor-nurse fantasy come to life, but—"

"That's not—"

Heather's affronted sigh was loud. "Look, you told Clay you wanted to find someone to build a future with. If that's not something you want—"

"I wasn't lying," he said. "I *am* looking to settle down."

"And what? You're too good for someone who works in a restaurant?"

He backed out of the spot and exited the parking lot, navigating his way out into traffic. "I'm not too good for anyone," he said. "I just . . ."

"What?" she snapped.

"I've already met someone."

Her tone immediately warmed. "Oh, that's great news. Who is it?"

Jet waffled for a minute then decided that since he'd already pulled his head out of his ass as far as Trix was concerned, he might be able to use her sister to help him secure another chance.

Because that was what this last week had shown him, that bottom line, his life was better with Trix in it.

Easy. Decision made.

Now how to convince Trix to give him another shot?

Jet was thinking that maybe Heather could help.

"It's Trix," he said when she made an impatient sound, and then he had the rarefied distinction of silencing Heather O'Keith. For a few moments, at least. Because she was smart and quick and never was knocked down for long—whether it was shock or in the business world.

"But Trix said—"

"We dated when we were working for Doctors without Borders."

More silence. Then, "Um, what?"

"We were together a year. I seriously fucked up. I—well, that's between her and me, but I wasn't thinking clearly. I said some shit, purposefully got reassigned away from her, and now . . ."

Sharp edges to her words. "Now, what?"

He deserved the tone and also knew that as Trix's sister, Heather would need reassurance that his heart was in the right place, that he'd recognized his mistakes and wanted to make them right.

"I'm not saying that we both didn't contribute to our breakup," he said. "But I certainly deserve the lion's share of the blame. I fucked up, Heather. It was easier for me to pretend that Trix was at fault, but I know now that's not the case."

"Hmm."

"I've apologized," he said. "And I'll continue to do my best to make it up to her, but . . ."

"You blew it."

"I overreacted. I cost us three years. I want—" He shook his head and pulled into the garage. "I guess I just want to prove that I deserve another shot with her."

"I think that's up to Trix to decide." Still frosty, but not quite as sharp.

A dulled arrow.

Still deadly, but marginally less effective.

"I agree," he murmured. "But she says we're friends now, that we'll forget the past and move forward."

"Sounds like she made her decision," Heather pointed out. "And that you're lucky to have her friendship at all."

Jet was starting to feel desperate now. Mostly because Heather was right. Trix had been gracious enough to apologize to him, and she'd never denied her past's role in their relationship—he got to shoulder the asshole burden on that front. First, for holding it against her and second, for doing such a piss-poor job of telling her he was sorry.

"I *am* lucky she gave me that much."

"Right," Heather said. "I'll give the phone back to Clay now. Let me know at some point if you want to go out with Molly—"

"I love her!" he blurted loud enough to make himself jump.

And he didn't think he would have been able to quantify what he was feeling into those words if he hadn't been so damned worried about Heather hanging up on him.

Probably her intention.

"Hmm," she murmured.

"Heather—"

"I know something about overreacting, unthinking men," she began.

"Hey!" he heard Clay say in the background. "I didn't—"

"*Anyway*," Heather went on, "my point is that people make mistakes. I get that. But I'm not willing to go behind my sister's back and betray her trust." She sucked in a breath. "I just got her back, Jet. I don't want to do something to make her leave again."

"Me neither," he said.

"So, I think I have to leave this up to—"

"I'm just asking for one thing," he said quickly, "and then if it doesn't work, I'll leave it alone. I'll even go on a date with Molly. O-or whoever else you want. I just need one shot. Pl—"

"What's the one thing?"

He told her.

Then waited for an interminable moment when all he heard was, "Hmm."

But just when he'd given up hope, Heather chuckled and said, "I'm probably going to Hell for this, but okay."

Jet breathed out a sigh of relief. "I promise that I'll never hurt your sister again."

There was a pause and then Heather said, "No one can make that promise, Jet. I just need you to love her like she deserves." His heart twisted. "If you can do that, I'll do the favor you asked for."

"I will."

No hesitation or reservations. No more waffling.

He'd made a decision, and Trix deserved the best he could offer.

"Okay, then," Heather said. "How do you want to begin?"

THIRTEEN

Trix

"GO ON ANOTHER BLIND DATE, they said," Trix grumbled, straightening the straps on her little black dress before slipping on her heels. "Because the first one went so well."

Yup. She was an idiot, but Heather had called and begged and cajoled and . . . Trix was going on another blind date.

Awesome.

Couldn't wait.

Rolling her eyes and wondering why she'd let her sister talk her into this, Trix picked up her purse and headed to the door.

She should be looking forward to the date with the gorgeous engineer, Monroe, that Heather knew via her work connections, but Trix just couldn't summon up the energy to be excited, even after seeing the man's picture.

Tall, dark, and gorgeous.

Exactly her type.

Except—

He wasn't Jet.

And *that* was a problem. Because, yes, she'd forgiven Jet for what he'd said, and they'd both taken ownership for the way their relationship had imploded. They'd moved on as friends . . . exactly as she'd wanted.

So there should be nothing wrong with her going on a date, and she certainly shouldn't be wanting that date to be Jet.

Friends.

That was it.

That was safer.

Her inner bullshit detector blared with that last thought, because she wasn't supposed to be making herself safer. She was supposed to be putting herself out there, being vulnerable, actually living her life.

Not safely.

"Ugh," she muttered and pushed out her front door. It wasn't even like Jet seemed to be interested in anything more than friendship at this point.

It had been just over two weeks since the almost kiss in the break room, nearly two months since the actual one, and he hadn't given her one heated look or lover-like caress or let his mouth come very near hers.

Absolutely nothing to indicate that he wanted her in a more-than-a-friend way.

She needed to move on.

Accept that his urge to fuck her had been closely tied with his anger about their relationship and now that the past and its ties were resolved, his desire had disappeared along with any ill feelings.

So, Date Night.

As in, she'd *finally* accepted Heather's set up and was going to get on with it, just mildly less "blind"—since she had seen the man in question's photo.

That would have solved a lot of problems for her before the last one.

Snorting, she shook her head and walked to her car, her cell chirping in her purse just as she'd unlocked the doors.

"Hello?" she answered, not looking at the screen as she climbed in and turned on the ignition.

"Hey."

Her stomach fluttered at the sound of Jet's voice.

Friends, remember? Nothing more.

That was what she wanted, what Jet wanted based on how he'd been acting over the last couple of weeks.

Friends were great.

She was great.

Everything was great.

Trix snorted as she checked traffic and pulled out onto the road. "Hi," she said belatedly. "What's up?"

She and Jet had texted a little bit and talked on the phone a couple of times, so hearing his voice on the other end of the line didn't make her feel awkward and clam up. Still, her pulsed picked up, her thighs trembled, and her fingers tightened on the steering wheel.

"Not much," he said. "Do you want to grab a bite? Neither of us has to get up at the crack of dawn tomorrow."

Their shifts mostly lined up, except when Jet was on call or she picked up overtime. For example, this week she'd worked Wednesday through Saturday and had today and Monday off, grabbing some OT on Tuesday. Jet had worked that morning, but wouldn't work again until Wednesday.

But now they were both free and she was going on this stupid date, and so she wouldn't be able to grab dinner.

She mentally smacked herself.

She should be excited about the date, not feeling pouty about it.

"I can't," she said, trying to stifle the pouty as she pulled onto the freeway and not succeeding.

"Oh," he said, and the disappointment in his tone was audible. "No worries. I'll—"

"I have a date," she blurted.

"Uh—"

"I'd rather be eating with you than this joker Heather is setting me up with," she muttered. "He's having us go to some fancy French place, and all I want is tacos."

He snorted. "Tacos always win."

"I know!" she exclaimed. "But apparently he's trying to impress me." Yes, it was a grumble. Yes, it was uncharitable. No, she didn't care. "At least that's what Heather keeps reminding me. Meanwhile, I think she just enjoys torturing me."

"Siblings, I think, are good at that."

"You're lucky you don't have any."

He stifled a laugh. "You wouldn't have said that if you'd met my parents. You'd have said I could have used a barrier."

"I—" Trix stopped, not knowing what to say, except, "I know the feeling."

Silence.

Then, "I know you do, babe," he murmured then his voice rose. "Okay, rain check on dinner. Call me if your date goes sideways, and I'll open a can of whoop ass on the son of a bitch."

"He seems perfectly respectable," she countered.

"They always do," he muttered. "They always do."

She laughed. "'Night, Jet."

"Night, sweetheart."

Trix hung up, feeling even less like going on this date, but she wasn't an asshole. She determinedly put Jet from her mind and forced herself to head for the restaurant.

She didn't stand people up.

THE SAME COULD NOT BE SAID of the engineer she was supposed to be meeting.

Monroe was an asshole who'd stood her up.

Trix sat at the table, looking hot as hell in her little black dress, thank her very much, and . . . she'd been stood up.

Cool.

Note to the universe, she was going to kill her sister.

Especially since she'd texted Heather and hadn't gotten a response. "Probably enjoying herself with her stupidly beautiful husband in her stupidly beautiful house in her stupidly beautiful life," Trix muttered, eating the last piece of bread in the basket the waiter had brought her.

With a pitying look.

Ugh.

She was in full-force that night, too, having had the time to go to town on her hair and makeup. Plus, her body was on point, mostly thanks to too many shifts and a lack of time to eat the stash of junk food in her apartment, but the fact was that she looked good.

And it was utterly wasted.

Fucking men.

Trix signaled the waiter and he came over, that pitying expression still fixed to his face.

She repeated, *fucking men.*

"I think I'm ready for my check," she said.

His expression didn't change as he nodded and left, returning a few minutes later with the bill. He left to process her card—because who carried cash anymore? And if they did, then they were way more together than her, *plus* way more prepared for this particular situation than she was.

Her cell buzzed.

Sighing, she pulled it from her purse, expecting it to be Heather and readying her diatribe. Or even better, maybe it was Monroe, appropriately apologetic for having made her wait.

It was neither.

It was a text from Jet.

How goes the date?

She debated how to answer that, but then the waiter returned, and she was signing a receipt for an exorbitantly priced glass of wine and two pieces of bread.

Well, at least she wasn't at risk of bursting out of her dress.

Her phone buzzed again as she put on her coat.

Either that means it's going perfectly or it's gone to shit.

Her heels *click-clacked* across the pavement as she strode to where her car was parked—three freaking blocks away and in front of a fucking Mexican restaurant, of all places. Fate was really trying to fuck with her that evening.

She'd bypassed tacos and . . . gotten stood up.

Monroe was—

Buzz. Buzz.

Okay, I'm probably intruding, but now I'm worried. Let me know all is good by responding. If not, I'll assume the bastard turned out to be a serial killer and hunt you down.

She hesitated and then smiled begrudgingly.

A miserable, embarrassing night that had ended up with her alone on a San Franciscan street corner, and she was smiling.

This man.

Okay, universe. So maybe not *all* men were horrible.

Snorting, she tapped the screen a few times and lifted her phone to ear, listening to it ring a couple of times.

Then Jet was on the other end of the line and all was right in the world.

"Am I speaking to Trix or the serial killer?"

She laughed. "Trix. Unfortunately. A serial killer might not get stood up."

Silence. Then, "Seriously?"

"I don't want to say, yes, but . . ."

"Fucking bastard."

"I'm okay, Jet."

"Where are you now?"

"Walking to my car."

He sighed. "No, I mean, where *exactly* are you?"

"I—" She broke off.

"You," he countered. Then waited, and Trix felt a pulse of irritation slide through her. Partly because he was pushing, but mostly because he'd always been really good at out-patiencing her.

"Ugh." She blew out a breath, stifled her sigh and told him her cross street. "But I'm heading to my car which is parked near your building. Right by Molly's and that really good hole-in-the-wall Mexican place."

"Is this the Molly's that everyone is so excited about?"

"Have not you eaten there?" she asked, incredulous.

"No."

"I know," she said, pausing at a street corner to check for traffic and then crossing against the light. Citizens of San Francisco didn't wait on corners in the cold if cars weren't about to mow them down. She glanced, she walked, and she did it with confidence.

"What?" Jet asked.

"I know you haven't eaten there because otherwise, you would know exactly why Molly's is the shit. They have the best pear and gorgonzola salad with candied walnuts." She held her coat closed against a gust of wind. "I'd say something about liking those nuts in my mouth—"

He snorted.

"—but exactly that reaction," she said with a giggle, rounding the final corner to where her car was parked. "Molly's is delicious, and if you haven't eaten there, then you need to remedy it immediately."

"I'll take it under advisement."

"You should—"

Trix skittered to a stop when she saw what was leaning against her car. Or rather, *who* was resting a hip against her passenger's door, ankles crossed, a brown paper bag dangling from one hand, his cell pressed to his ear with the other.

Jet.

He pocketed the phone when she stopped, pushing off the car and coming toward her.

"I—" She shook her head. "What are you doing here?"

"I live here. Well, *there.*" Jet smiled, jerked his head back over his shoulder.

"I remember," she grumbled.

Still smiling. "But the point is"—he held up the bag—"want to go up to my place and have tacos?"

Her jaw dropped open. "Um, what?"

"Did you eat?"

Another shake of her head.

"Good. I have tacos, let's go drink wine and eat them."

"I—"

He closed the distance between them and took her hand. "Stop thinking so hard. I've got chocolate ice cream in my freezer, a bag full of greasy deliciousness. Let's forget about the shitty night and do something fun."

That sounded like the best offer she'd heard all night. She rested her head on his shoulder, inhaled some of his yummy, spicy scent, and said, "Okay."

FOURTEEN

Jet

SHE'D SAID OKAY.

His heart leaped with joy, but he didn't gloat, or smirk, or tease her for accepting. Instead, he tightened his grip on her hand and started tugging her up to his condo. Quickly, before she changed her mind.

Less than five minutes later, she was in his condo and seated on a barstool with her favorite glass of wine and picking through the bag of food.

"Oh my God," she groaned and pulled out a burrito that was the size of her head. "You're a fucking god."

Jet bit back a smile.

He'd need to confess his part in the evening soon, but he figured it would be best to feed and water—or feed and alcohol—her first.

She pulled out three tacos, a bag of chips, along with guacamole and queso. "You sure bought a lot of food for yourself."

Yeah, he had.

Because the plan had always been to buy food for two.

"I can't believe that Monroe stood me up," she grumbled. "I waited in the restaurant for an hour, feeling pathetic with the waiters staring at me like I was a pity case." She pointed at the food. "Which do you want?"

Jet's gaze darted toward to the door, checking to make sure the dead bolt was thrown.

At least then he'd have a few extra seconds to stop her from storming out after he confessed his and Heather's part in this.

"Jet?"

"Hmm?"

"I'm starving. Did you want the burrito or the tacos?"

He moved to the fridge, pulled out a beer. "I don't care."

"Great." She grabbed the disposable wooden knife from the bag, sliced the burrito in half and took one taco then shoved the rest of the food in his direction. "We'll go, halvsies," she said, smiling up at him.

"Works for me."

Trix took a giant bite of burrito. "Mmm. God, I knew this place was good. I should have just skipped the date altogether and had this."

"This" sounded like "shmis" because she took another huge bite of burrito.

He smiled despite the guilt churning inside him.

He needed to own up—

She stopped, unbuttoned her coat, peeled it off, and tossed it over the back of the chair.

Which made his brain stop working.

She was wearing the dress from their blind date. *The* dress. The one that was low cut and skin tight and exposed the swirling, colorful lines tattooed on both arms. The dress left very little to the imagination. Imagination he didn't need because he had memories.

Memories that made his cock twitch.

Especially when she leaned forward to dig back into the burrito, and her breasts . . . *fuck*, but her breasts.

"Jet?"

"Hmm?"

Creamy skin, hard nipples in his mouth—

"*Jet?*"

He blinked. "Yeah?"

"You gonna eat?"

A nod and he moved jerkily to the stool. "Yeah." He picked up his half of the burrito and took a bite. "I like your dress."

Gray eyes on his, fire on their edges. "I seem to remember you making some comment about my *tits on display* the last time I saw you in this dress."

"I'm an asshole."

Silence.

His lips twitched. "Not going to disagree?"

"Nope." She lifted her arm to push back some of her hair and exposing the new tattoo he'd noticed a few weeks ago. But he'd only been able to see part of the curved blue and purple line then.

Now he saw the rest.

And his heart twisted. It was a stylized version of Odonnyew fie Kwan. The symbol basically meant that love never loses its way home and was a symbol of the Ashanti people of Ghana. "You got that?"

Her eyes shuttered. "Amare's brother did it for me." A shrug then a deliberate lightness in her tone. "Definitely not the most sanitary tattoo I've ever gotten, but still very meaningful."

He froze, dread circling in his gut at the underlying pain in her words. "When did you get it?"

Another shrug. "Doesn't matter."

"Trix."

She sighed. "That's why I was late coming home that night."

Shards of ice through his abdomen. There was no question as to what night she was referring to, at least not in his mind. She'd gotten it the night he'd left and—

"Do you like it?" she asked softly. "Don't think it's too much like cultural appropriation? I mean I wouldn't have gotten it at all, but Kwame said it was okay and Amare was so special and—"

He reached across the island and covered her hand. "I love your tattoos. Always have."

She stayed there for a moment, eyes damp, hand shifting so she could curl her fingers around his. "Yeah. Uh. Well, good," she said then muttered. "Not that you get a say because it's my body and you can just eat your half of the burrito and keep your opinions to yourself."

"I shouldn't have said that before—well, I shouldn't have said a lot of things, but in this case, I meant about your dress." He sighed. "I spent lots of time saying that you were pushing me away, but I did just as good of a job of shoving you away in return."

Silence as she studied him.

Then, "Yes." A murmur. "You did." A squeeze of his hand before pulling back and picking up her burrito. "But don't beat yourself up about it. We both made mistakes."

Mistakes.

Fuck. He'd made so many.

Including, leaving her alone in a restaurant to be pitied and stood up and—

"You okay?"

Jet nodded.

"You sure?"

He picked up the burrito, but his stomach was churning and so he promptly set it down again.

He needed to tell her about the date.

He should have already done so.

Fuck. So. Many. Fuck-ups.

By this point, Trix had some food in her belly, but not enough wine in her bloodstream. Which meant her stomach was happy, her mind was in top form, and thus, she was paying attention.

And knew he was being really fucking weird.

"Jet."

More booze. Yes, that was the solution.

He picked up the bottle to top off her glass.

He'd waited until she finished her wine and mellowed out and then confess—

She hopped out of her chair, which made every muscle in his body stiffen, but instead of moving toward the door, like he'd half-expected, Trix moved around the island, took the wine from his hand and set it down, then plunked herself into his lap.

Now he had the creamy skin of her breasts nearly at eye level, her bare thighs splayed across his lap.

He made a sound that was half-groan, half-pleasure, but somehow kept his hands at his sides. She hadn't invited him to touch and—

Her palm rested on his chest, the other rose to cup his cheek and tilt his face up. "Spill," she ordered. "Now."

Coconut. Flowers.

Curves.

Exposed skin.

His mind couldn't focus on her words with all of those distractions in front of him.

"Jet."

"I'm the reason you were stood up tonight," he blurted, totally tactlessly, completely opposite to how he'd planned to break the news to her.

"What?"

And the blurting continued. "I asked Heather to set up the date but only with you. Not with Monroe. I was going to meet you there, to show up instead of Monroe, and to . . . I don't know, swoop in and save the day."

Gray eyes fixed onto his. "Please, tell me you're kidding."

He winced at her tone. "I'd planned to come in after Heather texted me, but then Heather *never* texted me, and at first you didn't reply. But then you said you were leaving and had mentioned the taqueria and—"

Her body was actually vibrating with fury.

He grabbed her hips to steady her.

"You—" She gasped in a breath. "I—" Another. "How—?"

"I'm sorry," he said. "I don't know what I was thinking. I just wanted a chance to have another date with you, and—"

"Let me get this straight," she said, shifting in his lap and glaring up at him. "You got Heather to set me up on *another* blind date after our first one went so well"—lightning in those gray eyes—"but that date was one that I was supposed to be stood up—"

"I—"

"And then, when you were going to somehow come in and meet me there instead, *you* ended up standing me up instead?"

He winced. "I—"

"And now you try to bribe me with tacos and wine, like that was somehow going to make it all okay?"

Here she stopped talking and just stared at him.

"Um, yes?"

Her body was still vibrating in anger, bouncing on his lap in a way that he was certain she didn't intend. One that felt good and—

He was a total fucking perv.

"I—" A gasp. "Cannot—" One more. "Believe. You."

And then she burst into laughter.

Since that was pretty much the last thing he'd expected, Jet jerked so hard that he almost upset Trix and dumped her from his lap. Luckily, she reached for his shoulders, holding on and dropping her head to his chest.

He could feel her laughter through his shirt, hot, damp puffs of air soaking through the cotton of his button-down.

He was frozen in place, both in shock and scared to move and have the laughter turn back to fury. But then he thought back to her expression, to the sounds she'd made as he'd tried to explain and realized that she'd been laughing at him for much longer than he'd thought.

"You're such an idiot," she said, the words punctuated with giggles.

"I think that has been repeatedly established."

She stilled, face tilting up, eyes warm, lips curved. "You really wanted a date with me that badly?"

"Badly enough to concoct a scheme with Heather and make utter fools of both of us?" She nodded and there was no point in denying anything. "Yes."

"Idiot," Trix repeated.

"Yes," he said again.

Then she surprised him again.

Shifting in his lap, she stretched up and pressed her mouth to his.

FIFTEEN

Trix

A PLETHORA OF EMOTIONS. Too many damned feelings.

And all she wanted was her mouth against Jet's.

So . . . she kissed him.

The moment their lips touched, heat exploded throughout her body. Shooting south from her mouth, down her nape, her chest, her nipples beading against the fabric of her dress. It expanded in her stomach, arrowed between her thighs and—

He tore his lips from hers.

"Trix—"

She shifted in his lap, leaning back enough to slip one leg over to the other side, to straddle him. Of course, that meant he got a full view of what she was wearing under her dress . . . which wasn't much.

His eyes told her he liked the skimpy black cotton.

"Talk later," she murmured, shimmying close enough that her breasts brushed his chest so that she could reach up and weave her hands into his hair. "Fuck now."

Chocolate eyes went liquid, like hot fudge, and she shivered, thinking that particular fantasy was definitely moving to the top of her list.

Jet's lips were very close to hers. "What just went through your mind?"

She told him.

His hips shifted beneath hers, jerking up restlessly, and telling her all she needed to know about what he thought of that.

"Is that a yes?" she murmured.

"To the hot fudge?" he asked. "Or the fucking?"

"Either. Both." She grinned. "But how about just the fucking today? We need to stock up on supplies."

His expression was serious. "Are you sure, sweetheart?"

Her heart skipped a beat. "Yes, love," she murmured. "I don't think there's been a day when I *haven't* wanted you. Even when I hated you, I wanted you."

"Fuck, Trix. I'm so sorry." Regret chased desire from his face.

That hadn't been her intention, pulling him out of this moment, throwing the past in his face. "No," she murmured. "I didn't mean it like that."

He cupped her cheek. "You'd be better off finding someone else."

"Then I would continue to have this giant hole in my heart where you belong."

His lips parted, breath coming out on a long, slow exhale. "Baby," he murmured. "I'm—"

"Going to kiss me now," she interrupted, "and give me multiple orgasms because we're moving on from the past and going to see if whatever it is between us has a future." A shaky breath and she put all of that growth and effort to good use.

She'd spent months and years finding the strength to shed her armor, and now she was going to let it fall at Jet's feet. "Because I don't want to have this hole inside me anymore. I want you there instead."

His forehead dropped, resting against hers. "How did you get to be so smart?"

She inhaled his scent, the spice comforting and familiar and . . . home. "Probably because I got that 526 on the MCATs."

He laughed.

She laughed.

And then his mouth stole hers, swallowing her giggles, replacing them with his tongue as he kissed and kissed and kissed her.

There was absolutely nothing like Jet's mouth, his lips firm against hers, moving in tandem but never rough, always on the right side of demanding, of coaxing her to not get lost in the moment but to be an active participant. His tongue flicked and teased, then drew back, encouraging hers to move forward, to tangle with his in his mouth. Back and forth they went, mouths meeting, lips melding until Trix was so hot and riddled with desire that she was surprised she didn't turn into a puddle of goo and slide off Jet's lap onto the floor.

He released her mouth, allowing her to suck in some much-needed oxygen and not transform into that puddle on the floor. His lips moved down along her throat, nipping at her collar-bones. "Last chance, babe."

"I never had any chance when it came to you."

He froze, head coming up, eyes meeting hers. Their gazes locked for a long, pulsing moment before he smiled and said, "Likewise, sweetheart." The warmth in the words, on his face made her heart skip a beat, but then his arms were banding around her again, pulling her close and lifting her as he rotated and got up from the stool. "Up, baby," he coaxed, encouraging her a little higher so she could more easily wrap her legs around his hips.

And then his mouth was on hers and they were moving.

To the wall, to the floor. The couch. The bed.

Trix didn't give a fuck. His lips snapped the last threads of her tentativeness, burned away all of her control.

She needed him. *Now.* So, she told him with her tongue, with her lips, with hips rocking against his waist, her breasts rubbing over his chest, her—

He dropped her onto the bed, immediately following her down, and she was rewarded with the sensation of *all* of his hard body pressing against hers. Lips against hers, one hot, rushed kiss before his mouth ran along her jaw, nipping her earlobe, the spot behind her ear that always sent a shiver down her body.

Jet had forgotten *nothing.*

And he put it all to good use.

Fingers sliding up the outside of one thigh, slipping under the hem of her dress to knead her ass. Mouth moving down, kissing across her chest, nudging the straps out of the way as he moved. Then he reared back, reaching for the fabric covering her breasts, but in her surprise at the backward movement, she missed that he was moving closer, and for one horrible moment, she thought he was going to stop. To leave again.

That feeling faded as soon as she saw his face, but he knew. *He knew.* His eyes gentled, his mouth pressed lightly against hers.

"I'm here," he murmured.

Just *I'm here.*

She wrapped her arms around him, tugging him back down, soaking in the comfort of his warm weight. "I know," she whispered.

One pause. One moment. One remembrance of things gone wrong.

And then time shifted again, the past disappeared back where it belonged, and Trix slid her hands into his hair. Jet shifted enough to take her mouth, one hand braced by her head, the other tracing up and down her side.

When they broke for air, she smiled up at him. "You do know there's a zipper there, don't you?"

"Oh?" His fingers tickled her ribs lightly then gripped the pull, tugged it down. When he glanced up at her, his lips were twitching. "I guess I missed that."

He leaned back, and this time she didn't have that moment of panic.

Because he was reaching for the material, tugging it down her body and tossing it to the floor.

He froze and she felt unaccountably shy as he stared at her.

Then he met her eyes. "You're the most beautiful thing I've ever seen."

Instinct made her scoff.

"The. Most. Beautiful," he repeated.

Tears burned the backs of her eyes, but she blinked them away, touched his cheek. "*Jet.*"

"I will never waste this chance you're giving me."

She sniffed.

He winced then deliberately lightened his tone. "So, how good are my skills if I can make the woman I love cry in bed?"

Woman. I. Love.

She sucked in a breath, lips parting to—

She didn't know, didn't have time to process. Because his mouth was on hers, tongue sliding home, kissing her until her head spun. Only then did he pull away and make his way down to her breasts, taking off and tossing her bra to the side, before massaging them, then licking and nipping and finally sucking one nipple deeply into his mouth.

"Oh, God," she groaned, spine arching, hands gripping his head tightly.

Pleasure spiraled out from that one point, lighting her body on fire, making her limbs restless and heavy all at once. Then he switched sides and the process repeated, only this time it was even more intense because she was already spinning out of control, her desire on knifepoint.

"Jet?" she asked when he began to kiss his way down her stomach.

"Hmm?" He didn't pause what he was doing, and frankly it wasn't like she was going to complain.

"Can you—*ah*—" He nipped her hip.

"What, baby?"

She blinked. Focused. "Can you take off a few more layers?"

He glanced up at her and then his clothes disappeared. Okay, really, he tore his shirt over his head, kicked off his shoes, and leaned back enough to unbutton and kick his pants from his legs.

Meanwhile, she got to enjoy the show.

Jet wasn't bulky in any sense of the form, but he had a lean strength that made her fingers itch with the desire to trail them over his chest, to drift down the flat planes of his stomach, to slip under the waistband of his boxer briefs and—

He gently knocked her hands away when she reached for him. "Next time," he murmured and continued kissing his way down her stomach, tugging her underwear down. It flew off somewhere, but she was much less focused on where it landed because his slightly roughened palms were coaxing her thighs apart, trailing up the insides, one finger sliding through the wet heat of her pussy.

Then he bent and replaced his finger with his mouth.

And it was absolutely everything.

Her nerves had slowly been winding tighter and tighter as he'd kissed his way down her body, and by the time his tongue slid up through her folds and his mouth latched onto her clit, she was nearly nonsensical.

More. Need. Pressure. Harder.

Separate thoughts punctuated with gasps and moans, and Jet went down on her like he'd never forgotten a single thing about what she liked, what sent her spinning, what made her cry out in pleasure.

"Oh fuck, Jet!"

"Mmm." His groan vibrated against her clit, ratcheting her higher . . . until the next flick of his tongue sent her plummeting over the edge.

She groaned, head pressing back against the pillow, hips jerking, and pleasure burning through her.

"Fuck," she murmured.

Jet slowed his movements, softening his tongue, easing her through to the other side.

He crawled up next to her, tugging her close, holding her tightly against his chest. His cock was hard against her side, but he didn't press it closer, didn't arch against her, and she knew he wasn't going to make the next move. This was her show and for the most part, he was letting her call the shots.

"Have I mentioned that sometimes a girl just likes to be dominated in bed?"

Silence.

Then he slowly propped himself up on one elbow and bent so he could see her face. At her expression, one brown brow lifted.

"Is that so?"

She spun in his hold, resting one hand on his chest, feeling the light sheen of sweat beneath her palm. "Sometimes a woman just wants her man to flip her over and fuck her into oblivion."

His hands clenched on her hips, but his tone was light. "Oh? Do you know any men who might be up for that?"

Trix tapped a finger against her lips. "In this bed?" she asked innocently. "I don't think so—"

Her teasing cut off on a shriek when Jet lifted and threw her back onto the mattress. His hands were everywhere, cupping, teasing, sliding, and generally driving her insane . . . or at least, back up to the precipice. And he wasn't even inside her yet.

Head thrashing on the pillows, she moaned, "I need—"

"Hush." He nipped at her bottom lip. "I know what you need." And then he slipped a finger inside her, thumb pressing against her clit, arrowing pleasure through her body. In mere minutes she went from sated to writhing with need.

Up and up she went, climbing that mountain, muscles locking, heat blasting through her. She thought that Jet would slow, would pull back and reach for a condom, but he didn't. Instead, he kept working her, not pausing, not giving in, even when she gasped that it was, "Too much."

He just slipped another finger inside, circled his thumb more firmly, and . . . she catapulted her over the edge.

That was when he reached for his nightstand, grabbed a condom, and rolled it down his cock. Then he was lifting one of her legs up, wrapping it around his waist, and sliding home.

So. Fucking. Good.

He paused, glanced down at her, and she would swear the smile he gave her brought her halfway to another orgasm all on its own.

Then he was moving, and she was wrapping her other leg around his waist, and they were as close as two people could be —sharing bodies, sharing breath, sharing . . . ecstasy.

He groaned, head dropping to her shoulder while she cried out again, somehow finding more pleasure, but also feeling absolutely certain that being held in Jet's arms was the only place she'd wanted to be.

Forever.

SIXTEEN

Jet

HE WAITED until Trix was out before carefully slipping from the bed and heading back to the kitchen. It only took a few minutes to pack up the remains from their dinner, and it was probably a fruitless effort since they wouldn't be very good reheated anyway. But his fridge was pretty sparse, and unless she wanted to subsist on saltines and the rest of the bottle of wine, then a reheated taco was the best he could do.

"Hey."

His eyes shot from the fridge to where Trix had come out of the bedroom, one of his T-shirts slipped over her head, vulnerability written across her face.

"Hey, sweetheart," he murmured, closing the fridge and heading over to her. He wrapped an arm around her waist, tugged her close. "I was trying to salvage dinner."

The hesitation disappeared from her eyes. "I think that might be impossible."

"Probably," he agreed then turned her in his arms. "You okay?"

She smiled and nodded. "I had three orgasms, how could I *not* be okay?"

Except, the hesitation was still there, the shadows behind her eyes. She might not be aware of them, or was, perhaps, shoving them down because she didn't want to ruin the moment. The difference between the past and now was he knew that she deserved a partner who wanted to make that slice of uncertainty disappear.

"I'm not going to leave," he murmured. "I know it will take time for you to trust me, but . . . I'm not cutting ties ever again."

"Jet—"

He laid a finger on her lips. "If things end up not working for us, and I hope to God that isn't the case because you're the one woman I've had in my life that has meant enough for me to push beyond my past then at the very least, I don't want to lose you as a friend." He brushed his finger lightly back and forth. "You were the best one I ever had."

She sucked in a breath, her mouth moving against his finger as she pressed a kiss there. "What happened that made it so hard? I mean, I know your parents weren't great, but why—"

And there was the crux of it. He'd told her a little, but not enough.

Without warning, Jet scooped her up into his arms and carried her back to his bed. Only this time, he didn't drop her on the mattress and make love to her. Instead this time, he set her down, reclined beside her, and proceeded to tell her all of the fucked-up shit from his childhood.

"My parents had money," he said. "Like yours. And like yours, there were strings. At first, it was typical stuff. I could have the new bike if I got all As or the new video game or the new whatever was popular with my friends at the time." She nodded when he glanced down at her. "A lot of my friends were in similar situations. Buying affection and obedience with things, that's not out of the ordinary. Neither was me hardly seeing them."

Clarity began to shine in her eyes.

"My dad worked a lot. Typical. My mom was busy at the club and with whatever charity business or other things that kept her occupied. I was raised by nannies. Whatever, lots of people do that." He shrugged. "It's sometimes the only way."

"But?" she prompted when he hesitated.

"But, I can count on two hands the number of times I remember seeing my parents growing up. I'm sure it was more, that they were there and I just don't remember." He sighed. "But I do remember begging them to be there for my fifth birthday and Christmas"—he had been born on the 27th—"but them saying that fell during their trip to Vail, and I shouldn't inconvenience them. I remember that happening again for several years and getting the same answer." Jet shook his head. "Then asking to go with them to Vail. I'm guessing you know their answer already?"

She bit her lip and nodded. "I think I do."

"Yeah, it was a no," he said. "And a no to Father's and Mother's Day. A no to the presents I made them in school. I remember coming home so excited to give my mom a frame I'd made in class, some ugly thing made of popsicle sticks and paper flowers. My mom accepted it, but when I hugged her, she shoved me away and said I was wrinkling her outfit." A sigh. "And then I found the frame in the trash the next day."

Trix's eyes were glassy with tears. "Oh, Jet, I'm—"

"I'm not telling you this because I want you to feel bad for me," he said quickly. "I know it was fucked up, and I know I was an innocent kid who didn't deserve to be pushed away and emotionally abused and . . . frankly, neglected in a lot of ways. That wasn't right."

"No, it wasn't."

"It took me a long time to understand that and to come to terms with a lot of my life choices. My father wanted me in the family business, hated when I'd gone premed, but because it was a respectable profession, he'd allowed me to continue on." He rolled his eyes. "I should have gone my own way then, but instead, I kept trying, kept almost begging for the scraps of affection. I expected pride when I graduated as valedictorian, approval for getting into med school, and I never got any. Then they died in the accident and—"

He sucked in a breath, not wanting to say the words aloud, but Trix just put her palm on his chest and waited.

"And part of me was happy about it."

Her face didn't change. She didn't pull away. "I call that normal, Jet."

"Maybe," he said. "But I didn't understand it at the time. I felt so fucking guilty and horrible that I walled myself off. I would never let myself care about people like that, let people in who would disappoint and hurt me." He met her eyes. "They would be the ones begging for bits of affection. Not me. *Never me.*"

She wrapped her arms around him. "And then me. *Us.*"

"Yes," he said. "I didn't want to care, and then I couldn't help myself."

"And I was just as closed down, or at least I made a good show of acting like it."

"Yeah."

"So you cared too much and panicked."

He nodded. "Yes."

Trix shifted, touching her forehead to his. "And what's going to stop you from panicking now?"

Maybe once that would have pushed him away, made him freeze up and back away and be a real fucking idiot. But he knew what he was risking if he went down that road now.

And he wasn't going to lose Trix.

Not ever again.

"Because I love you," he murmured. "Because I did then and I do now, and I understand how precious and wonderful and special that is. I won't risk you, baby. Not when you mean so much."

Her eyes were wide, and no words came.

"Are you freaking out?"

She nodded.

"Are you going to run?"

She was silent for long enough that his intestines practically tied themselves into knots. But then she shook her head. "No, baby," she murmured.

"Okay."

Teeth pressing into a plump pink lip. "Okay."

"I'm going to show you that I mean what I say."

"Okay," she said again.

"And stop talking so you have some time to process."

"Okay."

"And—"

"Jet?"

"Yeah, honey?"

She nuzzled into his chest. "Stop talking and just hold me."

He grinned. "Okay, sweetheart."

"And stop saying *okay*."

"Okay."

Her head popped up, eyes narrowed. "*Jet*."

"*Trix*."

She dropped back down. "Night."

"Night, baby."

He tugged the covers up and held her while she drifted off to sleep, content that they had this second chance, that he'd laid it all on the table, that she understood and could forgive him enough to move forward.

He let his eyes slide closed, knowing that this was his future and it was going to be great.

And then he woke with empty arms.

Empty *fucking* arms.

SEVENTEEN

Trix

SHE WAS FREAKING OUT.

It was just after four-thirty in the morning, she was freaking out, and . . . she was doing a strange impersonation of a walk of shame in Jet's shorts, a T-shirt, and a pair of socks she was going to throw out the minute she got back to his place.

One, she needed to check on her car and make sure it was still there.

She couldn't remember if the street parking she'd pulled into had allowed for overnight parking.

Number two, she needed shoes that were not stilettos.

And clothes that fit.

Luckily, she had a go bag in the back of her car with extra sneakers and a change of clothes.

If her car was still there.

She rounded the corner, gut twisting, almost expecting to see an empty spot, but no, her little hybrid was still there.

Thank God.

She hurried over to the trunk and pulled out her duffle,

sitting on the bumper and peeling off the socks before swapping them for the pair in the bag, then slipping on her shoes. She was still in Jet's shorts and shirt, but a wardrobe change would have to wait for his condo. San Francisco streets did see a lot, but one thing they *wouldn't* see was her bare ass as she attempted to shimmy into some leggings.

Though . . . maybe Jet would like to see that.

Her smile was huge as she closed the trunk and stepped onto the sidewalk. Molly's was just a few shop fronts down, and it would open in—she pulled out her phone to check the time—less than fifteen minutes.

Great. She'd wait until then.

Grab coffee and some pastries then bring them back up to Jet. He'd certainly earned them.

She grinned again, probably looking like an idiot, but then again, the look matched her outfit. Last night had been . . . well, more than she'd ever hoped. Oh, she was still kind of pissed about the "blind date" Heather and Jet had conspired on, but she was also strangely touched that they'd gone to such lengths to convince her to give Jet another chance.

And then what he'd shared.

How he'd told her he loved her.

How desperately she'd wanted to say it back.

But by the time she'd gotten the courage, he'd fallen asleep, and after the long, emotional night, she hadn't wanted to wake him.

Well, tough. If he wasn't up by the time she got back, then he was getting shaken awake, coffee and pastries thrust in his face, and a declaration of love shouted into his ear.

Okay, maybe not shouted.

Whispered? Murmured? Spoken?

Ah, yes. Spoken.

That was the one.

Another grin, laughter bubbling inside of her. She'd never felt this hopeful, this happy, not even when they'd been together before. It was like the past had shed its heavy scales and now they could both move forward, lighter and free of its restrictions. "Oh lord," she muttered. "I'm way too poetic at five in the—"

She was so focused on her inner monologue, on watching the lights turn on one-by-one inside Molly's and the imminent deliciousness that was about to fill her belly that she didn't notice the footsteps until it was too late.

But she noticed the pain.

A sharp jab of agony across her skull, burning in her knees and palms as they scraped against the pavement. The snap of a bone breaking as her cell was ripped from her hand and her duffle yanked down her shoulder.

Finally, a raging hot slice of pain through her brain when the foot made contact with her head.

Then she felt nothing.

Blackness swept her under.

EIGHTEEN

Jet

HE WAS ALONE, and she wasn't coming back.

It felt like shit to be on this end of that gesture.

And thanks, karma, for granting him the opportunity to feel this horrible.

His cell rang, and he scrambled to grab it off the counter, hoping against hope that it was Trix, but after calling her cell six times and texting more than ten over the last hour since he'd woken, he already knew it wouldn't be.

It was the hospital, and even though he'd known it wasn't Trix, Jet still couldn't bite back the disappointment.

"Hello?" he answered, instead of chucking his phone across the room, like he really wanted to do.

"Can you fill in for me today?" Matt, or Dr. Harding, asked.

Not like he had anything better to do.

"Sure," he said, focusing on something besides the misery he felt. "Is everything okay?" Matt was solid and reliable but had a couple of young kids, one of whom had been pretty sick the previous week.

"Fine," Matt said and coughed. "Except the little germ machine has infected me with some horribly disgusting virus. I've got snot dripping out of every orifice."

"Not sure if that's possible," he said.

"It's not," Matt agreed. "But you get my point."

"Yeah." He stood and headed to the bedroom to change. "You on at seven?" It was just after five, but he was awake and might as well head into the hospital now.

"Yes, thanks, Jet," Matt said and broke off with a sniffle. "I owe you one."

"No worries, feel better." He hung up, dressed, and headed to the hospital. At least he had work to distract him from how royally fucked up his life was.

He didn't know if there had been a full moon the night before or if it was just his luck, but the department was absolutely slammed. Every bed was filled and there was a backup from admitting, which meant that patients who needed to go upstairs were taking up room unnecessarily. This happened for a variety of reasons, not the least of which—and also probably the most frustrating—was budgetary. As in, the med surge floor preferred the ED to take the budget hit instead of them and sometimes kept patients waiting until shift change.

The other reason for the packed ED was . . . sometimes shit just got weird in the department.

They'd be dead for hours and then as though everyone had been cued, multiple admits came at the same time.

The job kept him guessing, that was for sure.

And if he wasn't building clinics or treating people in remote parts of the world, then at least he had some excitement in his life. He stopped by the nurse's station, checking in to make sure they were all okay.

They were and he started to leave, but Rosario stopped him.

"Hey, I know you and Trix are close. I've been trying to get a hold of her for a few hours, but I—"

The hairs on his nape stood up, but he was already spinning around, trying to pinpoint exactly what had set his nerves on edge.

There was a commotion at the ambulance doors.

A shout.

Two figures staggered in, one being supported by the other, taking a few steps in through the doors, and then collapsing in a heap.

He ran.

Rosario ran.

The figures were two women. One, a tiny, plump female with a riot of brown curls spilling down her back. She wore a gray polo shirt that was soaked through with blood. Her skin was pale, sweat dripping down her face.

"Wouldn't let me call 9-1-1," she gasped, trying to get her shoulder back under the other female. "Should have—"

Brown hair. Thin. Tall.

He recognized the sneakers first.

Had seen them here. Seen *her* wearing them here.

Trix.

Oh God, it was Trix.

His hands started moving, searching and assessing her body for the injuries before his brain caught up.

A palm weakly grabbed his wrist. "Didn't—"

"Shh," he said. "I've got you."

He lifted her, rushing through the halls and setting her on the first available bed.

"Jet—"

Blood darkened her brown hair and the arm that wasn't gripping his wrist was completely at the wrong angle, bruising on her cheek, her throat. She was—

"Jet."

He glanced down, and gray eyes met his.

"I-I d-didn't l-leave."

He opened his mouth to tell her he knew that—

But then her eyes rolled back, and she stopped breathing.

HE WORKED on Trix until they kicked him out.

Then stayed in the hall until she was rushed up to surgery.

But the only thing that stayed with him after they'd taken her was the long, steady, unbroken beep of the heart monitor.

He'd lost her.

He hadn't, really.

And he'd lost her anyway.

NINETEEN

Trix

PEELING OPEN her eyelids took an immeasurable amount of effort.

But eventually she succeeded, blinking against the dim light as though she hadn't seen anything nearly that bright in a long time.

Her first wincing peek gave her the image of her feet covered by a pale blue blanket that she recognized instantly. Because it was an institutional standard, that tightly woven cotton covering, as was the way it was draped over her—secure but accessible to both change and view the patient underneath.

She closed her eyes and relaxed back into the pillows, trying to assess what was wrong with her body and how she might have ended up there.

Her arm hurt like hell and felt like it was immobilized in either a splint or a cast, her side ached, her head throbbed, and the skin near her hairline felt as though it were pulled tight . . . so stitches, a broken arm, bruised ribs, and maybe a concussion?

Okay, so it could have been worse.

The last thing she remembered was the wonderful night with Jet. Had she been in some sort of accident leaving his place the next day? All she could recall was waking up in his arms, too early but between the sun rising early and her biological alarm clock telling her it was time to head into the hospital . . .

Her breath caught.

She hadn't gone into the hospital.

She'd gone down to her car, to Molly's, and—

Her lungs froze. Someone had hit her from behind, knocking her to the pavement, kicking her in the side. She'd woken on the sidewalk, Molly next to her and frantic, her phone out and already dialing 9-1-1.

She'd refused to let the woman finish the call, had insisted Molly use Trix's car to drive her to the ED. It was only a few minutes away and not only would it have taken the ambulance longer to come, but it would have also been a waste of resources.

She'd reached for her phone to call Jet, but it hadn't been there.

And since she didn't know his number by heart, she'd figured she would get someone to call him for her.

But that was the last clear memory she had.

Now she was here—Trix forced her eyes open for another glance at the room and recognized she was in *her* hospital, only a few floors up from the ED. Molly must have driven her, and clearly, something hadn't gone quite to plan if she'd been admitted for bruised ribs and a mild concussion.

For one, she'd passed out again.

For another, she felt like she'd been run over by a Mack Truck.

Her eyes closed a second time and she sucked in a slow, shallow breath. As she became more fully awake, her pain level was increasing. She was tough, but it was already getting to unbearable levels.

"Hey."

A cool hand on her forehead.

She peeled back her lids, saw that Jet was there, pale, stubble covering his face, dark circles beneath his eyes. "Trix?" he asked hoarsely.

She started to nod, stopped when it made her pain ramp. "Jet."

Her voice was raspy. Admitted as well as been intubated.

"You hurting?"

"Yeah," she rasped.

"Here." He pushed the button on the line woven around the handle of the bed. She knew it was filled with a sensor that would administer pain medicine immediately.

"You scared me, baby," he murmured after the drugs had hit her veins, taking the edge off her pain. "But I'm glad you're awake."

She reached for his hand. "I didn't leave—" Her words cut off on a wince.

"It's okay," he said. "Don't try to talk. I know you didn't leave me. You were intubated." He brushed his knuckles lightly over her cheek. "I won't say I wasn't heartbroken there for a minute, but that quickly transformed into terrified when they wouldn't let me work on you."

Her eyes widened.

He nodded. "Dr. Joyce called and asked me to fill in. I was here when Molly brought you in—"

"I remember," she whispered in deference to her aching throat, his words sparking her memories. They had stumbled their way inside, Jet had picked her up, and—

"I'm sorry," she said. "I tried to call to warn—"

"You just spent eight hours on an operating table as the doctors worked to control bleeding in your abdomen. That, after coding twice in the ED and not regaining consciousness for three days, and you're worried about whether you tried to call me?"

Oh. So *that's* why she felt like shit.

"I guess," she murmured.

His eyes rolled to the ceiling and he cupped her cheek. "*Baby.*"

"I didn't get to tell you . . ." Exhaustion was creeping up within her as the pain medicine took fully. It weighed her limbs down, made her brain fuzzy.

"It's okay, sweetheart," he said softly. "Sleep now, you can tell me later."

"No," she said, wrenching her lips back open. "I have to tell you now."

"Okay." He brushed the hair back from her face. "Tell me what, sweetheart?"

Black was edging into her vision, fatigue sweeping over her. Unconsciousness was coming for her.

"I . . ." Her eyes closed.

"It's okay," he murmured. "Go to sleep. I'll still be here when you wake up."

She opened her eyes a millimeter, met his gaze, and in her final lucid moment, pushed out, "I love you."

Then got to see his face go soft before she passed out.

TWENTY

Jet

HE STOOD next to the bed, staring down at the woman he loved more than anything, the woman who had just said she loved him.

And she was unconscious.

Why did that seem absolutely fitting for their relationship?

Smiling, he shook his head then sat his ass back down in the chair next to her and pulled out his cell to text Heather. She'd been in the room almost the entire time since her plane had landed at the airport, after having flown home from Berlin when she'd heard the Trix had been hurt.

His cell buzzed with a response almost immediately.

Be there in fifteen minutes.

He tapped out a response.

She fell back asleep, but this is a good sign. She'll probably start being up a lot more.

His phone vibrated a few seconds later.

Okay, then I'll wrap up my meeting and come over. Do you think an hour is all right?

He'd all but shooed her away that morning, knowing that Trix wouldn't want her to be behind on her account, not if everything was okay.

I think she'll be happy to see you whenever you can make it in.

A reply a heartbeat later.

I'll be there within the hour.

Jet smiled. Heather really was a good sister.

He pocketed his cell, sat back in the chair, and watched his woman as she slept. Nothing else but Trix mattered at that point, not that the police had spoken with Molly—who'd apparently seen a flash as someone had run by her restaurant and then had seen Trix on the ground. It didn't matter that the detective had come to the hospital, leaving his card, and telling Jet that they were pulling the footage of the attack from Molly's cameras, nor that the person who'd hurt Trix was still on the streets somewhere.

The police were almost certain the attack had been random, based on the amounts of grab and go robberies in the city.

Not that it mattered. In fact, in a way, it was almost worse.

Trix had almost died because some asshole wanted an iPhone . . . and not even a new one.

Now she'd be dealing with potentially life-changing injuries for a very long time, if not permanently. People didn't just bounce back from major surgery, even if those people were as tough as Trix.

She had a long road to recovery ahead of her.

And he wasn't going anywhere.

"I'VE GOT IT," Trix snapped, clearly done with the amount of hovering that he and Heather were doing.

He recognized that and handed back the bag of popcorn she'd been trying to open. In truth, *struggling* to open. Because she'd been out of the hospital for less than a day and was weak after spending nearly two weeks prone in bed. Now, she'd been walked a little bit—yes, he'd thought that correctly, because Heather had made sure Trix had taken several faltering passes up and down the hall.

So, he got that Trix was two heartbeats away from losing her shit.

Heather, as smart of a businesswoman as she was, missed the cues and promptly snatched the bag of popcorn from Trix's lap, opened it, and poured it into a bowl, which she then handed over. And all the while, she kept talking about the nurse she'd hired against Trix's wishes—the irony of a nurse taking care of another nurse was not lost on him, considering he'd taken a few days off in order to help Trix while she recovered, also against her wishes—as well as the food delivery she'd set up.

The latter Jet wasn't sad about.

The first, he thought was overkill.

But he also knew that Heather's heart was in the right place.

That didn't mean Trix couldn't use a little backup in dealing with the overprotectiveness that was Heather. Plus, it wouldn't do for Trix to reinjure something while trying to throttle her sister.

"Two nurses and a doctor," he said, weaving his arm through Heather's. "That sounds like the title to a bad porno."

Trix's eyes met his as he led Heather to the door.

I got this, he mouthed and watched her shoulders drop in relief.

"I think one nurse and one doctor have got this," he went on. "Thanks for the gesture, but we're fine. We'll let you know if we end up needing help."

"But—"

He picked up her coat, helped her shrug into it, then opened the door.

"We'll be okay," he assured. "You go on home to your husband. He's missing you."

Heather nibbled at her bottom lip, but he just propped his door slightly ajar, and led her toward the elevator, pushing the button to call it. Thankfully, it opened right away and he . . . well, he basically shoved her inside the car.

"We'll call you," he said as the doors began to shut.

"I—"

She was cut off as they sealed shut.

He was at the condo's door when his phone buzzed.

I'm well aware that I've just been handled.

Jet grinned.

Another buzz.

You're good for her. You love her right.

Yes, he did, he thought as he walked back into his condo and saw her asleep on the couch, the bowl of popcorn untouched, her hair a mess, her sexy body clad in absolutely shapeless pajamas.

And still the prettiest thing he'd ever laid eyes on.

So, yeah, he loved her right.

And he was going to keep on doing it forever.

TWO WEEKS LATER, he walked through the door to his condo, hung up his jacket, and turned to see—

The table set.

Candles ready to be lit.

Delicious smells coming from the kitchen.

The woman he loved in a little black dress that made him crazy.

She was barefoot, headphones in, swaying to the music, and finally looking healthy and recovered for the first time since the attack.

God, he loved this woman.

He'd only returned to work a couple of days before, and this week was going to be hell on that front, as he began to make up for all the extra shifts the other docs had covered for him.

Then he'd come home to this.

Pretty, lovely Trix in his place, cooking at his stove, in a sexy dress, and more importantly, healthy and happy.

She spun, startling slightly when she saw him then tugged the headphones from her ears and strode over to him. "They got him," she said, throwing her arms around his neck, and for once the movement wasn't carefully calculated or punctuated with a wince.

"Got who?"

"Him," she said again, and then he understood.

"They arrested the guy who hurt you?"

She nodded. "They had his face from Molly's cameras, and they got him."

Jet blew out a relieved breath. "That's fantastic news."

"I know." She pressed a kiss to his cheek. "Also, I gave up the lease on my apartment, and so I'm moving in. And Molly was so excited to hear about the arrest that she brought a bunch of food up. I'm talking pastries and salads and this delicious potato and leek soup. I'm just reheating it along with some bread she baked."

His heart lurched in his chest. "What did you say?"

"That Molly baked bread?" Her head cocked. "That's not news, she does it every day."

"No," he said. "Before that."

Her lips twitched. "That I'm reheating soup?"

He shook his head.

"The pastries and salads and potato and leek soup—"

A roll of his eyes. "Enough about the soup."

"The arrest?"

"*Trix.*"

She smiled at him innocently. "Oh, that I'm moving in?"

He dropped his head, nuzzled her throat. "Mmm-hmm."

A shrug. "I decided I'm keeping you."

"You—" He straightened, happiness expanding in his chest, stealing his ability to speak. Never would he *ever* be able to predict what this woman would say or do. She'd keep him guessing . . .

Forever.

And that was just fine with him.

Because he could surprise her, too.

"As it happens," he murmured, nibbling at her jaw. She melted at his touch, leaning closer, brushing her breasts across his chest. "I found a different roommate, so that's not going to work—"

She gasped, leaning back. "How dare—"

Jet kissed her.

And then scooped her up into his arms and brought her to bed.

Luckily, Trix forgave him for his joke and kissed him back.

They wouldn't get to the food that Molly brought until much later.

But that was just fine with both of them.

TWENTY-ONE

Trix

"THAT'S THE LAST ONE," Heather said from her spot next to Trix at the apartment door. They were supervising the men moving Trix's belongings, cramming them jigsaw-style into the back of their various vehicles.

"Why aren't we paying someone to do this again?" Clay asked with a groan. "You're a billionaire and—"

Heather pinched his butt as he walked by.

Clay jumped but kept moving, though she thought his groan was warranted, considering he'd gotten the box filled with her books. And since she hadn't had much time to collect belongings while abroad, she'd been making up for lost time at the bookstores recently. That bin was filled to the top with romance and mystery and fantasy novels of various sizes.

She'd gotten her money's worth. That was for sure.

"Because manual labor is good for your abs," Heather said without missing a beat.

Clay gasped and whipped around. "Are you saying my abs are getting soft?"

"I'm saying that I love your abs," Heather said sweetly, turning to Trix with a wicked smile. "And I want it to stay that way."

Clay gaped for a heartbeat then tossed the box into the back of Trix's car and hauled ass over to them, not missing a step as he hauled Heather up into his arms and then proceeded to kiss the sass right out of her.

Jet grinned as he walked much more slowly over to Trix and slung an arm over her shoulders, leading them both away from the couple making out and into the apartment that had been home.

Her first ever real home.

Or maybe that wasn't right.

Maybe home had always been Jet.

"Do you know," she said when they wandered into the empty kitchen, "the reason that I rented this place?"

He stopped, glanced over at her.

This was the first time he'd ever been in the apartment.

She took his hand, led him to the window, positioning him exactly so he could see what she'd seen when she'd initially viewed the place.

Trix knew the moment he realized it. His shoulders jerked, head whipping around to face her. "That's—" He broke off, shook his head. "I don't—"

"I know," she murmured.

She'd felt a little bit speechless the first time she'd seen it.

It being the view of the hills in the distance, their tops dusted with pale brown, the fog crawling toward them, the ocean to one side, the spiked white tops of boats on the Bay on the other.

Just like *their* place.

Where they'd fallen in love.

On the coast of Africa, they'd stayed slightly inland at a small village surrounded by hills, a view of the ocean in the distance and a small inlet on the other side. There had been masts there, too, though not quite as tall and definitely not as modern.

But it was close enough to *their* place that she'd felt a sharp pang upon seeing it.

Then hadn't been able to imagine living anywhere else.

She'd pretended it was cheaper because that was easier than admitting she'd never stopped loving Jet, never stopped thinking about him or wishing that things would have turned out differently.

And now he realized that, too.

"Baby," he murmured, turning to face her and cupping her cheek in his palm. "This is—"

She covered his palm with her own. "We've talked a lot over the last few weeks, shared a lot about what makes us tick. We'll, *you've* shared," she added. "I've only yelled at you about what our relationship had meant to me."

"That's not true—" he began.

"It's true." She sighed. "I've shared bits and pieces, yes, but I don't think I ever explained to you why I was so closed down, why it's hard for me even now thinking about telling you, why I was scared to accept *anyone* fully into my life—whether it was you or Heather or friends or lovers."

He tugged her against his chest. "It's not an easy thing to lay yourself bare," he murmured. "And I can afford to be patient while you get comfortable."

"And was it easy for you to share?"

A chuckle that vibrated against her ear. "Hell, no. I still have to fight against the urge to keep everything as some sort of joke, to tuck all of those insecurities away, to not pretend my past didn't affect me."

Trix leaned back slightly. "I don't have a horrible neglect story like you."

He snorted. "Thanks."

Her heart twisted. "I didn't mean it like that—"

"I know, babe," he said. "There's me trying to lighten it."

"You're saying we should embrace our dark senses of humor?"

"I'm saying there's no other way."

She sighed, letting her forehead move forward to bump against his collarbone. "I felt alone a lot as a kid."

His arms tightened, chin tilting to rest on the top of her head, but he didn't say anything, just waited for her to gather her thoughts . . . or maybe for her to signal that now wasn't the time.

But Trix had realized that life was too fucking short for this to *not* be the time.

This was it.

She didn't want any more barriers between them.

She didn't want any more barriers between herself and the people who meant something in her life.

She wanted everything out in the open, the secrets that pressed so heavily down on her chest gone, their power reduced to ashes, whatever shameful hold they'd had on her for so long gone.

Trix was done being tied down by the past.

Lifting her head, she glanced over Jet's shoulder. "You might as well come in, too, Heather. You should hear this."

Heather, whose blonde hair had been peeking around the corner as she shamelessly spied on Trix and Jet, startled and jumped back. "I'm just—"

"Nosy," Trix said and smiled to soften the word. "But I know that it comes from caring about me." She turned in the circle of Jet's arms, held out her hand. "I didn't trust that for a long time, but when I finally realized the life I was living didn't make me happy, and I wanted to come home . . . where did I come?"

"California."

"No," Trix murmured. "To you." She smiled. "You were the one person who proved to me time and again that you actually gave a shit about me."

Heather's eyes went damp. "Come here." She took Trix's outstretched hand and tugged her from Jet's arms, wrapping her in a tight hug.

"You never stopped reaching out," Trix murmured. "Even when it pissed me off, when I was trying to get far away from here and forget everything that had happened, you always managed to track me down." She sniffed, blinking back tears. "I was so thankful for that . . . even when it was really fucking annoying."

They both laughed and held on to each other for a long moment.

"I am good at being annoying," Heather deadpanned and pulled back after they'd both chuckled.

"I never thought I was good enough," Trix said.

Heather's face sobered. "Trix—"

"No," she said. "Let me get this out?"

Heather nodded.

But she didn't really know where to start. How could she possibly begin to explain the black hole that had been inside her, the bottomless pit that sucked in every single good thing inside of her, making it disappear, leaving her empty and fragile and . . . not good?

How could she begin to put *that* into words?

She turned and glanced at Jet. His eyes were calm, his arms extended, his expression patient. "You're worth the time, baby. This doesn't have to happen today. But your pain is *your* pain.

You don't have to justify it. You're *allowed* to feel what you feel, no explanations required."

Her heart rolled over in her chest. "God, I love you."

His lips twitched at the corners. "I know."

She crossed to him, let him wrap his arms around her, and then she started talking.

She told them about being the *other* family, about her mother spending all the money, about living on a loaf of bread and a jar of peanut butter for two weeks—those being her mother's rations. She told them about mowing the neighbor's lawns and cobbling her piggy bank with her brothers' to pay the water bill while their mother came home with a new handbag or a pair of Louboutins. She told them about all the screaming, the way her brothers had left home as soon as they were able, and how she'd hated them for doing so, even while understanding their need to escape.

She shared how she'd gone to her father and asked for money to pay the power bill at fourteen.

And how he'd told her that her mother had already pestered him for child support for four kids he didn't even want.

She confessed about her mother's drinking. The hateful words that followed.

Finally, she told them about med school, not qualifying for loans because she had no credit and the market had crashed, because her parents made too much, because she'd spent every cent she earned putting herself through undergrad.

"He refused to pay," Trix said. "Refused even to sign a contract that it would be a loan, that I would pay back every cent. He said making a crew of useless Donovans was the absolute worst thing he'd ever done in his life, and *that* was why he'd refused to give us his name."

Jet had stiffened behind her throughout the monologue, but

his touch when he spun her in his hold and stared down at her face was as gentle as someone handling fragile crystal.

"I'm okay," she said, touching his cheek.

"Nothing about this is okay."

"I don't want his name," she murmured. "I never did. I just wanted a place where I belonged."

"You belong," he said. "Here. With me."

"And me," Heather said, voice watery. "I'm sorry. I didn't know—"

"How *could* you?" Trix said. "You were away at school, and it wasn't like I reached out . . . or even knew how. Our father is excellent at separating people."

Heather's gaze dropped to the floor. "Yes, he is." She sucked in a breath. "I just wish . . ."

"That things could be different."

Heather nodded.

"I know, me, too," she said. "But when I finished my last assignment and decided to come home—to come *here*—I didn't know what would become of it. I just knew that I wanted to find a family . . . and that I hoped the family would include you."

Heather closed the distance between them. "Our father is the absolute worst kind of asshole, but I didn't—I mean, I didn't go through what you did. We had money, fucking ridiculous heaps of it. I wish—fuck, I wish I knew that you were struggling. I could have—"

Trix stepped out of Jet's hold and took Heather's hands. "I don't blame you. I never have. Never."

"You should."

"*No.*" She tightened her hold. "I shouldn't. I never have, and I never will. This was never about some sort of you-had-and-I-didn't. This was me putting up walls to survive and then not realizing or being too scared to reach over the top for help.

That's what's changed for me. With you. With Jet. I'm not scared anymore."

Jet gently squeezed her nape. "I know, baby."

Heather gave her a watery smile. "Thank you, Trix. For saying that. I . . . I guess I never felt like my pain could mean anything. I wasn't abused. Yes, he was absent. Yes, he's never praised or told me he loved me. Yes, he was all about the business to the detriment of everything else—"

"That's abuse," Clay interjected, wrapping an arm around Heather's waist. "I'm sorry, I know this isn't my conversation to jump into, but, sweetheart"—he glanced down at his wife—"abuse comes in all forms. Just because he didn't leave physical bruises doesn't mean you don't have emotional ones."

Heather and Trix stilled, and Trix knew her sister was feeling the same pulse of shock that Clay had managed to reduce their feelings down to such a perfect explanation.

Face softening, Heather turned to her husband. "How'd you get so smart?"

"When you married me," he said without missing a beat then chuckled when she lightly smacked him across the chest. "Come on," he said. "Let's leave these two alone and take the first load to Jet's place."

Heather nodded, slipped out of his hold. "Just one more thing."

She came back over to Trix and pulled her in for one more hug, murmuring softly into her ear, "I know our father is really good at using our weaknesses to keep people apart. I also know I spent too long trying to find a reason for what could possibly motivate him to do such a thing." She sighed. "And I came to the conclusion that I'll never understand it. *Never*. I just know that I want *my* family to be different . . . and I really want you to be part of it."

Trix squeezed her lightly. "Well, good. Because you're stuck with me."

Heather dropped her arms, grinning. "I'm glad." A beat and she visibly exhaled the heavy moment from her features. "Now, don't forget to christen the kitchen counters before you lock up. Might as well make the most of your last day here."

Trix retched. "You know, I think that sisters are supposed to be grossed out by their siblings' sex lives."

"I've learned much in my years . . . and one of the most important is that a good orgasm can cure most ills."

Jet wrapped both of his arms around Trix's waist and rested his chin on her shoulder. "Bye, Heather."

"See you soon," she called, heading for the door. "Just not *too* soon."

The door closed behind her.

"You okay?" Jet asked.

Trix rotated in the circle of his arms. "I'm . . . not fine exactly, but I have you. I have Heather, and so that's a damned good start as far as I'm concerned."

"I agree."

"You would—*eek!*" Her hands fell to his shoulders when he swept her up and held her against his chest. "Jet! What are you doing?"

He spun, set her on the counter. "Taking Heather's advice."

"What?" Her brows drew down.

"We're christening these countertops."

"Um. No. That's not going to hap—"

"I love you," he said.

She shook her head. "I love you, but that doesn't mean we're going—"

He cut off her protest with a kiss.

And frankly, it didn't take much more convincing than that for her to play her part in christening those countertops.

Plus, Heather was right.

A good orgasm did cure most ills.

It also helped remove the hooks of the past and tuck it firmly back where it belonged.

So, Trix could focus on the future.

Exactly as it should be.

EPILOGUE

Jet, Six Months Later

HE WALKED into the restaurant five minutes late, eyes searching the area near the hostess stand for Trix.

He'd gotten stuck at the hospital, wanting to wait until a patient was admitted upstairs, and then running home to change because he wasn't going to meet his woman in dirty scrubs.

When he didn't spot her, he frowned. She'd left a note at the condo saying she was running an errand. It had probably just taken her a little longer than she'd expected. He'd sit down, order her a glass of wine, and wait.

He went up to the hostess and asked for his table. Five minutes later, he had drinks on the table and an untouched bread basket in front of him.

Ten minutes after that she still hadn't shown.

A little worried now, he sent her a text.

Five minutes after *that*, she still hadn't responded.

Knowing that she probably just hadn't heard the chime, but

his stomach churning anyway—because the last time she'd gone out of contact and it hadn't been because of work was when . . .

She'd been robbed and beaten.

"Fuck," he muttered, not giving a damn that he was in a fancy French restaurant and that it was impolite, he hit her number in his phone and brought it to his ear. It rang four times then went to voicemail.

His gut was churning now.

The server came over, a male in his twenties with a knowing look on his face.

Probably thought that Jet had gotten stood up.

And, he guessed in a way he *had*.

But that thought—Trix having gotten so wrapped up in her errand that she'd forgotten about dinner—was a much better one than her unconscious and bleeding out on the street.

"Would you like to order, sir?"

Jet shook his head. "No. I need the check. Thanks."

"Certainly." A nod. "Might I suggest you try some bread before you go?" He nudged the basket closer. That was weird, but the waiter disappeared before Jet could make heads or tails of the comment.

While he waited for his bill, Jet sent another text.

Still no response.

He pulled out his wallet, intending to just leave cash on the table, when the waiter came back, check in hand and handed it over.

"Did you try the bread?" the server asked.

For fuck's sake.

What the hell was the man's issue with the bread? Was it filled with fucking gold or something? His girlfriend might be out there hurt and—

The man nudged the basket, so it was almost on Jet's plate.

Was he fucking serious?

Jet glanced up, eyes probably sparking fire, a fistful of cash in one hand, and saw the waiter nod encouragingly.

To stop the insanity, Jet grabbed a fucking roll.

And froze.

A little black box sat underneath it.

His heart skipped a beat, the worry settled, and he reached for the box, a neatly folded square of paper taped to the top. He snagged it and at the same time, felt the server gently pry the cash from his other hand—which was mercenary but efficient, Jet supposed—before he was left alone at the table.

The paper shook as he unfolded it.

Will you promise to always share your tacos with me?

He snorted then obliged the arrow that was scrawled beneath the words and flipped the note over.

If so, open the box then come home.
-T

Jet snagged the box and stood, opening it as he strode out of the restaurant, knowing what was inside almost without looking, also knowing that it would go very well with what he'd bought a month before . . . because it was from the same jeweler.

A ring.

He grinned.

Never could predict.

Fuck, he was looking forward to a lifetime of that.

He moved quickly, legs eating up the blocks when his phone rang. He brought it to his ear.

"Hello?"

"So how did it feel?"

"How did *what* feel?" Being briefly terrified for her safety—they would have words about that later—or the ring that meant more to him than anything else ever had? Because she'd given it to him. No strings. No begging. She'd just . . . given.

And that, more than anything, was everything he'd ever dreamed of.

"Getting stood up," she said.

Which was pretty much the last thing he'd been expecting. Again.

The pieces shifted in his mind, coming together, Heather's insistence that she wanted them to go out for a good dinner—one she'd pay for, by the way, so another woman who he was going to have words with later, Trix not specifying her errand, not responding to his texts, his call.

"Oh, man," he muttered. "You play dirty."

He rounded the corner, instinctively knowing she'd be there. Leaning against a pole instead of her car, but phone to her ear, a paper bag of food in her hand.

He hung up, shoved his cell in his pocket, and closed the distance between them.

"You know, we're actually going to have to have a full meal at that restaurant someday," he said, brushing a hand down her cheek.

"I don't know." She shrugged. "Their bread is pretty good."

They laughed and he took the bag as they began walking up to the condo. "I didn't eat it."

She shook her head. "Wasting perfectly good carbs."

They hit the button for the elevator, headed up to their floor. "Looks like you have plenty of carbs in here."

"Had to spring for queso and guac, as per tradition."

He grinned, held the doors as they got off, and walked down the hall.

"So?" she asked when they went inside.

"So what?" he countered innocently.

"Jet!"

He smothered a smile but didn't answer her, instead moving to the hall closet, pulling down the bag he'd stashed there, the one that held an identical box. He turned around, extended it to Trix.

Who crossed her arms.

"I'm not taking it back."

"Good," he said and opened the lid to reveal the diamond ring inside. "Because I'm not taking this one back either."

Those pretty gray eyes dampened, her fingers reached out to touch the band. "You—?"

"Yes," he said when she faltered. "I had a whole day planned. The beach at sunset, a picnic, going down on one knee—"

"You can still do that," she blurted.

Jet grinned, dropping into the position and tugging the ring from the box. He took Trix's hand, slid the metal circle down her finger. "Will you . . . *share your tacos with me?*"

Her face had been soft, but at his words, she gasped and smacked him lightly.

"I love you, baby," he said. "Marry me?"

She dropped to her knees and wrapped her arms around him, lips meeting his, tongues tangling as they kissed and kissed and *kissed.*

When they broke for air, both of them were gasping.

"Is that a yes?" he asked, stroking one finger down her cheek.

"It's a yes," she confirmed, hands starting to undo the buttons of his shirt, mouth pressing to each inch of exposed skin. "To both the marriage thing." A kiss. "*And* the tacos."

He snorted.

She giggled.

And then they made love right there in the hallway.

Which was a good thing because . . . they hadn't christened that spot yet.

BAD WEDDING

BILLIONAIRE'S CLUB #9

ONE

Molly

SHE CHECKED the bread that was proofing in the oven, not opening the door and risking a disruption of those teeny bubbles that were still forming, but peering through the glass rectangle on the oven door and making sure those pale globes of bread were rising as they should.

Her homemade rolls were a top-seller, usually gone before ten in the morning.

That was because they were delicious, if she said so herself.

And she *did* say so, she supposed, snorting at her pun.

But puns were all she had at zero-dark-thirty in the morning. Zero-dark-thirty, otherwise known as four A.M. It was a stupid hour to be up and about, but she owned a bakery and that meant she had to get up early. Molly's—yes, she was egotistical enough to own a place named after herself, though in fairness, she hadn't come up with the name—served breakfast and lunch, with a limited staff and menu for dinner.

That limited menu meant she didn't have to work at dinnertime.

A good thing, too. Otherwise, she might as well live at the restaurant.

And while she loved Molly's, she also loved having a life.

Not that you've had much of that lately.

True.

But owning a restaurant in a big city was difficult, and even more difficult was to *keep* owning it. Molly had investors to reimburse, loans to pay off, wages to cover, and supplies to purchase.

So, that meant filling in if her evening cook had a date or got sick or worked only five days a week. Okay, so if she were being truthful, that meant she all but lived at the bakery an average of four days out of said week.

But that was better than seven, so there was that.

Seeing that the rolls were doing well, Molly turned back to the counter to finish up the rest of her prep. She had to toast some walnuts, get the *mise en place* ready for her soups—which were basically fancy words to say she was chopping up the onions and carrots, celery and potatoes and peppers, measuring stocks and creams, roasting cobs of corn.

Her rolls dinged, and she grabbed them out, switching them to the preheated oven, doing a little dance of adding another baking sheet in to proof, pulling out a tray of croissants that were done from a different oven and replacing them with peach turnovers. She packed up the *mise en place* and stored them in the fridge, then prepped several bowls of muffin batter—today would be lemon poppy seed, peaches and cream, blueberry, and double chocolate.

Once the turnovers were done, she divided the muffin batter into various tins then began rocking through baking them off while stocking the glass case next to the counter. It was a familiar routine. Her doors opened at five, but that was mostly for her few straggler early birds, and that wasn't typically more than five or six people, so she mostly let the first bell tinkling above the door let her know when she needed to pull her ass out of the kitchen. Which meant that she had to have the first batch of everything baked off before that. After her first employees clocked in at six-thirty, she could stay in the kitchen like she preferred.

Baking was her favorite.

The people weren't bad either. She loved getting to know them, to see them change, their lives grow full and happy, their kids get older. She loved *feeding* people, even if they weren't regulars.

There was absolutely nothing better than seeing someone's happy smile when they bit into something tasty.

Speaking of, the bell above the door tinkled as her first customer of the day strode into the bakery.

"I'll be with you in a second," she called, continuing to fill the case with lemon muffins.

"I did always love to see you like this."

Molly jumped, eyes shooting up.

It had been so long since she'd heard that voice.

I love taking bites out of you.

It had rumbled back then, too, rasping along her skin, skating down her spine, and making her shiver.

The first man she'd baked for.

The man who'd given her the money to open this place.

The one who'd *named* it.

And the one who'd left her at the altar. In the white dress. With the venue booked. With the caterer and the DJ set up. With the guests packing the pews on both sides of the isle.

Jackson Davis.

Jackson *Fucking* Davis.

"Jackson," she murmured and slid the back of the case closed.

"I'm back, honey."

She'd regret her actions later, but in that moment, with the memories of the full church and the people and their pitying expressions and *this man*. Not. Fucking. Showing. Up.

Molly snapped.

She threw the baking sheet at his head.

TWO

Jackson

IN FAIRNESS, he used to react faster.

His Molly seemed sweet and kind and levelheaded to the rest of the world, but with him, she always had a slice of fire.

He'd ducked a cookie sheet or twenty in their years together, but he'd been too long out of practice, too long away to remember how quickly she could launch that rectangle of steel, how it could unfailingly fly in perfect rotation toward his head.

Then it was there, inches away.

Jackson ducked at the last second, so the sheet glanced off his shoulder instead of his face.

Ouch. That was going to leave a bruise.

"Oh, my God," Molly said, hands coming up to cover the horrified expression she wore.

That was new.

The horrified reaction.

She never used to feel any remorse for losing her temper, for launching a sheet in his direction or cursing him out. For one, he always moved well before the sheet came close. For two, he always deserved her reaction.

He'd *curated* her reaction—poked and prodded and needled until she snapped.

Because there was something about seeing Molly pissed, watching the flush crawl over her cheeks, seeing her pale green eyes fill with sparks. She was beautiful normally, but she was absolutely stunning when she was pissed.

Not to mention her being pissed was usually trailed by angry sex.

And angry sex with Molly was the best.

Although . . . he didn't think angry sex was going to be on the plate with her today. Her hands dropped away from her face, those sparks faded away, and her pretty green eyes went damp.

"What the fuck, Jackson Davis?" she said. "What. The. Fuck?"

Then she spun on one heel and disappeared through the swinging door.

He stood there for a moment, staring after her, his heart hurting from the sight of her tears, regret a jagged and icy knife in his gut. He should have leveled with her from the second he'd found out, shouldn't have . . . done a lot of things.

Jackson sighed, shoved a hand through his hair.

He'd fucked up good.

Never let it be said that he didn't give it his all.

The bell above the door dinged and after a few seconds, he heard Molly's voice trail out of the back. "I'll be right out!"

Warm. As sweet as her cinnamon rolls and twice as calorie-laden. Or at least, that was how it had always felt to him. She just had to speak, and he was filled to the brim.

And he'd ruined that.

Fucking hell.

It was just after six in the morning. The case next to the register was full of various breakfast treats—croissants and muffins, fruit-filled Danishes, even a row of immaculately decorated flower cookies, the brightly-colored frosting punctuated with carefully placed sparkling sprinkles.

He knew she'd probably placed them with tweezers.

Because if there was one thing Molly was good at, it was caring about the details.

He'd once been one of those details.

Molly pushed through the door, another tray in her hands, her formerly askew ponytail carefully straightened and secured. She set the tray on the stainless-steel counter behind the case and smiled.

Not at him.

At the man who'd just walked through the door.

Fuck, Jackson didn't like that at all—her smiling at other men, even men who were well over seventy, had barely enough hair to cover an inch above each ear, and hobbled slowly in with a cane.

But he'd fucked up.

So, he didn't have a right to feel anything about her smiles.

"Ronnie," she said, still smiling, her eyes sliding deliberately past him, as though Jackson were nothing more than a piece of furniture, and an ugly one at that. "You want the usual?"

"Mornin', beautiful," Ronnie said then pointed at Jackson. "This young man was here first."

Molly smiled, though this time it was tinged with ice. "Oh, I've already helped him plenty." She tilted her head toward the windows. "Go sit at your table. I'll bring out your muffin and coffee."

"Black," Ronnie said.

"With only a half a pound of sugar," Molly added with

wink. "I know, honey. I'll warm you up a lemon poppy seed to go with it."

"You always know how to treat a guy." Ronnie put a five on the counter. "I wish I was forty years younger so I could marry you. Any man would be lucky to call you his wife." Then he grinned and made his halting way over to what was apparently *his* table, a small round top tucked into one corner.

It did not escape Jackson's notice that there was already a newspaper carefully laid there. One that Ronnie apparently expected, because he sat down and immediately got to reading.

It also did not escape Jackson's notice that Molly had stopped breathing.

That her face had paled, and pain had crawled across her eyes.

Because he'd once been the man who'd been lucky enough to marry Molly.

Fuck.

"Sweet—"

Her eyes flashed to his, hurt disappearing behind a mask of anger. "I think I made it clear when I sent you the paperwork. I don't want anything to do with you. Not now. Not *ever*." She bent, sliding open the back of the case and pulling out a muffin. Her movements were efficient, practiced, but wooden, and he knew she'd done the same thing a thousand times before.

She'd done the same dance many times over while hurting.

Because *he'd* hurt her.

Jackson didn't speak until she came back behind the counter. "Molly—"

Her head whipped up, but this time there wasn't hurt or anger on her face. Instead, it was determination and, fuck, he liked that expression even more than sparking furious eyes. "If you want more money," she said. "I'll find it. But I want you out of this business, Jackson."

Yeah, he was reading that loud and clear.

He'd gotten the papers the day before, couriered to his office, placed unceremoniously on his desk by his assistant, and they'd fucking pissed him off. An emotion he didn't have one right to feel about the situation, since it was entirely of his making, and yet, one he was furious about anyway.

What right did Molly have to cut this last tie between them? What fucking right?

Every right. She had *every* right. He knew that. He got that. He—

Couldn't bear to actually let her go.

A fucking joke considering he was the one who'd pulled the plug on their wedding, but also the truth.

Which is why he said, "I'm not going to let you buy me out," when he probably should have told her that he would sign whatever papers she wanted if she would only give him another chance.

But that wasn't his style.

Jackson wasn't altruistic. He wasn't good. He was selfish.

And he wanted Molly.

Green eyes sparked fire at his words, lush lips that fit perfectly against his flattened out, a muscle in her jaw ticked. She sucked in a breath, opened her mouth, and—

The bell jingled.

They both turned and watched a trio of men in suits walk through the door. Then the bell sounded again as another customer slipped inside. And then another. And another. They approached the counter, anticipation on their faces.

To talk to Molly. To eat her delicious food. To just soak in the warmth of her presence.

Jackson knew the feeling. He'd been stifling that urge for years.

Only he'd gotten really good at pretending he wasn't ruled

by those urges, that he didn't need the woman standing on the other side of the counter, her unruly hair escaping her ponytail, her curves unhidden even beneath the shapeless pastel pink apron she wore, the scent of all the delicious things she conjured up in the magical kitchen of hers surrounding him.

But he *did* need her.

He just didn't know how in the hell he was going to make amends for what he'd done.

THREE

Molly

SHE LEANED CAREFULLY to the side, peering through the round window at the top of the swinging door that led from the kitchen to the front of house, searching to see if it was safe.

It wasn't.

Jackson was still there.

When the morning rush had begun, he'd stepped away from the counter and she'd thought he would leave.

Thanked the baking gods that he wouldn't continue to darken her doorstep.

But instead of leaving, he'd picked up the plate with the lemon and poppy seed muffin she'd heated, snagged the coffee she'd poured and then dumped about a gallon of sugar into, and carried both over to Ronnie's table.

Now they were talking.

It had been nearly two hours. Jeanine, her morning shift cashier had come in, facilitating Molly's escape back into the kitchen. Ronnie had gone, the newspaper she left for him every morning folded carefully and tucked under one arm.

And Jackson remained.

Suit jacket off and draped over the back of his chair. Phone out, alternating between typing on it and placing it up to his ear and speaking into it. Yes, she could imagine the velvet rasp of his voice, practically feel it caressing her skin.

So many good times.

So much love.

And then . . . nothing.

He'd ghosted her to an insane degree, disappearing the morning of the wedding. His parents hadn't known where he'd gone, and neither had his groomsmen. She'd spent the day calling hospitals, organizing search parties, and driving the road between the hotel and the venue, looking for him or any sign of an accident. Eventually, she'd gone to the police department and filed a missing person report.

Then had received a phone call an hour later, asking her to come down to the station. She'd been panicked, on the verge of a nervous breakdown the whole way, thinking something horrible had happened to him. But then she'd been led into a room at the department, and Jackson had been standing there, whole and safe and . . . she'd run to him, thrown herself into his arms. *God.* She'd never forgot the humiliation of what had come next. The brusque way he'd set her away from him, his normally warm chocolate eyes having turned frozen and fierce.

"You have to stop, or I'll file a restraining order."

A restraining order.

While she'd stood there, heart shattering into tiny pieces, head spinning from his sudden transformation—her loving and devoted fiancé had turned into this cold and unfeeling monster —he'd calmly threatened her with a restraining order.

Calmly threatened.

Those two words shouldn't go together.

And yet, they did.

So, she'd gathered herself, lifted her chin, straightened her shoulders, steadied her voice, all while her heart was still breaking, and had slipped the ring off her finger.

The metal against metal sound of the band hitting the stainless-steel table had stayed with her for a long time. Because there had been a finality in the noise, a final nail in the coffin of what she'd always understood deep down in some dark corner of her mind was going to come. Jackson would leave her.

She'd known that.

She just . . . hadn't expected it to be on her wedding day.

Molly had left that tiny fluorescent-lit room and gone back to the apartment she shared with Jackson to find his things had been cleared out in the hour she'd been gone, a note scrawled in his handwriting left on the counter.

Lease paid up. Money in your bank account. Call this number when you need more.
415-555-6979
-J

She could admit now that was the moment she'd fully lost it. Her purse had hit the floor, dumping its contents everywhere. Her keys she'd launched across the room, leaving a huge dent in the wall. Her cell . . . well, she'd launched it hard enough to probably tear through the sheetrock and fly into the unit next door, but thankfully her aim was off, and it rebounded off the couch and dropped to the floor, ending up functional, albeit with a broken screen.

Functional but broken.

Yeah, look her up in the dictionary and that would be the perfect definition.

And after all of that, the being left at the altar, the panic and worry of the day, the unceremonious dumping, she'd been left with a wedding to dismantle, gifts to return, venders to pay . . . and been threatened with a restraining order.

Because that was Molly's life.

In hindsight, she could see it was for the best.

She'd been on the precipice of giving up on Molly's. It was too much work for too little reward, and she'd wanted to start a family. There was no reason she should be working the hours she'd been working when Jackson had the means to easily take care of them both.

In the end, Molly's had been a godsend.

Because she hadn't used the money he'd left in her account. Because she'd been too hurt and angry and upset to accept being bought off. And because it had given her the strength to transform from an insecure girl into a strong woman who knew her worth.

She'd packed her stuff that evening then moved it and herself out of the apartment the following morning, living in her office in the bakery until she could afford her own apartment, paid with her own money.

She'd become someone she could be proud off.

A capable businesswoman, a kind human being, a kickass baker.

Not a weak female who'd just roll over and be whatever Jackson wanted her to be.

And while she blamed him for leaving, for hurting her in such a dramatic and unnecessary way, part of her also felt grateful, because she was a different person today than she'd been four years before. Because she was a better, stronger person.

"Then why are you here hiding in the kitchen instead of dealing with the man?" she muttered to herself.

Because she might be stronger, but she wasn't immune to all that was Jackson Davis.

The voice that made her stomach dip, the body she'd known

so intimately, the memories of all the wonderful things they'd shared.

It filled her with *so* much longing.

Hence her hiding.

"Damn," she muttered and sucked in a breath, knowing she needed to go out there and deal with him. The rush had died down, the cases needed to be refilled, she needed to give Jeanine her first break, and she needed to get this conversation over with Jackson—

The timer for her final pan of rolls dinged.

Thank the baking gods.

Couldn't have that conversation right now. She had rolls to pull out, more pastries to bake, Jeanine to give a break, soup to get simmering. Jackson Davis would just have to wait.

Of course, what she didn't take into account was that Jackson didn't much like waiting.

FOUR

Jackson

HE'D SPENT the last hours biding his time.

Well, biding his time along with putting a few things in place. The reason he'd called off his wedding four years ago hadn't mysteriously disappeared, so he needed to put a few measures in place.

He hadn't had the means then.

But he had them now.

What he needed to consider was if those means were worth the risk of what they might bring into Molly's life.

His cell buzzed with a call, but the door Molly had disappeared behind after her employee had arrived swung open at the same moment, and he immediately forget about the phone, about his reasons for leaving, about his current means. Jackson could think of *nothing* except for how much he wanted Molly.

How much he'd missed her.

How much he'd missed out on.

The longing was sharp, a painful jab to his heart.

God, she was pretty and sweet and had once loved him like

no one else had ever done so. Leaving her had been the hardest thing he'd ever done, trailed a close second by staying away, by not contacting her to beg her for forgiveness. He'd kept discreet tabs on her, just to make sure she was safe, and those reports from his security combined with the risk he presented to her were what gave him the strength to not come back.

Until now.

Until the papers had been delivered, demanding he excise himself from the final hold he had on her life.

He couldn't cut that tie.

And now that he'd seen her again, seen what she built . . . *fuck*, he was so incredibly proud of her, proud of what she'd built. Without him. On her own. She'd always been smart and capable, but she'd lacked confidence. Jackson hadn't minded that, which probably made him an asshole.

But the woman in front of him wasn't just sweet and warm. She was comfortable in her skin, filling the space with an air of competence.

This Molly was different than the woman he'd almost married.

She was more.

Because he'd left.

Which then bore the question of whether or not he should just leave again. If he came back, would he ruin that?

He watched her check the case then disappear back through the door. His cell buzzed again, but he still didn't glance at it. She would come back and then—

She emerged with a large tray held in both arms, efficiently filling the rows of the case with a variety of pastries and sandwiches. After, she flipped a screen and turned the menu to reveal the lunch offerings then smiled at the petite brunette behind the counter who nodded, smiled back, and disappeared into the kitchen.

Jackson studied Molly's even motions, the way she moved. He knew she did it without thinking—wiping down the counter-tops, the register, scanning then restocking napkins and silver-ware on the unit that held the supplies, before making a sweep of the dining room with a gray plastic tub and collecting leftover mugs and plates then cleaning off the tables and picking up small plastic placards with numbers on them. In less than ten minutes the space was clean and ready for lunch.

Well, everywhere except where he sat.

The employee had come over to gather up Ronnie's plate and mug earlier, but she hadn't wiped down the pale white wood with him sitting there, and Molly had certainly given his table a wide berth before returning back behind the counter.

His phone buzzed again, and he glanced down, saw it was his assistant. Again. The office was probably freaking out. He didn't take days off, let alone disappear without his computer. Frankly, he was scared to think of what his inbox would look like when he got back to his office, the minimal replies he'd done via his cell akin to trying to put out a forest fire with an eye dropper.

The final patrons got up from the last occupied table and left. They disappeared out the front door, the quiet tinkling of the bell cheerful. And that was the only bit of cheerful in the whole space because when Jackson glanced toward the register, the look Molly gave him was chilly.

Probably, wondering why he didn't just sign the papers and follow them out.

He should.

He wasn't going to.

He'd done a lot of things wrong when it came to Molly and if he was going to fix that, then he needed to level with her.

Well, first, it would be good if he were able to get her to listen to him.

At least long enough to level with her, because if she didn't understand why he'd done what he'd done, if she didn't forgive him then he . . .

Would leave?

Everything inside him had stilled.

He'd done that. He'd buried himself in work, he'd eschewed his family, women, friends. He'd left everything behind.

And what had that gotten him?

Absolutely fucking nothing.

Well, he was done with nothing.

The papers arriving on his desk were a timely reminder that this was his chance to make things right. If Molly didn't want to listen to him, to forgive him, well, he wasn't leaving. He'd make her understand, make her realize he'd *had* to do what he'd done.

Make her understand that he hadn't wanted to, but that things had gotten complicated and . . .

He needed to make her see that things would be different now.

He *would* make her see that.

Decided, he stood, detouring to the table when the phone rang, picking up the plates and mugs, depositing them into the gray bin she'd carried around, grabbing the towel and spray she'd used to wipe the table, and giving everything a good clean.

He couldn't remember the last time he'd so much as cleaned up after himself. His dirty dishes were efficiently swept away, his toilet and sink scrubbed, his clothes picked up from the floor and laundered, his food prepared and placed in front of him fresh and hot no matter the hour he stumbled in from his office.

Coddled.

Surrounded by people.

And yet, alone.

Molly had never made him feel alone. She'd seen him as a

person, not a meal ticket, as someone to love rather than a commodity, as—

She'd loved him, and he'd had to shit on that love to make sure she stayed alive.

Now, he would do anything to have that love back.

He *was* going to do anything to get it back.

FIVE

Molly

SHE SAW Jackson get up and took advantage of the phone ringing to turn her back on him, relief pouring through her when the bell tinkled, signaling his exit.

Thank God.

He was a stubborn man, but she'd gone toe-to-toe with him plenty. He knew he couldn't out-stubborn her.

He'd sign the papers. Be done. Leave like he was so fucking good at.

Good riddance.

And no, that wasn't a fucking slice of disappointment she felt as she hung up the phone and carefully made a few final notes on the large catering order.

She'd been done with Jackson four years ago. She was still finished with him—

"I can't wait to get my tongue on your sweet treat."

Velvet. Rasp. Honey down her spine. A heatwave between her thighs. Molly spun and saw that she was wrong. Jackson hadn't left. He stood just feet away, leaning against the counter, one ankle crossed over the other and looking altogether too sexy for her own good. Tall and lean with narrow hips and defined arms, he was more swimmer than bodybuilder. But that was fine. That was her preference, her type.

Jackson Davis was her kryptonite.

But she wasn't a weakling, wasn't susceptible to a line that should have been sleazy and creepy, and instead threatened to melt her from the inside out. She had spine—spine that had become lined with steel over the last few years. Steel she took advantage of in that moment. "You're a fucking pig," she snapped.

He grinned.

Her stomach went a little more melty.

No, she wasn't proud of it. But thus was the power of Jackson. Her pussy knew exactly what he could do for it and was critically aware that it had been four years since her last orgasm of the Davis variety.

And those orgasms were special. He didn't need a road map to find her clit, his tongue was fucking magical, and . . . he knew her body almost better than she did.

Pathetic?

Probably.

Had she reaped the benefits during their time together?

Hell-fucking-yes, she had.

And there he stood, still grinning, not upset at her snapping, not pissed that she'd called him a pig. But then again, he'd always reacted that way. Provoking her then seeming to gobble up her anger, as though he craved her fury.

Her nipples perked up at the memory.

Pathetic round two.

She sighed. "Why are you here?" she asked, dropping her hands to the counter and letting her head fall forward as she rolled out her shoulders.

Silence.

Molly glanced up after a long moment, saw that he'd moved, but just as she processed that Jackson wasn't in front of her, that he might have gone, she sensed him behind her. His spicy scent surrounded her, and she started to spin.

But he caught her shoulders, stopped her motion. "I got you, honey."

Then those hands slid up slightly and began massaging the tight muscles there. She knew she should stop him, knew that with every brain cell she possessed, but the second he touched her, all common sense faded.

Because it felt good to have him touch her.

And seriously, how fucked up was she that it felt good to have this man touch her?

He knew exactly where her muscles ached, how the pain radiated into her neck, down her right arm. He remembered how hard to press so the knots went away, but not so hard as to hurt her.

He. Remembered.

Her spine softened, body instinctively arching to brush her ass against his pelvis, hearing his breath hiss out.

She got wet.

Just that easily.

But it was always like that with him. One touch and she was hot for him. One touch and she was hot enough to almost make her forget that she hated this man who had his hands on her.

"I didn't want to leave you," he murmured into her ear.

Cold washed over her, that heat gone in an instant. She spun, knocked his hands away. "Don't fucking touch me," she hissed. "Don't you *fucking* touch—"

"Baby—"

"No," she said, ice in her veins. "You don't get to call me

that. You don't get to put your hands on me. Not when you left like you did. Not when you—"

"Molly—"

"Leave me the fuck alone, Jackson." She shoved him back a step. "Just leave. You're really fucking good at that." Another shove, pushing him clear of the counter. "I don't need you in my life." One more and he was out from behind it, back on the customer side. "I don't need you here. I don't want—"

"They were going to kill you."

Her hands, raised and ready for another push, dropped to her sides. Her jaw fell open. Of all the excuses she could have imagined him to come up with, that was right up there with the last thing she would have expected him to say.

He hesitated then took a step closer, moving behind the counter again, and his voice dropping. "I got mixed up in a bad deal with some bad people. I realized it, but I was in deep." Another step. "Baby, I thought I could handle it, could get myself, my business out without any consequences . . . but then they involved you."

Molly froze.

"You," he whispered, taking another step toward her, until they were almost touching. "I couldn't let them involve you."

"H-how—" She cleared her throat. "How did they—?"

An expression crossed his face, one that she now realized she'd seen a lot during those final months they been together. Warring. He was warring with himself. But then he pulled out his cell, tapped on the screen a few times then held it out to her.

She'd just reached to take it when the bell above the door dinged.

They both whirled, saw that a group of women were bustling in. They were regulars, had been coming in since not long after she'd opened. Seeing Jackson behind the counter, they froze and Abby, a brunette with a baby on her hip, asked, "Are you okay, Molly?"

She forced herself to smile. "I'm good. You guys go ahead and take your normal table. Jeanine will come out to get your drinks." Then she took Jackson's hand and tugged him through the swinging door, finding her employee washing her hands.

"I'm just finishing . . ." Jeanine trailed off, no doubt stunned by the Tall, Dark, and Handsome suddenly appearing in the kitchen.

Another forced smile. "This is Jackson. We'll be in my office. Can you cover Abby and company? Michelle will be in for the lunch rush in just a few minutes."

Mutely, Jeanine nodded. But didn't move.

"They're at their usual table," Molly prompted.

Jeanine blinked, eyes flying from over Molly's head—and probably from Jackson's face—down to Molly's. "Got it," Jeanine said, and with another long, lingering look above Molly's head, disappeared through the door leading to the front of house.

"You do table service now?" Jackson asked.

She tugged his hand again, leading him toward her office. "Just for a few regulars."

Silence.

Her eyes slanted up to his, but she couldn't read the emotion there. "What?"

"You have regulars now."

Yeah, she did.

"Fuck, honey, you did it."

Her lungs seized. Just straight up froze in her chest, stopped moving, stopped functioning . . . because he was proud. She could hear it so damned clearly in his tone.

A shake of her head.

It didn't matter if he were proud of her. He'd left—

But maybe he hadn't wanted to go—?

Didn't matter.

But maybe it did. Hell . . . she didn't know anything except that she had to finish this discussion, that spending five minutes with Jackson might give her clarity and let her finally move on with her life. She was tired of just living for the bakery. She wanted more. But when Jackson had left, she'd built a wall around herself, an impenetrable barrier between her inner self and the superficial. She could charm an unhappy patron in a flash, had created a happy and relaxed work environment for her employees, but she hadn't opened herself up to the world. It was all fluff while keeping her vulnerable center safe.

She hadn't realized that she'd reached her office, that she'd stopped outside the door until Jackson's front came very close to her back, hand lifting to turn the handle and push open the door.

Heat on her spine.

Spice in her nose.

Longing between her thighs.

Blinking, she forced her feet to move, to enter her office, to cross around her desk and put some space between them, to give her a few seconds to clamp down on the effect his body had on hers.

She was a businesswoman. She had spine. She wasn't a weakling when it came to her desires.

But *how* she wanted to be.

Tamping down the urge and lifting her chin, she settled into her office chair, waving an imperious hand at the wooden one in front of her desk.

Jackson's lips twitched.

Then he ignored her wave, ignored the chair, and rounded her desk, propping his hip on it. "Molly," he murmured.

And she realized she'd made a critical error. Now, he was

between her and the exit. Now he was close, and she *wanted*.
Now . . . he held out his cell again.

She saw what was on the screen and the longing disappeared.

She saw the image and the bottom fell out of the world she thought she knew.

She saw the image, and so many pieces fell into place.

SIX

Jackson

HE REALIZED about two heartbeats after Molly saw what was on the screen that he'd bungled this.

Words would have been better than the image that had been the final straw.

The photograph had convinced him to leave her.

It was of Molly, taken in her kitchen four years before. The construction on the bakery had just been completed, and everything was new and shiny. But that wasn't the part that had made him pull the plug on their relationship. No, the reason he'd finally capitulated to the threats he'd been receiving with ever-increasing frequency was because of the red dot centered on her forehead, and the angle of the photograph.

They'd been in her shop.

They'd had a gun trained on her.

And his Molly had been wearing her headphones, her gaze on the dough on the table in front of her as she carefully deposited perfect slices of apples. She'd had a smile on her face, completely oblivious to the fact that a bullet could have torn through her skull.

A smile on her face when a gun had been pointed at her head.

He'd received that image the morning of the wedding.

And that was the moment he'd stopped trying to handle things on his own. That was the moment he called in the best, most expensive security he could afford for Molly. That was the moment he'd contacted the authorities.

And *that* was the moment he'd known he had to cut Molly loose.

In a way that was public.

In a way that made it absolutely clear he no longer had feelings for her.

In a way that made it certain she'd keep her distance, that she wouldn't bring herself back into the crosshairs of the. Fucking. Russian. Mafia.

Who knew that finding a long-awaited investor for his software company would be his undoing?

Fuck. He'd been so thrilled to finally have been able to roll out his new product.

He just didn't realize that doing so would put the woman he loved at risk from a corrupt foreign power who had no compunction about killing anyone in order to get their way.

"Wh-what is this?"

"It's why I left, Mol."

Pale green eyes on his. "I-I don't understand."

"I fucked up, sweetheart," he said. "I accepted some money from people I shouldn't have then dismissed the threats until they made it clear that I *couldn't* dismiss them." With that photo.

She dropped the cell to her desk, pushed up from her chair,

and paced away from him. Five steps from him she stopped, spun around. "When?"

"What?"

"When did you find this out?"

His brows drew down. "They sent the picture the morning of the wedding."

Her eyes slid closed then opened slowly, understanding in their peridot depths. "That's why you didn't show."

"I couldn't."

"This wasn't the first threat."

Her words weren't a question, but rather a statement, and he knew he owed her nothing less than the absolute truth. "No."

"Ah." Molly tilted her head back and was so still that she could have been a statue. But then she released a long, shaking breath. "And is there a reason that you didn't tell me that any of this was going on?"

The question was deceptively calm.

"I—"

It was probably just as well that she only let him get that one syllable out. Because he *didn't* have a good reason, other than the fact that he'd thought he was doing the right thing by protecting her.

"Your life was threatened. *My* life was threatened," she said, pushing past him and pacing again. "And you thought what? That I couldn't handle knowing? That I was too weak to know the truth?" She turned, closed the distance between them, and jabbed a finger into his chest. "I was going to be your wife. We were supposed to be partners, and the fact that our lives were at risk didn't register even a mention on your list of things you should talk to me about?"

She had a valid point. One he hadn't quite grasped until that exact moment.

"Baby—"

"Molly," she corrected.

"Molly," he said. "You're right." He reached for her hand, but she stepped back, not allowing the contact. "*Of course*, you're right. I wasn't thinking clearly about any of it. Everything got so big and out of control so quickly, and . . . I didn't know what to do."

"No."

He blinked. "No?"

She shook her head. "No, Jackson. You didn't keep this from me because you were scared or were trying to protect me. Or not *only* for those reasons," she added when he opened his mouth to reply. "You didn't think I could handle it."

He froze, started to tell her that, no, he hadn't thought that. Except . . .

This Molly, the one standing in front of him, the one who was so capably running a business, who was taking this news without hysteria and tears, without fury, was a very different Molly from the one he'd been engaged to. *That* Molly had been a little fragile, already under stress from the wedding and the new business. That Molly had loved him with a depth he'd never doubted . . . and if he was admitting it, he'd liked that devotion.

It had fed his ego to have someone so utterly committed to him. He'd *liked* that she'd almost been more involved in his life than her own, that she knew what clients he was meeting with every day, that she sent deliveries to his office tailored to what they preferred. He liked that she'd made dinner every night, that she had picked up his dry cleaning, that he'd never once had to make a run for food or stop at the grocery store on the way home from work.

Fuck. He was an even bigger asshole than he'd thought.

She sighed, dropped into her chair, leaning her head back and closing her eyes. "Anything else?"

"What?" His gut was churning from what he'd just realized, guilt swelling within him, a wave that had begun when he'd received the papers, one that had continued to gain height as he'd debated coming to the bakery, then had grown bigger as he'd seen what she'd built. One that was pounding into him, trapping him against the rocks that lined the shore as it beat against him again and again and *again*. He'd hurt her without realizing it, hadn't appreciated her, had taken and taken and would have *continued* to take if he hadn't broken things off.

He would have sucked her dry until she was nothing more than a shell of herself.

And that made him fucking despicable.

"Is there anything else you kept from me?" she asked, eyes still closed.

Throat tight, he said, "No." It was the truth. There was nothing except for the fact that the photograph had shown him how much of a close call she'd dodged when he'd called off the wedding.

Molly sighed again, eyes opening, those pretty green eyes locking with his. "I hated you for what you did. For a long time, I absolutely hated you." She pushed up from her chair. "But honestly? You did me a favor, Jackson. I wasn't . . . fully formed four years ago. I was living off you, making my whole life yours. I was *weak*." One step and she was close enough that her scent surrounded him.

Sweet. Fuck, she always smelled so damned sweet.

But also . . . in that moment, he'd never felt more sure that she was too fucking good for him.

Another step, her moving past him toward the door again.

He'd spent the day getting his fill. He'd leveled with her. He'd made it clear it wasn't her fault.

Should he have done that four years ago? Fucking, *of course*, he should have.

Could he build a time machine and go back, fix what he'd done? No.

But could he make it better for her now, take a worry off her shoulders, remove himself from her life, one he had no right interfering in? Yes.

Jackson heard the *click* just as he opened his mouth to announce that he was going to sign the papers and remove himself once and for all. He frowned and spun toward the sound.

"You hurt me."

Then, suddenly, Molly was there, within arm's reach, looking so fucking beautiful that he couldn't imagine how he could have ever left her.

But he'd been a different man then.

"I know I did," he said. "And I'm sorry. I was wrong . . . about so many things."

Her expression hardened. She took another step toward him. "Yes."

"If I could change it, if I could go back and—"

She rose on tiptoe, eyes coming level with his, hurt swimming in their depths. "You can't go back." A beat. "*We* can't go back, Jackson."

"I—"

Molly kissed him.

SEVEN

Molly

SHE WAS PROBABLY AN IDIOT.

Hell, she was *definitely* an idiot.

But he'd shown her that photograph, she'd seen the dot on her forehead, and terror had gripped her for long enough that her lungs had frozen and she'd felt her mind swim from a lack of oxygen.

It was a violation, and just because it was a violation from four years ago didn't mean she couldn't understand.

Jackson hadn't been thinking.

He hadn't broken it off because of her.

And . . . she'd felt no little amount of relief.

Not her. Not her. Not—

He'd gone still when her lips had touched his, rigid like a metal statue, his hands at his sides, their bodies not touching except for their mouths. But now he unfroze and exploded into a flurry of motion that sent all thoughts of idiocy and relief and *not her* from her mind.

Because this was Jackson, and this was her . . . and *this* had never been their problem.

His hands came up, one clamping onto her hip, the other sliding up her spine to weave into the messy ponytail at the base of her neck that was containing her riotous brown curls. A second later that elastic disappeared, and his fingers were combing through her hair, the pads resting against her scalp.

God, she'd missed that, missed him cradling her against him, angling her head just slightly so their lips were perfectly aligned. Missed how just the touch of his mouth against hers somehow righted everything in the universe.

Then his tongue brushed against the seam of her lips.

She didn't think, didn't hesitate, just parted and let him in. Their tongues tangled and stroked. He tugged her more firmly against his body and then they kissed and kissed and *kissed*. Eventually, though, he started to slow the flurried movements of his tongue, began to loosen the grip on her hip, ease his hand from her hair.

No.

She didn't want him to stop, to slow, to pull back.

She leaned in, throwing her arms around his neck, plastering herself against his chest.

He tore his lips away. "Mol—"

"Kiss me, Jackson. Make me forget."

A long moment of hesitation, his deep chocolate eyes locked onto hers, but then she tilted her pelvis, brushed against the hard length of his erection, and he groaned, banded his arms more tightly around her then dropped his head.

Lips on lips.

Hard against soft.

Duel moans. Hers because this was as right as she'd felt in the last four years. His because . . . well, she hoped he felt an inkling of the same.

But Molly didn't stop to process or think. She weaved her hands into *his* hair, climbed up his body, wrapped her legs around his waist, and kissed him. She nipped at his bottom lip, tilted *his* head, swept her tongue deep to taste the spiced heat of his mouth.

The flavor of the cinnamon gum he preferred.

The bitter tang of the coffee he must have drank that morning.

The faintest hint of mint from his toothpaste.

Ambrosia.

Jackson.

Right.

He straightened from the desk, lifting her into his arms and spun, shooting an arm out, sending her keyboard clattering to the floor, dumping the cup of pencils, the small wooden cylinders hitting the tile with a series of rapid *tap tap taps*. The next second she was on her back, splayed out like she was a plate of chocolate cookies placed in the center of a group of very hungry, PMS-ing women.

Hot eyes, reddened lips. An erection outlined by the thin material of his slacks.

She wanted him, wanted him to make her feel like she used to, wanted to forget everything that had happened.

For one moment, she just wanted to feel good.

"Mol—"

"Fuck me, Jackson," she said, heart pounding, breaths coming in short bursts. Her need was on a razor's point, almost painful. This close to him, so long since she'd felt anything as remotely strong as the pull they had when they were together. "I need you to just fuck me."

His fingers tightened on her hips, jaw tightening. "That's not—"

"Help me," she moaned. "Help me forget." She wrapped her legs around his waist, drawing him close.

He groaned, thrust against her then stopped, head hanging, breath in rapid gusts. "Baby, we—"

"Please." She reached for him. "Please, Jackson."

Only the briefest hesitation before he bent, lips pausing a hairsbreadth from hers. "Okay, baby." He brushed her mouth. "I got you."

He reached for the button of her jeans, flicked it open, and slid his hand inside.

"Oh fuck," she moaned. That hot, roughened palm sliding under her underwear, fingers slipping through her wet pussy was the best ever.

Well, until his thumb circled her clit and pressed.

Hard.

She arched off the desk, nipples beaded and aching, moisture pooling between her thighs, which kept trying to spread but were hindered by the stiff material of the denim. Jackson slipped his hand free, and she made a noise in protest, but just as the sound passed her lips, he reared back and yanked off her sneakers.

They hit the floor one after another, were followed by her jeans, by her underwear.

And then Jackson was on his knees, shouldering her thighs apart, mouth descending . . .

"Fuuuck," she breathed, head clonking back against the desk.

No one could tongue fuck her like Jackson could.

He slid his tongue through her labia, stopping to suck at one spot on the right side that never failed to make her squirm and groan, to ratchet her arousal to epic proportions before continuing up, kissing and licking . . . and sucking her clit like it was a hard candy he was determined to finish before the principal caught him with the sweet treat between his lips.

I can't wait to get my tongue on your sweet treat.

What should have been the cheesiest, worst line in the history of all lines, sent heat skittering down her spine for a second time.

He had his tongue on her and when he murmured, "So fucking sweet," against her pussy, Molly imploded.

Just that easily.

Because with Jackson, it had always been heat and speed, ease and comfort, allowing herself to be swallowed by the wave of his presence.

Pleasure exploded from her center, flying through her limbs, pulsing outward, filling her with fire. She moaned loudly and found his hand covering her lips to stifle the sound, even as his tongue coaxed her through to the other side, gently caressed her down from the precipice.

That wave covered her, comforted, even as it sucked her under.

It was only when he reached for her panties and started to tug them over her feet that she realized what he was about.

Stopping.

"Jackson," she said.

"I'm going, baby."

Was he fucking kidding? He was going to blow back into her life, eat her out like it was his fucking job, and then leave her wanting him?

No.

Not this time.

She was driving this.

And she wanted the man's cock inside her.

Maybe it was selfish. Maybe it was using him. Maybe she

was pissed and hurting and overwhelmed and this was the stupidest thing she could do.

But fuck it all.

She'd spent too long being unselfish with this man.

For once, she could reach for what *she* wanted.

For once, that could be okay.

Molly moved, kicking off the underwear, pushing off the desk, and grabbing the front of Jackson's button-down. She yanked him against her and rose up to slant her lips across his.

He kissed her back and it was all teeth and tongue, nipping and stroking, sparking her sated desire back into an inferno. He grabbed her hips, pulling her snuggly against him, grinding the hardness of his cock against her.

She reached down, opened the button of his slacks, yanking at the zipper, fighting with the material until . . . *finally*.

His cock was hard and scorching her hand.

Molly shoved at his pants, getting them past his hips before lifting a leg and wrapping it around his waist, angling him until he was positioned just right.

"Baby—"

She tilted her pelvis and took him inside.

Fuck. Yes.

They both hissed out a breath as he stretched her wide, the burn of him amping up her pleasure. It had been so long, and this felt so fucking right.

She jumped slightly, wrapped the other leg around him, taking him deeper.

"Fuck me, honey," she moaned, arching back, feeling him bottom out, a harsh guttural curse vibrating through her.

Then there were no more words. No delays or hesitations.

His hands came to her ass, and he spun them, pinned her between the wall and his chest.

And then he moved.

He pounded into her, a little hard, a little rough, not smooth and sweet and gentle in the least. It was fast and intense . . . and it was the best fucking ever.

Literally.

The. Best. *Fucking.* Ever.

The hard circles of his shirt buttons were digging into her chest, the strap of her apron was abrading the skin of her neck, his zipper scratched her thighs . . . and those little pains didn't take anything away. In fact, they heightened the experience, elevated it. He kept thrusting, hard and thick and hot, his scorching breath puffing against her skin, his groans vibrating through her.

"Fuck, baby," he gritted out. "Baby, tell me you're there with me."

"Almost," she panted. "I need—"

He knew what she needed even before she finished the sentence. He altered the angle of his thrusts, so that each time he bottomed out, he rubbed against her clit, and then he shifted one hand, fingers sliding along the crease of her ass, moving in, pressing against her with his thumb until he was fucking both of her holes, finger and cock moving in unison.

"I'm—" She broke off. "Jackson— *Fuck!*"

She was there, her orgasm exploding through her.

He ground into her once, twice, a third time and groaned, holding deep, his cock pulsing as he came inside her.

They stayed like that for a long time, Jackson still hard and planted deep, their breathing rapid and staccato, their skin sticky with sweat.

But the longer they stayed like that, the harder it was to keep her mind focused on just feeling. Memories kept creeping to the forefront of her mind. How she'd felt when he hadn't shown up at the church. The panic of searching the hospitals. How broken she'd been after the scene in the police station.

Her breathing had been slowing, but now it started to speed up again, horror washing through her.

This was either her getting swept along with the tsunami that was Jackson or it was her taking advantage of a man's guilt just so she could have a couple of orgasms. "You—"

Jackson moved without her finishing the sentence, slipping out, steadying her as she found her feet.

Then her panties.

She slid them up her thighs, made a grab for her jeans and yanked them up her legs.

"We shouldn't have done that."

He'd stolen her words, taken what *she* should have said.

"You're right," she agreed then added, "You should go."

At the very least, she could say that.

Because if she told him to go then she wouldn't ask him to stay.

Jackson's eyes drifted up, moving to lock with hers, holding for a long, drawn-out moment. But he didn't ask to stay either.

He just finished doing up his pants, straightened the cuffs of his shirt, and headed for the door, pausing with his hand on the knob. "For what it's worth, I know that I did the wrong thing, and I'm sorry for that." He turned the handle, opened the door. "But I'm not sorry it kept you safe."

He stepped out into the hall, closed the wooden panel behind him.

"Not sorry," she muttered, doing up her own pants, smoothing her apron. "That sounds about right."

But she didn't mean the words.

Of course, she didn't.

And anyway, she was too wrapped up in the conflicting thoughts in her mind to really mean anything.

Was she the user or the usee?

So, instead of thinking about it further or the fact that she'd had to go to the bathroom to put in a tampon, rather than spending the remainder of the day with the reminder of Jackson dripping out from between her thighs, she took care of the problem, washed her hands, and deliberately ignored the random pulses of pleasure that continued to crop up as the hours passed.

Instead, in what was probably a sick circle of events, she spent the rest of the day making apple turnovers, the same ones she'd been making in the photograph that had torn them apart.

Only this time, there wasn't anyone around.

Or at least there wasn't anyone around who had the urge to shine a bright red laser on her forehead.

Molly was wrong about the last.

She just didn't find out how wrong until much later.

THE NEXT DAY she woke up early, got dressed, and stumbled through her morning, the early hours feeling all that much earlier because she'd hardly slept the night before.

Jackson Davis.

Not the bad guy she'd made him out to be.

Especially when, shortly after five in the morning, as Molly was finishing up loading the case in the front of the bakery, the bell chimed over the door and a young male in an expensive suit strode inside.

"Molly Miller?" he asked, approaching the counter.

"Yes?" she replied, confusion drawing her brows together.

"These are for you from Mr. Davis." He extended a manila envelope in her direction.

"What—?" she began to ask.

But by then she'd opened the flap and recognized what was inside.

The papers she'd had couriered to Jackson—signed,

although with an addendum saying she'd bought Jackson out for a dollar instead of the fair market price she'd offered previously.

Signed.

Done.

Out of her life.

Perfect. That was exactly what she wanted.

And if she thought that perhaps, deep down, she might not *actually* want Jackson out of her life for good, if it were the sliver of a thought, the barest thread of a wish, Molly was great at pretending she didn't see or feel it.

She was excellent at pretending.

She'd made it her life's work.

EIGHT

Jackson, A month later

HE STRODE out of his office after nine at night and bit back a curse when he saw the man waiting in the reception area.

"Dan," he said, shoving his cell into his pocket and coming to a stop. "Do you take some pleasure in sneaking into my office?"

This late at night, the building was locked down, the floor to his office doubly so.

Dan shrugged. "Gotta keep your security on their toes."

At the mention of security, one of Jackson's expensive as hell security team members appeared in the hall, his body tensed and readied as though he were heading into battle. Jackson caught the man's gaze and shook his head. "We're fine."

Dan waited until the guard left, who backed slowly down the hall with a glare at the sneaky agent, before he turned to Jackson and gestured the opposite direction.

Jackson took the hint, led the way to the corner office that had become his home away from home. His company had recently taken over the top five floors of this building, retrofitting and modifying the space, and moving in just a few weeks before.

All at prime San Franciscan prices.

The location was more about the perception of power rather than actual power, but Jackson *had* managed to secure some truly reliable—and not criminal—investors in the last few years, ones that didn't want to use his product to conduct corporate espionage or to unleash an army of bots to try and divide the American people online.

He'd gotten better at discerning, and his business had grown.

But old problems persisted.

Case in point, the man in front of him.

"It's good to see you, Davis."

"I wish I could say the same, Plantain," he muttered, because apparently they were switching to last names. He strode through the door to his office, leaned back against his desk and tried to ignore the memory of doing the same on Molly's desk . . . and what had happened after. "What are you doing here? Pretending to be in town to watch your sister play again?"

Dan's sister was a goalie for the San Francisco Gold, the newest expansion team in the NHL.

But hockey didn't run in the family.

Dan was part of a nameless government agency, a member of a team that had shown up about eight hours after Jackson had called the FBI to report the threats and the dirty investors in his company.

He was also part of the team that was supposed to have already taken down the investor and dismantled the criminal organization, a clan of the Russian mob called the Mikhailova, that had provided it.

"You're clearly not a sports man," Dan said. "It's not even hockey season."

Jackson sighed, didn't take the bait. Truth was, he *wasn't* much of a sports man. He was too busy saving the business he'd almost torpedoed and then doing his limited part to root out the bad guys involved. "Why are you here?"

Dan sprawled into one of the chairs and announced, "We've had a setback."

Fury tore through him. "This shit was supposed to have been done two fucking years ago."

No sympathy on the agent's face. "Sorry to be the one to tell you this, but life doesn't always work out the way you want it."

Jackson cursed and thrust a hand through his hair. He knew that. He'd lived that life for the last four years, had tried to stop himself from having to live it for the previous year before that. All for nothing. In the end, he'd had to give everything important up anyway.

Molly gone.

His business in tatters.

"You are *not* going to tell me to make lemonade out of lemons."

"How about lemon cake?" Dan said, still sprawling though he smacked his lips. "Fuck, I love lemon cake. In fact, I could go for—"

"What's the setback?" Jackson said, interrupting him before he could go full soliloquy on the merits of lemon cake. Having heard more than a few of Dan's tangents over the years, he knew they were neither short nor particularly meaningful.

"You."

Jackson frowned. "What the fuck are you talking about?"

"You shouldn't have gone to see her, man," Dan said, and that one sentence twisted Jackson's stomach into knots.

He pushed up from the desk and got in Dan's face. Probably not the smartest thing, especially when he could see the outline of a weapon on the other man's hip. But fury had overshadowed common sense, at least for the moment "What. The. Fuck. Are you talking about?"

"They saw you go to her."

Jackson's heart seized and his throat constricted. "It's been four years."

"They saw."

"It was only a couple of hours." Hours riddled with both pleasure and guilt.

"Time doesn't matter with these guys."

"Fuck." He leaned back, paced the length of his office. "*Fuck!*" He turned back. "What are we going to do?"

"I've got protection on her."

Jackson snorted. "The same protection that resulted in her having a fucking gun pointed at her head?"

Dan sighed. "My advice is to continue staying away. Leave her to her life, make sure these guys know that she doesn't mean anything to you, make sure they don't use her to get to you. Leave her alone so she can be safe."

"I did that already, and it didn't work."

"You went back."

"I—" Jackson cut off his excuse. He'd been about to say he'd had to talk to her about the papers, but that was a lie. He could have signed and been done without seeing her. He could have left when she'd so clearly wanted him to. He could have not fucked her against the wall in the single best sexual experience of his life before finally abiding by her wishes and leaving. He'd ruined so much, taken so much—

"Just stay away."

How could he? He'd tried that for four years. Then one morning in her presence, and he was right back where he'd begun. Obsessing about Molly, thinking of her every waking moment, fighting with himself to not go back to the bakery, to not beg and plead and make her understand that his life without her was meaningless.

Maybe if he hadn't seen her, he could have continued to resist. Maybe the urge to go back wouldn't be so acute.

But he *had* gone back.

And now Jackson was in agony.

"You can't stay away, can you?" Dan asked quietly.

Silence.

Then, "No."

"Fuck." Dan pulled out his cell, considered for a few seconds then began typing. Within a half-minute of him hitting the final key and placing it on his thigh, there was a buzz, signaling a response. He nodded. "If I told you to give me three more months, could you do it?"

Jackson stifled a curse. *No*, he couldn't do it. But could he also risk Molly just because he might be in agony for another ninety days?

Also, no.

"Fuck, no, you can't," Dan muttered, typing on his cell again. "Okay, here's what we're going to do. *This* is no longer your office. Your office is the bakery. Your ass is in a chair at Molly's place anytime she's there. Your presence is known and expected and constant."

Jackson frowned.

"It's not a deterrent so much as a declaration. Molly is yours. If you're always there, they'll see she belongs with you. That they have to fuck with you to get to her."

More frowning. "They've made it pretty clear they don't mind fucking with me. Isn't this going to just unleash more shit onto her?"

"The shit's already coming, Jackson. But we can just use this to our advantage. Push them to make a move sooner than they're ready." Dan shoved his phone in his pocket. "It's not foolproof. It's dangerous. But the *whole* situation is dangerous. So, if you really can't give me a few months then you have to be prepared to be all in."

"I've *been* in. *Fuck*, Dan. I've done everything you've asked of me. I left the woman I loved. I stayed away from her for years." He paced away again. "I gave you access to my company, to every document and email and bank account. I did *everything—*"

"And you've got nothing to show for it," Dan said quietly. "I know, brother. I know what that's like."

"Fuck," he hissed, knowing that he had to make a decision.

Knowing the decision was already made.

Molly.

It was all for Molly.

He sucked in a breath, released it slowly. "Tell me exactly what I need to do."

NINE

Molly

ZERO-DARK THIRTY.

Stumbling out of bed.

Attempting to corral her hair, to pull on clothes that coordinated—sort of—shoes that matched—occasionally proving more difficult, especially when comparing black to navy.

Today, she settled with plain gray sneakers with jeans and a T-shirt that was emblazoned with the bakery's logo.

Easy. Simple.

Necessary.

She hadn't slept well since the day a month before when Jackson had walked back into her life, her dreams punctured by memories of him, by memories of *after* him.

Which made getting up at three-thirty in the morning seriously unforgiving.

Thankfully, she'd managed to hire a second baker, so her early mornings were now limited to the three middle days during the week—Tuesday, Wednesday, and Thursday.

Being able to sleep until six on the other days made it so she could function.

She may not be thriving, but at least she could function.

And she knew that was a win.

Head down, move forward, keep going, and things would be okay, wounds would heal, shattered hearts would be pieced back together, a spine would be strengthened and able to hold a head high.

Her coffee pot was already percolating, that first mug filled, her travel carafe next to it, readied for its own supply.

Molly made the switch, set the maker to go another time and it began rumbling, popping, and hissing as it filled the To-Go cup that was the second necessary piece of her wake-up routine.

The first being that initial mug ready to go.

She picked it up, blew on the hot liquid, then drank quickly, ignoring the burn of the too-hot coffee, relishing the spike as the caffeine hit her system, shaking the clouds from her mind and enabling her to locate her purse, keys, and cell.

By the time the travel carafe was full, her mug was empty, and she was awake enough to operate a motor vehicle.

She set the empty mug in the sink, grabbed her stuff—and the To-Go coffee—then headed out the front door of her duplex.

And almost mowed down a man.

The scream caught in her throat, then dissipated when she saw it was Jackson, her mouth dropping open.

What. The. Fuck?

Before she could unstick enough to verbalize that thought, he stepped close, *real* close, and brushed his mouth across her cheek, very near her ear, in which he whispered, "I'll explain in the car." Then he swept her purse from her hands, wrapped an arm around her waist and started leading her to a vehicle that was not hers.

She repeated. What. The. Fuck?

But when her feet started to skitter, to fight the forward motion, Jackson bent again and nipped her ear. "Don't fight me. It's not safe. Car, baby." Her eyes flew up, saw that his jaw was tight, his body stiff, even though his voice had been gentle . . . and so it seemed smarter in that moment to *not* argue, to just walk to his car.

To allow him to open the door and help her inside.

To wait until he'd started the engine and then pulled out of the spot to burst out with, "What the fuck, Jackson Davis?"

His gaze cut to hers then returned to the road, navigating the nearly empty streets with all the care of a professional driver navigating the world's most important race.

"I'm here," he stated calmly.

That was it. *I'm here.*

As though that were supposed to bring some clarity to the situation when he'd disappeared and come back then disappeared again—

You asked him to go.

Yeah, there was that.

So, she stifled the temper that only seemed to ramp when Jackson was around and forced herself to calmly ask, "Why are you here?"

Silence for an interminable stretch.

Then, "It goes against every grain in me to tell you this, when I feel like I should be protecting you, not telling you something that will make you terrified," he said, and just that precursor to the explanation was terrifying. Add in the careful tone, the stiffness in his jaw, his body, and the hairs on the back of her neck rose. "But I promised myself that I wouldn't carry anymore secrets. You deserve to know the truth of what's happening."

Molly swallowed hard then asked, "And what's the truth?"

"The truth is that when I came to the bakery a month ago, I brought you back into the focus of the Russian mafia."

Oh, fuck.

"When I came, when I stayed, they realized you still had value to me, and they'll exploit that connection to get what they want."

Double fuck.

"The government knows, they've been following you and protecting you since they found out from their source that you're back in the crosshairs, but they're also close to shutting this cell down, close to giving the group a death blow that will put them out of commission for many years, if not forever."

That was great. Eliminating the mafia forever sounded like a good thing.

Yet Molly couldn't help but focus on one word in particular. "Crosshairs?"

He pulled into the small parking lot of the bakery, slid his car into a spot, and turned to face her. "I'm sorry, baby. I didn't think they were still following me so closely. I hadn't heard from the government or gotten any threats from the mafia for more than a year. I'd thought they'd moved on from me or I would have never come to visit you."

Her hands were trembling, her heart pounding.

Crosshairs. Following. Government. Mafia. Threats.

It should have been the starting plot for a movie.

Instead, it had been Jackson's life for the last four years.

"Baby." He cupped her cheek. "Please know—"

She turned her head, met his chocolate eyes that looked so dark in the shadowed dimness of the early morning. "Why are you here?" she asked.

He frowned. "I—"

"No, I mean, today. *Now*. Why are you here this morning?"

"I need to be where you are."

Simple words she once would have given anything to hear. But now they seemed to have a different meaning.

"Because I'm in danger?"

He nodded.

Unbidden, her heart sank. "I see." She reached for her purse, slung it over one shoulder. "Let's go in. I can't get behind." She pushed out of the car, her travel carafe still in her hand, the contents untouched, but her brain all too awake.

More danger.

More martyring.

Only this time, instead of leaving, Jackson had forced himself to come back.

Being forced to spend time with a woman he'd left behind.

Every. Girl's. Dream.

She extracted her keys as she walked to the back door, slipping them into the lock, pulling open the heavy metal panel, pretending not to notice that Jackson was right behind her, his body inches from hers, the smell of cinnamon and mint tangling in her nose, her spine tingling with the urge to allow herself to melt back and lean against his hard chest.

Instead, she punched the code for the alarm, waited for him to trail her in, then hit the dead bolt she'd installed after he'd shown her the picture a month before.

Yes, *she'd* installed it. She'd gotten good with a drill over the years, and while she knew the lock wasn't foolproof, that it wasn't even the door through which the photograph was taken, it still gave her some peace of mind. No one was getting through the back door.

She stashed her purse in her office, grabbed an apron from the hook in the kitchen, then placed her phone in the cradle to start her morning playlist of whatever was upbeat and pop and could help her channel sweet and light vibes.

Because it reflected in sweet and light pastry dough.

Lie.

But also, she was the boss, her baked goods were the shit, and thus no one was going to argue with her. She got to listen to her saccharine music. She got to bake. And everyone else got to eat.

The fast beat blared to life through the wireless speakers as she washed her hands and started gathering ingredients.

Flour. Eggs. Yeast. Butter. Milk—

The music stopped.

She spun. Seriously? The man was invading her life. Not because he wanted her—not that *she* wanted *him* either, but still! He'd waylaid her outside her duplex, had bustled her to his car, and was only here because he felt guilty for bringing something down on her that he didn't have any control over.

"Why are you pissed?"

Molly froze. "Why am I pissed? *Why am I pissed?*" She threw her hands up, began weighing out flour into the giant stainless-steel bowl in front of her. "Oh, I don't know, maybe because my ex-fiancé has popped back into my life twice now in a month, after not seeing him for *years*. And only because he was pissed that I wanted him out of *my* life for good." She shook a little more flour out, checked the weight. "Or *maybe* that my ex just declared that he's staying around because he's got a misguided notion that he can protect me? Did you take a superhero military man course in the time we've been apart and can now go Captain America on any bad guys who might bother me?"

She set the bag of flour to the side, moved on to the yeast and milk, warming the latter, allowing the former to soak in the warm liquid while continuing to measure the remainder of the ingredients.

"No."

"So, what makes you think that you can protect me better than I can protect myself?"

Silence.

"I'll hire some security," she snapped. "Up our actual system here, take stronger precautions, but I don't need you, Jackson."

And she most especially didn't need him just because he felt obligated to protect her.

Once everything was weighed out, she went over and started the music again then headed to the sink to wash her hands for a second time.

Good hygiene was important.

But just as she'd picked up a knife to start cutting butter, the music cut off again.

Was he fucking kidding?

She slammed the knife down, spun to face him.

He came very close. "Still not sure why you're pissed, sweetheart."

"You—"

He bent. "The agent said I needed to be here, and I'm going to be. End of story."

The *agent* said he needed to be there.

Her heart pulsed with pain, but fury quickly trailed that pain. Jackson shouldn't be able to have this power over her. She shouldn't feel so much longing toward this man who'd broken her. And yet, it was there. Because no matter how much she fought it, an invisible thread tied them together.

Or at least tied her to him.

Because apparently, Jackson was only here out of some misguided notion of duty and because some government agent told him he should be.

They were over. Done. Four years and gone. Finished. Out

of her business with a spectacular goodbye fuck included as a Happy Meal prize.

Now she just needed to take a hacksaw to that thread and get him to leave.

And *then* she needed to bake some fucking rolls.

Jackson dropped his hands to her waist, jostled her lightly. She glanced up, had to force herself to not get lost in the melted chocolate of his eyes. "You can be pissed all you want. You can argue and launch your cookie sheets—"

"Sheet pans," she snapped, smacking his hands away and stepping back. "Or baking sheets, not cookie—"

A flash of white teeth, but he didn't reach for her again, just crossed his arms and leaned against the counter, seeming so calm and composed when she felt like there was a tornado exploding to life within her. "You can launch your *sheet pans* at my head all you want, but I'm not leaving."

She was tempted to go find a sheet pan, just so she could take him up on the offer. "I've heard that before." A beat. "Or no, I guess I actually *haven't* heard it because we never got to the *till death do us part* portion of the festivities."

Chocolate eyes cooled. Hardened. "I didn't want that."

"I know!" She slammed her hands down on the table, nearly upsetting the bowl of flour and not caring in the least.

"I *don't* think you know," he murmured. "I don't think you believe me when I say that not showing up at that church was the hardest thing I've ever done in my life. That I wanted nothing more than you—"

"Except, you *didn't!*" she screamed. "Because if you'd really wanted me then you would have come, or you would have *talked* to me earlier. You could have explained. You c-could—" She stopped talking, dropped her gaze to the flour, and focused on breathing, on just . . . breathing.

No tears.

No more fucking tears.

"I should have talked to you."

Molly snorted then started dumping ingredients into the industrial mixer. Flour in, salt in one corner, eggs, the milk, and bloomed yeast. Each part coming together, each part doing its job, each—

"I—"

She flicked the knob, drowning out the rest of Jackson's sentence.

Which was just as well. Because that tornado was still spinning inside her, upsetting all the carefully built structures within her—the confidence she'd laid brick by brick, the insecurities she'd buried deep, the—

He turned off the mixer.

She saw red, fingers came up to grab the bowl, but instead of launching it at his head like she really wanted to, Molly walked a few feet and chucked it into the sink.

"You don't understand—"

And that was when she lost it.

"I have a fucking job to do!" she screamed. "Why can't you understand that? Maybe the job isn't something you think is valuable, but I do, and I'm going to do it without you interfering. Okay? *Okay?* Or is that too much for me to ask, you arrogant, egotistical, selfish bastard—"

"I'm not leaving," he said and crossed his arms, jaw tight, stubborn expression on his face.

"Fine." She tossed her hands up. "Fine! But I have shit I need to do. Things you're preventing me from finishing because you're in my face and turning off my music and mixer. If you want to park your ass at one of my tables, fine. Then *park* it." She forced herself to take a breath. "Just stop sabotaging my business, shut your fucking mouth, and let me do *my* fucking job."

His expression went unfathomable. "You've changed."

She rolled her eyes. "Real shocker there. People grow and change and—"

"No, you've changed because of me."

A sigh. "No, Jackson. I changed for *me*. I changed because I realized I wasn't fully formed, that I couldn't truly be a partner in anything—in business, in love, in friendship—unless I finally became my own person." She turned the mixer back on. "So, kudos to you for making that happen," she said over the noise.

"I'm sorry for my part in it. Sorry for all the mistakes I made." He moved toward her, but this time didn't touch the mixer. "I've changed, too. I wasn't fully formed, either. I was a taker and as much as I would have loved to make you my wife, I would have drained you dry."

Her breath caught.

His fingers brushed lightly over her cheek. "I didn't— I'm glad I didn't have the chance."

He stepped back. "I'll be here for as long as the threat is. And then I'll excise myself from your life as painlessly as possible."

That didn't sound painless.

It sounded horrible.

But by the time she realized that, he'd turned, flicked on the music, then picked up a messenger bag she hadn't seen him carry in and slipped out to the front of house.

The lights flicked on.

Her heart pulsed to the beat of the music.

But today, it didn't make her feel light and sweet.

And neither were her rolls.

In fact, she had to throw the whole batch out and start again.

TEN

Jackson

WELL, no one could say he hadn't deserved the verbal lashing that Molly had dished out.

He did and then some.

His only hope was that she'd gotten out the hurt, that she'd heard his apology, that they could navigate their way forward.

Because while he was impressed with the woman who'd built this place, who'd now opened two additional locations to much success, that angry female who'd unloaded on him in the kitchen wasn't anything like the Molly he'd fallen in love with.

She was more.

And yet, he knew that if she couldn't let go of what had happened between them, they had no hope of moving forward.

They couldn't keep rehashing and tearing each other apart.

They needed to navigate new terrain.

Which meant that *he* needed to help her see they could have something great between them again. That it might not be the same as what they'd had, but that it could be more and wonderful and—

His cell rang.

He glanced at the screen, saw that the number was Dan's, and picked up. "Yeah?"

A beat of hesitation, then, "You okay?"

Pinning his phone between his shoulder and ear, he began pulling out the things he'd need to work from Molly's shop—laptop, mobile hotspot (since he couldn't trust his business to an unsecured WIFI network), pad and paper (because sometimes his mind worked better via old school methods)—and replied, "Fine. What did you need?"

Another pause. This time longer.

"What, Plantain? I've got shit to do—"

"That was a pretty intense fight," he said. "I just wanted to make sure—"

Jackson almost dropped his phone. "You were inside?"

"No. I . . ." He sighed. "We have eyes and ears inside the bakery. Just to make sure—"

Dan kept talking, but Jackson stopped listening, or stopped *actively* listening, because he was replaying the fight with Molly, hearing the soundtrack of what she'd said, what *he'd* said, and wondering how many fucking people had just heard them airing their shit.

And fuck, did they have eyes and ears in Molly's office? Had they seen them?

"How long?" he asked, not giving a shit that he'd interrupted.

"What?"

"How long have you been surveilling her here?"

"Since last night. The team put them in while I came to your office," Dan said. "There was an active threat, and—"

Jackson stifled his sigh of relief.

They might have heard and seen him getting yelled at, but

at least they hadn't seen Molly when they'd been together in her office.

"I understand," he said. "It's smart, but I need to tell Molly. I promised her I wouldn't keep any secrets, and I'm going to keep my word."

"I was afraid you'd say that," Dan told him. "I get it, man, I really do. But know if she freaks out and has us take the audio and visual out then we won't be able to protect her properly, or *you* for that matter."

Jackson didn't have a death wish, but his well-being was much lower on his priority list than making sure whatever risk had bled over from his life into Molly's was taken care of.

He wanted her safe.

He wanted her happy.

He wanted to figure out a way to move forward.

"I'll do my best to help her understand that it's important for her safety," he said. "And temporary."

"Temporary is a good point to focus on," Dan said. "That and chocolate—" He broke off. "Okay, she probably has plenty of chocolate. How about alcohol? Or really expensive shoes?"

"Alcohol and kitchen accessories are my safest best, I think," he muttered, hitting the button to boot up his laptop. "The woman can never turn away from a new spoon."

A beat, then, "Kinky."

Jackson snorted. "So, were you just calling me for a heart-to-heart, or did you actually have something important to discuss?"

"Heart-to-heart."

He rolled his eyes. "Cool. Well, some of us have real work to do."

"I resent that comment," Dan said, then his voice went serious. "One of us will always be watching, and listening, and close. We'll send in the troops if something goes down."

Fuck, that didn't sound good.

"Do you think something is going to go down here?"

Because fuck what he'd said about not interfering with Molly's business. If she were at more risk here, if the bakery were targeted, then he was bundling her ass up and shipping her off to Alaska.

"No," Dan said. "They'd be stupid to risk something at the bakery. There are too many neighbors, too much cross-traffic. They'd be much more likely to make a grab at her duplex, since it's a corner unit and semi-isolated." He paused for a second. "Probably also something you should talk to her about. Think she would stay at your place? It's more secure."

No. She wouldn't like staying with him at all, but he didn't say that, just entered his password into the laptop's lock screen, and said, "I'll find a way to make it happen."

"Booze and kitchen accessories."

"Right," he muttered.

"This will all be over soon," Dan said. "Just remember that."

He'd placed his online order for the local kitchen store, along with one for the local wine shop, and he'd arranged for his assistant to pick both up and bring them to him by lunchtime.

He might have actually gotten off cheaper if he'd been looking to buy Molly expensive shoes or purses because, turned out, kitchen shit was expensive.

Or at least the brand he'd remembered her liking was.

Anyway, the collection of spoons and scrapers (not spatulas, because he'd at least learned *that* minimum piece of information from Molly during their time together), came bundled together like a bouquet of flowers. But apparently the wooden handles were "*to die for,*" according to the reviews, and he knew she'd appreciate the bright and cheerful display of llamas printed on the silicone head of the scraper.

The wine was just that. Something else she'd appreciate.

A medium-bodied Pinot Noir with fruity tones they'd discovered while wine tasting years before.

Once, it had been her favorite.

Today, he hoped she wouldn't launch it at his head.

A little after six, Molly came out of the kitchen with a tray in her arms and started filling the case.

Jackson hadn't consciously moved, but one second, he was in his seat, and the next he was at her side, lifting the tray—the *sheet pan*—from her arms and holding it so she could arrange the case. And when the sheet was empty, he pushed through into the kitchen, set it on the counter, and retrieved two more trays filled with muffins. Molly murmured "thanks" when he reappeared with them, but otherwise they didn't speak as she carefully filled the display case with the variety of treats she had managed to whip up in just under two hours.

When he carried the last of the empty pans into the kitchen, he came out to find she'd moved toward the front door, scooping up a newspaper that had been dropped through the slot, and was carefully folding it. With a look rife with different emotions —fear, tentativeness, frustration, hope—in his direction, she had set it on Ronnie's table.

"Coffee?" she asked.

He nodded.

"Have a seat," she said. "I'll bring it out."

And she had, along with a banana chocolate chip muffin that had him seeing stars it was so delicious. But then again, she'd probably known that, considering she'd remembered bananas and chocolate were his kryptonite. However, before he could thank her for the food and the coffee—also made exactly as he'd preferred—the morning rush began. Jackson had pretended to keep his eyes on his laptop, but in reality, he'd watched Molly as she worked.

In reality, he couldn't *stop* watching her.

Her personality filled the space with comfort, with caring. She had a bright smile and a kind word for everyone who walked through the door, and he knew it wasn't an act. He knew she *did* care.

She wanted her customers to have full bellies and satisfied taste buds.

She wanted them to feel comfortable enough to linger.

She was the lifeblood of the space. The reason it was so successful.

So, his eyes might have started on his laptop screen, but they'd drifted up to the counter more often than not.

Which meant his emails piled up.

It almost meant that he couldn't find the strength to care.

Ronnie, the older man he'd met last month, strode in, stopping at the counter to order, even though Molly clearly knew what he wanted. She'd had it over to him about ten seconds after Ronnie had sat down at the table with a placard of his name on it. The nameplate was new, apparently, and because it adorned the table next to the one Jackson had chosen, Ronnie told him all about how Miss Molly spoiled him and how she was so wonderful.

"There's a woman who shouldn't be single," Ronnie said.

"She's not," Jackson blurted.

Rather stupidly. Okay, *exceptionally* stupidly.

Ronnie's eyebrows lifted, but just as Jackson was about to blurt out something else, something along the lines of he'd fucked up and was trying to get Molly back, Ronnie nodded, picked up his paper, flicked it open, and said, "Good." Then he began reading.

Feeling like he should clarify, Jackson opened his mouth. "I—"

"No disrespect, son, but I don't come into this place to talk. I want to read my paper in peace."

Jackson's teeth clicked together.

Hadn't come in to talk?

This from the man who'd spent the last five minutes waxing poetic about Molly? Who'd talked his ear off during his last visit? Ronnie ignored him, eyes on the paper as he carefully turned the page. Okay, then. Jackson turned back to his computer, clicked to open a random email in his inbox, and started reading—

"My Molly deserves someone who'll take care of her."

Jackson glanced over. "Molly can take care of herself." Ronnie's brows drew together, but before he could reply, Jackson said. "But that doesn't mean I'll let her."

The older man's face relaxed, and he nodded approvingly. "Good man."

Jackson's eyes flicked back to his laptop. "Not sure about that, but I'm trying."

"That's about the only thing you can do when you meet a woman like that," Ronnie said. "You keep trying. You keep giving. You keep caring . . ." He paused, waited for Jackson's gaze to come back to his. "You keep on caring until they believe they're worth it."

He folded the paper and pushed to his feet with a groan.

"Only then will you know that you've done your job right."

ELEVEN

Molly

SHE STRETCHED HER ACHING NECK, taking a short
break from decorating the row of cakes she had spaced out on
the tables in the kitchen.

Breakfast had come and gone, lunch was in full swing—the
newest chef she'd hired doing a great job of putting together the
hot and cold sandwiches and salads that dominated the lunch
menu. The only major differences between lunch and dinner
were the prices—lunch was cheaper—and the portion size—
dinners were larger. Well, that and they'd thrown a seasonal
pasta dish on there in the last few months, but that had been her
marketing and accounting guru, Shannon's idea. She'd stumbled
across a fresh pasta shop a few blocks over, and when Molly had
tasted the offerings, she'd known they would need to feature
their pasta.

So now there was fresh, bulk pasta for purchase in the case
and a pasta dish on the dinner menu.

That was part of why she loved this city—the nooks and

crannies, the hole-in-the-wall restaurants, the food that never failed to make her moan in pleasure.

It fed her soul.

Just like this row of cakes was going to feed the bakery's bank account.

She stretched again, ignored the ache in her shoulders and neck, and picked up the edible flowers, choosing the prettiest ones and carefully arranging them on each of the white buttercream frosted round cakes.

That done, she gave everything a final inspection, boxed the cakes, and then carried them over to the walk-in. A few seconds to make sure everything was labeled correctly for the pickup that would happen after she left for the day, and she was done.

Well, with the cakes at any rate.

She had to start another batch of soup simmering, bake off the last of her roll dough, and check that her food order was ready to be sent off for delivery the next day.

Then she was done.

Sighing, she dropped her head forward, taking just one more moment to stretch the ache, enjoying the cool air of the walk-in, then straightened and reached for the soup ingredients.

Warm hands on her neck.

Jackson's warm hands on her.

"Sorry," he murmured, when she jumped and squawked. "I didn't mean to startle you."

"It's okay," she whispered, stilling as his fingers began massaging.

Frankly, *anything* was okay if he continued to rub the aching soreness out of her neck and shoulders. For the most part, she was used to bending over for hours, but that didn't mean she didn't still hurt when it came to the end of the day. Especially when she'd given up sitting on the stool because she couldn't reach properly. Frankly, her back needed a break.

"Those are beautiful," he said, voice still soft, warm breath hitting her nape.

"Mmm," was all she could muster.

The man knew her body, could hit every spot, soothe every ache, and while this massaging was what got her into trouble last time, she didn't pull away. Instead, she allowed herself just a few more seconds of the delicious contact.

Eventually, when the urge to spin in his arms and have him demonstrate the rest of his skills—only this time in a way that would definitely get her in trouble with the Board of Health—grew to almost a tipping point, she slipped free and grabbed the soup ingredients from the shelf.

She didn't protest when he immediately snagged them from her.

If he wanted to lug the heavy tub, fine.

Plus, if his hands were busy holding things, he was a lot less dangerous to her willpower.

"Where do you want it?" he asked.

Everywhere.

That was the problem.

"On the counter by the sink," she said, and if he caught the edge of need in her tone, Jackson didn't comment on it. Instead, he nodded and left the walk-in, and Molly would be lying if she said she didn't take an extra minute in the cool air of the refrigerator, trying to temper her desire.

Bad for her.

Jackson was very, very . . . good—

No. *Bad.* He was bad for her. He'd broken her heart. He constantly made her lose her temper. He'd said cruel things and shown up just because she wanted him out of the business.

But . . . he wanted to protect her, was here because—

"Because the federal agent told him to be," Molly muttered to herself.

The cold of the space finally penetrated her mind and body because . . . *that* was reality.

He wasn't here for her. He was in her bakery to assuage his conscience.

He didn't want her at risk.

But he also didn't want her—

Then why did he come back? her brain countered. *Why is he here rather than some burly bodyguard? Why is he lugging soup ingredients and massaging aching shoulders?*

Because they had chemistry. Because the sex was good, a bonus byproduct to doing the right thing.

Sigh.

Molly couldn't tell if that disappointed sigh came from her brain or her heart, but what she did know was that she had to grasp on tight to the reality that Jackson wasn't here for her, not really.

He was here for *him.*

Head on straight, keeping a firm hold to the truth of his presence, she left the walk-in. There was work to be done.

She'd best get to doing it.

"Ready?" Jackson asked, just under two hours later.

She glanced up from the stack of order forms she'd been double-checking and saw he was leaning against her open office door. Since he'd clearly interrupted her while she was in the middle of noting something on the page, no, she wasn't ready to go. "Nope."

Her eyes dropped back down to the page, but her ears still worked.

Hence the reason she heard his sigh.

"What?" she snapped, eyes flashing up again.

"You're at twelve hours."

Her brows drew together. "What?"

"You've been working for twelve hours straight," he said, coming fully into her office and shutting the door behind him. "I haven't seen you so much as take a bathroom break, let alone stop for lunch or to rest for a few minutes."

"I seem to recall you rubbing my shoulders a couple of hours ago."

His lips pressed flat. "So, a sixty-second massage is a replacement for actual rest and nourishment?"

"I went to the bathroom," she pointed out. "Several times. And I ate."

"One croissant. Four cups of coffee," he said, crossing his arms. "Oh, and one half of an apple that was left over from the turnovers you made."

"I ate more than that . . ." She trailed off as she thought back. Hadn't she? She *had* started to pull together lunch.

"Your salad you made for yourself is in the trash."

Her jaw dropped open.

How did he know that?

"Because I just threw it away," he went on. "After seeing it sit untouched on the counter in the front of the bakery for three hours."

Damn. That salad was her favorite.

Kale and colored bell peppers, slivered onions, and a chipotle vinaigrette. And homemade—because, duh—parmesan crisps.

She'd been on track for a normal day, for a normal lunch, but then her employee, Todd, had been telling her about the new play he'd just landed, and telling her with a certain amount of flair. So much so, that he'd flung out an arm in dramatic fashion, and accidentally knocked over the gum paste flowers she'd crafted for the large cake order she'd finished earlier. They'd hit the floor, and what few hadn't shattered had needed to be tossed —because, well, they'd hit the floor.

Luckily, her client had been understanding, especially when she'd shown them a pic she'd snapped of one of the cakes with the edible flowers carefully arranged on them.

Vibrant. Elegant. Striking.

Something that was challenging to do with gum paste.

Something that nature made easy.

It wasn't the first time a kitchen disaster had struck, and it certainly wouldn't be the last time.

Nor was it the first time her lunch had ended up in the trash.

Stuff happened, she pivoted and coped, and made the best of it.

Then she got on with her day.

The final part of which was this order.

"Two things," she said, setting down the pencil she'd been holding. "Or three, rather. First, thanks for throwing that away." His face clouded, lips parting like he was going to interject, so she talked right over him. "Second, I know *you're* not talking to *me* about working long hours."

"I—"

"Third, I have to finish this order so that I can leave, and you once again interjecting yourself into my life is delaying me."

He crossed over to her, bypassing the extra chair as he rounded her desk, and leaned back against it, his thigh six inches from hers. Her stomach clenched, heat pooling between her legs . . . because this man breathed and she wanted him, especially when his eyes were hot and angry, his jaw tense. That intensity had always translated into pleasure for her.

And her body knew it.

God, she was so fucked up.

"Don't look at me like that," he growled.

She tore her gaze away from where it had been slowly drifting down, tracing the buttons of his shirt, sliding toward the brushed nickel of his belt.

But she didn't have to look lower to know he was hard.

Molly let her eyes close, slowly inhaling, and trying to reason with herself. A month ago, she'd thought to take control, to fuck him, to get her pleasure, her taste, and then they could be done.

They weren't done.

Not by a long shot.

Fingers brushing across her cheek, drifting down her throat. Breath hitching, pulse thundering, lips parting.

"Are you going to hate me forever, honey?"

Her eyes flew open, and Jackson was there. Right there. Kneeling next to her, his mouth so freaking close, his scent so overwhelming, the heat from his body so intense that she forgot about the order she was going over, forgot about her wounded heart, about the painful past.

She leaned forward and sealed their mouths together.

It was a spark in dry tinder.

Heat exploding into fire, into *need*.

His hands came to her face, angling her head, pulling her out of her chair and into his lap, her desk rattling with the force of him colliding back into it. But then his tongue was in her mouth, then he was kissing her like he wanted her as much as she wanted him, and . . . she forgot.

That she was in her office.

That this was four years after she'd been dumped.

That this wasn't her and Jackson and what they'd had before.

His tongue stroked hers, his lips alternated between firm and soft, coaxing and demanding, his fingers clenched on her hips. Molly moaned and reached for his chest, starting to tear at the buttons on his shirt, pelvis canting, wanting, *needing* to get closer.

Jackson caught her hands, tore his mouth away.

Unceremoniously stood then deposited her in her desk chair.

He stood, towering over her for several heartbeats, eyes blazing, chest rising and falling in rapid succession.

Then he dropped his chin to his chest.

Inhaled and exhaled one long, slow breath.

His head came up, face placid, though his eyes still burned. "Finish your work so I can drive you home." He strode for the door.

Anger flared through her, hot and furious and overwhelming. She wanted to snap at him for coming back into her life. To scream and yell and throw things because he'd shattered the perceptions she'd held on to as an excuse to keep the world away. His fault. It was all his fault.

Except . . . it wasn't.

She knew that. Logically.

It was just easier to continue being mad, rather than acknowledging that he might have had legitimate reasons for leaving.

Safer.

If she were locked down, then she couldn't get hurt.

But there. *That.* The slight dip in his shoulders as he walked, the way he was holding himself.

It was far too familiar.

Because he was hurting, just as she was.

And *finally,* she was able to look beyond the anger enough to realize that Jackson had been wounded, too.

Perhaps even more.

Because while she'd been able to burn him in proverbial effigy, he'd had to be the bad guy, the one who'd separated them, and not because he wanted to, because he'd been trying to keep her safe.

Should he have talked to her? Should he have looped her in and not just broken things off without thinking it through?

Yes.

But could she understand wanting to keep the Jackson she'd loved safe, being willing to do *anything* to protect him, even if that meant breaking his heart?

Also, yes.

And was this anger too much, was it eating her up inside so she felt like she was constantly on edge, always just a hair trigger away from exploding? Was she done with holding on to the fury?

Yes.

No, she couldn't just forget it all, pretend it hadn't happened.

But she *could* put it aside, help him figure out the situation that was putting them both at risk, and then move on from it.

Healthier. More whole.

"Jackson?" she called when he reached for the doorknob.

He spun. "Yeah?"

"I want to hate you," she told him. "I want to hate you so you can never hurt me again." Honest words, albeit harsh. Still, she knew that she owed it to both of them to also give him the truth.

"I know, Mol." He swallowed hard, eyes dropping to the floor.

"But—" His gaze flew back up. "I can't," she murmured. "I can't hate you, Jackson."

His chest expanded, hope exploding across his face. "Honey—"

Put it aside. Move on. Stop being angry.

Yes to all of those things.

But . . . saying yes to all of that didn't also mean saying yes to opening herself back up to the potential world of hurt that was Jackson Davis.

"I need to finish this," she interrupted. "Then you can drive me home."

His expression dimmed slightly, the hope disappearing, and she told herself that she would not feel guilt. She. Would. Not. Feel. Guilt.

She felt it anyway.

But she didn't stop him from reaching for the doorknob this time, nor from turning it and pulling the wooden panel open. Nor from disappearing back into the hall.

Enough anger.

But her walls were staying up.

TWELVE

Jackson

I CAN'T HATE YOU, Jackson.

I want to hate you.

Fuck.

His plan for winning Molly over wasn't exactly going smoothly.

But at least she didn't hate him, or *couldn't* hate him. That was something.

He was waiting in the hall outside her office, thankful that she'd introduced him to her staff after the morning rush as an old friend who'd be hanging at the bakery working for the present. Because of that, no one was questioning his presence in the staff-only spaces.

It had been twenty minutes since he'd retreated from Molly's office, only leaving to grab his messenger bag with his work materials that he'd stowed behind the counter, and then running out to his car before returning to lean against the wall while answering the slew of late afternoon emails that always seemed to appear when everyone was preparing to leave for the day.

The plus was he could do that from his cell.

The minus was that it was hard to type with one hand, because the other was holding the bouquet of kitchen accessories.

He'd met his assistant at lunchtime, stowed the case of wine in the trunk of his car, along with the "flowers" he'd just retrieved.

Paired with Molly's declaration of *I can't hate you,* he hoped that he might be able to make up some ground here. They had the chemistry, that was for damn sure, and he knew it would stay there even if her anger faded, because they'd always been good together. He was tempted to use that chemistry to his advantage. To keep pushing at her until she exploded again and he was able to get his hands on her, his cock inside her.

But that wouldn't solve the mess between them.

He needed her sweetness, the caring that filled the bakery. He needed her to trust him to not hurt her. He needed her to understand that he wasn't going to take.

He needed to prove that *he* could be the one to give.

So flowers, of the kitchen variety, anyway. Along with moving slowly and carefully, so that Molly would be able to trust him.

And make sure she was safe.

But Molly had been right about more than one thing as they'd gone toe-to-toe that day. He hadn't suddenly turned into a superhero. He didn't have the skills to keep her safe.

All he had was Dan and the security at the office.

He didn't have a bodyguard anymore, and he only knew that supposedly Dan's team had eyes on both him and Molly. Obviously, they would be easier to watch if they were together, and hopefully Dan was right about Jackson's presence being a deterrent since Molly was already on the mafia's radar. But he needed to figure out what else he could do, what other precautions he could take to ensure Molly was safe.

He'd been focused on the security of her heart, when he needed to be equally attentive to her physical well-being.

There was movement inside Molly's office, and Jackson quickly sent a text to Dan, asking him for some resources and recommendations he could use to protect her, money not being any object, then he pocketed his phone.

Molly tugged the door open, expression distracted, ponytail askew, eyes tired.

She stopped short when she saw him standing there.

"Oh," she said. "Um—"

He thrust the kitchen implements under her nose.

Not the smoothest transition in the least, but at least he didn't accidentally gouge her eye out with one of the wooden spoons.

"Oh," she said again.

"I figured you'd had enough with flowers today."

She glanced down at the cellophane-covered utensils, wrapped in a pink ribbon. Then her mouth twitched. "Llamas are a favorite I picked up only recently. How did you know I was into them?"

"I didn't." He shrugged when she looked up. "They just seemed bright and cheerful like you."

Her mouth fell open. "*You* think *I'm* bright and cheerful? I've yelled at you for a good portion of the two days I've seen you in the last four years." Her hand closed around the bouquet, one finger trailing over the pink patterned silicone.

He grinned. "Okay, maybe not around me," he agreed. "But you've created this incredible space, Mol. People love coming here because the food is good, but they hang around because you fill the space with warmth, because you give them a place they can gather and feel happy. I'm so proud of you."

Her eyes widened. "That's the second time you've said that."

"That's because it's true." He slid a finger under her chin, lifting gently when her eyes would have gone to the floor. "You're impressive, honey, and you've done a hell of a lot more than create a program that is equal parts useful and dangerous."

She canted her head to the side. "Last I heard, you'd gathered investments totaling over five hundred million dollars."

"Last *I* heard, the military threatened to pull out of our contract because I wouldn't give them a backdoor access into the program."

"What's backdoor access?" Her cheeks went a little pink. "I mean . . . in *this* sense. Not the"—she coughed—"why would they threaten to pull out—?" More pink.

Jackson's cock twitched, and he bit back a smile.

His Molly wasn't shy in bed. His Molly knew what she liked, and sometimes that did involve a bit of backdoor play. But *his* Molly outside of the bedroom blushed. God, he loved seeing that pink on her cheeks.

Especially when it reminded him of the pink spreading down her throat, across her breasts, over—

She smacked him lightly. "Stop looking at me like that," she said, echoing his words back to him.

He lost the battle with his grin. "Hard to ignore, isn't it?" He brushed a kiss across her forehead. "Backdoor access, in this sense, is a way into the program if they're locked out or someone has their security or privacy settings battened down. It would give them a key into anyone's data, at any time.

Molly frowned, opened her mouth, but at the same time, Jackson clued into the dark circles under her eyes, the fatigue dragging down the smooth planes of her shoulders, and knew she was so much more important than the latest crisis that had jammed his inbox full of emails and his calendar with conference calls.

"Let's get you home," he told her. "If you still want to know more about the program and can stay awake through the explanation, I'll tell you on the way."

"Let me just check in on the staff and we can go."

He wanted to argue, to batten her down and rush her home, to force her to rest until she didn't look tired.

But this was her business.

She'd worked incredibly hard for her success.

And so, he wouldn't piss her off by hefting her over his shoulder and carrying her out to his car. He wouldn't discount her hard work by presuming to tell her what to do.

No.

He'd save that for when he told her that she was coming back to his apartment, and that she was staying there until Dan told them it was safe for her to leave.

And . . . then Jackson was going to tell her she *still* had to stay.

Because he'd gone four years without Molly Miller.

He wasn't going without any longer.

PREDICTABLY, his telling Molly about her change in living situation didn't go well.

Thus, there wasn't any further talk of back doors.

However, there *was* plenty of talk of her threatening to disembowel him with the new spoons he'd bought her.

Thank God he'd stuck with blunt instruments.

They'd had a few minutes of peace, the time between him showing her the case of wine in the trunk and then until the point during the drive home that she realized he wasn't heading to her place—read: ten whole minutes.

Then she'd clued in. *Then* he'd told her she was staying with him and that was just the way things were going to be.

She'd responded to that appropriately: "Fuck off, Jackson!"

To which he'd replied, "I will, if it means you'll see some goddamned reason and stay in a place that's safe!"

Her lips had parted, eyes furious, and then she'd softened and shaken her head. "You're the most infuriating man I've ever met." Another shake. "You know that, right?"

He'd pulled to a stop at a signal, opened his mouth to say, who the hell knew what, but he didn't get a chance.

Molly leaned over the console and pressed her lips to his.

He was pissed and frustrated and worried . . . and hard as a fucking rock, but that didn't mean he was going to pass up a chance to kiss this woman, to show her every one of the conflicted and confused and intense emotions she made him feel at any given time.

Her tongue was fierce. Her mouth was hot. Her lips were demanding.

Her hands pressed to his chest, moved down—

A horn blared behind them.

They both jumped, and Jackson's eyes flew up just in time to see the light change from green to yellow. He hit the gas, slid through the intersection a heartbeat before the signal turned red.

Whoops.

Out of the corner of his eye, he saw Molly was grinning.

Well, hell. He didn't think he would ever understand this woman.

But if she kept grinning like that, then Jackson didn't think he cared.

THIRTEEN

Molly

OKAY, so she'd lost her head for a second.

Kissing Jackson wasn't exactly keeping her distance.

But also, kissing Jackson wasn't exactly *not* keeping her distance.

Which didn't even make sense.

Mentally shaking her head, she knew that a lot of the last day, the last month, the last year, didn't make sense. *She* didn't make sense when she was with Jackson.

Always a push-pull. Always trying to align her heart and body with her mind.

Yet, all she knew was that when he'd yelled at her, when he'd finally lost some of the cool veneer in telling her all of the reasonable, *logical* reasons to stay at his place—better security, easier for the federal agents to keep tabs on them, not surrounded by woods that she normally loved, but with the threat of the Russian mafia potentially coming down on her that could be dangerous (also something she was willing to go without for a bit in the name of her safety)—and yelled, she'd finally clued in.

This wasn't about *just* keeping her safe.

This was more.

And perhaps that shouldn't have made her heart leap with joy, shouldn't have made her frustration at the order fade.

But it had.

Paired with the wine and the cute llama spatulas, and her irritation had fled.

Perhaps, that said terrible things about her. That she could be bought, that a few nice words and kitchen utensils meant she would lose all the fight she'd gained over the years. Or perhaps . . . it meant that she could finally be a grown up instead of a spurned, heartsick ex-fiancé, and understand his concerns, know that they were valid.

And so, she'd kissed him.

It had seemed like the most expedient way to end the argument, especially since they'd slid to a stop at one of the city's interminable red lights. Though that had backfired as they'd kissed through the green signal and probably left a trail of furious drivers behind them.

Her bad.

Though, the kiss had been very, very good.

But back to more pressing matters. She turned to Jackson and said, "I want to meet this federal agent you're working with."

At the same time, he kept his eyes on the road and said, "If you're already pissed at me, you might as well know that the bakery had cameras and microphones installed."

She *hadn't* been pissed.

The news circled her back around.

"Um, *what?*" she exclaimed. "Cameras? Did they—? Oh my God, is there some video out there of us having sex?"

"What? No!"

"You said there are cameras and microphones. Oh, fuck, who's watching them? Did they hear—?"

One second Jackson was driving, the next he'd pulled the car into an impossibly small spot on the street, thrown the transmission into park, and then turned to her. "Mol. *Stop*. Everything was only installed last night. There isn't a tape or a recording of us."

Horror filled her as she remembered what she'd said, how she'd acted. *Fuck*. To think someone had watched her freak out, seen her rage at Jackson as she'd aired the dirty laundry of their relationship. "Where are the cameras? Are they in my office? Did they see—?" She saw his face change, knew someone had been on the other end of the feed, witnessing her throwing herself at him, casually viewing her losing her mind and all semblance control when he'd kissed her.

Embarrassment was a hot poker through her mind, and she covered her face with her hands. "Oh, God," she groaned.

"It's not a big deal," he said, carefully peeling her fingers back. "Nothing is saved. Everything is deleted after forty-eight hours. They just want to make sure they have eyes and ears on you, just in case something happens."

She glanced up into his chocolate eyes. "Do they really think something is going to happen?"

Because if federal agents thought she might be at risk . . .

Well, then this entire thing was much more serious than she'd been giving it credit for, and *shit*, now she wasn't just embarrassed, she was a little terrified.

It's the Russian mafia, idiot, her mind said snarkily. *You'd be a moron to not be scared.*

Well, moron or not, she hadn't exactly been firing on all cylinders since Jackson had reentered her life. Everything was mixed up—her emotions, her job, her memories, her future . . .

none of it was simple or made sense, and now her bakery was full of microphones and cameras.

"I need to talk to the agent," she said again.

Molly needed to understand everything.

She needed to stop freaking out about a broken heart and a canceled wedding and start worrying about the fact that the Russian mafia was interested in her enough that federal agents had put cameras in her bakery to keep an eye on her.

Now you're getting it.

Jackson nodded. "I'm sure I can arrange that." A beat. "Are you going to keep the cameras?"

"Or what?" she asked. "I mean, seriously," she added when his face clouded. "What's my alternative? I take them out and risk some scary mafia guy sneaking up on me? At least if the feds are watching and listening then I'll be safe."

She hoped.

Jackson's expression darkened. "I'm sorry I came back," he said. "If I'd just signed those papers. If I hadn't gone to the bakery—"

Molly squeezed his arm. "I'm guessing you didn't know it would bring me back into this."

He shook his head. "No, sweetheart. I thought they were done with me. They'd gone quiet for two years. Dan said it was all but done, and . . . it's stupid, but I just figured that with everything turned over to the feds, with my security team in place, that there wouldn't be any risk." A sigh. "But then Dan showed up at my office last night, and he doesn't show up anywhere unless shit is serious."

That sounded ominous, and she couldn't help wondering how many times Jackson had seen Dan, and thus, how many times shit had gotten serious over the last few years.

But she didn't get a chance to ask because Jackson kept talking. "If I— *Fuck*. I should have just—"

"Had the benefit of hindsight?" she interrupted.

"I *knew* better."

"The universal human condition."

His brows drew together.

"You're experiencing the universal human condition of wanting to change the past even while knowing that it's impossible. Reliving and analyzing and thinking back through every single thing we did, in order to try to make sense of how things turned out. I'm well-versed in that. I swear, I could have gotten my PhD in the process after you broke things off." His face clouded and she brushed her fingers across his jaw. "I'm not trying to make you feel guilty, especially not when you've perfected the process. What I *am* trying to tell you is that I'm not mad you came back."

He snorted.

"Okay, not *all* mad. I'm so incredibly furious that you didn't talk to me about this years ago. But I'm also . . . I don't know . . . understanding? Or, at least, I finally have some clarity as to why."

"Yeah," he muttered, turning his eyes back to the road.

"I'm also going to try to not hold it against you quite so much."

She saw the corner of his mouth closest to her turn up. "I think I've earned your anger."

"Well, *I* think you've played the martyr for long enough," she countered.

He'd just flicked on the signal, started to check for traffic, but at her words he turned back to face her, jaw dropping open. "*That's* what you think I've been doing? Getting some sick pleasure out of sacrificing myself for you?"

Molly shrugged. "I don't know what else to think, Jackson. Your reasons for breaking things off might have been noble in the past, same as your reasons for parking your butt in my shop now, for ordering me to stay at your apartment. An order I happen to agree with," she added when it seemed like he'd argue with her. "I don't want anything to happen to either of us, and if me staying with you for a little bit makes that more of a certainty then fine, I can stand sleeping on your couch for a while."

"You're not sleeping on the couch," he growled.

A roll of her eyes. "I'm not arguing with you about that. My point is, the reason you ended things wasn't because you were crazy in love with me and were desperate to protect me, it was because you felt like you needed to punish yourself."

"That's—"

"And you *continue* to want to punish yourself. I don't know why. I could never love you enough to convince you to let me in that deep." Her gaze flicked to her hands, to the faded burns, the scars, the callouses. She'd earned the hardened skin, had dealt with the stitches, pushed through the pain to keep growing. Her eyes lifted, found his. "I wasn't strong enough then to chisel my way through the barriers. I was dealing with my own insecurities, was too scared that if I did push then I might lose you."

She sucked in a breath, lifted her chin.

"The difference is that I *did* lose you, and I went through some really dark times—no matter that it was ultimately for my own good or to keep me safe . . . I get that. But, I'm also different now. And I don't want a man in my life who's only here because of a misguided duty." She took another breath. "I want a man who loves me as much as I love him."

"I—"

"Feel like you have a duty to protect me because you brought this down on my head."

"Yes, but—" He broke off, shook his head.

She waited for him to say something, part of her terrified that he might suddenly declare his love for her and that she might be weak enough to forget everything and jump right back into how she'd been in the past. The rest of her knew she was too strong to do that.

"I'm not here just because I feel obligated," he finally said. "I care for you."

I care for you.

Probably the only words she'd accept at face value in that moment.

But also, words that hurt.

He cared. People everywhere cared—a person cared for a puppy, or a stranger who fell in the street, or a woman who'd once held a piece of his heart, even as he'd kept the rest of the pieces safely locked away.

"I care for you, too," she said and left it at that, not giving voice to the way those words sliced deep, so tired of being angry, of being hurt. "I won't fight you on our safety. Granted that you do arrange that meeting with Dan," she added then paused as she considered her options. "I want to know everything that relates to me. I *deserve* to know that much."

"I'll make it happen."

Molly nodded. "Thank you."

Jackson's eyes moved forward again, his hand for the turn signal, but then he paused. "I broke something inside of you when I called things off," he murmured. "I didn't realize it before. I thought that I could just piece it back together and make everything all right again." A beat. "But that's not how this works, is it?"

She shook her head, another wave of sadness washing over her. "No, honey, it's not."

He swallowed. "And even if I manage to piece it back together, it'll never be the same."

Molly hesitated for a few moments before eventually saying, "Sometimes staying the same is overrated. Sometimes the pieces have to be broken in order to become something better."

"Fuck." A quiet curse, under his breath, almost not reaching her ears.

"I'm okay," she continued. "Everything worked out."

"Except, I broke something I should have known was precious," he muttered, "and you can't go back to what you were before."

"I don't *want* to go back."

His jaw clenched, the muscle twitching just in front of his ear the only sign of how agitated he was.

"Jackson?" she whispered.

His gaze flicked to hers, frustration in his eyes.

"I think we were both broken. Back then, I mean."

He stiffened, and she braced herself, instinctively knowing that she'd touched a nerve. But then he sighed, and the tension left him. "Yeah, I think we were, too." A nod, pain flashing across his face before he turned, started to check his mirrors.

"I guess what we need to ask ourselves is . . . if we're both still broken now?" She nibbled at the corner of her mouth. "And if we *are*, then can we find a way to be whole again? Or will that brokenness continue to chase us for the rest of our lives?"

His hands convulsed on the steering wheel, knuckles standing out in sharp relief against his skin. Then they relaxed, and he flicked on his turn signal, maneuvering out of the tiny spot and back into San Francisco traffic.

"There's one broken person in this car," he said, the words almost icy they were so devoid of emotion. "And I think we both know it's not you."

She inhaled sharply, opened her mouth to say . . . what?

But she never got the chance to find the words.

Because Jackson's cell rang.

"Answer it," she said when he glanced at her.

Relief and disappointment slid through her when he did as she said, when he answered the call over the Bluetooth in the car and began advising his assistant on rearranging his meetings for the following day.

Relieved because the conversation had been another heavy, exhausting, mind-melting one, and they'd had enough of those for one day.

Disappointed because she finally felt like they were getting somewhere . . . and because she might finally have the courage to *keep* pushing until she made it through his walls.

Until he told her the secrets he was holding on to so tightly.

The ones that made the shadows cross behind his sad chocolate eyes.

The ones she knew were the key to understanding both where they'd been and what they could be moving forward.

It took some effort, but Molly convinced Jackson to make a detour to her condo.

She needed to pack up her things, to get a change of clothes and her toiletries, and despite his promises that he'd have his assistant pick up what she needed, Molly liked the idea of a strange man going through her underwear drawer almost as much as she liked the fact that the mafia had somehow entered her life.

That was, not at all.

So, he'd made a quick call to the mysterious federal agent, Dan, letting him know what their plan was, gotten the okay, and they'd made the detour.

In. Out. Just the essentials.

It had all gone to plan without any hiccups until she'd asked Jackson to grab her Kindle from inside the bedside table.

She'd forgotten what was inside.

Something she'd gotten so used to that she barely saw it anymore.

But . . . there was a reason she'd never thrown it away. Because this was another photograph that had changed her life, albeit of one showing her and Jackson, him down on one knee, ring in one hand, love written over his face. Her expression had been shocked and partially obscured, her hands coming up to cover her face.

Jackson hadn't hired a photographer to take pictures.

Rather, a stranger had snapped it and then later had come up to congratulate and pass the photo along. A kindness for no other reason than to be kind. And Molly had cherished that picture for a long time, but then it had become a painful reminder, tucked into a drawer.

Eventually, though, it had become a distant memory.

A pang, and yet, not the agony it once was.

Although, it wasn't so distant with the man pictured, standing in front of her of her with a tortured expression on his face didn't slice across her heart.

Because she got it now.

"I remember being so fucking scared," he said, voice rasping as his eyes came up to meet hers, small smile on his lips. "That you would say no. I knew even then that I didn't deserve you . . . and yet, I couldn't let you go." His expression darkened.

"Jackson," she began, stepping toward him.

His eyes came to hers, freezing her in place. "Like now. I don't deserve you now."

"That's not—"

He dropped the picture back into the drawer, picked up her Kindle. "Anything else?"

She wanted to argue, to push, to demand her talk to her . . . but walls.

Hers, that was. The need to strengthen and keep them up.

But also, *his*. The impenetrable ones she'd never been able to find her way over or through or around. One look at his face told her all she needed to know on that front. His walls were still in place, and they were stronger than ever.

Maybe it was better this way.

No. It was most definitely better this way. Stay smart, keep her head down, continue moving forward. Right.

But maybe it wasn't better? Maybe they could—

A shake of her head, a stifled sigh, then Molly zipped up her bag, and said, "That's enough for now."

She meant the clothes.

But also maybe . . . she meant the two of them.

But also maybe . . . she didn't.

FOURTEEN

Jackson

HE GRABBED the case of wine from the trunk of his car, shouldered his bag and Molly's, despite her protests, then closed and locked everything up before leading the way over to the elevators.

She held the kitchen bouquet and trailed him silently.

Silence.

He'd thought he'd been used to it after the last few years spent working late in the office after everyone else had gone home then returning to a silent, empty apartment.

But he wasn't used to Molly being quiet.

Their relationship wasn't filled with long moments of comfortable silence, of two people sitting in quiet reflection or mutely observing the world around them. Molly was a chatterer —talking about her day, about her business, about a new recipe, about a news article she read, about a podcast he just *had* to listen to—and he'd loved it.

As an only child of two working parents, he'd had a lot of quiet.

His mother worked eighty-plus hours a week at the doctor's office she'd founded, and his father had traveled, so much so that he'd once received an award from his preferred airline for the most miles flown in a year.

Jackson had been used to doing things himself, had run feral and roamed his house and neighborhood, living off an obscene amount of peanut butter and jelly sandwiches while getting himself to school on time, making his own lunch, and oftentimes, his own dinner.

Oh, there'd always been food available, plenty of jars of peanut butter and strawberry jelly, multiple loaves of bread, apples, bananas, graham crackers. Plenty of snacks for a kid.

There just hadn't been dinner around a worn wooden table, discussing his homework over vegetables he'd been forced to choke down, someone to check that he'd brushed his teeth at night, or hell, even someone to make sure he went to bed at a reasonable hour.

He'd fended for himself.

Which was probably why he'd been so drawn to Molly in the first place.

She had been caring personified, thinking of him and his needs, filling the space around him with laughter and conversation, and meals were never in short supply. He'd fallen hard, latched on, and . . .

Sucked her dry.

The elevator opened with a *ding*, making him blink and blindly step forward, following Molly onto the car then pushing the button for the eighth floor. After a few seconds, the doors slid closed, and she sighed.

"What's wrong?"

Had she gone back to being mad about his high-handedness? Or was this something else?

"Nothing," she said. "Or nothing *new* anyway." The last was a quiet addendum, barely reaching his ears.

He turned, locked eyes with her, thought about pushing her for an explanation.

But fuck, hadn't he put her through enough? Hadn't this day been long enough for her? He didn't need to add his bullshit to her—

"It's that," she said.

His brows drew down. "What?"

"The wall." He didn't understand what she meant, and luckily, she seemed to read that loud and clear. "*Your* wall, Jackson. The one I could never get through when we were together, the one I told myself I would be able to eventually one day find my way around, or even if I didn't, then the one I was okay with being between us because I was too scared to push, if that meant I might lose you." She cleared her throat. "It's also . . . if I'm being truly honest with myself, even though I'm twisted into knots, even though I keep alternating between being terrified and wanting to push forward, it's also the wall I don't want between us now."

He clenched his hands into fists, considered what had been running through his brain, the promise he'd made to himself to tell her everything from this point forward. He'd already told her he was broken, so he might as well confess the rest. "I—"

The elevator doors opened, and, instinctively, he put his free hand out to prevent them from shutting, holding the metal panel so Molly could get off.

She took one step, stopped. "Um."

Jackson's eyes flew up from the box of wine he'd been concentrating on not dropping and he skidded to a stop, elevator doors closing behind him, his chest only millimeters from Molly's back.

Then he quickly moved in front of her.

The man who stood so casually, leaning back against the wall opposite, one ankle crossed over the other, smirk on his lips, outweighed him by at least fifty pounds, and while Jackson was on the tall side of average, this man had a good six inches on him. His black suit was expensive and tailored to his body like a second skin.

Which revealed a body well-honed and riddled with muscle.

Fuck.

Molly slipped her fingers into the waistband of his slacks, holding steady, even as her breath came in rapid exhalations he could feel on the back of his neck.

The man took a step toward them, and every nerve in Jackson's body went on red alert.

"*Privyet,*" the man said, leaning toward them.

Russian for hello.

Fucking hell. Where was the security Dan had promised? Jackson shifted to the side, slowly backing away, nudging Molly away from the man, closer to his condo. If he could get her inside, she could be safe and call for help.

"Mr. Davis," the man went on, Russian accent heavy. He came close enough for him to smell the expensive cologne, see the fine stitching on his suit jacket. "My boss would like to—"

The elevator doors dinged open.

The man's head swiveled in that direction.

Jackson didn't look to see who was on the car, who'd inadvertently interrupted the man's sentence, and he didn't delay, just nudged Molly toward his door, shoved his key in the lock, and got her inside.

Wine box he somehow still held on the floor. The door shut. Locks engaged. Dead bolt thrown. Cell in hand to call Dan.

Knock-knock.

"Go into the bedroom," he ordered. "Lock the door and call—"

Before he could finish his sentence, a familiar voice penetrated the wood. "It's me."

Dan.

"It's okay," he told Molly, checking the peephole before opening the door enough to peek through the gap. When both showed no sign of the mafia member, he shut the panel, pulled off the dead bolt, and opened the door.

Dan slipped through, gun at his hand.

In another few seconds, the door was closed, the bolt back in place, and his gun was back in his holster.

He pulled out his phone, pressed a button, lifted it to his ear, and said, "Shit's getting spicy. Let's call in another team. Report back on their ETA." Then he hung up, glanced between Molly and Jackson. "Should we order a pizza?"

Fucking unbelievable.

Jackson shoved past him, going over to where Molly was standing, her face pale. He slipped an arm around her waist and gently pulled her trembling body against his.

"Who was that?" she whispered.

"*That* was Maksim Petrova," Dan said, "Underboss of the Mikhailova clan, and a guy you really don't want to meet in a dark alley."

"I don't give a fuck *who* that was," Jackson growled. "You told me it was safe to bring Molly here."

"It is."

Jackson snorted.

Dan pocketed his cell. "We have cameras along every stretch of the hall, in the elevators, the parking garage, the stairwells, and guards stationed in the condo next door, watching the feeds," he told them. "Plus, I was there the entire time, ready to step in if there was an issue and me bringing in another team at this point will mean double the manpower."

"I think a fucking mafia guy getting in the face of *my* woman is an *issue*," Jackson snapped and felt Molly stiffen. "He could have—"

"I'm okay," she said. "It's . . . I'm not going to say fine—"

"It's *not* fine," he snapped.

She squeezed the hand around his waist. "That's why I'm not going to say it's fine, but he"—she nodded at Dan—"said he was there, that we were safe the whole time."

Jackson forced his grip on Molly to stay light, when all he really wanted to do was yank her against him, hold her tight, and pretend the rest of the world didn't exist. He glanced down at her instead, took a breath, and kept his voice even. "That's what he said four years ago before I got that fucking photograph."

Her lips parted. A long breath slipping free. Clarity dawned on her face, and she leaned a little more heavily against him, rested her head on his shoulder.

And he . . . settled.

His terror at her being in the same space as that man, as *Maksim*, faded enough for him to think clearly.

"If you want this over with then we need intel," Dan said. "We need to figure out where they're going next, how they managed to sidestep our net. If we can find out how high this goes, who's working with them in our government, then we can take them down." Dan came toward them.

"You've been trying to take them down for more than four years," Jackson said. "And it's not working. Give me one reason why I shouldn't just pack us up, fly us to some deserted island, and hunker down until the threat passes."

"What?" Molly exclaimed. "The bakery. I can't just—"

"Because they will find you, and they will do *anything* they have to in order to get you to give them what they want," Dan interrupted, blue eyes icing over. "And if you're in the middle of fucking nowhere instead of here then *I'm* not there, and your chances of getting you and Molly out of this situation alive are nil to fucking zero."

"He's scary," she whispered.

Dan's expression warmed, lips twitching. "I don't like the fucking Russian mafia. I don't like not getting the job done. I especially don't like not getting it done for four fucking years." He leaned back against the wall and crossed his arms. "And I *really* don't like people getting hurt or threatened when they're under my protection."

"I still stand by my statement of saying you're scary," Molly said, her voice wobbling just slightly, and Jackson knew she was forcing the lightness in her tone.

But he was still so impressed with her all the same.

He hadn't been nearly so composed the first time he'd come face-to-face with one of the Mikhailova, or the Vory as they were sometimes called. He'd been a wreck, and here she was cracking jokes with a federal agent, laughing when he stuck out his hand and said, "Oh, I'm Dan, by the way."

She smiled. "I figured." A beat. "So, *you're* the one who's been spying on me at the bakery and trying to steal my secret recipe for my rolls?"

Dan chuckled. "The mafia would be smarter to do that. One of my team bought a box of them yesterday. I'd be five hundred pounds if I had access to that recipe."

"If you can get Jackson and me out of this, you have a lifetime of anything you want from the bakery on the house."

"Sweetheart—" Dan began, but cut off when Jackson narrowed his eyes at the other man. The idea of him posing a threat to the agent was probably right up there with suddenly possessing some superhero skills, but the other man wasn't a dick. He'd cooled it on the endearment and said, "That's kind of you to offer, Molly, but I've always paid my own way."

"You just want to keep your six-pack," she teased. "Now"—she clapped her hands and pulled out of Jackson's hold—"Jackson is going to show me where the kitchen is. You boys are going to plunk your asses in chairs, and then we're going to figure out how to take down these mafia guys, once and for all."

Dan grinned then glanced from Molly to Jackson.

And Jackson didn't have to be a superhero to read what was in the other man's mind.

Molly was incredible.

Molly was special.

Molly was . . . *his.*

Something that Jackson knew he communicated to Dan, lack of superhero skills or not.

Molly, not waiting for him to point out the kitchen, started down the hall, and so Jackson did what he had to after his woman had worked her ass off for twelve hours then had faced off with a mafia man, followed by joking with a federal agent—he scooped her up, cradled her against his chest, and told Dan, "Get on ordering that pizza."

Then while they were waiting for the delivery, the three of them hashed out a plan to keep Molly and Jackson safe while Dan's teams hopefully worked their magic.

Because they all wanted this thing done.

Jackson just hoped that during the process he could figure out a way to win Molly back.

Unfortunately, he didn't think he'd be able to do so without laying absolutely everything on the line.

The question was: could he man up enough to actually do it?

FIFTEEN

Molly

SHE WATCHED Jackson walk Dan to the door, the two of them continuing to talk about the additional security from the company that Dan recommended.

Apparently, they were a mix of former government agents and military personnel who specialized in tricky situations like this. Not at all like a celebrity seeking a bodyguard, which Molly would have probably ended up with if she'd done the hiring, but people who had serious experience in dealing with bad guys like the mafia.

The pizza had been delivered—well, picked up by one of Dan's team to make sure it was safe—and they'd eaten as they'd discussed the additional security measures.

Jackson was going to continue to stick close to her, working from the bakery so Dan's team only had to cover one place. They were going to hire some additional protection and keep the microphones and cameras in place. And she'd given over her keys so his team could install some devices there, just in case the mafia came looking and happened to reveal something useful.

She liked the idea of cameras and microphones in her business and home about as much as she liked burning a batch of rolls, but it was a necessary inconvenience and so she was going with it.

Some part of her kept expecting to break down, to freak out about the fact that, for all intents and purposes, she was being followed by the mob.

A scary, Russian branch of it.

And yet, she was somehow holding it together.

Probably because Dan and Jackson had looped her in. She knew as much about the ongoing investigation as Jackson—which was basically that they wanted his program so they could use it to support their illegal businesses by selling private information and blackmailing prominent users. But just as Jackson had refused to allow the government backdoor access to the data, he wasn't letting the mob have it.

He'd turned everything physically to do with that program—all the servers, the computers, the storage—over to Dan's group, and any work was conducted remotely, carefully shrouded behind some seriously intense firewalls.

She had to admit that she hadn't quite understood all of what Jackson's company did until that point.

She'd known it was technical, knew that four years ago while he and his team had begun garnering more attention in the tech world, that it was valuable. She just hadn't understood exactly how much so.

He'd basically figured out a way to glean tiny bits of data from users and to monetize that.

Most of the time it was fairly innocuous, like whether or not someone was thinking about purchasing a specific brand of shoes, or if they preferred a pug to a corgi when searching for puppy videos. But it could also be used to follow other user trends—was someone at risk of being radicalized or thinking about hurting themselves or someone else.

Information that was valuable and could save lives.

But also some intense big brother shit, especially if someone who didn't have their users' best interests in mind got involved and starting gleaning data that was a serious breach of privacy.

The program was a dangerous beast, but it was safe, and Jackson's company was focusing on other ventures—including several security products that consumers could use to protect themselves from just the type of data gleaning that everyone who was after the program wanted to exploit.

"Basically, the consumer product would have fail safes to capture and delete information that might put people in danger before it can be picked up and sold. Kind of like armor for your online habits," Jackson had told her when she'd asked him about the irony of designing programs that would counteract each other. "But I've learned that protecting a consumer's data is more important than me making a few bucks from selling it to companies or governments—"

"Or the mafia," Dan had chimed in.

Jackson nodded. "Definitely that. So yeah, similar programs are already out there. Maybe mine is more efficient at stockpiling data, but I also don't want to be the face of a company that wants to exploit people or their personal information. I want to be proud of my work." He shrugged. "So, it was a no brainer, we made the shift."

That had taken her breath away.

She didn't think she'd ever heard Jackson so passionate about something. Yes, he'd always been driven, wanting to make his place in the world, always seeming like he needed to prove himself worthy.

But this was different.

He'd changed, too.

And she began to wonder what it might be like to be with this Jackson, what it might be like to have this man want the woman she was now.

Because he ticked all the boxes—protective, honest, passionate, thoughtful.

If only he didn't have people willing to hurt him in order to get their hands on his program.

"I thought they were done with me," Jackson said. "It's been almost two years."

Dan nodded. "We thought they'd turned their attention to other things, too. But the Mikhailova clan was recently caught up in a big sweep in Spain, and several of the higher ups were arrested and jailed," he told them. "That's why we have the oh-so-pleasant Maksim on our hands now."

"He's expanding their investments," she guessed.

"Seems likely," Dan agreed. "Many of their assets are tied up in Spain. They need money."

"And data, especially blackmailable data, sells at a premium."

Dan tapped his nose in agreement then changed the subject back to their safety, and while she could appreciate that was probably the more appropriate topic at hand, it was also more worrisome.

It was much more fun to be contemplating the mafia's assets than considering how their expansion of them was going to impact her life.

Case in point, the conversation Jackson and Dan were wrapping up.

She should probably be over there, going over the final details, making sure she understood every single thing she could. But it was nearing nine at night. She'd been up since three-thirty that morning, and her eyelids felt like they had concrete blocks attached to them.

Relaxing back into the cushions, she let them slide closed for just a second.

Then felt like they'd barely closed when she felt Jackson scoop her up into his arms.

"Couch," she murmured, so tired but also knowing that she'd promised herself she wouldn't take his bed. "I'm sleeping on—"

"Shh," he said.

Maybe she was weak, maybe she had just hit her limit on stressful scenarios for the day, or perhaps the long, emotional hours had just finally caught up with her. Regardless of the reason, Molly didn't protest further. Rather, she relaxed against Jackson's chest and let her eyes close again, not protesting when he set her on the bed and tugged off her shoes then her jeans. She didn't even make a peep when he reached under her shirt and unhooked her bra, slipping its straps down one arm then the other before tugging it off.

Her head hit the pillow, blankets were tugged up to her chin, and she swam out of the fog of her sleepiness to summon a response to his hushed, "What time do you need to wake up, babe?"

"Three-thirty."

Then she let the darkness swarm back over her and sleep tug her under.

SHE WOKE up to her cell blaring too damned early.

But that was what happened when someone got up in the early hours of the morning . . . or really, the late hours of the night before.

It took her several long moments to remember she wasn't in her bed, her condo.

It only took one more beyond that to realize she wouldn't have her coffee.

God. No.

Coffee . . . she needed. She wanted.

Regardless, she slipped out from beneath the covers, flicking on the light that had her blinking against the brightness grumpily. The bedroom was larger than hers, nicer than her. Same went for the condo.

It might be nicer, but it didn't have her carafe of coffee.

Rolling her eyes at herself, she stumbled over to her bag, which was sitting on a bench at the foot of the bed then slipped into fresh clothes. A shower would have to wait, considering she'd seen what looked to be a dozen knobs inside the glass-enclosed space, and she wasn't fucking with all those knobs at three-thirty in the morning.

Knobs.

Heh.

Also, three-thirty brought out her inner innuendo.

Tugging on a sweatshirt, she slipped her feet into her sneakers, zipped to the bathroom to brush her teeth and wash her face then spent several minutes attempting to contain her hair in a ponytail.

By the time she came out, she was in desperate need of coffee.

But, it would have to wait until the bakery.

At least then she'd have a vat of the stuff.

Feeling marginally better at the thought of copious amounts of the glorious, steaming beverage, Molly quietly slipped from the bedroom. The plan was to text Dan, who would drive her over and stay until Jackson came over at a more reasonable hour.

Jackson hadn't been thrilled.

But he also wasn't used to the hours. He needed sleep to keep running his business.

So compromise.

Except, the second she strode out of the bedroom, she realized that his agreement had been a means to end the fight.

Because Jackson was awake and dressed . . . and he held out a cup of coffee in her direction.

She took it, sucked back a huge sip.

Then another.

By the time the caffeine hit her blood stream and she opened her mouth to tell him to get his butt back to sleep, Jackson had her carafe in hand, his jacket on, and he was striding to the door while texting someone—presumably, Dan, because a few seconds later there was a knock on the door.

Jackson checked the peephole then crossed back over to her, switching the mug for the carafe. "Time to go, sweetheart," he said and set the cup on the side table.

"You should—"

He cupped her cheek. "You're there. I'm there."

Her heart skipped a beat and she wanted to ask him if it was because he wanted to be, or because he felt he *had* to be.

However, instead of that question coming out from between her lips, "You know how I take my coffee?" emerged in its place.

Early.

It was early and she hadn't had enough caffeine.

That was the only explanation for the nonsensical question.

Jackson glanced down at her, eyes melted chocolate, and then he brushed his knuckles over her cheek. "Yeah, baby, I do."

Clink.

A chunk of her wall crumbled and hit the dirt.

Before she could focus—or in reality, *panic* on that realization, he grabbed her hand, tugged her to the door, and whispered, "Time to make some of your sweet treats, baby."

She was woman enough to admit the raspy words made her shiver.

Made her want.

SHE FELT him a second before he slipped the tray from her hands, holding for her as she filled the case with warm muffins—double chocolate chunk, raspberry with a cream cheese swirl, her ever-popular lemon poppy seed, and, though she wasn't admitting it to the universe (or herself) banana chocolate chip for Jackson.

It had been three days since she'd begun staying at his condo, and those three days had been filled with . . . right.

Jackson was there.

It was the same and yet different.

They'd always fit. Within a few seconds of literally bumping into each other on BART nearly seven years before, they'd fit. Numbers exchanged, coffee grabbed, movies seen and shared tub of popcorn consumed. It was always easy, their bodies in tune in the bedroom and out of it.

And perhaps that *easy*, the way they'd slid into each other's lives seamlessly, how they'd liked the same TV shows and food, how they'd just plain gotten along from the beginning had hid the problems in their relationship. Because they got close and they did it fast and within a few short months, Molly hadn't been able to imagine a life without him.

She'd gotten attached.

She'd been afraid to lose that close if she pushed to delve deeper than he was willing to give.

So, they'd existed. They'd continued on that path and she'd been happy.

But after Jackson had broken up with her, once she'd lost that connection anyway, Molly had realized how unhealthy it was. She shouldn't be afraid to push the person who she was going to spend the rest of her life with.

She should be free to be her.

And maybe now she could be?

Before she could focus fully on that, he'd gone and returned with another tray. "Here you go, baby," he murmured, holding it up for her to load the next shelf. She glanced up, got lost in those chocolate eyes, warmed and shining down on her. There was something there, something different and open and deeper . . . and it gave her hope that—

The bell over the door tinkled, and Ronnie walked in.

"Go," Jackson told her. "I'll finish up."

Her favorite regular (shh, don't tell anyone) made his way to the counter, put down his traditional five, ordering his coffee and his lemon poppy seed muffin—there was a reason she made them every day, and it wasn't just because they were delicious and sold well.

They were Ronnie's favorite. His wife had made them for him and he'd had them for breakfast every day for the last fifty years of his marriage.

When his wife had gotten ill, he would come in and buy two of them every morning, packed up to-go, and take them home. But eventually . . . he'd come in and bought only one lemon muffin, then he had begun to stay and eat it while drinking a cup of coffee, his expression lost and closed down and . . . well, it had told her enough.

So she made them.

Every day.

She bantered with Ronnie, told him to grab his table, and poured his coffee, but then when she turned to grab the muffin, Jackson already had one readied on a plate.

He remembered the lemon poppy seed.

He remembered.

Clink.

Another piece of that wall chipped away, fell to the ground.

Although, this time it wasn't so scary.

"No!" She sat bolt upright in a cold sweat, heart pounding, head spinning, and totally confused as to her whereabouts for several long heartbeats.

But then a gentle hand touched her cheek, a soft, raspy voice reached her ears, "It's okay, baby. I'm here," and she calmed enough to be coaxed back down onto the mattress, to allow herself to be tucked into Jackson's arms.

Probably, she should have moved, used her moment of alertness to go out into the living room and sleep on the couch like she'd told him she was going to do, like she'd told him *every* night she was going to do since she'd begun to stay here.

But it didn't matter if she got tired and drifted off on the couch or if she fought tooth and nail with him about not sleeping in his bed, she still ended up there.

Hell, just that evening she'd threatened to order a bed online to fill the empty second bedroom, but Jackson had argued he liked his empty room because it showed off the windows.

Showed off the windows.

What the hell did that even mean?

He'd just been trying to annoy her. And know what? It had worked. She'd flounced off into the bedroom, taken a long soak in his huge bathtub, and she'd crawled into his bed, eyes sliding shut almost before her head hit the pillow.

Tonight, however, she hadn't woken alone.

Tonight, she'd woken up with Jackson in bed with her.

And . . . his arms felt good.

Too good.

He was snuggly and warm, and she didn't want to move. She wanted to stay in his embrace forever, especially when he held her like she was precious and whispered soothing endearments in her ear. So words that made her forget all about the dream that had woken her, heart racing.

The fear disappeared because . . . God, she'd missed sleeping with this man.

"It's okay," he kept murmuring, one hand rubbing up and down her back. "It's okay, honey. Just sleep. I've got you."

"Do you want me?" she asked, and later she would blame the combination of his snuggly arms and the lingering drowsiness from her nightmare, but mostly it was just that she *needed* to know.

His hand froze. "What?"

"It's just . . . when you picked me up and brought me to the bakery last week, you said you were staying near me because Dan told you to, not necessarily because you wanted things to work out between us. Is that . . . is that still the case?"

Silence.

Arms slipping free.

Her gut sinking.

Then the light flicked on, blinding her for several seconds.

"What the hell did you just say?" he asked, gaze furious.

She sat up, tugging the blankets with her when she remembered she wasn't wearing a bra. "I . . . it's okay, Jackson. I mean, I get it if too much time has passed, and things have changed for you. I just thought . . ." She trailed off.

"Molly. What. The. Hell. Are. You. Saying?" Each word was clipped out, like raindrops plinking against metal.

"I just— I guess I was wondering if you thought that when this is all over . . ." Here she lost her steam, gaze flicking to his face and then away, but when he didn't say anything, she kept talking. "Um . . . I guess I thought we could see about maybe . . .

if you and I, these new, changed, *better* versions, might have something special . . . like we used to?"

She finally clamped her mouth closed, trying to not analyze the mess she'd just spewed.

Her cheeks felt hot, her skin too tight, her discomfort growing by the second.

Because Jackson didn't say anything.

Anything.

Know what? That couch sounded pretty good right about now.

She shoved herself off the mattress, took one step toward the bedroom door, and found herself tugged back against a hard chest. "What did you just say?" he asked again, and Molly only shook her head in reply. She'd already done the verbal vomit. There was no way she was going back and repeating for a second round.

Thankfully, Jackson didn't actually seem to need her to repeat it.

He spun her in his hold and said, "Are *you* seriously asking *me* if we can have another shot?" A hard shake of his head. "Honey, I'm the one who should be begging you for that. I'm the one who'd planned on begging you *for that.*" He cupped her cheek. "I just spent the last three hours ordering you llama-emblazoned towels and potholders, and more spatulas and a stand mixer with llama decals for my condo, because you've always liked it when your kitchen stuff matched, and that doesn't even touch on the llama pajamas and the grocery order for your favorite ice cream and chocolate-covered pretzels, or the bath stuff in your favorite scent—"

"You were able to find Bourbon and Strawberry?" she asked, which was totally not the important part of what he'd just said.

He nodded anyway.

"But it's discontinued."

The ghost of a smile. "I have my sources." A beat. "Honey, I spent the time looking for your favorite things because I spent this week hoping I just could get you to not hate me, forming a plan in my mind, a long, hard-fought quest to get you to just give me one more shot to make you happy, and then you just turn to me and casually ask if we could see where things go?" His eyes warmed. *"Fuck, baby.* Nothing like ruining my process."

She didn't take offense to the last because it was said lightly, his eyes teasing. Instead, Molly pressed for some clarification. "But in the bakery, you said that you were only staying because Dan told you to."

"He did advise that," Jackson said.

A sigh.

Because why the subterfuge?

He understood the meaning of her sigh without an explanation. "Because you were so angry, baby. I thought . . . well, I thought it would take ages to convince you to give me another chance."

Her gut tightened, and she let her eyes drift away.

She'd spent barely a week with this man in the last four years and had asked him to give them another shot.

Was she insane?

Or worse, had she gone back to the same pathetic weakling she'd been in the past?

But then she thought of the conversation with the first night in his condo, the way he helped out at the bakery, how he didn't minimize her work. Then she thought of Jackson staying up for hours, saw his laptop on the nightstand, the screen showing a page of models wearing bright, colorful pajamas, and she knew he'd spent time looking for things she liked, knew he was expending effort to show he cared.

And she knew this was different.

Being included, being treated as a partner, not something fragile to be taken care of.

She thought of why he'd done what he'd done.

How they'd both changed.

And she knew this wasn't old habits or the past repeating itself. This was a shot at something different.

Something more.

Jackson didn't pretend to not notice the internal war waging no doubt reflected in her expression. Instead, he said, "I know. I know I changed things between us, that there is something irrevocably altered that we'll never get back, but also, Molly, please just know that nothing has to be decided tonight," he added. "Let me take you on that quest to convince you to give me another shot. Keep your heart safe and secure until I've earned your trust back."

He meant it.

And that's when she finally believed everything.

"You know," she murmured. "I always had this complex when it came to how I compared myself to my family."

He frowned.

"I know you didn't know." She shook her head. "Sorry, I know that probably doesn't make sense. I just mean, I was so ashamed to feel inferior, knew logically it wasn't something I *should* be feeling, that I should be confident and comfortable in my own skin . . . but I wasn't." She sighed. "I knew it was bad to think that way, so I didn't tell anyone. Not even you."

"Mol—"

"Let me finish?"

He nodded.

"You know my family," she said, and he nodded again. "You know they're wonderful, that they never consciously made me feel inferior . . . but I still did. I mean, my siblings are so successful, and I didn't get into a great college. I wasn't athletic or popular like them. I loved to read and bake and stay home." She nibbled her lip. "And they didn't ever say that was a bad thing. My parents were supportive of going to culinary school instead college, bought me loads of books. I—I just never shook the feeling of being an ugly duckling."

"Your parents are proud of you, honey," he said. "They came to the opening and tried all the food, and they could hardly contain their pride. Anyone could see it."

"Except. Me."

He froze.

"I know we've both said that we've made changes over the last years, and I know we both meant it," she told him. "But my changes came from therapy. After . . . *us*, I went into this dark place, similar to this unhealthy place that I've spent the last week dipping my toes into, only it was much worse." She took a breath. "I thought you dumping me was the culmination of all of my unworthiness. I just *knew* that you were too good for me and that it was only a matter of time before you moved on—"

"That's bullshit."

She smiled. "I didn't say it was logical. It was fucked up thinking, something destructive I'd been holding on to and feeding for years, including the years we were together."

"Honey—"

"But therapy taught me that those feelings, as you so eloquently said, were bullshit," she said and touched his cheek. "It took me a long time to believe that, but I won't lie that seeing you after all of this time, confronting the feelings you brought forth within me, I backslid a bit." She thumped a fist on her chest. "I hoped. I *wanted*. But I wasn't free of those thoughts, of thinking that you weren't here for *me*. I went to the dark side again, even if it was just briefly."

Jackson gently placed his hand on her nape. "If I make you

feel that way, we shouldn't give this another chance. I don't want to be the one to destroy you."

The truth was there in her heart.

"Don't you see?" she asked, moving closer. "Don't you see that you don't have that power anymore? *I* took it back. Or . . . maybe you never had it in the first place, maybe it was always me, letting this self-destructive monster lose in my mind and heart."

"I don't know if I believe that, Mol." He shook his head. "I don't see how I can care about you as much as I do and let you risk yourself. I should back off, should—"

"And *there*," she said.

He frowned.

"There's *your* self-destructive monster."

His eyes widened.

"Mine reduced me, shrank all of my wants and needs and accomplishments and pride in myself and my work into a tiny, damaged ball." She stepped closer. "Yours takes all of the good qualities you have—your heart, your protectiveness, your ability to care and feel deeply—and makes you fall on your own sword."

He inhaled sharply, and she wrapped her arms around him.

"I want to give us another chance. To see if we can slay these fucking monsters and move forward as something better," she said. "But, honey, you have to know your own mind." She hugged him tight. "I think you need to level with yourself about what you really *do* want, if the thing you truly desire is us in a real relationship. Or . . . if us being in a relationship again will just be another iteration of you sacrificing yourself for the good of others."

"That's not—"

Her cell blared, her very early alarm telling her it was time to head to the bakery.

She stepped out of his arms, reached for her phone, and silenced it.

"Don't tell me now," she murmured. "Think about it, and we'll talk later." His face darkened, and she hugged him again, tight and quick. "You owe yourself the time, honey. And you owe it to me, too."

His lips had parted, protest no doubt at the ready, but at her words, he stopped, eyes softening, and nodded.

Molly knew she was doing the right thing by giving them time.

What she *didn't* know in that moment was that later she would wish she'd heard him out . . . because *later* she didn't have the chance to hear anything from him at all.

SIXTEEN

Jackson

THAT DAY he was given a stool in the kitchen to park his ass, rather than his spot in the front of house, along with one half of a stainless-steel table he shared with extra takeaway boxes to park his laptop and cell phone. Molly kept the coffee flowing and the pop music blaring, but Jackson had learned his lesson.

Don't touch the volume.

Don't interrupt her when she was working her magic.

Surprisingly, being up at the ass crack of dawn wasn't terrible. He was definitely tired, especially after spending so much of the last week with minimal sleep and maximum worry, but being awake so early also meant he had a chance to actually reduce the number of emails in his inbox instead of just trying to tread water.

Being allowed back into the kitchen for more than a few minutes meant Jackson was able to step into Molly's office for a few minutes (and close the door to drown out the sound of Ariana Grande's latest), to take any necessary calls, as well as, to check in with the security company Dan had recommended.

The team he'd hired had joined forces with Dan's and was plugging any holes they could pinpoint.

They were safe.

As they could be.

The rest of the time—that being time not spent on the phone or managing his inbox, he did what Molly had asked of him that.

He thought.

It *should* be simple.

She knew how he'd grown up, that his parents had been uninvolved, but he could see how he minimized the impact of such a childhood. Any time he'd spoken of his past, he'd always framed it in the vein of independence was good for him—it had allowed him to think outside the box, to do things for himself instead of relying on his parents.

Now he wondered how much of a coping mechanism that was.

Instead of being pissed that his parents had considered their careers more important than him, he'd made the decision to think it was for his betterment.

Maybe that wasn't all bad.

He'd met plenty of people who'd blamed the world for all of their problems, and they weren't exactly pleasant to be around. So, he'd buckled down any leftover hurt, framed his vision for the positive, and moved forward.

That was a good thing.

Except . . .

How could it be a good thing when that buckling down meant that he'd hurt Molly?

That he'd craved the kind of love and care she'd given him to such a degree that he'd only been able to accept her affection, rather than reciprocate in any meaningful way? Hell, he hadn't been a total ass. He'd celebrated the holidays, her birthday, their anniversary, but last night had been the second time (sadly, both times having come in the last week) that he'd taken the time to shop for things that weren't necessarily expensive or showy, but rather, a few items he thought would bring a smile to her face.

Not buying something just because he thought it was the right thing to do, because it was what a man should give to a woman, but instead giving her something that showed he understood her, that he *knew* her. That he paid attention and cared.

And that it wasn't necessarily the right thing, but something that would make her happy.

She was right.

He hadn't been capable of giving her *that* before.

He hadn't been able to look past all the expectations for how things should be between a man and woman, between people who loved each other. He'd only been able to give what he thought was the right thing.

And the truth was that there was not *one* right thing.

Not a certain engagement ring or eating dinner together or having a career that provided for them. Not even her favorite ice cream or a llama-printed scraper.

Because nothing would be right so long as the wall remained.

If he held on to that solid barrier between him and the rest of the world . . . it would protect him, certainly, but it didn't discriminate. It separated him, just as effectively, from Molly.

So, yes, he'd hated breaking things off.

He'd hated not having her in his life.

But he'd also been broken.

Which meant he'd been able to keep a portion of his heart safely ensconced behind that wall.

So, he had to decide, did he take a sledgehammer to those bricks, did he punch a giant hole in the barrier, grab on to what he wanted, and let her in—*all the way* this time—past, present, and future?

Or . . . did he do what he did best?

Throw himself on his sword in the name of making her life better, while his remained empty and cold and devoid of anything except peanut butter and jelly sandwiches.

Fuck. That.

Jackson closed his laptop, rose to his feet, and turned to Molly, who was singing softly to the music as she measured out flour into a giant silver bowl.

He opened his mouth.

Then saw the red dot floating across her chest.

He didn't think, just moved.

The sound penetrated his senses when he was still too far away.

Pop.

"Mol—!"

A burning pain.

Darkness sweeping up.

Yanking him under.

The last thing he heard was Molly's ear-piercing scream.

SEVENTEEN

Molly

TURNED out that seeing one's ex-fiancé getting shot was overwhelming.

Molly remembered screaming and dropping the bag of flour, but she didn't remember the men flooding into the room, didn't hear the yells and gunshots that left holes in the bakery walls, had shattered glass and destroyed equipment.

All she knew was that she came back to herself when Dan roughly yanked her off Jackson, shoved her to the side, and began administering first aid.

She didn't even know how she'd ended up on top of Jackson, covered in a pink paste-like substance . . .

Pink. Paste.

The flour. The *blood*.

She shuddered, tried to hold down the bile that rose suddenly in the back of her throat.

Blood. So much blood.

On her hands. On her clothes. On her hair.

On the floor and the table and—

"Hey."

Molly blinked, glanced up at a tall blonde with startling blue eyes.

"Let me clean your hands."

She started to lift them, swallowing hard when she caught a glimpse of her palms stained with that mix of flour and blood, but then a pair of firefighters burst through the swinging door leading to the kitchen, and she was shifted to the side again.

Not delicately.

Not gently.

They needed her to move out of the way so they could help Jackson.

Which cleared her head enough for her to get to her feet, to make her way to the sink, and to wash her hands.

Soap and hot water, not looking at what was coming off her skin.

But then they were clean.

She grabbed a paper towel, dried them, then steadied herself and turned to see what was happening.

The firefighters, along with Dan and several men she didn't recognize, had surrounded Jackson's prone form as they worked on him. Stained gauze, opened packages, pieces of wrappers from the medicine they were using littered the space between them.

And all the while Jackson just lay there. Unconscious.

But still alive.

She *had* to believe he was still alive because they continued to work on him.

She had to—

As if Jackson knew she was on the verge of a mental breakdown, suddenly his head turned in her direction, eyes open and alert and riddled with pain.

Molly didn't stop to consider the ring of medical staff, the stained floors, or supplies. She just closed the distance between them and took up position by his head, bending and telling him, "You're okay. Everything will be okay."

His face evened out.

His expression softened.

But then his eyes rolled back, his chest arched off the floor, and she lost him.

Right there.

Someone coaxed her back as sharp questions and answers rang out, as more equipment was brought in, as gauze and IV fluids morphed into a defibrillator and CPR, a stretcher and then a rushed trip back out the door with Jackson strapped to it.

Molly wanted blackness to come up and claim her.

She wanted to go back and find out what he'd been about to tell her just a few hours before.

She wanted to demand they close the bakery and that Jackson haul himself off to an armored house where he would be completely out of reach of the mafia.

She wanted . . .

Him to be okay.

"Mol," Dan said, coming over to sit next to her where she'd scuttled back out of the circle of healthcare workers, not needing to be moved brusquely this time, knowing they had needed the space to help Jackson, not her in the way impeding them.

But she also thought that perhaps she should have stayed.

Because Jackson had been so pale, so still . . . and she wasn't sure she would get a chance to touch him, his skin, his hair, smell the spice of his scent, see him smile, or watch those chocolate eyes melt.

"I should have closed the bakery," she said. "I should have locked him in his condo, not have allowed him out to put himself at risk, and—"

Dan set his hand on my shoulder.

"If we're taking blame, it falls on me," he said. "I'm the one who's supposed to be protecting you both, making sure you are safe. And I've done a shit job of that."

"Yes, you have!" she snapped, turning and glaring at him. "You *promised* it would be okay. You had all of these plans, and not a single one of them involved Jackson getting hurt or dying and—"

He tugged her against his chest.

Well, she didn't want to be comforted, didn't want to be coddled or held. She was scared and angry and . . . just wanted Jackson to be okay.

"Let go of me," she snapped, beating on his chest. "Let. *Go*."

Dan didn't, just held her as she continued to struggle and said, "I could tell you all of the reasons why what the Mikhailova are doing doesn't make sense, that I've never seen them be so fucking careless or stupid before, that this doesn't fit their M.O.—"

"I don't care," she growled.

He slid his hand to her nape, tilted her head so her eyes met his. "I could also tell you that our intel is so fucked right now when it comes to them and how they're acting because the pieces we have are somehow fitting together and yet the puzzle they've formed is all kinds of fucked up." He shook her lightly. "I could tell you that we've taken down bigger and worse groups of bad guys and come out with everyone who we've protected along the way alive. I could tell you that I would have never knowingly put either of you at risk if I seriously thought they come in here again with loaded guns." Her gut sank, eyes sliding closed. "But—" He waited for her to open them again. "All I can honestly say is that I'm going to do everything to keep you safe, not just because I promised Jackson that, but because I'm promising *you* that."

"And Jackson?" she asked coldly. "What kind of promise can you give *him?*"

His expression clouded, and his eyes turned scary. "That we're going to take these motherfuckers down, once and for all."

THERE WAS a box of with a dozen lemon poppy seed muffins, Ronnie's newspaper, and a note for her favorite patron taped to its top sitting outside the bakery's front door. This was paired with a sign in the window saying that Molly's was closed for unexpected repairs

Lies.

But she figured it was better for her patrons to think a pipe burst or some ovens went down rather than knowing that there were bullet holes in her kitchen. Thankfully, Dan's team was handling the investigation quietly.

Not that there was much to investigate.

They had tape of the man entering the bakery, of Jackson getting up from his stool in the kitchen, glancing from her to the door, then sprinting toward her, and . . . going down.

It hadn't been him they were after.

It was *her*.

She'd demanded to see the tape, much against the advice of pretty much everyone, but eventually Dan had relented and shown her, and it had taken everything in her to not throw up.

He'd fallen to the ground like a sack of bricks.

Like a dummy.

Like a dead body.

Shuddering, she kept her eyes on the road, focusing on the traffic rather than those slightly pixelated images on the screen of Dan's cellphone.

She hadn't gotten in the ambulance with Jackson, hadn't

ridden to the emergency department. She hadn't been thinking straight enough for that. And by the time Dan had felt things were secure enough to drive her over, he'd gotten a call from one of his team that Jackson had already been taken in to surgery.

She'd still wanted to go to the hospital and wait.

They hadn't let her.

She got it, or at least, part of her did. Jackson had taken that bullet for *her* and putting herself at risk, acting like a sitting duck in the waiting room and making it easy for someone to come in and finish the job was not part of the plan.

Jackson was alive.

That was most important.

But it was absolutely killing her to not be there.

So, she'd spent the time cleaning up and shutting down the bakery then diverting the impending food delivery and outstanding cake orders to her other locations. Once the hour had reached a reasonable one, Molly had called her staff and informed them of the sewer line break—Dan's idea—telling them they'd work as much as possible at the other locations, but even if they didn't get the hours, they'd still have two full weeks of pay. While she was thankful she had enough in her reserves to actually be able to afford that without the business going under, she still couldn't believe she'd been focused on her business when Jackson was unconscious in the hospital.

Still, none of it had been distraction enough to completely erase the images of what had happened from her mind, what was happening with Jackson.

Then she'd gotten word he was out of surgery.

That he was alive.

That he was awake.

And she was thankful Dan had pushed her to get her affairs in order. Because her mind had needed the distraction while things were uncertain and because after the news had come in she wasn't in any way capable of doing it.

The adrenaline had faded.

Molly felt shaky and frightened and one push away from losing it completely.

Part of that was because she still had crusted, sticky flour in her hair. Her clothes were . . . ruined was probably the simplest description because even if she *did* manage to get them clean, she didn't think she'd ever be able to put them on without thinking of what happened.

Destined for the trash.

Just like all of her dough.

The rest of her just needed to see with her own eyes that Jackson really was awake and okay and—

Her phone rang and she glanced to Laila, the driver of the vehicle she was riding in, the blonde who'd kindly wanted to clean her stained hands that morning, and who was currently escorting Molly to the private hospital where Jackson had been transferred after he'd gotten out of surgery.

"Who is it?" Laila asked.

"My friend, Shannon," Molly told her. "She works for me, does marketing and accounting, and—" She stopped her explanation there, seeing Laila's eyes start to glaze.

"Go ahead and answer it," Laila said, flicking a switch on a box positioned on the dashboard. "No details of where you are or are going."

"Okay."

She swiped a finger across the screen, and Shannon's cheerful voice filled the airwaves. "I saw a missed call from you. Did you burn an oven full of goodies and need me to ride in on my white stallion and save the day?"

"There's been a sewer leak."

"What?"

"A main burst and flooded back into the kitchen. The whole bakery is shut down," Molly said, repeating the lie she'd perfected over the morning. "It sucks, but I'm going to take advantage of the time to tackle those outstanding repairs we budgeted for."

"*What?*" Shannon said again.

"Consider yourself to have the next two weeks off," Molly told her. "Let's touch base about details in the next couple of days. I'm too tired to break everything down again today."

"Okay, hun." Shannon's voice was concerned. "Are you sure you're okay?"

"Yeah. It'll all be fine."

She hoped.

"Well, I'm around if you want to come over later and share a pizza."

"I'll let you know, but I think I'll be at the bakery until late."

"I can bring—"

"What? Hold on a sec." She covered the receiver, made some muffled noises then got back on with Shannon. "Sorry, Shan. They need me to go look at something. I'll call you tomorrow, okay?"

"I—"

She hung up before her friend could get out the rest of her sentence, which was just as well. Molly had been lying all day and, sadly, they were starting to come easily, almost without having to really think about it.

That wasn't the kind of person she wanted to be.

She didn't want to be able to lie as easily as breathing, or to have to keep track of some complex web of half-truths.

And yet, here she was.

"You're doing really well," Laila said. "Most civilians would have fallen to pieces if they'd been through what you had today."

"No offense," Molly muttered. "But I'm not sure I want that particular compliment."

Laila grinned. "Noted."

She changed the subject. "How long have you worked for Dan?"

Brilliant blue eyes flashed over then back to the road, the grin widening. "Dan works for *me* actually."

"*Now* we're talking."

Laila snorted. "I'm just kidding. Kind of, anyway. We're more like equals. He and I both head teams. Mine is the one that was called in for extra support." She glanced into the rearview. "Though I am sorry to say that we didn't make it in earlier. Otherwise, the response time this morning would have been much quicker."

Molly frowned, not sure what she meant.

"Our plane was delayed because of fog, and we were just arriving at the command post when the cameras picked up on the intruder. If we'd been there, we'd have had more bodies on the ground, and he would have never got that far."

Molly's frown deepened, for two reasons.

One, it hadn't occurred to her to even think about the man who'd shot Jackson or where he'd ended up. Two, she wondered if the reason that they'd come into the bakery that morning was less about the Mikhailova breaking protocol and more about the fact that they'd somehow known reinforcements were coming.

Had they taken a chance to act before Dan's team had gotten back-up?

"What happened to the man from this morning?"

Laila scowled. "He must have clocked our guy on the corner because he slipped out the back door and got away"

"There wasn't anyone there?"

A shake of the other woman's head. "There was supposed to be, but he'd been knocked unconscious. Serious laceration that took sixty stitches and a handful of staples to close up." Laila scowled. "He's lucky he's not beside Jackson, recouping in a bed for the foreseeable future."

"I see." But what Laila told her made the hairs on the back of her neck prickle.

"What's put that expression on your face?" Laila asked as she steered the car off the freeway, coasting along an exit ramp that wrapped through a large grove of Redwoods.

Molly shook her head. "It's probably nothing."

"I've been in this career for too long to think that *nothing* is really nothing." She turned the car to the right. "Tell me."

Knowing it was unlikely she'd thought of something the agent hadn't already analyzed six ways to Sunday, Molly told her what she'd been thinking. "I just . . . none of this really adds up. First, why take a shot at me if they want Jackson to cooperate? I'm not trying to be an egotistical asshole, but Jackson doesn't have a lot of people in his life that he cares about, and if they killed me, I can't imagine he'd be motivated to help them."

"Go on," Laila said when she paused.

"So, I guess, I'm just thinking that piece doesn't fit. The killing me piece. Dan thought it more likely that they'd try to kidnap me and force Jackson to hand over the program. Killing me gets them nowhere."

Laila nodded, navigating the car up a twisting road. "Okay, I'd agree with all that."

"The other piece that doesn't add up for me is that maybe the Mikhailova's behavior this morning wasn't them being careless. Maybe they were told the team was coming in by someone on the inside and decided to act before that back-up came . . ." She trailed off, realizing that she was basically telling this woman she hardly knew that one of her co-workers might be a mole or, worse, a member of the Russian mafia.

Laila was quiet for a long time.

For a long, *long* time.

For long enough that Molly started to get nervous, to begin considering options for tucking and rolling and getting the fuck out of this car if Laila turned out to be the one who'd betrayed everyone.

"And now I'm wondering how all of us, how the people who do this for a living, could have possibly missed that." Laila gripped the steering wheel tightly as they approached a huge metal gate. "We've been chasing shadows, dodging and trying to capture an enemy that always seemed one step ahead. And not once did I consider that one of us might be helping them."

"It might not be that at all," Molly said. "I just bake for a living. It's not like what I'm saying is anything other than a guess."

Laila rolled her window down, punched a code into the keypad, and the gate began sliding open. "It's intuition. It's *logic*. And it bears chasing down." She hit the button to close her window, let the car move forward. "Because if what you said pans out, Molly Miller, then you may have just cracked a federal investigation."

"I—"

"Do me a favor?" Laila glanced over.

Molly nodded.

"Don't mention this to anyone but Dan or myself until we know for sure, okay?"

EIGHTEEN

Jackson

HE WOKE SLOWLY, eyes heavy, every part of his body feeling like he'd been run over by a train.

But then his thoughts sharpened, focused into one thing:

"Molly!" he said, voice hoarse, bolting upright in bed and then nearly collapsing right back down to the mattress when the bolt of red-hot pain shot through him.

Soft hands on his face, a beautiful face he knew better than his own. "Shh. Jackson, I'm here," Molly said, and helped him lie back down on the mattress. "Easy, baby. You're hurt."

He didn't give a shit about being hurt.

He wanted to make sure she was okay.

And that didn't have anything to do with the fact that he was being a martyr or sacrificing the things he wanted because he thought they were the right thing to do, that if he could be good or kind or brave enough then someone would love him.

This wasn't about the monster inside him—or in his case, the little kid who needed approval and understanding from his parents and then the world.

This was about a man and his woman.

A woman who'd had a red laser beam pointed at her chest.

So no, it wasn't martyrdom or approval-seeking. This was making certain that the woman he loved was unscathed.

"Were you hurt?"

"No," she said, hands running carefully over his face, down his arms. "I'm fine. But, Jackson, you're *not*. You need to calm down before you pull out your IV or something."

Frowning, he glanced down, saw that he was indeed hooked up to an IV, to several monitors.

"Where am I?" It didn't look like a hospital, not with the heavy drapes, the plush carpet he could see peeking out from beneath the bed, which definitely didn't look like something he'd expect to see in an institutional setting.

"Dan pulled some strings and had you moved to a private hospital."

His brows shot up.

"Yeah," she murmured. "Pretty plush for a hospital."

"Somehow, I didn't expect this of the federal government," he said.

"I know," she agreed. "When Dan said private hospital, I was thinking something more along the lines of beige walls and peeling paint."

"Exactly."

Jackson wanted to sit up again, to tug Molly down onto the bed next to him and hold her close, to physically feel her in his arms, to touch every inch, and reassure himself that she really was okay. But the burst of adrenaline he'd had upon waking was rapidly fading, and the pain was creeping back in.

"What happened after . . .?"

"What do you remember?"

He shuddered, remembering the red dot of light, how it had danced across the embroidered chest of her apron, but the shuddering had him wincing, and then Molly said, "Never mind. Just rest, baby. We can talk more later."

No. They needed to talk more *now*.

She needed to understand the shift that had happened in his mind. Who knew how much time they had, or if the mafia would come, guns blazing, into this hospital?

"I love you, Molly," he said, making sure it was the first thing he told her, in case the world imploded. "I loved you four years ago, but I *love* you now." He sighed. "I know that probably doesn't make sense, but I wasn't capable of loving you then like I do now." He took her hand. "You were right. I had something inside of me that kept me carefully separate from the rest of the world. It's just not a monster . . . it was a little kid, wanting to be loved first, by his parents, then by you. But at the same time, I was too scared to accept that you *could* truly love me, not when the people in my life who were supposed to do that from day one, couldn't."

She tilted her head to the side. "But you told me that you and your parents had a great relationship, that they had to work a lot, but—"

"I lied." He let his head fall to the pillows, exhausted, but knowing he had to make her understand. "I . . . they were neglectful. There's no other way to frame it. I wanted to call it independence or building character, and I pretended it was for my betterment." He laced their fingers together. "But it wasn't. It was for *their* betterment. Their lives, their careers, even their friends came before me." He squeezed lightly. "And I did that to you, when we were together. Partly because it was all I knew, a pattern to be repeated, but also because if *I* controlled our interactions, if I only let you into the carefully crafted pieces of me, then you'd love me and wouldn't leave."

Her face was soft. "Jackson, hon. We don't have to do this now. You should rest and—"

"No," he interrupted. "We need to do this now, because this morning I was getting up out of a stool, coming over to tell the woman I want to spend the rest of my life with, the woman I love more now than I ever could before . . . that she was right. That I'd been hiding." He lifted his free arm to cup her cheek, and it took way more effort than it should have. "And then I saw that dot on your chest, and I knew—I fucking knew that I'd missed my chance to tell you."

Yes, he was choked up.

Yes, maybe it was from the drugs, from the injury.

But also, yes, it was because he'd almost lost this woman again, and that was unbearable.

"You done?"

He chuckled in disbelief at the sharp edge of Molly's tone.

But that chuckle was short-lived because it was immediately punctuated by a groan. "Don't make me laugh."

Her eyes flashed. "I wasn't trying to," she snapped. "What I was *trying* to do was to get the dumb ass man that I love to rest after he took a bullet for me, after he almost lost his spleen and then spent several hours in surgery to control internal bleeding." She pulled her hand free, paced away. "Internal bleeding!" she exclaimed. "Do you know how serious that was? How *scared* I was that I might lose you when we were finally finding our ways back to each other, and it was so *much* better than before?"

Hands on her hips, she spun back to face him and glared.

"Mol—"

Her jaw ticked.

"You love me?"

She softened, eyes gentling, fury disappearing from her expression. "Yeah."

"But Mol . . . you actually really do love *me?*" he asked. "The man who's kind of a wreck, who's only just figuring out that the way he's lived his life for the last thirty years was shit?

The same one who's going to have to figure out how to move forward without repeating the same horrible pattern?"

Her feet were silent as they trailed across the carpet, bringing her back to his bedside. "I love the man who ordered me llama-printed scrapers because he thought they would make me smile, the same one who remembered my favorite wine, who knows my preferred brand of ice cream."

She sank into the chair next to the bed, bringing their gazes more level.

"I loved the man from four years ago, deeply, irrevocably, but *this* man, the who cares about my likes and dislikes, who gives freely, who tells me the truth even when it's scary, and says he's proud of me, *this* man has the potential to be loved so much more deeply." She trailed her fingers over his jaw. "Because you're not doing it to punish yourself or alternately, dolling bits of your heart out bit by careful bit. You've given me *you*. And Jackson, I know exactly how precious of a gift that is."

He was frozen. Her words washing over him, filling him to bursting.

He was terrified and relieved, both in equal measures.

Because they had a fresh start.

Because he might screw up again.

He lifted his hand, cupped it over hers on his jaw. "I'll do my best to not fuck it up."

"Don't you see?" Molly leaned down and brushed her lips across his. "Don't you understand by now that neither of us is perfect? That we'll both definitely fuck up." Another brush of her mouth. "Plus, it's the making up that will be the most fun anyway." She straightened, smile escaping. "Only this time, I won't have to throw sheet pans at your head to test your reflexes."

Jackson chuckled then groaned. "No more making me laugh, remember?"

"I remember." A beat. "Only, I'm so funny, I think that's impossible."

He snorted but held back the laughter. "So, it's this easy? We just declare ourselves and move forward?"

"What do you mean?" Her head was tilted to the side in question and ridiculously cute. But then again, he found everything about this woman adorable, including her uncanny ability to throw large metal objects.

"We had all this hurt and history and bad memories." Jackson started to shrug but caught himself. "So, we just pretend it didn't happen and move on?"

"No."

He frowned.

"We remember it. We don't go back. We move forward and build something better."

"I can do that," he nodded.

She propped her head on her hand, resting her elbow on the bedrail. "I know you can."

"And you'll be able to do it?" he asked. "You're able to believe I've fallen back in love with you?"

"You took a bullet for me," she said matter-of-factly, though her eyes were warm. "I don't think there's much clearer of a gesture of true love."

His mouth tipped up. "So, I could have just done that in the first place? Get shot?"

Molly sighed, shook her head. "You're an idiot."

"I'm *your* idiot."

Another sigh, though this one was trailed by a smile. "I'd take your brand of idiot any day of the week, Jackson Davis."

"Good," he murmured, lids heavy. "Because I'm not letting your brand of special go." He let his eyes slide closed, sleep beginning to close over him.

"Plus, baby," she said, sounding just as tired. "I think the truth that neither of us were willing to admit a month ago was that years might have passed, but we both never stopped being in love with each other."

She was right.

Though, that shouldn't be surprising with his Molly.

She had a knack for being right.

But then there was no more thinking.

Sleep tugged him under.

And the events that were about to crash into them would prove that Molly's knack for being right was even more honed than Jackson had given her credit for in that hospital room.

NINETEEN

Molly

FUNNY STORY.

There were contractors that specialized in bullet holes and blood stains.

Okay, so maybe that wasn't funny per se, but it *was* interesting. And despite the bullet holes in the kitchen and her wall of ovens, along with two that somehow had ricocheted inside the walk-in to hit the Freon line and cause the whole thing to have to be replaced, the holes had been filled, the stains cleaned up, and the front of house had gotten a facelift with new tables, paint, and a larger glass case.

All expenses she'd been planning on.

All expenses she'd been planning on in a *few* months.

But Dan had smoothed the way with the insurance company, and they were covering the replacement of the walk-in while the tab for the industrial cleanup of her kitchen was going to be covered by Dan's budget for the venture.

Which she was starting to suspect . . . okay, was beyond

suspecting and had moved into near certainty, that Dan and Laila didn't *actually* work for the federal government. For one, they seemed pretty free and lose with the rules—getting the insurance company to cover something they'd initially refused to, using their so-called federal dollars to clean her place up, the fancy private hospital, being able to install cameras and microphones that were absolutely undetectable, all in the span of a couple of days.

Molly thought that meant they had big bucks.

And she didn't think big bucks and a federal investigation mixed, especially with all of the budget cuts she'd been hearing about lately.

So yeah, she intended to press Dan for details, and use her instincts Laila had praised, to get to the bottom of the mystery.

And soon.

But right now, she was waiting for Jackson to wake up.

He'd slept through the night, through the checks on his wound, his blood pressure, his temperature with a scary sort of intensity . . . as in, he didn't groan or move or show any indication that someone was touching him. Instead, he just slept on, and it would have been seriously frightening if not for the fact that the nurses and doctor who checked on him were not concerned in the least.

But Molly didn't think she'd rest easy until he was back to feeling more like himself . . . and acting less like a Sleeping Beauty.

Knock-knock.

She glanced up and saw Laila was standing in the doorway.

"Can I come in?"

"Yes, of course." Molly closed her laptop with a sigh of relief. She'd been trying to weed through the spreadsheet Shannon had sent with the bakery's finances while attempting to appear as though she weren't counting every breath that Jackson took.

Laila had a bag from a fast food restaurant in one hand, a tray with two coffees in the other, and Molly wasn't going to lie, her stomach rumbled.

Yes, it was fast food.

Yes, she would have turned her nose up at it just the day before.

But today, coffee paired with an egg sandwich and greasy hash browns sounded just about perfect.

She reached for the bag then stopped when Laila held it against her chest.

"This isn't for you."

"O-oh." Molly's cheeks went hot. "I'm sorry. I thought—"

Laila grinned then held out the bag. "I'm just fucking with you. I'm guessing this is utter shit when compared to the stuff you make in your bakery." She set the tray on the small table next to the bed. "Wasn't sure how you take your coffee?"

"Just black," Molly told her. "I have enough sugar throughout the day."

Laila handed over a cup then proceeded to dump no less than six sugars and four little containers of cream into her own coffee. "What?" she said when Molly stared at her, eyebrows raised—because, seriously, Laila gave off tough, military badass vibes. She did not give off six sugars and four creamers vibes.

"Nothing," Molly said. "You do you."

Laila took a sip and sighed in pleasure. "I will. Also, let it be noted for the universe that I do not get enough sugar throughout the day, so I stock up on it first thing."

"Well, next time you're in the neighborhood, and when our little mafia problem is solved, come into the bakery, and I can provide you enough sugar to jumpstart your system for the day."

She nudged the other woman's shoulder. "I also promise that it'll be tastier than a fast food coffee and breakfast sandwich."

Laila snorted. "Twist my arm why don't you?" A beat. "You make croissants?"

"Chocolate-filled and traditional, every single day," Molly told her. "Flakey pastry, buttery layers—"

The egg sandwich was an inch from Laila's mouth, but at Molly's words she set it back down on the paper wrapper and frowned. "No fair, Ms. Baker."

"Hey, *I'm* the one promising you tasty treats."

"But you're not the one *with* tasty treats," Laila said. "So, eat your breakfast sandwich, drink your coffee, and tell me when exactly you're going to relax enough to sleep so that when this one"—she pointed at Jackson's still-sleeping form—"wakes up, he won't kill me or Dan for letting you run yourself into exhaustion."

"Um. That's not . . . " She trailed off when Laila's brow lifted.

Okay, so maybe she was counting breaths and freaking out about Jackson and the possibility of infection, or the chance of some stitch coming free and him bleeding out, or maybe that the surgeons had missed something—

"You don't have much of a poker face, do you?"

Molly sighed. "I'm guessing you don't need me to answer that."

Laila reached over and squeezed her hand. "I'm not going to tell you to stop worrying," she said. "But I'll just tell you that it'll get better."

"I'm guessing you're speaking from experience?"

A nod. "My line of work is not an easy one at times."

"I could see that," Molly said then asked softly, "And the nightmares? Do they ever really go away?"

Jackson shifted slightly in the bed, drawing her gaze before Laila could answer, her shoulders tensing as she waited to see if he would finally wake. When his eyelids fluttered and slid open, Laila stood, grabbing her food and drink. "Looks like that one is going to give you some peace of mind." She nodded at the untouched sandwich on the table. "Just make sure you *finally* eat something."

"Molly?" Jackson's voice was groggy.

Laila smiled, headed for the door. "For the record, the nightmares *do* go away. Over time they tend to fade on their own," she said. "*Though*, I have found that having someone to hold you while you sleep makes that process go by a little faster." A beat, a smile curving the corners of her mouth. "Lucky you, I think you have a volunteer." Another pause. "It also helps to actually *eat something.*"

Then she was gone, and Molly focused back on Jackson.

His chocolate eyes were molten and hot.

"Nightmares?" he asked.

"Um—"

He cut her off before she could answer, asking, "*Actually* eat something?"

"Uh—"

Jackson's gaze flicked to the nightstand and he leaned up enough to grab the sandwich Laila had brought then shoved it into Molly's hands. "Food," he growled. "Then sleep."

"Jack—"

"*Food.*"

"Are you trying to be a caveman?" she snapped. "Because it's not attractive."

His expression went thunderous. "Your skin is pale, those circles under your eyes are darker than that black coffee you like to drink, and your hands are shaking," he said. "You need to eat and rest."

Molly's eyes flicked down, saw that her hands were indeed trembling.

"*You're* telling *me* to rest."

His eyes narrowed. "Eat the fucking sandwich before you pass out, Molly."

Her temper flared, but also . . . she found she couldn't argue further with the man who'd taken a bullet for her, who'd been rushed into emergency surgery, who'd slept the last eighteen hours, and had done it hard, after declaring his love for her because his body needed healing.

She picked up the damn breakfast sandwich and started choking it down.

Yes, she was being dramatic and a fancy bitch about the fact it was from a fast food restaurant. It wasn't *that* bad—so the bread and egg and cheese wasn't her chocolate croissants or apple turnovers, but it was warm and food and filled her belly.

Add in some much-needed coffee, and she was feeling much better by the time she finished it.

"Happy?" she asked, setting the cup down on the table. "I ate—*oof!*"

One minute she was straightening from putting the coffee down, the next she was yanked forward, sprawling on the bed, instantly trying to get up, to move away from Jackson, lest she hurt him.

"Stop squirming," he ordered then huffed out a pained breath.

Molly immediately froze. "What the hell are you doing?" she whispered.

"Getting you to rest," he whispered back.

"I can't rest *here*," she said, still whispering.

"Nightmares," he replied softly, as though that were an explanation that made any sense. "Also, why are we whispering?"

"I don't know," she whispered then forced her voice back to normal. "Jackson, you had surgery yesterday, and you have a wound that's just barely begun to heal. You need space to do that."

"How am I supposed to rest if the woman I love isn't eating or sleeping?" he asked. "If the situation were reversed, would you be able to just go back to sleep?"

Well, put it that way.

He touched her cheek, his expression telling her that he knew he'd won this round.

"Glad you're going to see reason." He tapped her lightly on the nose.

She narrowed her eyes at him.

Jackson grinned. "Why is it I find it incredibly sexy when you glare at me?"

"That's not supposed to be the result of my glare," she muttered. "I still think I should move back to the chair. It reclines enough for me to lay down and—"

A finger to her lips. "Let me do this for you, love," he murmured. "I can't do much else, can't make this problem go away, can't suddenly manifest superhero powers and whisk you off to somewhere safe. But I *can* hold you if the nightmares come."

And how could she disagree with that?

"I'm not hurting you?"

"Having you in my arms feels nothing short of right."

Carefully, she shifted to her side, making sure to not put any part of her body near his wound, near the IV that was still pumping him full of saline and antibiotics. After a moment, he ignored her minute, tentative movements and just closed his arms around her, tugged her against his chest, and ordered, "Sleep."

Because it felt right to be held by him, because he sounded

drowsy himself, Molly didn't fight the order or bother to comment on his caveman-like tactics.

Instead, she closed her eyes and for the first time in days, fell asleep without a deluge of worry downpouring through her dreams.

TWENTY

Jackson

BEING SHOT SUCKED.

Just in case anyone was wondering.

He'd spent the last week hunkered down in the hospital trying to pretend that his injury was no big deal, all while feeling pathetically weak when his legs shook as they carried him to the toilet.

Because his first conscious action after making sure that Molly had gotten some food into her, as well as some rest, had been to get the fucking catheter out.

Going to the bathroom on his own seemed a necessary skill.

First, peeing on his own.

Second, making sure they were safe.

Also second, building on what he and Molly had started.

And third, world domination ... *bahaha!*

He rolled his eyes at himself, knowing he couldn't blame the pain medication any longer for the horrible joke. Nope. That was all him and his stir-crazy brain.

Seven days confined to a bed, with only a few short breaks

and halting traipses down the private hospital's hallways to continue building his strength. Seven days where Molly had taken care of *everything* from managing to get into his laptop to get in touch with his assistant—he'd discovered that on the second day in bed, after sleeping for the majority of those two days, that he'd apparently developed appendicitis and was recovering. So, aside from a few calls to his CFO and COO, handing over the big projects, and an inbox that could never quite get to zero, Jackson didn't have much to do.

No meetings.

Nothing needing his approval.

Lots of sitting around, twiddling his thumbs, and watching some bad reality television show Laila, leader of the second team Dan had called in, had put on TV, and although he'd never admit it, Jackson was starting to see the appeal.

Molly, meanwhile, had not.

She wasn't used to time away from the bakery, wasn't used to not being on her feet all day, creating delicious masterpieces from flour and eggs and butter.

She had taken stir crazy and raised it one delivery of supplies to the hospital's kitchen, seven batches of different muffins, two of croissants, and one of apple turnovers.

Dan and Laila and their respective team members taking a turn at the hospital had been thrilled.

Jackson had kept his mouth shut.

Because the IV had come out shortly after the catheter and because that day he'd finally managed the strength to hobble down to the kitchen and check on her . . . and had gotten some treats for his trouble.

Plus, between the baking and the managing of her business, she didn't fight him on sleeping in his arms every night.

Slow and steady, rebuilding that trust, getting to hold her close, to smell her, to feel her against him. To admit that, he too, had nightmares and when she was next to him, he slept better because he knew she was safe.

But by tomorrow, he'd at least be allowed to return to the condo—now retrofitted with more security and additional body-guards. Dan's team was apparently tracking down a final few leads before they took action. "If we cast the net wide enough," he'd said, "we might finally be able to put this thing to an end once and for all."

An end once and for all sounded good.

Jackson was done with looking over his shoulder. He was finally ready to live his life.

With Molly.

Who breathed out a long-suffering sigh when the older female on screen lamented about the man she was supposed to be marrying—all without having ever seen him—and their seven-year age difference.

Again.

"I can't take this any longer."

She pushed up from her chair, nodding at Laila who was currently on watch and was somehow giving the impression of both devouring the train wreck on the television while also being aware of everything around her.

Case in point, she was on her feet, positioning herself between them and the door several seconds before the knock came at the door.

"Identify," she called.

This didn't worry Jackson because it was something that had happened the entire time he'd been awake to witness it. This time, like all the others, they heard a familiar voice rattle off a string of numbers and letters, which had Laila relaxing and the door opening after she said, "Cleared."

Dan poked his head in. "Hey," he announced. "I'm here to rescue you from reality TV."

Molly sighed in relief, Laila made a noise of protest, and Jackson stifled his response that it wasn't really saving if he wanted to know where the TV show was going.

Regardless, Mol saved him from blurting that out by announcing, "I'm going to bake."

"I'll walk with you," Laila said. "Suddenly too much testosterone in this room." She grabbed her stuff as Molly bent and brushed her lips across his, murmuring, "I'll be back in a little bit. Going to finish making those pumpkin muffins."

He watched them leave, mind prickling.

Maybe it was the testosterone comment from Laila, having learned over the week that the woman had spent most of her life surrounded by males and was certainly no stranger to rooms filled with testosterone—and that *those* rooms most definitely didn't have trashy reality TV shows blaring in their backgrounds.

Or maybe it was the pumpkin muffins.

Because Molly had told him she'd finished the batch that morning.

Unfortunately, by the time those two oddities punctuated his brain, by the time he mentioned them to Dan, and by the time they both tried to reach Molly and Laila, respectively, it was too late.

They were gone.

TWENTY-ONE

Molly

"WHAT IS IT?" she asked the moment they were out of earshot of the room, heading down the hall toward the stairwell that led to the kitchens.

"Wait." Laila tugged open the door, started heading down the stairs, with Molly following. They stopped about halfway down, Laila's gaze going above and below them, silently searching for long seconds until her eyes returned back to Molly's.

"It's tomorrow," she said. "They're going to make their move in the morning when we head to the condo."

Molly's breath caught. Shit. That sounded ominous. "So, we're not going to go? And why aren't we discussing this with Dan and Jackson?" she asked. "Shouldn't they know that—"

Laila reached out and squeezed her shoulder. "I'm worried that Dan might be in on it."

"What?" Molly's mouth fell open. "No." She shook her head. "That can't be right. He's been trying to solve this for four years. He's—"

"There's someone on the inside," Laila interrupted.

"I was right?" she asked carefully.

Laila nodded, releasing her arm. "I intercepted a coded message, encrypted on our server in a language that is supposed to be strictly for us—" A door opened above them, footsteps coming down. Laila tensed, her body between the person's and Molly's but when Laila saw who it was, she relaxed and stepped to the side.

It was a male agent Molly hadn't seen around before.

"Daniel," Laila said when he hesitated before moving by them. "Have you met Molly yet?"

"No." He stuck out his hand, and Molly shook it, intimidated by the sheer size of him. This was a man who could crush her like a toothpick. "Hi, I'm Daniel. Also known as the bigger, *smarter* Dan."

Laila grinned. "Who goes by *Daniel* because two Dans in the group is two too many."

"Rude." He winked. "Actually, I go by Daniel because it's more sophisticated."

"Also, he lost the game of rock-paper-scissors."

"A *tournament* of rock-paper-scissors."

"To-may-to, to-mah-to," Laila said. "Daniel and I go way back. Stitches come out?"

He nodded. "All recovered."

"Glad to hear it. I missed your dumb ass," Laila said, grinning to soften the insult, though Daniel didn't seem the least bit perturbed by it. "You heading out back?" she asked.

Another nod. "Yup. I'm on watch while Ryker gets some shuteye." He glanced at Molly, smiled. "Nice to meet you."

"You, too." She inwardly frowned, trying to understand why her brain was pinging, but then Laila turned and pushed through the door into the kitchen, studying the space for several long moments before waving Molly in then closing and leaning back against the door.

"I need you to be careful," Laila said. "The reason we're not up in that hospital room telling this to Dan and Jackson is because the message I intercepted was in Dan's code."

Molly gasped.

"I don't know if the person on the inside is really him, or if it's someone else who's trying frame him," Laila told her. "All I know is that this whole situation smells like high heaven, so I need you to stick close to Jackson, to me, and most of all to be careful."

She nodded. "I can do that."

Laila squeezed her arm.

"Good."

"You're not with the FBI or the CIA, are you?"

"If I told you that then I'd have to kill you."

Molly laughed.

Laila didn't.

In fact, her face might as well have been made of granite. Her blue eyes cold and unfathomable, her jaw tight, her shoulders rigid. She reached into her pocket and pulled out her cell phone.

Oh shit.

"Never mind," Molly said. "So . . . um . . . I'll just start mixing batter?"

Yes, the last was a question. No, she hadn't necessarily underestimated Laila, the other woman was clearly capable and strong. It was just that with all the reality TV and joking around, she'd sort of forgotten that the other woman was dangerous.

Okay, so she *had* underestimated Laila.

She wouldn't be making that mistake again.

Her eyes darted to the door, mentally calculating her chances of getting by Laila if *she* turned out to be the mole.

Maybe she could put her sheet pan skills to the test?

But just as she'd started to inch toward the stack of them near the oven, Laila grinned and bent over laughing. "I'm just fucking with you."

Molly didn't find that nearly as amusing. "That's not funny."

Laila was still laughing as she straightened. "It is to me." She threw an arm around Molly's shoulders. "But seriously, all I can tell you is that I work for an entity that has a particular interest in making the world a better place."

"Does this entity fund this hospital?"

"Sometimes the work is dangerous and certain accommodations need to be made."

"How wonderfully vague," Molly deadpanned.

A flash of white teeth. "We're good at vague. But we're also good at keeping people safe." She rolled her eyes. "Or usually, anyway," she muttered. "When we don't have someone on the inside working against us." She dropped her arm, reached for the door. "Okay, so let's skip making the pumpkin muffins and get you glued to Jackson's side, so I can kick some ass and figure out—"

Laila didn't get to finish the sentence.

A puff of air blew past Molly's ear, and as she whipped around to see it, she heard Laila grunt, heard the soft, "*Fuck. Run, Molly.*"

Then it was too late.

Another puff of air.

A sharp pain in her stomach.

She glanced down, and there was a bright red dart sticking out of her abdomen. Then she looked up, saw the hulking

Maksim, who'd been waiting outside the elevator at Jackson's condo.

He didn't wait this time.

He came toward her.

And the last thing she saw before her brain went fuzzy and her legs weak, were his huge, beefy hands reaching for her.

Then the world went black.

TWENTY-TWO

Jackson

THE CALL CAME after Dan and his team members had torn the hospital apart, not finding a single sign of Molly and Laila, aside from Laila's cell phone, unlocked, an emergency code on the keypad, but not sent.

One agent, Daniel, said he'd seen them as they'd headed for the kitchen, when he'd been on his way to the back of the hospital for a guard change. But by the time the agent he'd been relieving had made his way back inside, they been gone. The phone the only clue that something was wrong.

Jackson had long given up the hospital gown, had forced his ass out of bed to help search as much as Dan would let him.

But he hadn't turned down the chair Dan had offered *after* he'd helped.

And now, Jackson's cell was ringing.

He glanced at Dan, who looked to the agent next to him with furious dark eyes and an expression that said he was going to kill whoever was responsible. "Ready for the trace?" The man nodded. "Okay," Dan said turning back to Jackson. "Answer, but on speaker."

Jackson swiped his finger across the screen, hit speakerphone. "Hello?"

A voice heavy with a Russian accent said, "Point Bonita Lighthouse. Midnight. Bring the hard drives currently in KTS's possession."

"Where are Molly and Laila?" he asked. "I need to hear that they're—"

Click.

"Fuck," he muttered, tossing the phone onto the desk. "Fucking hell."

"It's clearly trap," the pissed off man at Dan's side spat.

"Yeah, Ryker," Dan said. "I know." He glanced at his watch. "But we have three hours. We need to get the drives here, so we have something to negotiate with. Daniel?" He turned, nodded at the other agent. "Can you call headquarters? Tell them that we need some leeway." He glanced at Jackson. "If you work fast, can you make them look like the program? Something that looks real enough that we can hand over for the switch? If we use dummy drives to get Molly and Laila out—"

Look, Jackson got it.

He'd been staying mostly to the sidelines for the majority of this investigation, letting the agents lead the way since that was their expertise.

But this?

No. No more.

"Absolutely fucking *not*," he snapped. "I'm not putting the woman I love at risk just because some politician with something to hide might get outed from my program. I've sat back for too long, letting you guys drive this, but I'm done." He shoved to his feet. "They can *have* the fucking program, can use it to glean whatever fucking personal information—porn habits, racist comments, search habits—they want. I don't give a shit any longer." He slapped his hands on the desk. "Because I'm done risking Molly's life for this. I'm done risking my own life and everyone else's. Is it the most noble thing in the world to turn it over? *No.* But *no longer* will I give up everything important to me for a program that someone else is going to make in a few years anyway."

Dan stared at him, eyes intense pools of deep blue.

Then he turned and nodded at Daniel. "Make the call. Get the drives here."

Daniel nodded and left.

Dan waited until the door shut then came over and clapped Jackson on the shoulder. "I promise that you're done having to give things up." A beat. "Nice speech by the way."

Then before Jackson could ask Dan what in the fuck he meant by that, the agent began talking.

And suddenly, a hell of a lot more pieces fell into place.

Less than an hour later, the drives were in the back of an SUV, Jackson was sandwiched by a pair of muscled military guys, and they were heading to the lighthouse at Point Bonita.

This time he wasn't going to sacrifice to get Molly back.

He was going to fight for her.

Until his last breath.

TWENTY-THREE

Molly

SHE WOKE to someone nudging her hard in the side.

To someone hissing in her ear.

"Molly! Wake up, now!"

Boulders were attached to her eyelids, but she managed to wrench them open, to see that she and Laila were . . . *somewhere.*

She sniffed and inhaled salt. Looked around and saw trees and dirt and darkness barely punctuated by moonlight. Listened and could hear waves crashing at a distance.

Were they near the ocean?

"*Molly.*"

She blinked, focused on the someone in front of her. On *Laila* in front of her, arms bound, eye swelling, and normally contained blond ponytail scattered to hell and back.

"Laila," she whispered, instinctively keeping her voice low in volume to match the other woman's. "Where are we?"

A shake of her head. "No time. The guards have finally gone. I need out of these restraints."

Molly glanced at the zip ties that were wrapped around Laila's wrists, her arms pulled tightly behind her back. Her own wrists were free, but that probably had more to do with her not posing a threat.

Too bad there weren't any sheet pans around.

"Is there a trick to getting them off?" she asked quietly.

"Yeah," Laila said, her teeth flashing in the dim light. "A knife."

Molly shifted to her knees. "Well, I don't happen to have one of those."

Another flash of white teeth. "Well, I *do*. Reach into my bra, but carefully. There's one sewn into the band."

"Sewn in?"

"You never know when it might come in handy." Laila gave a small shrug. "And it's usually missed because the people searching are too focused on other things. Here," she added when Molly didn't move, just stared at her incredulously. "Under my shirt on this side."

"Got it," Molly said.

"Be careful," Laila told her, "I can feel that it's come loose of the sheath."

Nodding, she put her hands under the T-shirt and moving up to the band of Laila's bra then sliding between the fabric and her skin, trying to find the knife without stabbing herself or feeling Laila up.

She didn't succeed on either effort.

"Ouch!" she muttered, feeling the tip dig into her finger then carefully shifting back and working at the other end. "How are you able to move without stabbing yourself?"

"Lots of practice," Laila quipped. "Though usually it stays in the sheath."

"I'm guessing there aren't a lot of females in your can't-tell-you-without-killing-you entity," she said, running her finger carefully along the edge of the knife.

"Not so much."

"Well, tell whoever it is that designed this thing to go back to the drawing board," she muttered. "This could kill you."

"In fairness, I'm not usually in this particular position when I'm trying to retrieve it."

"*In fairness,* I don't think they're all that familiar with the inner workings of the female bra."

Laila snorted. "I think they're probably more familiar than either of us."

Molly froze then thought of the muscled badasses she'd seen over the last week, "Okay, fine. You're probably right."

"What a sad thing to be right about."

Molly snorted then, "Got it!" She tugged at the handle, feeling it come loose of whatever string or casing it had gotten stuck on. "I keep thinking someone is going to step out of the trees and call 'Cut!' at any time," she said, carefully sliding the blade from beneath Laila's bra and T-shirt. "Then ask me to do it again, only with more fondling."

"Not sure that's possible," Laila said.

"Hilarious." She held up the blade, thin and slender, but also scarily sharp, as her bleeding finger could attest. "How should I do this?" Last thing she wanted was to cut Laila.

"Just slip it in and tug," Laila said.

Molly blurted, "That's what he said."

Then froze and her gaze met Laila's, smiles breaking out on their faces. "I didn't think I'd be the type of person who'd be making jokes when I'm about to die," Molly said, shifting around and doing as Laila instructed—shoving the blade in the gap and yanking it toward her. It took a surprising amount of force to cut through the tie, and she suspected Laila's wrists didn't come out of the endeavor unscathed.

She didn't complain though, didn't do anything other than spin, take the knife from Molly's hands, and say, "You're not going to die. That's the first thing you need to remember. Second," she said. "Laughter is a way to cope with stressful situations. Keep it so you can freak out later instead of now."

Molly nodded, sucked in a breath. "Okay. Pretend to be a badass now. Cry later."

A punch to her shoulder. "Exactly." Laila shimmied and pulled the knife's sheath from her bra, covered the blade, and then stuck it in the back of her pants. "Ready?" she asked.

"For what?" Molly was blinking, stunned at how fast Laila had moved.

"For your first lesson in badassery."

And then she showed Molly how to launch herself over the cliff.

TWENTY-FOUR

Jackson

"DOESN'T MAKE ANY SENSE," Daniel muttered as they all piled out of the SUV. "Why would they knowingly corner themselves?"

They had pulled into the parking lot, and the lighthouse was a short hike ahead of them.

A short *dead-end* hike.

"Because they're not planning on being cornered," Ryker muttered. "It's a trap, dude."

"Yeah," Dan agreed, checking the straps on his backpack. "They want the drives. The rest of us are collateral." He glanced at Jackson. "You sure you're up for this?"

"Yup." Jackson adjusted the bulletproof vest he wore, the one he was all too aware didn't protect his head in the least, and tried to summon up some of the same confidence these guys had when he didn't have a gun . . . not that *having* a gun would mean anything, since he had no clue how to use one.

But he digressed.

Because they had a half-mile hike ahead of them, one that

would be easy on a normal day, but one that seemed daunting in the dark, especially when he was recovering from a bullet wound.

Jackson didn't say any of that.

Instead, when Dan said, "Fifteen minutes. Let hit it," he followed the other man who followed Daniel, and was trailed by Ryker.

Quiet.

It was very quiet as they walked.

Well, *they* were quiet, not making any noise as they moved, not the crunching of rocks or a stick being broken beneath their boots, not a muttered curse as they tripped over a bump in the path.

Nope. All the noise came from Jackson.

And knowing that, he tried to walk carefully and silently . . . but he just didn't have the skill.

He was also slowing them down, not just because of his injury but because these men could move.

Post-bullet Jackson wasn't currently in the best shape of his life.

But then, his ineptitudes turned out to be a good thing. Because the path narrowed and turned a corner, a metal bridge seeming to spring up out of nowhere as it spanned a huge gulf below them.

Shouting erupted. Shouting in *Russian*.

Flashlights flicked on, bouncing through the dark in the distance and then closer.

Footsteps pounded along the metal bridge.

Before Jackson could open his mouth to ask what they should do, he was yanked back and to the side, Ryker moving in front of him. "Down," he hissed, and Jackson didn't hesitate, didn't question the order. He hit the dirt, wincing when his stitches protested. "Stay," Ryker snapped.

Jackson stayed.

The footsteps pounded closer then closer then . . . Dan made a gesture with his hand and Daniel *moved*. He grabbed the first man that came over the bridge, wrestling him to the ground while Dan took the next, and then Ryker took the third. They were silent, the three men between him and the mafia as they silently immobilized the figures sprinting over the bridge.

Then he felt something hit his shoulder. Hard.

But not where the guys were focused. Not in front of them.

It came from *beneath* them.

He twisted, felt his eyes go wide, and had to bite back a curse. Because beneath the bridge, clinging to the edge of the craggy cliffside were Molly and Laila, the latter with a knife clutched between her teeth.

Jackson didn't think.

He moved, shimmying forward and reaching over the edge. He grabbed Molly's arm, the back of her pants, and yanked her up next to him on level ground, but when he turned to help Laila, he saw she was already up, hustling toward the group of men, joining the fray with a sharp word to Dan.

Ryker froze for a heartbeat, his hands around the neck of one of the men who'd come over the bridge, then he moved, tearing a gun out of another one's hands, as Laila slipped between them.

The *pop-pop* of silenced gunfire.

Flashlights shining, blinding him for long moments before his eyes adjusted again.

Scuffling on the path.

The sound of fists meeting flesh.

But the entire fight was quieter than he would have expected, certainly quieter than a fight scene in any action movie he'd ever watched.

And then it was over.

A line of bodies on the ground. Laila, Ryker, Daniel, and Dan standing over them.

"Any more?" Dan asked Laila.

"Not sure," she said. "Unconscious until ten minutes ago."

"You climbed a fucking cliffside when you were unconscious?" Ryker snapped.

Laila rolled her eyes. "I know you'll reconsider the logic of your words later," she muttered. "For now—"

If Jackson never saw another circular, red light for the rest of his life, it would be too soon. But this dot wasn't on Laila or Molly or Daniel or even on Ryker. It was on Dan, squarely in the center of his chest.

He glanced down, cursed.

Footsteps coming over the bridge. The light drifting up from the bulletproof vest, centering on Dan's forehead as Maksim emerged from the shadows. He stopped out of reach and his gaze slipped from Dan and the group of agents, over to Jackson, who tucked Molly behind him.

"I'll take the hard drives now."

He knew.

Maksim somehow knew that none of the badasses had the drives. He knew they were in the backpack that Jackson was carrying.

"Why do you want the hard drives so badly?" Laila asked, attempting to draw his attention, but Maksim didn't shift his focus from Jackson . . . or move his gun from Dan's head.

"How fast can you duck, Agent Plantain?"

Dan's spine went stiff.

"Also," Maksim said. "I don't give a shit about the program that fucking pain in the ass made." His word hardened. "I want those fucking hard drives."

"What's on them that's so important?" Laila asked.

Maksim smiled, but it wasn't a happy smile. This was laced

with cruelty, anger, and . . . satisfaction. His eyes flicked between the agents. "Well, aside from it having information that is critical to Alexei's innocence—"

"Read: there is blackmail material on someone in Spain that will get him out," Laila muttered.

Maksim's expression shifted, more satisfaction creeping in. "I think that is what you Americans would call splitting hairs." He shifted his gun, moving it from Dan over to Molly. "I was going to only wound her before," he said to Jackson. "Just to *motivate* you to come to the right conclusion and hand over what our money bought."

"I returned the investment," Jackson said. "Once I figured out what you wanted, I gave it all back."

"But you couldn't return the investment of our time." He sighed, shaking his head. "You Americans always want and want, but never are willing to give. Although, perhaps that isn't fair. I have found one individual here who is—"

Daniel was going to move.

Jackson didn't stop to process how he knew that. Instead, he watched in horror.

Daniel yanked Laila's knife from her hand and threw it. The blade flew through the air and . . . struck home, cutting off Maksim mid-sentence. His body crumpled, collapsing to the metal frame of the bridge.

"What the fuck was that?" Dan spun, grabbing Daniel's vest and shaking him violently. "We had him. We fucking *had* him—"

Laila got in his face, followed by Ryker, and the conversation got heated.

Daniel shoved them away, turned to Jackson. "Give them to me," he snapped. "Now."

"Daniel." Laila's tone was devastated. "*No.*"

But the man who had stopped just a few feet away, didn't

react, didn't seem to care that while her knife was in Maksim's chest, Daniel might as well have stabbed it directly into Laila's heart. "Hand it over."

Jackson felt a tug on the backpack and let his shoulders relax, his arms to fall so that Molly could slip it free. Fine. Daniel could have it.

If it meant they would all be safe then—

Molly stepped to the side, holding the backpack, and drawing Daniel's focus. He took a step toward them, hand extended, and . . . Molly launched the backpack over the cliff.

"No—"

The sentence cut off abruptly as Daniel was momentarily detained by Ryker, but then he was free and he was running—not toward the parking lot, but over the bridge.

His footsteps clambered across the metal, followed by Dan, Ryker, and Laila's as they gave chase.

But Jackson couldn't focus on that, couldn't take more time to think, to process the roar of a boat's motor as it came to life and then faded away. Instead, he just needed to feel and react and live without walls between him and the rest of the world. He spun, took Molly into his arms, and hugged her tightly.

"It's over," Dan said, when he came back, Daniel conspicuously absent. "For you, it's finally over."

And for the first time in four years, Jackson knew that when the other man said those words, it was the truth.

Just as he believed Dan when he added, Laila and Ryker coming up behind them, "For us, this is just beginning."

TWENTY-FIVE

Molly, A Week Later

"HOW ARE we just supposed to go back to real life when we've spent the last couple of weeks playing commando?" she asked Jackson, stepping between his legs as he sat in "his" stool in the bakery's kitchen.

"Easy," he said, slipping his arms around her. "Because we weren't *actually* the commandos."

She wrinkled her nose. "But, I *did* climb a cliff in the dark of night, after being drugged with a poison dart—"

"Don't remind me." Jackson shuddered.

"I also finally got to put my sheet pan throwing skills to good use."

He grinned. "True. Who would have thought that all those years of throwing things at my head would be useful?"

Molly laughed, leaning against his chest. "I love you, baby."

"I love you, too." He touched her cheek. "But when I think what could have happened . . . Promise me, no more cliff climbing, no more playing at being a commando. I don't think my heart can take it."

As if she was suddenly going to go to badass school. She had rolls to bake, muffins to perfect. "I promise," she said. "Any more cliff climbing will be in a perfectly controlled environment. With ropes and a safety net and—"

He kissed her. "No climbing."

She kissed him. "No more arguing."

"What's the fun in that?"

He had a point. Which was why she nipped his bottom lip and said, "I think I may take up target practice . . ."

Jackson growled and tugged her close, tickling her lightly on the ribs, which turned into tickling a different body part that she very much enjoyed. Still, it was the middle of the day and they both had work they should be doing, so she kissed him lightly on the lips then straightened. "I know something that *my* heart can take."

He nuzzled her throat. "What's that?"

"You taking me on a first date—" She stopped, and shook her head. "Or another first date . . . a *second* first date?"

Jackson grinned, brushed her hair out of her face. "What if I already said I had it planned?"

"I'd ask if it includes chocolate and alcohol."

"As a matter of fact . . ."

"Mmm." She nipped his jaw. "Well, then I'd say I accept."

"Friday," he told her. "When you don't have to be up so early and can sleep in the next day."

Molly's heart swelled, because aside from the whole Jackson-nearly-dying and the her-being-kidnapped thing . . . these last few weeks had been something special. Because he had let the walls down, because he learned and paid attention to the little things—her schedule—and the big things—how she was in love with him but wanted to have the time to get to know him again, for them to learn each other. Because they deserved to take the time, they deserved the space and ability and even the lovely fluttering feeling that came from building a strong foundation between them.

Even if it heavily featured a crumbling cliffside in the First Act.

Or Second Act. Or maybe it had been during the finale?

The point was . . . this was their chance, whether it be the start of the sequel, or just the lovely paved road that led to their happily ever after.

And know what the awesome thing about sequels was?

That sometimes they began with a plot twist.

Which was why she tugged Jackson off the stool, took him by the hand and led him to her office. The cameras had been removed. The microphones were gone. The bakery was closed, her employees long gone as she'd gotten ahead on the following day's baking while he caught up on his emails.

"What are you doing?" he asked.

She closed the door, pushed him back against it. "Well, funny story. I did some research about gunshot wounds . . ." She let her hand drift down his chest, coasting over the waistband of his slacks, dipping under. "Turns out that while sex is still off the table"—she dropped to her knees—"blow jobs aren't."

"Mol—"

He groaned when she freed him. "Consider this you getting lucky before the first date."

Then before he could argue further, she closed her lips over his cock, sucked him deep, and Molly showed him how lucky he was about to get.

And when she finished, coaxing him through to the other side, Jackson nudged her back onto the desk, dropped to his knees, and *then* he showed her exactly how lucky she already was.

But then again, she already knew that.

EPILOGUE

PART ONE

Jackson, One Year Later

THE WHITE DRESS.

The flower arrangements.

The glittering diamond ring.

They had absolutely none of that.

Instead, they had croissants and apple turnovers. They had a minister standing in the front of bakery's display case. They had Molly's patrons as witnesses.

The only thing that was frilly and white was the apron Molly wore courtesy of her friend, Shannon.

But right now, he needed to pull the woman he loved away from the *thing* she loved most in the world . . . or perhaps, the second most. Well, frankly, he wasn't sure where he fell on the scale some days, certainly not when she was talked so sweetly to her rolls as she shaped them or her dough as it rose.

First or second, that was fine with him.

Because Jackson knew that at the end of the day, Molly came home to him and the rolls, they stayed at the—okay, sometimes they came home, too.

And that was fine.

What was not fine, however, was the sight of his woman, the one he was waiting to marry in the other room, crying.

He rushed over. "Baby, what's wrong?"

"I can't do this," she said. "I-I just can't—"

His heart sank. His stomach twisted itself into knots. His first instinct was to tell her that they didn't have to go through with this, that they could give themselves more time, that he'd step back and let her get her head together.

But . . . fuck that.

He was done with *that*. Done with stepping back and not fighting for the things he wanted.

Jackson had Molly back in his life and this last year had been, hands down, the best one of his life. So, no, he wasn't going to step back or send his woman on her merry way. He loved her, wanted her as his wife, as his partner, as his best friend.

"I'm going to marry you," he said, and, yes, his tone was sharp. But when Molly's eyes shot up to his, surprise lifting her brows, he kept talking. "No, we don't have to get married today, if it feels too soon. No, we don't have to get married next week or even next year. But I love you, Mol. You're *it* for me." He brushed a finger under each eye, wiping away the tears. "So, you *are* going to marry me, you *are* going to keep building our life together with me, and you *are*—"

She kissed him.

Long and wet and hot, and when she finally pulled back, his lungs burned, desperate for oxygen.

But before he could suck in enough air to regain his voice, Molly spoke. Thus, further proving how much more of a badass she was than him. Cliff-climbing, minimal need for oxygen, crafting deliciousness from flour, sugar, and butter that had taken the whole city by storm, no big deal.

"You silly man," she murmured, lips close enough that they brushed his when he spoke. "I wasn't talking about marrying you."

He frowned. "Then what?"

She backed up, shifting to the side, and Jackson noticed what was on the table. "*This.*"

"What is it?" he asked, staring at the blackened circles sitting on the counter.

Molly's cheeks went red. "Our wedding cake."

"I thought you didn't want to bother with a cake," he said, cautiously poking a finger into the pan, into what once had resembled cake, and now resembled a brick.

"I didn't," she said, flush spreading fuller. "But *you* did."

That was true.

He might not have given a shit about the dress or the church or even writing their sentimental vows.

But *he* cared about the cake.

Stupid.

And still, he'd always imagined his wedding punctuated with a cake, cutting it with their hands laced together over the knife, then messily feeding Molly a morsel, kissing off a dollop of buttercream frosting from her nose. It was the one thing he'd been able to picture with crystal clarity from the beginning.

Chocolate cake. White frosting.

That was it.

A small thing in the grand scheme of things, but he had also wanted Molly to have something sweet that she didn't have to make herself. So he'd offered to order one from a different bakery.

She'd flipped. He'd let it drop.

And she'd made him a cake anyway.

His lips began curving up.

Well, *burned* it.

"Honey."

She wrinkled her nose. "I blame it on the bullet holes in the oven."

"I thought the oven was replaced."

"Shh." A shake of her head. "We're ignoring that detail. It was the bullets. Most definitely. They must have made the timer malfunction."

Jackson tugged her against his chest. "Nice try, baby." He bent and nipped at her lips. "What was it really?"

Her expression softened, but she didn't argue or defer further. "I got distracted."

"You?" He lifted a brow. "When baking?"

A shrug. "It happens to the best of us."

"But not to *you*." Shifting, he brushed his lips over her cheek, dragged them down her throat, nipping at the spot just above her collarbone that never failed to make her shiver.

"Not to me," she murmured. "Or not usually anyway." She laced her hand through his. "It's just . . ."

His stomach clenched, but he'd grown a lot over the last year, had gone to therapy, had committed to tearing down the walls and forcing the little boy inside of him to grow up. Because of that, he was able to ask without being too terrified of the answer, "Just what?"

"Just thinking about . . . *this*," she said, and took their joint hands, placed them on her apron covered stomach. "Because it turns out this is actually going to be a shotgun wedding."

Jackson felt his mouth drop open, but inside his heart soared.

"Really?"

She grinned, nodded. "*Really* really."

His eyes burned, but just as he'd done over the last year, he embraced the burn, the feelings, the intense emotions instead of boxing them up or keeping them out or running scared. Still,

he wasn't exactly eloquent. "Mol," he murmured. "Baby, that's .
. ."

Amazing. Wonderful. Unexpected. Frightening. The best
fucking news of his life.

But she knew.

Knew that all of those thoughts were running through his
head even though the words might not be flowing through his
lips. She knew. Knew him and his heart. Knew how much
building a family and future together meant for both of them.

Which was why she simply lifted up on tiptoe, pressed her
lips against his briefly, and then took his hand, saying, "I know,
Jackson. I know."

He stared into those gorgeous green eyes for a long moment.

Then he straightened and tugged her toward the front of the
bakery. "Forget the cake. It's time to get married."

She didn't argue.

They said their I Do's, they kissed in front of a cheering
group of customers, and then . . . Jackson kissed a dollop of
apple turnover filling from Molly's nose.

For the record, it was every bit as tasty as buttercream
frosting.

EPILOGUE

PART TWO

Kate

DISGUSTED, she walked out of the bakery.

Mostly with herself for being jealous over the clearly happy couple.

Although, partly because they were so ridiculously happy. Come *on*. Who looked into each other's eyes with such devotion and joy while getting married in a freaking bakery with mostly strangers looking on?

No dress or cake—counterintuitive as that sounded, considering they were getting married in a freaking bakery.

No flowers, which would be Kate's weakness because she loved gardening and arranging flowers, having spent most of her extra money on sprucing up her backyard.

The inside might be a disaster.

But the backyard was a lush, gorgeous retreat.

Not that it mattered because she didn't have anyone to share it with. Least of which a gorgeous hunk of a man who stared at her with love in his eyes and tenderness in his smile.

Yes, she was bitter.

So, it was the perfect time for her cell to ring, her mother on the line.

Deal with the torture now? Or wait until it frothed to full power later?

She was already cranky and jaded and in a bad mood, so she might as well deal with her loving, but very nosy and interfering mother now. No sense in wasting a good mood later.

Because there *would* be a later.

Her mother loved her, that was never in doubt. What could *possibly* be questioned was the amount of attention she gave to her children's lives.

Attention that was now squarely focused on Kate.

On the fact that she was single when her two younger siblings were happily married, and her younger sister had recently popped out a kid.

Impressive. Beautiful—which she knew because she'd been in the delivery room.

But also . . . not *her.*

Hence, the increase in motherly calling.

Sighing, Kate swiped a finger to the screen and put her phone to the screen. "Hey, Mom."

"I've got the perfect man for you to bring to the Christmas party. He's a doctor and . . ."

Her mother continued talking, expounding on all of the wonderfulness that was this doctor. The trouble was that Kate was done with being set up. Her family were great at finding their own soulmates, their own happily ever afters . . . unfortunately that same ability didn't extend to her.

Either *by* her or *for* her.

It never failed to end in disaster. Both for her *and* for her date.

So, as much as she longed to have a man who she could call her own, one who'd call her his in return . . . she was taking a break from dating, from men, and most definitely from being set up.

"Mom," she began. "I'm not actually—"

"He's a doctor, isn't bald, and can have a conversation about something other than himself, Katie," her mother said. "He is a catch."

Who would turn into the world's worst asshole when he was around her.

Because that was her superpower.

Transforming seemingly *wonderful* men in lying, cheating, arrogant, self-centered, mansplaining, assholes.

And being that lightning didn't tend to strike the same place multiple times, Kate had decided on a hiatus from the opposite sex. Some time to sort out what was happening inside of her to make everyone she dated turn into a jerk.

This wasn't about all men on the planet being the bad guys, or her always picking wrong, or even about her family trying to set her up with a bunch of douche canoes. There was something wrong inside of *her*, something intrinsically wrong with the way she interacted with the men in her life.

So, a break.

Time to figure her shit out.

It was just . . . Christmas.

All of her family in one place. The huge party with the whole neighborhood. Everyone paired off and happy and gathering under the mistletoe her mother hung in each and every doorway.

And her.

Alone.

The pitying gazes plentiful.

Or worse . . . the copious conversations where all the happy people constantly threw every single male with half a brain cell in Kate's direction.

My cousin is in town and fresh out of a relationship . . .

I have a coworker who's new to the area. He's looking for someone . . .

My ex-husband would be perfect for you—he's actually a great guy . . .

And more.

Kate just couldn't take it, couldn't stand the idea of another Christmas party at her parents' house matched with someone who didn't fit her, or worse spending the entire extravaganza alone and in the corner, playing wallflower.

She wanted excitement.

She wanted someone who could be unequivocally hers.

She wanted someone who saw inside her and didn't run off in a panic.

". . . and Katie, love, he's going to be at dinner this Friday so that you two can get to know each other better—"

Fucking hell.

Family dinner *and* the Christmas Extravaganza?

Please. God. *No.*

"Um, Mom—"

"Remember he's got all his hair—"

"Actually, Mom. I'm kind of seeing—"

"And his stomach doesn't hang over his belt—"

"That's not—I don't really care about that—"

"*And* he's got the loveliest blue—"

"I'm engaged!" she screamed, cutting off her mother's soliloquy of all things doctor, and successfully drawing the attention of random strangers on the sidewalk. Which was a hard thing to do in San Francisco—because it was San Francisco and these streets had seen a lot of shit—but also could only further confirm that she'd screamed it like a complete and total lunatic.

Shrieking *I'm engaged* on street corners.

What every man wanted.

"Katie?" her mom asked. "Did you say you're engaged?"

No. No, she wasn't. Not even close. She was on a break from anyone with a Y chromosome, mostly to save them from herself.

But also . . . there was joy in her mom's tone.

Absolute joy that she had never heard directed at her. To her brother, when he'd announced he was proposing to Chelsea, then again at his wedding this last summer (during which Kate had fended off the worst setup of all setups, The Can't Take No For An Answer Setup). Her mother had expressed that joy when her sister had announced she was pregnant, and again after her adorable niece had been born.

But she'd *never* given it to Kate.

Which was probably the reason she let the crazy keep rolling along.

Why instead of saying, "No, Mom. You heard wrong," she said, "Yes, I am, and you'll get to meet him Friday at dinner."

Horror flowed through her as intensely as her mother's excitement poured through the airwaves, expressing her joy at meeting him, her joy at Kate having finally found a slice of her own happy.

"What's his name, honey?"

Oh fuck.

"What's that?" Kate asked, panic swarming to overtake horror. "You're breaking up."

Oh shit. Oh shit. She hadn't thought this through. She needed—

"I asked his name—"

"Hello?" More panic. More horror. More pretending the call was cutting out because she had to end this conversation now. Hell, she should have never picked up the call in the first place. "Mom? *Hello?*"

"Katie!"

Shit. Shit. *Shit.* "I can't hear you," she said. "If you can hear me. I'll call you later." She hung up.

Or never.

As in, she'd never call her family again. As in, she was moving to a deserted island and changing her name and—

Fuck.

Because despite all of the setups and the pity and the fact that they'd found their happy, she loved her family. So. Damned. Much. And she also loved that stupid fucking Christmas party, even when she was lonely.

"*Ugh.*" Kate groaned, feet sliding to a stop on that dirty San Franciscan sidewalk.

She had a choice here.

She also knew she wasn't going to make the right one.

Because, instead of calling her mother back and telling her she'd heard wrong, that she wasn't engaged, Kate opened Instagram, tapped on the profile of a man she'd been following for a while now, who'd followed her back and commented on a few of her posts, and . . . sent a message.

Later, she'd want to pretend she'd been drinking.

But in *that* moment, the only thing she was consumed with was desperation.

And lust. She couldn't deny lust was also her downfall.

Because surprisingly, shockingly, *insanely* the man from social media, the one whose abs had made her fall just a little in love with him . . .

He said yes.

And suddenly, Kate had a fiancé.

EPILOGUE

PART THREE

Dan

HE SLIPPED OUT of the back of the bakery, after having watched Jackson and Molly finally find their way to the happy ending they deserved.

No big church or puffy dress this time.

Just two people who were in love.

People who had almost missed their chance because he couldn't get his shit done.

"Fuck," he muttered, so damned tired of the guilt and yet knowing that it was just part of the job. When he'd been cherry-picked from the FBI a few years before and folded into the private sector, Dan had already been well-familiar with the failures that were common in this line of work.

Not every case was solved.

Not everyone came out alive.

Not every ending was happy.

Dan got that. He . . . just hadn't expected to find it so fucking depressing to be working for an agency with a bigger reach, who took on bigger bad guys from around the world.

Because despite the larger budget, the greater access to resources. Sometimes the bad guys still won.

And the only thing he hated more than the bad guys winning was when that unhappiness or death or boulder hanging over someone's head he was supposed to be helping was *his* fault.

"I knew you'd be here."

Dan didn't react. He might feel like a failure when it came with taking down the Mikhailova clan, but he was damned good at being aware of his surroundings, of keeping himself alive.

So, he knew that Laila was there, had slipped out the back door of the bakery, having felt the same connection with Molly and Jackson, and wanting to see them happy.

Because happy didn't happen often enough in this industry.

But just as he knew Laila had emerged from inside, even though she'd hardly made a sound when opening that heavy metal door, Dan also knew that Ava had come out behind her.

Ava.

Peaches. Humid summer days. Whisky and lemonade and—

Fuck. *Ava.*

She strode over to him, curves in a compact body, shining brown hair swept up into a ponytail that swung behind her shoulders as she moved, strength and confidence . . . and so many painful memories.

Her eyes looked right through him, minimizing everything that had happened between them two years ago.

Then those eyes narrowed, focused on him, seared straight into his soul.

"We found the hard drives."

A beat as Laila came forward and crossed her arms, expression furious.

"And we know what's on them."

BAD BRIDESMAID AND RIDING THE EDGE

Get your copy of Bad Wedding at www. books2read.com/BadWedding

Get your copy of Riding The Edge at www. books2read.com/RidingTheEdge

Now, keep reading for Bad Marriage, a never before released novella.

BAD MARRIAGE

A BILLIONAIRE'S CLUB NOVELLA

ONE

Abby

THE BABY WAS CRYING.

Again.

Groaning, she tossed the covers back, pushed herself out of bed, and blearily stood up.

Then promptly tripped over some sort of Lego creation and fell to the carpet.

"Abbs?" came Jordan's groggy voice. "I'll bring Emma to you."

"I'm okay. Go back to sleep," she said, knowing he would do so, and immediately at that. It was almost annoying how quickly the man could slip into unconsciousness.

And he needed it.

Emma had decided it was her tiny six-week-old's task to ensure the entire household was running on fumes—of the energy sense.

Or perhaps the diaper fumes sense.

Snort.

Rolling her eyes at herself, Abby pushed up to her feet,

Emma's cries growing in volume with each second that passed. She stepped over Carter's rendition of a Duplo house this time, snagged her robe from the chair by the door, and slipped out into the hall, still somewhat in awe of how dramatically her life had changed in just a few years.

She had a daughter.

And two sons.

She finally had a family after she'd always felt so lost about her place in the world.

She wouldn't say that her identity was solely based on being a wife and mother, but it had given her the confidence to live out her dreams.

So she could add boss, businesswoman, and partner to her list of attributes.

Along with sleep-deprived.

Pushing into Emma's bedroom, she saw that her daughter was red-faced and squalling—well, she'd heard that last part already, but now she could see the squished-up unhappiness of her expression.

"Oh, baby," she murmured, sweeping over and scooping her up. "I've got you."

The swaddle had come loose, and since Emma's diaper felt full, Abby took her to the changing table and completed the dirty end—literally—of the business. Then re-swaddled her and sat down in the rocker.

Emma had quieted, as she always did once she was picked up, though it was punctuated by tiny cries that told Abby her daughter was hungry. She unsnapped her nightgown and lifted Emma to her breast, rocking her softly and humming a nursery rhyme she didn't know all the words to. Which was okay. Her daughter seemed to like the melody even without the words.

Eventually, Emma finished and lay drowsily in Abby's arms while she tried to summon the energy to cover herself and begin the careful task of setting the baby in the crib without waking her.

Maybe arduous was more like it.

"Here, sweetheart." The soft words had her looking up at her husband, Jordan, who was wearing just a pair of boxer briefs and looking all too much like Thor when she was feeling very blah and stretched out and saggy. He slipped her nightgown back up, buckling the snap with practiced hands. Then he lifted Emma out of her arms.

"I told you to sleep."

"And I told you I'd bring the baby to you," he whispered, pressing a kiss to her forehead. "You're exhausted."

"You've got a membership to that club yourself."

He smiled, and she felt that quirk of his lips like a physical caress, a heat blooming within her that reminded her why they had three small children—though she'd only birthed two of them.

The third, Hunter, they'd adopted. Biologically, he was Jordan's nephew, but in all ways that truly mattered, he was their son.

A son that would need to be driven to school in—she glanced at the clock—three hours.

Dear God.

There was a reason sleep deprivation was considered torture.

She hadn't even realized that her eyes had slipped closed or that Jordan had successfully made the baby-to-the-crib transition until she felt the rocker move, until she felt herself being swept up into his arms.

"Wh—?"

"Hush," he whispered. "The little beast is finally asleep."

She dropped her voice to barely audible. "I'm too heavy."

Flashing blue eyes had her hiding her face in his chest. She hadn't meant to say that out loud, hadn't meant to let the insecurities that were building in her mind outside her brain. She'd just given birth six weeks before. Of course, her body had changed.

"Bull. Shit," he hissed.

She didn't reply, knowing that there wasn't much she could say. She was putting up a good front, but two babies in three years meant that she was feeling more than a little insecure.

Things—skin, breasts, hair—hung differently. Her stomach was . . . well, it might as well be a roadmap for how many lines crisscrossed it.

And she'd lost track of the last time she'd showered or worn a shirt without crumbs or spit-up or poop on it.

Hell, her hair probably had poop in it right now.

A tear leaked out of the corner of her eye.

"Abbs?" Jordan asked softly, navigating the mess of toys like a professional. No Godzilla-esque Duplo destruction for him, that was for sure.

Meanwhile, she—

"Sweetheart," he said, setting her on the bed and wiping the tear—okay *tears*—away. "What is it?"

She shook her head, knowing the inner voice was fueled by exhaustion and hormones. It would pass, and she'd feel more like herself.

Eventually.

"I'm okay," she whispered, hoping eventually would come sooner rather than later.

"You're not," Jordan argued. "But you're also too tired to argue about it now." He swept the covers up and over her, tucking them tightly around her. "Sleep, my love."

"But—"

He slid in next to her, pulled her against his chest. "Sleep."

And truly too exhausted to argue, she did as he ordered.

TWO

Jordan

SHE LOOKED LIKE A FUCKING ZOMBIE.

Dark circles, shuffling gait, pale skin as she staggered to a chair in the kitchen and sat down.

After making sure it wasn't too hot, he put a mug of tea in front of her and then a plate with toast, cinnamon, and sugar—her favorite of late.

Then he sat next to her.

Tired hazel eyes drifted to his. "Is Hunter up for school?"

He nodded. "I dropped him already."

Those eyes flew to the clock. "I'm sorry," she said. "It was my turn. I must not have heard the alarm and—"

He covered her hand. "I turned off your alarm, sweetheart."

She frowned. "Why?"

"You're not getting enough sleep."

"I'm fine."

He lifted a brow. "We're starting the bottle tonight."

"But—"

"No buts," he said. "You're running yourself ragged

between Carter and Hunter and Emma, and you need at least one chunk of solid sleep every night." Squeezing her fingers lightly, he shifted closer to her. "You don't have to be Super Mom. I'm here, too. Let me help."

"But you've been taking more of the nighttime feedings and that isn't fair."

He loved this woman, but she was talking crazy. "You mean I've been carrying Emma around and changing a few diapers while you're *feeding* her," he said. "Tell me which of those is more important."

"Jor."

"I love you," he said. "But this isn't a scoreboard. Your body needs to rest and recover, and you've been pumping, so why not use the milk?"

"What if we need it?"

"More than we both need sleep?"

She froze, and he knew he'd scored a point. Jordan understood she was exhausted—he wasn't feeling particular chipper himself after Emma's weeks of exercising her lungs—but Abby had been through a difficult pregnancy, a difficult delivery, and now a difficult few weeks. She needed more rest than she was getting.

Even if she was trying to pretend otherwise.

"I'm just not sure if it's too soon . . ."

He brushed back her hair from her face. "How about we just try? If it doesn't work out, then we'll go back to the other way."

"Okay," she said and picked up her cup of tea, lifting it to her lips.

Right on cue, Emma, who he'd had set up in the vibrating, musical swing in the corner, began crying. Which was promptly followed by Carter, who had been building a tower of wooden blocks that collapsed.

He glanced at his wife, lips twitching.

"What was that you said about rest?" she asked, fighting a smile.

"We'll look back at these days at some point, right?" He kissed the top of her head, moved to the swing and picked up Emma, bringing her back to Abby and shifting the mug well out of the way of flailing little arms. Then he scooped up Carter, hugging his son and talking him down from the tower edge before they sat on the rug together and rebuilt an even better one.

"You're a good dad," Abby said, coming over to them and kissing his cheek. "Even if you are a stubborn husband."

"I learned all of my stubborn skills from you," he deadpanned.

She laughed, and even after all these years, it was still the best sound on the planet. "I love you and your stubbornness." A waggling of her brows. "*And* your hammer."

He snorted. "My *hammer* is what got us into this mess."

"True," she said. "But it was worth it."

Jordan stared at his little family—minus one because Hunter was at school—and had to agree.

They were worth every hour of lost sleep and the gray hairs and the vomit and poop and fallen block towers.

But a week later, he had to wonder if Abby felt the same way.

She was getting more sleep, Emma having taken to the bottle like a champ and giving them each a block of almost four hours. It felt like nirvana, like the skies had cleared and the sun was shining down on them.

Or at least it did for him.

Abby had grown steadily quieter, even as the dark circles beneath her eyes faded.

Hormones, perhaps. Or a case of the baby blues. He'd read somewhere that they didn't always come on right after birth, that depression could slide in later.

He made a mental note to keep an extra close eye on her.

He'd just returned from dropping Hunter at school and was looking forward to a nice, hot shower and maybe a cup of coffee sans the side of tears, in that order, so he traversed the stairs as quietly as possible, slipping into the bedroom to not wake the beasts—er, his lovely, beautiful children.

Then tiptoed through the bedroom to not wake his lovely, beautiful *wife*.

He pushed open the door.

Abby was naked and in the shower, her gloriousness visible through the glass panes, and he was abruptly reminded of how long it had been since he'd held his wife, the water pouring down on them, her silken curves against him. She was still the most gorgeous woman he'd laid eyes on, and he needed to hold her. His gaze flicked to the left, to the monitor that showed his younger two children were still sleeping.

And he seized his opportunity.

He stripped down and slid into the shower behind her, slipping his arms around her waist and pulling her back against him.

"Jordan!" she shrieked, trying to squirm away.

"Hi, beautiful," he murmured, flicking his tongue out and tasting the shell of her ear.

"I—" She kept squirming, and he released her, frowning when she stepped out of the spray and reached for the towel hanging over the side, using it to cover herself.

"What is it?"

She shook her head, clutched the towel to her like it was a

lifeline and she'd just fallen off a ship in the middle of the ocean. "I—uh—the baby is up." She stepped out of the shower.

Emma wasn't up.

He could see that much, but he could also see that his wife was uneasy about something. Jordan wasn't sure whether she thought he was trying to get lucky—he certainly wouldn't turn her down, but he wasn't expecting anything, especially this soon after she'd given birth—or if she was uncomfortable with her body or if she was still tired and hormonal and just off, but any idiot could see that she needed some space.

"I'll hurry up and shower and grab her," he said, reaching for the bottle of shampoo.

"No!"

His eyes shot to hers, hands covered in suds, soap dripping down his temples.

"I—uh—" She was wrapping her robe around her still towel-covered body. "I've got her."

"Okay, sweetheart," he said.

But inside, he recognized the tell she'd just given him.

And he filed it away to deal with later.

Because he knew exactly how to deal with it.

THREE

Abby

SHE WAS A MESS. An absolute mess.

She was running away from her husband, had jumped like a cat trying to escape a bath when he'd touched her.

Stupid, she knew that.

He'd said time and again she was beautiful . . . but when he'd put his hands on hers, when it had felt different—

She'd just not been able to handle it.

Hustling into the closet, she wrestled her way into her maternity jeans, the stretchy top making her feel like she was trying to squirm into leather leggings for how difficult it was.

Not that she'd ever worn leather leggings.

That was more Seraphina's style.

Her buxom best friend would probably bounce back from pregnancy and slip right into her jeans—or leather leggings.

Meanwhile, Abby was wearing stretch-top clothes and hiding the post-partum bump that still wouldn't go away. Sagging skin, a speed bump, and a husband who looked like a god.

What was she going to do?

The monitor lit up, Carter talking to himself in bed. She watched him, his little feet in the air, kicking back and forth as he chattered. Soon Emma would be awake and hungry, and Abby wouldn't have time for this train of thought, for the nasty thoughts she couldn't seem to stifle in the quiet moments.

She knew they were too harsh, knew she shouldn't think of herself like that.

But she couldn't seem to stop the thoughts from coming.

Especially when Jordan was being so wonderful.

The damned man was being *too* wonderful—taking over the nighttime feeding, bringing her food, doing the laundry and most of the cooking, calling her beautiful, and driving Hunter to school—

With a groan, she yanked a T-shirt out of a drawer and tugged it over her head. Abby knew she was being silly. What sane person complained their partner was doing too much?

The online groups she was part of were filled with posts of men shirking their duties, leaving their wives to fend for themselves with a newborn.

And she was complaining that Jordan was being an actual partner—stepping in when something needed to be done, taking charge of the kids or schedule, not constantly asking her if she needed help.

Instead he was just doing it.

Plates and cups overflowing in the sink? They got washed and put in the dishwasher.

Laundry hampers filled to the brim and then some? They were empty, washed, folded, and put away—more neatly than she could probably do it in her state.

The fridge empty? He got groceries.

The kids were hungry? He cooked.

She'd gotten the fucking Holy Grail of husbands.

And she was absolutely miserable.

Because somehow him being nice and understanding and responsible, him stepping up without a word from her, made her feel like she wasn't pulling her weight.

She didn't look the same for him any longer *and* she wasn't doing enough.

Double, double, toil and trouble.

"And great," she muttered, hurrying out of the closet and down to Carter's room, "now I'm going as mad as Macbeth and company."

"Mama!" he called, lifting his arms up.

She went over to him, hugging him close. "Hi, my lovely boy," she whispered. "Good morning. You hungry?"

"'Gry!" he exclaimed.

"Should we have bananas and oatmeal?" she asked, grabbing him a set of fresh clothes and getting him ready for the day.

"Yes!"

Emma had begun fussing by the time they emerged into the hall, making animal sounds—"A dog goes woof!"—so they detoured to grab her and then made their way down to the kitchen.

Jordan was on the phone when they came in, and he slipped out with one finger raised, but he'd already prepped the oatmeal with a side of bananas and put her nursing pillow on the table beside her chair.

And her heart squeezed again, guilt sliding through her.

The man was doing too much.

How in the hell was she ever going to make things even between them again?

FOUR

Jordan

HE HUNG up the phone after confirming that the others thought his plan was sound and then went back into the kitchen, ruffling Carter's hair as he determinedly spooned oatmeal into his mouth.

Well, about half of it made it into his mouth.

The rest was on his face and the highchair and his clothes and the floor.

But he loved feeding himself.

Jordan had just gotten in the habit of making twice as much so that a reasonable amount made it into his son's stomach.

Emma was also eating happily, and he sat next to Abby at the kitchen table. "You hungry?"

She bit her lip, nodded. "But I can get it—"

He stood. "Cinnamon toast and tea? Or are you sick of that yet?"

She smiled. "Is it even possible to get sick of cinnamon toast and tea?"

"I'm guessing the correct answer to that question is no."

"Exactly, but Jor—" She stopped. "You really don't have to wait on me hand and foot. You're already doing so much and—"

"This is my family, sweetheart. I couldn't carry Emma"—he grinned—"and thank God for that, but let me at least take care of you in this way."

Guilt flashed in her eyes. "Are you sure you don't mind?"

"Yes." He tucked a lock of her hair behind her ear. "In fact, it makes me feel like I'm finally doing something productive."

More guilt. "Baby—"

He bopped her lightly on the nose. "Hush."

More guilt in her expression, but Jordan decided not to comment on it or push further. He had a plan, and he was going to stick to it. Or at least, he'd put the plan in place and had to trust that the rest of the Sextant would pull their weight. So, instead of worrying about something he couldn't change, he poured a cup of coffee for himself, brewed her some tea, and then set about spending the rest of the day making sure she got as much rest as possible.

Because his woman had plans that evening.

Whether or not she liked it.

SHE WAS GOING to kill him.

They'd been married long enough for him to see that much in her face, but he simply ignored the glare and opened the door a little wider to allow Bec, Sera, CeCe, and Rachel in.

"Hi," CeCe said, kissing him on the cheek and whispering. "Heather's going to call. She's in Berlin."

He smiled. "Thanks for the assist."

"Aunt CeCe!" Hunter yelled, dropping his pencil onto the kitchen counter and tearing through the room to hug Cecilia tight.

"Oof!" she exclaimed, teetering back on her heels before Jordan snagged her arm to steady her. "How did you get so big?"

"It's my new heart!" he said, or really, yelled, sprinting back to the kitchen, but not before yelling some more—this time over his shoulder, "It makes me a superhero, CeCe!"

"I see that," she said in what someone on the street might think was an indulgent tone.

But Jordan knew better.

Hunter *was* a superhero.

Less of the Hollywood variety and more of the real-life type. He'd been sick for much of his life, and it wasn't until he'd received a heart transplant a few years ago that he'd been able to be a real kid.

It was still hard as hell to let him play sports and skid through the house, especially after Jordan had spent so much time at Hunter's bedside, but Abby was the one who'd actually helped him see that his nephew wouldn't be able to live a full life unless he loosened the protective hold a bit. He'd already been more son than nephew—Hunter's biological dad and Jordan's brother had died before he was born—and Abby, too, had given him the courage to adopt Hunter, to be a true family, and he was forever grateful for her.

And the woman thought she wasn't doing enough?

Ha.

She'd changed his life for the better, made it something he was so damned thankful to be living, made it—

Perfect.

Even with her glaring at him from across the room.

"Where's my little squishy?" Sera asked, hanging her coat on the rack and squeezing Jordan's arm at the same time.

None of the Sextant—and somehow, he'd gotten in the habit of calling Abby and her friends that, even though it was a ridiculous name thought up after too many drinks and an ill-fated

Google search—but regardless of that silly name, none of the women were still at guest status, as Abby liked to call it.

They strolled right in, Sera scooping up Carter and kissing his chubby little cheeks, CeCe moving to look at Hunter's homework, Bec grabbing drinks from the fridge and snacks from the pantry, and Rachel carefully snagging Emma from Abby's arms, ordering her to go upstairs for a nap.

"But—"

"But, nothing," Rachel said, in her no-nonsense, efficient tone. "We want to chat and hang out, but not until you've slept a bit more."

"I'm not tired—"

Except, Abby's protest was cut short by a yawn.

Bec, who was setting a pile of snacks on the table, merely raised a brow. "Want to try that line with another group of dirty old ladies?"

Snorting, Jordan moved into the kitchen, grabbing some ingredients for spaghetti, one of the few meals he could cook—and the only one that would work for a large group that Hunter and Carter would both eat as well. But while the cooking was necessary, it was also part distraction.

Letting Abbs' friends take her in hand.

Because sometimes a man needed to call in the experts, and as much as he loved his wife, he knew there were things she still held back from him, still kept close to her chest.

Part because of her asshole of a father.

And part because she felt a responsibility to do everything by herself.

Stubborn woman.

But still, he wouldn't take her any other way. He just knew that sometimes he needed a little help to get through that shell of hers.

When Hunter left to put his homework in his backpack,

CeCe came up next to Jordan, leaning a hip against the counter as he sliced vegetables. "It's not often a *man*"—her green eyes danced—"calls an emergency Book Club meeting."

"You mean Wine Club?" he deadpanned.

"Yes, exactly."

He sighed, dropped the veggies into the stockpot. "She says she's not doing enough," he said softly. "Like giving birth and nursing Emma, all while taking care of Hunter and Carter isn't enough."

CeCe snorted.

"Exactly," he said. "But I don't think that's all of it. That's why I called Sera. There's something else going on."

"Yeah?"

He thought about the way she'd jumped away from his touch, the guilt in her eyes, the way she'd avoided being close to him all day.

And his worry was that it was more than being tired or feeling like he was taking on too much. Jordan worried that she was unhappy because of something he was doing and just hadn't found a way to tell him.

Which worried him further.

Because if their communication had broken down that much, if she couldn't just talk to him as a friend and wife, then . . . fuck, he was *definitely* doing something wrong.

Hence the big guns.

Hopefully, if she couldn't talk to him, she would at least talk to her friends.

"We'll sort her out, Jor," CeCe murmured, squeezing his arm. Then she smiled. "After her nap, that is."

"Did Bec get her to go lay down?"

A nod. "Already out, poor thing."

He stirred the pot, began adding tomato sauce. "Emma has decided that sleep is far too overrated."

"I thought you guys were going to hire a nanny."

"Abby wants to wait until she goes back to work."

"A night nurse?"

He shook his head. "Couldn't get her to agree to it."

"Stubborn one, isn't she?"

"It might be her superpower."

CeCe chuckled. "We'll turn the screws, get her to talk."

"How will you torture her?"

"I'll threaten her with a glass of wine," CeCe said.

"That'll do it," he said, feeling better already. Not because of the wine—Abby couldn't stand the stuff, even though the rest of her friends could suck it down like punch—but he felt better because they cared about Abby, because they knew her, because they would help him get to the bottom of this.

And if it ended up that he was the problem that was making his wife so miserable, then Jordan would fix it.

Whatever it was.

FIVE

Abby

BY ALL MEASURES, she should be furious at her husband.

Inviting people over when she was exhausted and had given birth just a few weeks before—six was a few, right?—but regardless, the house was a mess, her body was a mess and—

They were her best friends in all the world.

And Jordan had invited the cackling group of six over *then* had entertained them for a glorious two hours when they'd forced her into a nap.

The house sparkled—or if not that, then it had at least been picked up and organized. How long it would stay that way was questionable, given that it was now home to three kids, but they'd come, they'd cleaned, they'd made her rest, and Jordan had cooked and fed everyone.

Her reheated plate was in front of her, along with a small glass of rum, copiously mixed down with Diet Coke. Sera had said she'd checked the measurements carefully so as not to interfere with her breast milk.

Which was beyond sweet.

Her friend, not the milk. But then again, it wasn't like she went around tasting it. Her milk could be sweet and delicious and—

Her mind threw the brakes on that particular train of thought.

Maybe someone would get their jollies off it, but she'd spent the better part of the last few years feeling like a cow—either because she was nursing or because she was pregnant and as large as one.

It didn't feel very jolly.

Or sweet.

But her friends and Jordan were.

He'd taken the kids upstairs, put the littles to bed, and he and Hunter were camping out in the bedroom rewatching the latest season of *The Mandalorian* before it was his turn to go to sleep.

Abby had to admit she was a little jealous to not be part of the rewatch party—it was so good—but also, it was nice to be hanging with her friends. She'd sat and let the chatter wash over her, a Hallmark movie playing in the background, listening to Bec talk about a new case—and the other lawyer's attempts to circumvent her.

"Which won't work, of course," Bec was saying. "It's practically a juvenile move, and I'd already prepped my clerk to file if he made that move." She cackled and rubbed her hands together. "I only wish I could see his face when that filing goes through."

"You're too smart for your own good," Sera said.

"Nonsense," Heather said, her voice slightly tinny as it came through the speakers of CeCe's phone. She was sitting cross-legged on her bed in Berlin, dressed for the day and wisely abstaining from a drink, as it was breakfast time there. "It's never a bad thing to be smart."

"So says the two smartest women I know," Rachel said.

Bec buffed her knuckles on her chest. "It's a hard cross to bear, that's for sure."

Sera swatted Bec on the shoulder. "Hush you."

"Hey!" Bec swatted her back.

"How's the real estate market right now?" Abby asked quickly, before they could digress too far down the swatting track. She, Bec, and Sera had all been friends since boarding school—and sometimes they still acted like it.

Sera lifted a brow, but her lips were curved. "Putting your mom powers to use?"

"I've become an expert at breaking up fights."

CeCe tsked. "My little squishy and Hunter don't fight. They're angels."

"Hmm," Heather said.

Abby snorted.

Rachel giggled.

And Sera spent the next few minutes telling them about her latest sales—then a few more complaining about a couple of very challenging clients.

After which, Abby tried to turn the conversation to Rachel.

Because if she could just delay enough, give the other women their turn to talk, Heather would have to go to breakfast, and she wouldn't have to give her recap of her life.

Which was a mess.

And not in terms of the state of her house.

Her mind was muddied, tangled and twisted, and she kept going in circles, warring with herself about things she should know logically didn't matter, but things that still continued creeping in anyway.

She wasn't ready to divulge those thoughts.

Not when she was in a room of happy, smart, beautiful women.

Not when she felt none of those things.

Not when she knew she *should* be feeling all of them because she was so fucking lucky and privileged and—

"The reason you have that look on your face is why I'm not going to answer the question," Rachel murmured, reaching over Sera and squeezing her hand. "What's going on?"

What *was* going on?

So much and yet nothing she could pinpoint.

Annoying and destructive thoughts and yet a wonderful husband and family.

No sleep and feeling like a cow and—

She started crying.

"Oh God," Abby said, wiping frantically at her eyes. "Ignore me. I'm fine. I just—" A sob bubbled up in her throat. "I'm just tired and hormonal."

"Maybe," Bec said, "but it's not *just* that. Otherwise"—she waved a hand in the direction of Abby's face—"you wouldn't look like that."

"Like what?" Abby asked, affronted.

"Miserable," Sera said. "Do you think you have PPD?" she asked. "You got pretty blue after Carter was born."

Abby's first inclination was to immediately deny she felt depressed. Not because it was a negative thing. She knew it was common, and she truly *had* felt very sad after Carter's birth, perhaps even depressed. But Carter had slept better than Emma, and she'd had CeCe around to help.

So maybe it *was* just fatigue.

Maybe she should hire the night nurse like Jordan suggested.

But then she would be doing even less, and the scales would be tipped even more in her favor and . . . she wouldn't be doing anything or enough or—

"I don't think I'm depressed," she murmured, wiping the tears away.

"Then what, honey?" Sera asked. "For all intents and purposes, you have everything you've ever wanted."

Abby stared at her hands. "Then why does it feel as though it's all going to get torn away? Like any second it will be gone, or Jordan will get tired of me and move on, or my kids will get sick or I will, or we'll all get struck by lightning!" She sighed. "I know it's ridiculous," she said. "But every instant of the day, my thoughts are in this cycle. What if Jordan doesn't like my body now? I'm heavier and stretched out and—God—he saw me poop twice on the delivery table. Twice!"

"Abbs," Sera began.

"And I *know* it's ridiculous," she repeated. "Jordan loves me and doesn't care what I look like. But he's a fucking Greek god with a six-pack and I've got a flattened, lumpy *keg!* And—"

"Didn't he used to have the mystical eight-pack?" Heather asked.

A strange question from the man's sister.

Abby blinked and glanced down at the phone. "Um . . . yes?"

"And you don't love him less just because he has two less . . . packs?" Heather asked.

It was such a ridiculous question that Abby just looked at her.

Then eventually answered, when Heather stared back through the screen at her, brow lifted, inscrutable expression in place.

"Of course not," she finally said, albeit a bit mutinously.

"Well, that's that," Heather said, rubbing her hands together. "He loves you, sickeningly, so if he's willingly invited our lot into your place to take over and fuss and eat and drink him out of house and home. And that's just from a friend perspective," she added when Abby began to shake her head. "From a sister perspective, I know I've never seen my brother happier."

"It's true," Sera said. "Even from that first night in the bar, he's never had eyes for anyone but you."

"And," Rachel murmured, "the way he looks at you is . . . right. He's not worried about the varnish on the surface, he loves what's within."

Silence.

Then Bec grinned and shook her head. "Damn Morris, you're good."

Rachel smiled. "It's Scott now, but I'll take it."

"I thought you were going to stay Morris?" Abby asked. Rachel had been married before, to a man who was a special brand of asshole. She'd vowed to never change her name again.

"I've decided I like being a Scott," she said, eyes full of love.

"I bet you do," Bec chortled.

"How's Luke?" Rachel asked innocently.

They all laughed when Bec's—or Becky as Luke called her —cheeks went pink, but she was a true New Yorker and didn't back down, teasing Rachel about Bas and Sera about Tate, and Heather about Clay, just for good measure.

"Also, fuck the notion of having to do it all," she said, turning her laser-sharp focus onto Abby. "That's just some bull-shit patriarchy hangover. Jordan isn't working, but you are, or will be soon. He can definitely pick up the slack. And even if he *was* working and you weren't, you just spent the last nine months puking your guts up and then pushing a watermelon out of something that's the size of a lemon"—here, she shuddered —"and you've been playing milkmaid with all the nursing and then when you go back to work, I know you'll be pumping. He can do some of the work around here."

"It's more than some."

"So what?" Heather said. "Plus, my brother has never been shy about expressing himself. If it gets too much, he'll tell you."

Abby bit her lip. "He wanted to hire a housekeeper to come in once a week and maybe someone else to do the laundry, but I told him no."

"So no to the night nurse, no to the laundry service—which sounds amazing, by the way—and no to the housekeeper," Sera said, ticking the items off on her fingers. "Why don't you want the extra help?"

"I—" She sighed. "It's just such a waste of money, and I should—"

"And there goes my bullshit meter, scaling right off the charts," Bec said. "Jordan sold off his multi-billion-dollar company a few years ago to sit on a beach. He found you instead and wants to make your life easier."

"But that's just it exactly," Abby said, jumping to her feet. "He wanted to be on a beach and instead, he got me pregnant and now he's saddled—"

She broke off.

Not quite able to finish the statement.

Unfortunately, someone else did.

"Saddled with you," Jordan said from the hall, a bowl of popcorn in his hands and hurt marring his expression. "You think *I* think I'm saddled with you?"

"Oh shit," Heather whispered.

Abby's heart sank. "That's not what—"

"Dad?" Hunter called. "Is the popcorn done?"

He swallowed, glanced up the stairs and smiled. "Just finished. Be right there, but it's probably only one more episode before bed."

"Aw, man!" But his voice faded, his footsteps drifting back down the hall.

"That's not—" She broke off again, took a step toward him, and stopped.

"That's not what you meant?" he asked quietly. "You don't actually think that?" His eyes were hopeful, as if he wished she'd just been spewing nonsense in the heat of the moment and none of it really meant anything.

She wanted that, too.

Except, she couldn't quite bring herself to say that she didn't mean it.

Because deep down, some part of her did wonder if he wished he'd ended up on that beach in the tropics instead of her working for his former company, their home just miles away from what had once been his office, their family growing by the year.

Maybe he wanted mai-tais and margaritas instead of leaking nipples and poopy diapers. Maybe he wanted his freedom instead of being tied to the school calendar and extracurriculars. Maybe he wanted to find someone who wasn't a nerdy, sock-loving, pajama-wearing cow-equivalent.

Maybe he wanted more than her.

And he must have seen those thoughts on her face because he swallowed again, and it looked painful, even from the far side of the room.

"Jordan," she began.

"I should get Hunter the popcorn," he said, lifting the bowl.

She bit her lip but didn't know what to say, how to make him understand this wasn't about him.

It was her.

All her.

He held her gaze for another few seconds then nodded and disappeared. She listened to his footsteps on the stairs, disappearing down the hall, until finally, the bedroom door clicked closed.

"Shit, Abbs," Bec said, breaking the silence that had fallen.

"I know you didn't mean to," Sera whispered, "but I think you hurt his feelings."

Abby *knew* she had, and she felt awful about it. This whole thing was supposed to be about her and her messed-up head. Jordan had been nothing but wonderful and understanding and helpful and . . . now she'd hurt him, made him think that she thought that—

Fuck.

She needed to untangle this mess of thoughts in her mind and go fix things with her husband.

Now.

She went to stand, then realized she was still on her feet, still frozen in place and staring at the empty hallway.

But her friends weren't frozen.

They'd stood too, were gathering up glasses and bowls and napkins, carrying everything to the kitchen. CeCe began washing up, Sera loading the dishwasher. Bec returned snacks to the pantry, and Rachel had retrieved the re-useable wine stopper and was plunking it in the bottle of pinot grigio they'd opened, before stowing the plugged container in the fridge. In less than five minutes, they had the space spic and span again. Then they were bundling into their coats and slipping out the front door.

"We'll give you some privacy so you guys can talk," CeCe said, pulling her in for a quick hug.

"It'll be okay," Rachel murmured, hugging her after CeCe had slipped by.

Bec kissed her on the cheek. "Just talk to him," she said. "He's a good guy. He'll understand where your head is." Then she tugged lightly on the end of Abby's ponytail and walked down the path to the driveway.

Sera stopped on the threshold, weaving their fingers

together and squeezing lightly. "Honey."

"I hurt him," Abby whispered. "He's been the perfect fucking husband, and I just hurt him."

"I think you need to talk about exactly why that hurt him so much—"

"I—"

"Not with me," she said, not unkindly. "With him. Because you two are the product of some pretty messed-up families. Not that mine is anything to write home about," she added. "Because God knows, my parents are a special brand of dysfunctional."

"I don't think this is about our childhoods."

Or maybe it was. Shit. This had just gotten so infinitely complicated.

Sera smiled, touched her cheek. "I think you just realized that maybe this is deeper than you first thought."

Abby sighed, nodded. "I think you're right."

"I know I am," Sera said lightly. "But, babe, what you need to think about more than my all-knowing rightness is whether you're actually worried that Jordan is unhappy *or* if this has more to do with your dad's special track record of making new families every couple of years."

Abby sucked in a breath.

Fuck.

Fuck.

Because if Abby's dad was bad about using women like tissue and discarding them just as easily, then Jordan's dad was even worse.

And if part of her was worried, however stupid and illogical she knew that was—even in her emotional, hormonal state—that she might end up like one of those tissues . . .

Then Jordan must think that *she* thought he was like his father.

And that might be the worst insult she could ever give him.

SIX

Jordan

HE WAS PRETENDING TO SLEEP.

Like a child.

Lying in bed, the popcorn propped on his chest, next to his son, and pretending to drift off.

Because he knew that Abby was going to come up.

Her friends were too intuitive to not have recognized the wound his wife had unintentionally—and he knew it was unintentional because she was too damned nice to hurt him on purpose—but they were too smart to stick around after that.

And sure enough, he had barely made it to the bedroom before he'd heard the footsteps and the dishes clattering then the front door opening and goodbyes being given.

Then fifteen minutes later, footsteps on the stairs and Abby had crawled into bed.

Luckily, he'd begun his fake sleeping already, so Hunter had just whispered loudly—*loudly* because it seemed like no matter how kids tried to lower the volume of their voices, it was still ear-piercing, "Dad's sleeping!"

"I see that," came Abby's lilting voice, at a much more reasonable volume. The bed shifted as she crawled onto the mattress. "Can I join you for the last little bit of this episode? It's one of my favorites."

"It's epic!" Hunter said over a certain not-quite-Jedi wielding her saber.

"It is at that," she whispered.

And Jordan didn't chime in.

Because he was pretending to be asleep.

Pretty soon the episode was over, and Abby left with Hunter to tuck him into bed, but when she returned, he immediately knew the jig was up.

Mostly because she sat down next to him on the bed and said, "I know you're awake."

He stifled a sigh but opened his eyes. "Hey, sweetheart, you ready for bed?"

She just looked at him.

He just looked at her.

And then she released a deep breath and said, "I know I hurt you, and I'm sorry."

She had, but it hadn't been on purpose. He knew that. But he'd been so convinced he could just easily fix this little bump in the road she was having if only he took enough off her plate and got her some sleep and time with her friends. He never considered that the real issue would be . . . her worrying he would leave her.

Some part of her honestly thought he would leave her.

Like his father.

Like *her* father.

Fuck, but that stung.

But it wasn't like either of them had great examples of men in their lives. It wasn't a surprise that there would be some deep-seated anxiety and fears. Or that she would be especially vulnerable during times like these, when she was exhausted and there were all sorts of hormones flowing through her.

It was just . . .

He wasn't his father.

He knew that. *She* knew that.

So, he didn't need to make it even harder for her.

Shifting, he slipped an arm around her waist and tugged her close, taking solace in the feel of his wife near him while shoving the slice of pain away.

"I know, baby," he said. "It's okay."

She sighed, her arm coming around him. "It's *not*."

"You said something in the heat of the moment," he told her, running his hand up and down her back. "I'm not hurt."

He wasn't hurt.

Not really.

It was the fatigue talking. For both of them.

Soon things would settle down and they'd be back to normal and he wouldn't feel like this, like he'd been scoured from the inside out. He would be totally fine and it wasn't a big deal and—

"Don't lie to me, Jor," she said, sitting up enough for him to see her face.

He brushed a finger over her lips. "What's that they say about eavesdroppers?" He forced himself to smile. "That they won't like what they hear? I'm fine, sweetheart," he added lightly, needing her to know that it was . . . and it would be. But more than that, he knew he didn't need to add his hurt feelings to her burden. Especially when it would all be fine. He'd get over it. "Though what's *not* fine is you thinking that your body isn't beautiful."

A roll of her eyes. "It's hard to feel beautiful when you're a cow."

Opening his mouth to protest, he didn't manage to actually get that protest out before she covered his lips with a finger.

"That's not in the sense of I'm fat and disgusting—though I won't lie and say that I love all the new stretch marks and sagging bits, especially when you seem to only grow more handsome as the years go by—but I feel like a cow with all the feedings. No"—a shake of her head—"not just *that*. It's this sense of my body not being my own, like I'm standing in front of the mirror and seeing someone else."

He squeezed her arm. "You've had a lot of changes since we got married. Getting pregnant with Carter and becoming an instant mom to Hunter, the new job, another baby. I feel like that would throw anyone for a loop."

"But it's not like you haven't had any changes."

"Don't you see?" He sat up, tugging her up with him, heart full of so much love for her. "I didn't start actually living my life until I saw you in that bar. I'm so thankful to have you, to have our family, our kids, even your friends."

Her eyes went damp. "I'm so thankful to have you, too. I love you so much. It's just . . ."

"Just what?" he pressed when she just trailed off.

"Just"—she bit her lip—"I just worry that you want that beach."

He snorted, thinking of how delusional he'd been, selling his business, buying an island—an actual island. Jordan had wanted privacy and quiet, or so he'd thought. Because he knew himself well enough now to recognize that he would have been absolutely miserable.

"This life I have with you . . . it's more than I could have ever imagined. I wake up every morning feeling so fucking lucky to be next to you."

She sniffed. "Even if it's being woken up at three A.M.?"

"Even if it's being woken up at three A.M. paired with the sounds of a child vomiting."

They both shuddered, remembering the worst throwing up incident of their marriage. At least, he figured she was remembering the same thing as him—avocado exorcist a la Carter.

"Even if your wife says something unforgivable?"

"Even if my wife is obsessing over something that isn't a big deal," he said, deliberately meeting her eyes. He believed the statement, too, even if it still smarted, because it wouldn't be a big deal.

At some point, it wouldn't be a big deal.

He knew it.

He just needed to . . . something. He needed to get some sleep, let some time pass, and the pieces would settle into place.

And it wouldn't hurt so much.

And part of him would stop worrying that deep down he was like their fathers.

Because he wouldn't let that happen, *couldn't* let that happen. Not when he had so much. Not when he knew the worth of having Abby and Hunter and Carter and Emma in his life. Not when they both had so much more than the men who'd contributed half of their DNA to them. Jordan knew the worth of that, of the family they'd built, and wouldn't ever take it for granted.

"I love you," she whispered, hugging him tight.

"I love you," he whispered back. "Come on," he said, coaxing her down next to him, "let's sleep before Emma decides she's up to party."

Abby giggled but curled up into him. "I shouldn't be tired," she murmured, resting her head on his shoulder. "I had two naps"—a yawn interrupted her statement—"today."

"Sleep, sweetheart."

And after a few moments, she did.

But he lay awake, turning her words over in his head, wondering how he could make her see that he wasn't ever going to leave her.

Wondering how she could even think that when he felt so tied to her, to their life.

Wondering how he had gone his whole life thinking he was so different, but even his wife was worried that he was the same as them.

Sleep stayed out of reach, her words clawing into him, the barbs locking in deep.

And he continued to wonder.

As the sun rose, dawning on a new day, he hadn't gotten any closer to the answers. Instead, he just wondered how he was going to prove to her—and perhaps to him as well—that he wasn't like their fathers.

SEVEN

Abby

SHE'D FUCKED UP.

Yup.

She'd known it from the moment she'd seen Jordan's face but had relaxed after their talk that night. He'd seemed to understand, had promised he wasn't hurt.

But now, as the week had gone on, she knew he was a big old liar.

He *was* hurt, and he was trying to prove that he wasn't.

The reality of what she'd said, what she was feeling, how she'd so hurt the man she loved had prompted her into action the next day. So she had called her doctor and made an appointment. They'd discussed her emotions and insecurities and fatigue and had agreed that if she still felt so unsettled the next week, she would try some antidepressants and meet with a therapist.

But her words had been the catalyst that yanked her out of the fog.

Well, that and the sleep. And the fact that she'd finally had enough energy to start going to the gym. With all of those things, she was finally thinking clearly and feeling better and not so caught up in her own head and insecurities to not see the rest of the world around her.

Slowly but surely, she was feeling more like herself.

Still, she'd kept the therapist's number. Just in case she started feeling so twisted up again and needed more help.

But while she was starting to feel more like herself, he was on edge, something fragile about his emotions, even as she tried to show him that she knew he wasn't like his father, that her freak-out had been about her and not him.

And they were both doing it without really talking to the other.

Oh, they *were* talking.

About everything except the giant fluorescent pink elephant thundering beneath the surface—Carter and his new words, Emma and the fact that she was actually sleeping thanks to Jordan's insistence on giving her that late-night bottle, on Hunter capturing the lead in his class's play as Professor Rock, oh and the new nanny they'd interviewed based on CeCe's recommendation who would be starting in a few days.

Everything was settling in, calming down.

And yet, nothing was.

Because her husband was hurt, even though he was putting on a great front.

Abby sighed and pushed off the chair in the back yard where she'd been enjoying the feel of the afternoon sunshine. She knew that she needed to figure out a way to take back those words.

Or not take back, she supposed, since she knew that was impossible. Instead, she needed Jordan to know that she knew that he wasn't like their fathers. But, fuck, just thinking that tangled line of thoughts was confusing, let alone trying to prove

something just so someone else could let go of their biggest insecurity wasn't easy.

As a woman who'd spent nearly all of the last two months in
that cycle of self-doubt and uncertainty, she knew one conversation couldn't break it.

She'd needed Jordan and her friends, then the blow of
seeing his face, then talking with her doctor, followed by several
nights of thinking and journaling, and then several more conversations with the Sextant to get her head on straight.

Oh, and she'd needed sleep, too. And the gym.

Because all those pieces together had finally unsnarled the
tangle.

Or maybe rather than untangling, she'd passed the snare
from her to Jordan, like some perverse game of emotional
telepathy.

He was sitting at the kitchen counter, his laptop open, a file
from Heather open on the screen that he was reviewing for her.
But his eyes were shadowed, and when he heard her come in, he
jumped up and crossed to her. "Hi, sweetheart," he murmured,
tugging her close and giving her a peck on the lips. "Need
anything?"

"No, thank you, baby," she said, squeezing him back. "I'm
just going to start dinner."

"It's already in the oven."

She froze. "I told you it was my turn."

"I was here and knew the recipe."

"Jor—"

He hesitated, uncertainty on his face, and she hated that
she'd made him doubt himself. "Yeah, sweetheart?"

Which was why she said, "Thank you" instead of anything
else.

And then the same later, when he ran her a bath and rushed
to gather up the kids so she could have private time—definitely

much-appreciated, aside from the thread of vulnerability in his eyes, the slightly-desperate tone of his voice.

But it was his expression this morning that made her shift her thinking from this would pass—that it would just take some time to convince him she didn't think of him as his father or hers, for that matter—to recognizing this wasn't just going to fade away. She could be as patient as possible, could keep trying to reassure him that she knew the difference between him and their dads, but he wasn't going to absorb that.

Because she'd hit at his greatest vulnerability.

And that wasn't something that was easily erased.

Luckily, she had an idea.

EIGHT

Jordan

THE KIDS WERE ASLEEP.

And so was his wife.

But he was sitting at the kitchen table, putting the finishing touches on the file for Heather and wondering if he'd done enough over the last couple of weeks to prove to Abby that he was in for the long haul or if he needed to do more.

Did she know?

Did she feel how desperate he was to keep her? To prove to her he had staying power?

He hoped for the first, not for the second two. No man wanted to be seen as desperate, and certainly not by the woman he was desperate for.

At least, he thought that should be the case.

But it was becoming harder and harder to not just tell her that he was still thinking about what she'd said, that it was affecting him still, that he wanted her to know that—

Ping.

An email hit his inbox, his eyes flashing to the corner and seeing that it was a message from . . .

Abby?

"Uh," he muttered, not particularly eloquently, but his fingers moved over the trackpad, and he clicked on the message anyway.

Jordan,

I know I hurt you. I've seen it in your eyes, even though you've tried to pretend everything is fine. Take it from someone who has plenty of experience pretending, none of that will make any difference. It will keep eating at you, keep making your thoughts all twisted up and impossible to let go.

But I was lucky enough to have a husband who understands and cares and loves me unconditionally, friends who push me to get my own head out of my ass, and a wonderful family I feel absolutely privileged to be a part of.

And yet, I know that sometimes all of those things don't make a difference.

Sometimes your mind won't let you out of that tangle. So, I've decided to yank you out myself—with a journey. ;) Hopefully by the end, with all the evidence, you will see you are not like them. I hope you will see all you mean to me, how much I love you, how strongly you've stitched yourself into the fabric of my soul. Forever.

That's your first clue. Now here's your second.

You started with a chain, then a slip, and a single and a double.

—Your love,

A

He sat for a moment, staring in wonder at the email, reading it through again, and feeling his heart squeeze tight.

He hadn't been fooling her, not for a moment, had he?

Just as she hadn't fooled him with all of her "I'm fine" nonsense.

Jordan hadn't been able to sit back and watch her zombieing through life all uncertain and lost. Just as she, apparently, couldn't stand to watch him unravel. Stubborn, the both of them, but also stubborn in the best way.

God, he loved this woman.

And he knew exactly where the first clue was leading him.

He closed his computer and walked into the family room, heading for the basket she used to keep by the couch, but was now kept on one of the built-in shelves.

Tucked in between two skeins—see? He *had* learned something from his wife's crochet lessons—of yarn, was a small folded piece of paper with his name written on the outside in Abby's messy handwriting.

> *Your clue is a wall we created out of love, one that I insisted upon, but one that you insisted was laid out in crisp, even perfection. Every time I look at it, I feel my heart grow full at what we've made.*

His gaze flew up, locking onto the wall where Abby had nixed hanging his favorite painting and instead insisted upon hanging family pictures when they'd moved into this house. It had begun small—starting with just the two of them, then the addition of Hunter, then adding Abby's pregnant belly, then Carter, then another pregnant belly, and then . . . a new addition that hadn't been there earlier in the day.

The five of them gathered together on the couch, Hunter tickling Carter, Abby holding Emma, who was smiling, and him, his face turned toward his family, love shining brightly in his expression.

His heart thumped.

Then he walked over and grasped the slip of paper tucked under one corner of the picture.

I love you and our family, more than words can express. For your next clue, go peek in on our newest and find her favorite lovey.

He smiled and quietly went up the stairs.

Then just as quietly, he slipped into Emma's room, moving to the ugly stuffed dog that had once been Abby's childhood toy and was now Emma's absolute favorite thing to stare at. Currently, it occupied the rocking chair, another slip of paper folded underneath its right foot.

He opened it.

Our littlest is trouble, just like her mama, but I know you love us both very much. Now, for your next clue, find little squishie's favorite book, and further that, his favorite page. :)

Jordan tiptoed over to the crib, brushing a soft finger over Emma's nose. She frowned, just like her mom did when he touched her while she was sleeping. Laughing softly, he left her room, walked down the hall, and moved into Carter's room.

Who was passed out in his toddler bed, his butt stuck in the air, same as he'd slept since he'd been able to roll onto his belly to get into that position.

Navigating the stuffed animals and books and Duplos littering the floor, Jordan went to the bookcase and pulled out *Goodnight Moon.*

"And a comb and a brush and a bowl full of mush," he whispered to himself, opening up to Carter's page, heart thudding when his fingers brushed another slip of paper.

I knew you'd find it because you're a great father, because you pay attention to the details. You always remember the important things, and we are so lucky to have you. Now before I cry (damned hormones!), you'll find your next clue in the last-minute project you ran out to get supplies for.

He'd known it was coming, that logic told him he'd be next journeying to Hunter's room. But, considering he'd been cursing to himself about having to craft a mission out of popsicle sticks and craft glue only hours before, this made him smile.

After quietly closing the door behind him, he moved to his oldest son's room, heart expanding with love when he saw the mini-me of his brother sacked out on top of the covers, a book open on his chest. Such a voracious reader, just like Abby was. And . . . just like Zach had been. Though he missed his brother intensely, Jordan knew he was beyond lucky to have Hunter in his life.

Carefully, he put a bookmark in to keep Hunter's place— he'd lived with bookworms long enough to not make that mistake—set the book aside and tugged the covers up and over his son.

Then he moved over to the dreaded mission project to read the note propped up outside its front door.

If you were like our dads, you wouldn't have known about my crocheting or the photos. If you were like your or my father, you wouldn't have known about the lovely or the favorite page in the book or Hunter's last-minute project. If you were like them, you wouldn't know where to find me now.

So for your final clue, your wife will be in her favorite place. The one you made so special for her.

"Fuck, but I love you, Abby," he whispered, pocketing the note, and continuing down the hall. Past their bedroom and into the small study that he'd converted into a reading nook.

White shelves stacked high with books. A comfy chair with colorful throw pillows and fluffy blankets. A space heater because the blanket was never enough.

And his wife.

Sitting on that chair, with a fuzzy throw covering her, a book in her lap.

In her favorite pajamas, cozy socks on the feet sticking out from beneath the blanket.

She set the book aside. "Hi," she whispered.

His heart was full. "Hi, baby," he said, crossing over to her. "How—" He broke off, not knowing what to say except, "I love you."

Her eyes were gentle. "I love you, too. I'm sorry if I didn't show that to you before, or at least not how I *should* have." She brushed her fingers over his jaw. "I'm sorry I hurt you."

He took those fingers in his, squeezed lightly. "Honey, don't say that. I'm fine. I—"

"*Jordan.*" Her voice was firm. "Don't sweep this under the rug. I hurt you."

He started to shake his head, then stopped, knowing he owed them both the truth. "Okay, I *was* hurt. I felt . . ." A sigh, but she was silent. "I think part of me has always worried I'll turn out like them, even though I know exactly how valuable our life is."

"But you're not like them." She took his hand, squeezed it. "And I'm so sorry that I made you think that."

"It's o—"

"Not okay," she said sternly. "Certainly not okay. But I'll do what it takes to prove to you that my insecurity was about me, about my childhood baggage, and had nothing to do with you."

His heart was full, that jagged cut not nearly so painful. Because of the notes and the journey, because of the love and care in her eyes, her touch, her words. He cupped her cheek. "I'm familiar with baggage, childhood and otherwise, but it's so much easier to bear knowing I have you and the kids. You make my life full. And the notes . . . baby . . . the things you said." His voice cracked, but he pushed on. "I don't think I've ever felt more loved or appreciated, and I want you to feel that same way, to be secure that I'm not going to leave you like our fathers did, trading wives and families like baseball cards." He brushed her hair back from her face. "I want you to know that I'm here for the long haul and don't care what you look like or how many kids are running around our house or whether or not I have to go out for wood glue. I love *you*. The person you are inside. The person you've helped me become. The family we've built. The—" His throat went tight, words stoppering up at the top of it. "I just love you," he finished, not too poetically, but it was the truth.

And probably the most important truth.

"I love you, too," she said, lips curved into a soft smile. "Throughout these last couple of weeks, I realized I was living in comparisons." A shrug. "I know that doesn't make much sense, but basically I was comparing my body to how it looked before kids, comparing the things we're not doing with what we used to do, comparing everything I felt for you and how much it has changed. And it *is* different." She bit her lip. "I was worried that because my love felt different from a few years ago, it meant yours did too and that it would mean your passion would fade or that you would eventually want something different."

"Abbs—"

"But now I understand my mind, my feelings better," she said, squeezing his hand. "We're not in the first bloom of love, we're in the *forest* of it. We're the tall trees growing up to the sky, the flowers sprouting beneath, the animals and critters weaving and running in between. Clearly, I'm not one for poetry." A laugh as she shook her head. "But suffice to say, I've realized comparing our life now to how it had once been without thinking of how much it has expanded is unacceptable. It may be different, but for all the differences, it's so fucking incredible that sometimes I feel like I'm at risk of waking up from the best dream ever. Because"—she leaned forward, brushed her lips across his—"I have you and Hunter and Carter and Emma and my nosy friends, and we've made our own family that's not in the shadow of what we grew up in. It's fully in the sunshine and it's wonderful."

"Fuck, sweetheart," he groaned, the words broken, tears dangerously close to spilling over. "You're killing me."

"Good," she whispered, "because I'm about to kill you some more." And with a wicked smile, she shimmied out of her pajama pants then undid the first button of her top, then the next and the next and the next, until she was clad in only a silken black negligée. "I've decided to love my body for the cow it is"—her smile turned mischievous as she brought his hand to her breast—"but I might need you to remind me of that every once in a while."

"Once in a while?" he rasped.

"Yes," she said, arching into his touch. "And also right now."

Then she kissed him, slipping her tongue into his mouth, love and passion and desire mixing together until he broke apart to pay gentle homage to those glorious breasts, until he'd skimmed his fingers over the soft curve of her belly, the gentle slopes of her thighs.

"Get me naked, baby," she whispered, squirming against him, against the light strokes of his fingers.

"In a minute." Another stroke that made her gasp. One more that made her groan. Then he slid the straps from her shoulders, tugged it off her body, and showed her exactly how much he loved her body—stroking her naked skin, kissing his way down her torso, licking her between her thighs. He pulled out every last trick he knew.

"Oh God!" she moaned, gripping his shoulders, tugging him down over her. "Enough, Jor. I want you inside."

Since that was where he wanted to be too, he made short work of removing his clothes, crawled back onto that big chair, and then slid inside.

"Yes," she groaned, holding him close. "God, I've missed this."

He was too close to the edge to risk any words. Instead, he concentrated on gaining control and not blowing his load. And then he concentrated on bringing her to that edge with him.

Then beyond it.

Thank fuck, she made it over the precipice.

Because in the next second, he exploded, pleasure flooding him for an eternity, before he collapsed on top of her, barely having the presence of mind to roll to the side so he didn't crush her, as he caught his breath.

Long minutes later, she stiffened in his arms.

"Sweetheart?" he asked.

"Please, tell me we didn't just make baby number four," she said, eyes wide.

Because . . . birth control. *Right*. They hadn't worried about that much over the last years of pregnancy.

"Shit," he whispered.

But then her lips curved, her arms wrapped around him, and her mouth found his, laughing as she broke away and shook her head. "Well, if we hop aboard that train, I'm glad I have you with me."

"First-class cabin all the way."

And as they both laughed, Jordan hugged her tight, knowing that truer words had never been spoken.

He was so glad to have her with him.

BILLIONAIRE'S CLUB

Bad Night Stand

Bad Breakup

Bad Husband

Bad Hookup

Bad Divorce

Bad Fiancé

Bad Boyfriend

Bad Blind Date

Bad Wedding

Bad Engagement

Bad Bridesmaid

Hate missing Elise's new releases? Love contests, exclusive excerpts and giveaways?

Then signup for Elise's newsletter here!

http://eepurl.com/bdnmEj

BILLIONAIRE'S CLUB

Did you miss any of the other Billionaire's Club books? Check out excerpts from the series below or find the full series at www.amazon.com/gp/product/B07JVRRGCT

Bad Night Stand
Book One
www.books2read.com/BadNightStand

Abby

"I'M THE BEST FRIEND," I said and lifted my chin, forcing my words to be matter-of-fact. I'd been through this before. "You might be fuckable to the nth degree and perfect for Seraphina, but I refuse to set her up with a liar."

In a movement too quick for my brain to process, my stool was shoved to the side and I was pinned against the bar, heavy hips pressing into me, a hard chest two inches from my mouth.

Seraphina whipped around at the movement and I could just see her over Jordan's shoulder, her blue eyes concerned.

"Hi, Seraphina, I'm Jordan," he said, calm as can be, gaze locked onto my face then my eyes when mine invariably couldn't stay away. "I'm going to borrow your friend for a minute."

"Abs?" she asked, and I knew she'd go to bat for me right then and there if I needed her to.

"Weasel or no?" I managed to gasp out. For some reason, I couldn't catch my breath.

Not that it had anything to do with Jordan.

No, it had *everything* to do with him.

"Weasel?" he asked.

I shook my head, focused on my best friend. Weasel was our code name for the men trying to weasel, quite literally, their way into my pants and then into hers.

I was just about ready to say fuck it—or me, rather—even if Jordan was a Weasel. He smelled amazing. His body was hard and hot against mine.

And it had been way too long since I'd had sex.

"No chemistry on my part—" Seraphina began.

"Your friend isn't who I'm attracted to," Jordan growled out. "You are, and it's fucking pissing me off that you don't believe that."

———

Bad Breakup
Book Two
www.books2read.com/BadBreakup

CeCe

"You're even more beautiful than I remember," he said, and the rough edges of his accent hacked at the words, making them more of a growl rather than a soft sentiment.

Her breath caught, and she found her eyes drawn to the stormy blue of Colin's.

And she stared again, utterly entranced before she remembered how it had all ended.

Her in a white dress.

Alone, except for the priest who'd given her a pitying look and invited her to stay as long as she needed.

But it had always been like this, Colin's gruff words winning her over. They were unexpected from him—he was typically so reserved and taciturn. And that compliment, freely given as it was, chipped away at any defenses she managed to erect.

The problem was that his words weren't always followed up by action. In fact, they were typically trailed by pain for her and fury for him.

The hurt of those memories—of Colin so angry, her so broken—helped shore up her resolve.

"Don't say things like that," she snapped and started to pop her earbuds back in. Her friends at home had filled her phone with a slew of romantic audiobooks and she decided that she much preferred fictional heroes at the moment.

At least if they broke their heroine's heart, it was only once.

Colin had already broken hers twice.

She wasn't looking for a round three.

—Get your copy at www.books2read.com/BadBreakup.

Bad Husband

Book Three
www.books2read.com/BadHusband

Heather

"I'm getting drunk," he said, but allowed her to pull him inside the car so that her driver could shut the door behind them.

"You're already drunk," she said.

He stiffened. "*More* drunk."

"Fine," she said, half-worried he was going to launch himself from the sedan. She'd never seen Clay like this. Usually he was so cold and uncompromising, impenetrable even under the toughest of negotiations. He was . . . well, he was typically as *Steele*-like as his last name decreed.

She wrapped her arm through his in order to prevent any unplanned exits from the vehicle and gave the driver the name of her favorite bar. "If you really want to drink, let's do it right."

And *then* she'd drop him at his hotel.

Except it didn't happen that way.

Yes, they hit the bar.

Yes, they drank.

Yes, they got plastered.

But then they woke up . . . or at least, *Heather* woke up.

Naked.

With a softly snoring Clay Steele passed out next to her in bed.

That wasn't the worst part.

Because Heather woke up naked and with a softly snoring Clay Steele in her bed *and* she was wearing a giant diamond ring on her left hand.

Still not the worst part.

That came in the form of a slightly crumpled marriage certificate tucked under her right cheek.

And not the one on her face.

She pulled it from beneath her, a cold sweat breaking out on her body, dread in every nerve and cell.

She *still* wasn't prepared for the horror she found.

The marriage license had been signed by . . . Heather O'Keith and Clay Steele.

Holy fuck, what had she done?

—Get your copy at www.books2read.com/BadHusband.

Bad Hookup
Book Four
www.books2read.com/BadHookup

Rachel

The man didn't take the hint. He didn't leave.

Why won't he leave?

She dropped her chin to her chest.

"So," he finally said after another lengthy—and silent—moment. "Gay, taken, or not interested?"

"Oh my God," she moaned, one hand coming up to push her bangs off her forehead. "This is *not* happening."

"I—" A beat then his voice was incredulous. "I *know* that moan." Warm fingers grasped her wrist, tugged until she could see him in all his yumminess.

Her moment of weakness. Her hookup because she'd been feeling desperate and lonely and—

"It's you," he said softly.

Yes, it was *her*. Rachel, the good girl who didn't sleep around, who *certainly* didn't hook up with random strangers in a bar.

Rachel, who *had* hooked up with a stranger.

The sex had been damned good. Incredible, actually.

But it had been just that. Sex. And she hadn't been able to let go of the guilt. She'd now slept with a grand total of two men in her life, and one of them was her husband.

"I—" She tugged at her wrist. "I need to go."

—Get your copy at books2read.com/BadHookup.

Bad Divorce
Book Five
www.books2read.com/BadDivorce

Bec

Bec really didn't expect to see another person waiting for her when the doors opened with a soft *ding* and she stepped off.

But there *was* another person waiting just outside her front door.

A person she never expected to see again.

Luke Pearson.

Her ex-husband.

It was one-fucking-thirty in the morning, and her ex-husband was sitting on the floor outside her apartment.

Asleep.

Fuming, she marched over to him and kicked his shoe. Hard.

"Luke. Why in the ever loving fuck are you here?"

His lids peeled back and sleepy green eyes met hers. "Becky," he murmured. "You're gorgeous as always." The drowsiness began to fade from his expression. "Did you just come from work?" He glanced down at his phone. "Do you know what time it is?"

"Of course I know what time it is—" Bec bit back the words. Fuck, but wasn't this conversation an exact replica of the broken record one they'd had *way* too many times over the course of their relationship?

She crossed her arms. "Never mind that." A glare that had withered balls much bigger than Luke's "Why did you break into my apartment?"

He stood. "First, I didn't break into your apartment. This is the hall. Second," he hurried to say when she opened her mouth to argue semantics, "I didn't break in. You used our anniversary as the code."

Oh for fuck's sake.

Well, she was changing that tomorrow . . . today . . . fuck, *yesterday*, now that—

"Go away, Luke," she said, pushing past him and unlocking her door while blocking his view of the keypad that was identical to that of the elevator. Her front door's code was not the date of her anniversary with her ex.

But Luke probably already knew that, given that he had been sitting on the floor of her hallway rather than on her couch, beer in hand, feet making prints on her glass coffee table.

Men.

Fucking men.

She slammed the door closed behind her and threw the dead bolt. The knock approximately one second later did not surprise her. Bec dropped her briefcase to the floor then opened it just enough to shoot angry eyes at him through the narrow gap the dead bolt allowed.

Serious green eyes fixed onto hers. "We need to talk."

"Luke," she snapped. "I'm exhausted. It's the middle of the

night. I wouldn't have any patience to talk to my best friends right now, let alone my ex-husband."

"Funny story about that," he said, his lips curving. "Turns out that I'm not actually your *ex*-husband."

—Get your copy at www.books2read.com/BadDivorce

Bad Fiancé
Book Six
www.books2read.com/BadFiance

Seraphina

Sera was alone, pining after a man who'd created the latest social media craze.

Yup. Her life was *ah-maz-ing*.

Tate cleared his throat, and Sera realized she'd been staring at him dumbfounded for a good couple of minutes.

"How can I help you today?" she asked. "I do hope"—*Do hope? What was she, British? Ugh.*—"I-uh . . . I hope you were able to find a house. The agents I passed along are very good at finding unique properties, and I even gave them a few locations to start with . . . " She bit her lip, attempting to stop the ramble.

"No."

Just no.

Um. Okay.

He lifted a hand, rubbed the back of his neck. The movement made his shirt lift, exposing several inches of flat stomach and tan skin and, oh God, a trail of blond hair leading south. Her mouth watered, desperate to trace that path with her tongue—

Sera sucked in a breath, popped to her feet.

"Ah. I'm sorry." She picked up a random file, pretending to know what was in it. "I'm actually really busy, so this will have to continue another time."

Like never.

She rounded her desk, forced a smile. "Mr. Conner," she said when he didn't move. "I'll have my assistant schedule something soon."

"Seraphina."

She shivered at the sound of her name on his lips—soft, a little raspy, and deep enough to conjure all sorts of unhelpful fantasies in her mind.

Shaking herself, she moved to open the door.

Suddenly, Tate was there, hand on hers, body inches away, spicy scent inundating her senses.

Sera's breath caught. "What are you—?"

He seemed to be arguing with himself then finally, those piercing blue eyes locked onto hers. "I need you to marry me."

—Get your copy at www.books2read.com/BadFiance

ALSO BY ELISE FABER

Billionaire's Club (all stand alone)

Bad Night Stand

Bad Breakup

Bad Husband

Bad Hookup

Bad Divorce

Bad Fiancé

Bad Boyfriend

Bad Blind Date

Bad Wedding

Bad Engagement

Bad Bridesmaid (March 1st, 2021)

Gold Hockey (all stand alone)

Blocked

Backhand

Boarding

Benched

Breakaway

Breakout

Checked

Coasting

Centered

Charging

Caged (March 12th, 2021)

Love, Action, Camera (all stand alone)

Dotted Line

Action Shot

Close-Up

End Scene

Meet Cute (April 5th, 2021)

Love After Midnight (all stand alone)

Rum And Notes

Virgin Daiquiri

On The Rocks

Sex On The Seats (April 26th, 2021)

Life Sucks Series (all stand alone)

Train Wreck

Hot Mess

Dumpster Fire (February 15th, 2021)

Clusterf*@k (August 16th, 2021)

Roosevelt Ranch Series (all stand alone, series complete)

Disaster at Roosevelt Ranch

Heartbreak at Roosevelt Ranch

Collision at Roosevelt Ranch

Regret at Roosevelt Ranch

Desire at Roosevelt Ranch

Phoenix Series **(read in order)**

Phoenix Rising

Dark Phoenix

Phoenix Freed

Phoenix: LexTal Chronicles **(rereleasing soon, stand alone, Phoenix world)**

From Ashes

In Flames (January 25th, 2021)

To Smoke (October 18th, 2021)

KTS Series

Fire and Ice (Hurt Anthology, stand alone)

Riding The Edge (December 7th, 2020)

Stand Alones

Someday, Maybe (YA)

ABOUT THE AUTHOR

USA Today bestselling author, Elise Faber, loves chocolate, Star Wars, Harry Potter, and hockey (the order depending on the day and how well her team -- the Sharks! -- are playing). She and her husband also play as much hockey as they can squeeze into their schedules, so much so that their typical date night is spent on the ice. Elise changes her hair color more often than some people change their socks, loves sparkly things, and is the mom to two exuberant boys. She lives in Northern California. Connect with her in her Facebook group, the Fabinators or find more information about her books at www.elisefaber.com.

facebook.com/elisefaberauthor

amazon.com/author/elisefaber

bookbub.com/profile/elise-faber

instagram.com/elisefaber

goodreads.com/elisefaber

pinterest.com/elisefaberwrite